Praise for the historical fantasies of Judith Tarr

Devil's Bargain

"Meticulous historical research." —*Booklist*

"Impressive. . . . Tarr brings [her story] to life with believable characters, romance, and intrigue." —*VOYA*

"Delightfully mixes tales of Arabian magic with real, although alternate, history and a solid understanding of the period to create a fascinating tale." —*University Review* (Philadelphia, PA)

Pride of Kings

"An eerily beautiful, sometimes frightening undercurrent to this engrossing, thoroughly satisfying novel. . . . Tarr smoothly blends a dazzling array of characters from both history and myth. . . . A totally credible delight." —*Publishers Weekly* (starred review)

"A new tapestry of myth and magic. Gracefully and convincingly told." —*Library Journal*

"*Pride of Kings* offers decisive proof that heroic fantasy can still be more than an exercise in fancy dress and moonbeams." —*Locus*

Kingdom of the Grail

"Tarr spins an entertaining and often enlightening tale." —*The Washington Post*

"Eloquently penned mythical history. . . . Drawn with depth and precision, Tarr's array of characters are as engaging as her narrative is enchanting." —*Publishers Weekly*

"A lyrical and exciting story . . . richly woven narrative." —*VOYA*

"With her customary artistry and feel for period detail, the author of *The Shepherd Kings* weaves together the legends of Camelot and the *Song of Roland*, creating a tapestry rich with love and loyalty, sorcery, and sacrifice. Tarr's ability to give equal weight to both history and myth provides her historical fantasies with both realism and wonder. Highly recommended." —*Library Journal*

continued . . .

"[*Kingdom of the Grail*] is fun and exciting and was the first Arthurian related tale that I've enjoyed in a long time."
—*University City Review* (Philadelphia)

The Shepherd Kings

"Never one to gracefully deposit the reader at the beginning of a new story, [Judith Tarr] starts this one with a bang. Tarr has once again created a powerful female character . . . with the brains to match her beauty. [She] brings all her research skills to the fore as she dramatically describes the final battle. . . . *The Shepherd Kings* has more excitement, color and spectacle, undiluted sex, intrigue and adventure than one ordinarily finds in several novels by less talented storytellers."
—*The Washington Post*

Throne of Isis

"In this carefully researched, well-crafted novel about Antony and Cleopatra, Tarr weaves . . . a marvelously entertaining tapestry."
—*Booklist*

"Tarr's historical outline is unexceptionable, her wealth of cultural detail impeccable."
—*Kirkus Reviews*

Pillar of Fire

"A book that can be savored and enjoyed on many levels—perfect for beach reading, what with its lively portrait of enduring love between two who can never publicly acknowledge their commitment, and for such higher pleasures as those afforded by finely wrought characterizations and insights into the minds and hearts of the mighty."
—*Booklist*

"With her usual skill, Tarr combines fact and fiction to create yet another remarkably solid historical novel. This is a highly entertaining blend of romance, drama and historical detail."
—*Publishers Weekly*

King and Goddess

"A dramatic tale."   —*Publishers Weekly*

"Pleasingly written . . . provides fascinating insights into Egyptian history and daily life. Readers lured by history in general and Egypt in particular will enjoy it."
—*The Washington Post*

"This historic fiction brings the turbulent era alive."
—*St. Louis Post-Dispatch*

The White Mare's Daughter

"Culture clashes, war and goddess worship set the stage for Tarr's well rounded and lively prehistoric epic. Tarr's skillful juxtaposition of two vastly different yet spiritually similar societies give a sharp edge to this feminist epic. [Her] fully fleshed out characters and solid, intricate plotting add depth to an entertaining saga."   —*Publishers Weekly*

Queen of Swords:
The Life of Melisende, Crusader Queen of Jerusalem

"Tarr vividly portrays the contrast between the self-righteous, primitive Crusaders and the cosmopolitan, sophisticated residents of the sun-blasted land the Franks call Outremer."
—*Publishers Weekly*

Lord of the Two Lands

"Her prose is lean and powerful, and she exerts admirable control over an impressive cast of characters, some imaginary, others not."   —*The Washington Post*

HOUSE OF WAR

JUDITH TARR

A ROC BOOK

ROC
Published by New American Library, a division of
Penguin Group (USA) Inc., 375 Hudson Street,
New York, New York 10014, U.S.A.
Penguin Books Ltd, 80 Strand,
London WC2R 0RL, England
Penguin Books Australia Ltd, 250 Camberwell Road,
Camberwell, Victoria 3124, Australia
Penguin Books Canada Ltd, 10 Alcorn Avenue,
Toronto, Ontario, Canada M4V 3B2
Penguin Books (N.Z.) Ltd, Cnr Rosedale and Airborne Roads,
Albany, Auckland 1310, New Zealand

Penguin Books Ltd, Registered Offices:
80 Strand, London WC2R 0RL, England

First published by Roc, an imprint of New American Library,
a division of Penguin Group (USA) Inc.

First Printing, November 2003
10 9 8 7 6 5 4 3 2 1

 REGISTERED TRADEMARK—MARCA REGISTRADA

Library of Congress Cataloging in Publication Data

Tarr, Judith.
House of war / Judith Tarr.
p. cm.
ISBN 0-451-52900-6
1. Jerusalem—History—Latin Kingdom, 1099–1244—Fiction. 2. Richard I, King of
England, 1157–1199—Fiction. 3. Wizards—Fiction. I. Title.

PS3570.A655H68 2003
813'.54—dc21   2003046617

Printed in the United States of America

PUBLISHER'S NOTE
This is a work of fiction. Names, characters, places, and incidents either are the product of the
author's imagination or are used fictitiously, and any resemblance to actual persons, living or
dead, business establishments, events, or locales is entirely coincidental.

HOUSE OF WAR

CHAPTER ONE

The leper followed them into Gehenna. They had passed him as they came out of Jerusalem by the Zion Gate, skirting the ashpits and the middens with their reek and their buzzing of flies, where the lepers and the beggars and the sick and mad wandered like damned souls in the Christians' hell. Beggars knew better than to trouble a pair of children with one horse between them, who looked like runaways and were trying not to be obvious about it, but the one leper trailed after them as they went down into the steep and stony valley.

He was not begging, and he was not being furtive. He shuffled behind them in his dusty rags, with his wooden clapper and his veiled face. He was only going the same way they were. That was all. He was not following them with any kind of intent.

The sound of his clapper echoed below the Mount of Zion until they left the road and took a narrow path up the rocky slope. Then it fell abruptly silent.

Teleri had not known she was holding her breath until she had to let it go. Something about the leper made her flesh creep.

"We should go back," Benjamin said for the hundredth time. "We're not supposed to be here. We're not even supposed to—"

Teleri stopped short. She was on foot; Benjamin was riding the bay mare. The mare fussed at Teleri's grip on her bridle, but once Teleri unlocked her fingers, the mare sighed and lowered her head, nosing about for scraps of grass and thorny scrub.

"See how calm Aliyah is," Teleri said. "We're safe out here. Nobody ever takes this path: they all stay on the road."

"I'm not worried about bandits," Benjamin said. "I'm worried about what will happen when your mother and my father find out where we've been. You know they said—"

"Mother doesn't care what anyone does since Owein died," Teleri said flatly. "Uncle Judah is all in a fuss about the family coming for Passover."

"Maybe so," said Benjamin, who could be just as stubborn as Teleri, "but your father is coming back, and when he gets here, you won't be able to put a foot outside the house."

"He's not here yet," Teleri pointed out. She planted her hands on her hips. "Do you want to find the lost Ark or don't you?"

"I still think we should look under the Temple," Benjamin said. "That's inside Jerusalem, and therefore technically—"

"That's too easy," Teleri said. "Someone would have found it. It's not in the city. You know that; we've talked about it. Get down and help me. There are caves under here, I feel them. They make my feet itch."

Benjamin set his chin. Teleri held her breath. Teleri was

gifted in seeking and scrying, but Benjamin had the knowledge in his blood.

Just when Teleri started to grow dizzy from lack of air, Benjamin swung his leg over the pommel and slid down. He was much taller than Teleri, and much thinner. He was scowling, though from the way his face suddenly changed, he was feeling the same thing as Teleri.

It would be stronger for him. This was his country far more than it was Teleri's. Teleri had been born here, but her parents came from elsewhere. Benjamin had been born in York, far away in England, but his ancestors had built the Temple and fashioned the Ark.

Teleri stooped down and began to clear a circle. Benjamin did not move. Teleri hissed. "Get over here! We'll never get this started if you don't help."

Benjamin shook his head. "Be quiet," he said. "Listen."

Just as Teleri opened her mouth to declare that there was nothing to hear, she heard it. It was a soft scraping, like a sandal sliding on stone, and a sound like labored breathing.

She had thought they lost the leper when they turned off the road. There were stories, which she had never believed, of the hatred of the afflicted for the whole. In her experience, which was not slight, lepers were either too prostrated by their condition to feel anything for anyone else, or so resigned to it that their whole life was a prayer. They were not monsters, nor were they evil. They had a sickness of the body, not of the soul.

In spite of everything she knew from growing up in or near a hospital, her skin had begun to crawl again. The place they had come to was hardly an hour outside the walls of Jerusalem, but a trick of terrain made it seem that they were in the deep desert. There was nothing to be seen but a steep stretch of stony hillside and the brief level on which they stood. The path that had brought them here had bent abruptly before they found the level space. Anything that came along it would be almost close enough to touch before they could see it.

That was bad strategy, as her father would not have failed to remark. Worse, the path ahead narrowed to a goat track and headed up the steep hill. Aliyah was a desert horse, fast and surefooted, but she could not carry both of them up that. They were trapped, if anything wanted to catch them.

Hastily Teleri drew a ragged circle around the three of them and muttered the words that raised a wall of protection. It was not much, but it was better than nothing. She was regretting now that she had eluded the protectors who watched over her at her mother's command. They would have told her mother what she was up to, with inevitable consequences, but she—not to mention Benjamin—would have been considerably safer.

It was only a leper, she told herself, or maybe not even that. It could have been a rock sliding down the hill, or a gust of wind. The wind blew oddly in these places. Sometimes it could seem like a living thing.

The dragging steps drew nearer. Her wards began to hum just below the threshold of hearing.

The shrouded shape rounded the bend of the hillside and stood still. It was wrapped in ragged black. Its shoulders were narrow and hunched, its back bent.

Teleri felt eyes on her. They stripped her skin away from the naked soul.

Benjamin was praying behind her: *"Baruch Adonai . . ."*

The thing in the leper's rags cared nothing for prayers, Hebrew or otherwise. It wanted her—her heart, her soul. It craved the magic that was in her and the blood she had inherited: child of two great mages, dweller in two worlds, protected of the powers of air.

It was a hungry thing—ravenous. It sucked at her through the frail shield of her wards. She reached inside of her and drew up power from the earth.

She should not have done that. She knew it just as the force that she had summoned coiled like snakes about her feet and dragged her slowly, inexorably, toward the thing that waited for her.

In pure desperation she sent a cry ringing up to heaven. She longed to hear the clap of great wings above her, and see—

Hooves rang on stone. The shadow-thing wavered, distracted. Its grip on her weakened. She lashed out at it.

A monstrous shape swooped down out of the sky. A pair of horsemen rounded the hillside at a perilous pace. A bolt of lightning struck the place where, an instant before, the shadow-thing had been.

It was gone. All that was left of it was the leper's clapper, charred and smelling faintly of brimstone.

Teleri burst through the wards. A prince of the jinn hovered above her, a terrible shape of wings and fangs and claws, as dearly familiar as her mother's face. His reproach was silent, but she felt it like a pang of guilt deep inside her.

Her father sat on his white Arab mare in the jinni's shadow. His turban was spotless and his robe perfectly clean, as if he had not been on the road for days. The man behind him was travel-stained enough for two, regarding Teleri with the same silent reproach as the jinni.

"Father," Teleri said, stopping short. "Mustafa."

"Daughter," said her father. "Benjamin. We thank you for this child's rescue. That bolt of yours was a strong working, and well aimed."

Teleri rounded on Benjamin. His cheeks were scarlet. "It was all I could think of," he said. "Uncle Ahmad, if you're going to punish her, you'll have to punish me, too. We came out here together."

"That will be settled later," Ahmad said. He held out his hand. Teleri let him pull her up behind him on his horse. Benjamin mounted the mare Aliyah. They rode together with the jinni flying slowly above them, away from that accursed place.

Teleri's mother was not at home. She was in the hospital as usual, the servants said. One of them would have gone to tell her that her husband had come to Jerusalem earlier than expected, but Ahmad stopped him. "She'll be back soon enough," he said. "Let her finish her work."

The servants exchanged glances. Teleri knew as well as they did that her mother might not come back at all that night, or tomorrow, either. She had not wanted to be in the house for more than a few moments since Owein died.

None of them said anything of that to Ahmad. The servants were protecting him. Teleri was protecting herself.

He did not confront her immediately. He sent a servant to take Benjamin home, and another to prepare a bath for Teleri. She was deeply glad of hot water and herb-scented soap, washing off the dust and the terrors of Gehenna.

Her father found her tucked up in bed with a posset. He had taken the time to rest a little himself, and to take off his turban and put on a house gown and silken slippers. He sat on the side of her bed.

Even knowing that she was about to pay the reckoning, she flung her arms about him and hugged him tightly. He returned the embrace with one just as strong.

She drew back. There were a few more threads of grey in his beard than there had been when he was last in this house, a year ago, but his face was as finely drawn as ever, his skin barely lined. She noticed these things now, as she grew older.

Parents were human, that was her latest discovery, and they were mortal, though maybe hers were less so than most.

He was studying her, too. There was more to see, since she was still growing and changing. He did not speak of it, only smoothed the curl that persisted in falling over her forehead.

She braced herself. Now it was coming.

"Tell me," he said with deceptive mildness, "what you were doing in Gehenna."

She could not lie to him. He was not one of the servants, to believe in wide eyes and studied innocence. "We were looking for the lost Ark," she said.

His brow rose. "Indeed? Did you find any sign of it?"

"There wasn't time," she said. "We were just beginning when—"

She found she could not go on. Her throat closed; her eyes stung with ignominious tears.

He was kind enough not to remark on the tears. "Surely you are aware of the things that live in the earth of that valley. It was a black place long ago, soaked in blood. The souls of the lost still wail on the wind. What in the world would persuade you to search for that particular treasure there?"

"Because of the blood," Teleri said. "Because it was a place of sacrifice. What better place to hide the Holy of Holies?"

"Is that your conclusion or Benjamin's?"

Teleri's cheeks warmed. "Benjamin's," she admitted. "But I made him go. He didn't want to. He hated the place."

"Well he might have," Ahmad said. "Some of his ancestors no doubt died there."

"Was that what that thing was? Was it a ghost?"

"It was not a living thing," Ahmad said, "but it was not a dead one, either. It was something between. Something . . ." His voice trailed off.

"Something evil," she said. "Something born out of blood and hate. But it didn't come from the valley. It followed us from the Zion Gate. We thought it was a leper. We didn't know until it was on us, what was underneath the robe."

She was shuddering. She could not help herself. He drew her into his arms again and held her. "You are not to blame for that," he said. "For slipping out when you were strictly forbidden to ride outside the walls without a protector, you will pay as full a price as your mother or I can conceive. But you did not summon that thing, whatever it was."

"I made it worse," she said in a small tight voice.

"You'll pay for that, too," he said, "but not tonight. Tonight we thank Allah that I came when I did."

"Thank Allah," she said. Even with the threat of retribution still to face, she was glad, very glad, to be in her father's arms tonight, and not in whatever hell of pain the dark thing had meant her to inhabit.

CHAPTER TWO

Sioned was exhausted almost beyond rational thought. If she drove herself just one more hour, she could fall onto a cot somewhere and sleep, please the gods, without dreams, until one of the apprentices woke her for yet another day of healing the sick.

Even Master Judah knew better than to try to send her home. Home was memory. Home was a death she could have prevented, if only—if only—

She must not think. She must not remember. This wound to dress, that boil to lance—and there was a fever, which needed bathing and dosing. The sick woman needed comfort, too, but that was beyond Sioned. She left that to the other physicians.

None of them spoke to her. She knew, distantly, that Master Judah had ordered that she be left alone. Someday she would thank him.

She sat down for a moment to take a breath before she

went on to the next sufferer. When she looked up again, her husband stared gravely down.

He often came to her in dreams, or they walked together outside of the world, if time and duty separated them as it had for the past year and more. It was one of the greater blessings of their magic, and it had been a great comfort when she was lonely or when the world was more than she could face.

But not since Owein died. She had turned her back on dreams, and on Ahmad, too. It was not that she blamed him. All the blame was purely her own. She could not face him. If he was coldly angry, her heart would break. And yet if he shared her grief without recrimination, all of her would break, purely and simply.

Ahmad did not speak. If he was alarmed, he did not show it. He lifted her with that easy strength of his, although he was neither tall nor broadly built, and carried her unresisting from the hospital.

His father had named him Yusuf, but his mother called him Owein. It was not in the bargain they had made when a witch from Gwynedd married a princely sorcerer from Syria. She would name the daughters, they had agreed, and he would name the sons. Teleri was firstborn, and he had honored the bargain. But when Owein was born, after a difficult pregnancy and a labor that came near to killing his mother, she never could remember to call him by the name his father gave him.

Teleri was like her mother: a dark, sturdy child with clear oval features and evening-colored eyes. Magic crackled off her like sparks from a cat. Owein bore a striking resemblance to his maternal grandfather. He was, the gods and Allah be thanked, considerably less irascible than Henry Plantagenet had been, but he had that careless brilliance and that gift for bending people to his will. Ahmad, father of many sons though he was, was as pleased with him as if he had been the first.

His mother adored him. Her daughter was as dear to her as her own self, but her son touched a part of her that even Ahmad had never come near. She said to her brother Richard once, "Now I understand your mother."

"God help you," Richard said with feeling. She laughed, because she was too happy to be annoyed with him. There was a little wryness in it, too, that she of all people should find a common ground with the terrible Queen of the English.

It was Owein's birthday. He could count them: five fingers on his hand, five years in this world. His father, in collusion with Mustafa, had given him his first horse, an exquisite little mare of the pure desert strain. Her sweet temper and smooth gaits pleased his mother, but her speed and fire were more than enough to delight a spirited young manchild.

He had been riding since before he could walk, borrowing or begging or occasionally stealing anything that would carry him. Grey Safiyah won from him a roar of delight and a swift and entirely anticipated demand: "I want to ride her out!"

His father concealed a smile behind a stern expression. "And are you confirmed enough in discipline to do such a thing?"

"I can go with Mustafa," Owein said. "The jinn can fly with us. I'll be as safe as castles."

"Mustafa may have other obligations," Ahmad said.

"He does not," said Owein. "It's my birthday. The king said he could spend it with me. He knew I'd want to ride out. Look at him, he's laughing at us. He knows you're going to say yes."

Ahmad lowered a glare at Mustafa. That most trusted of the king's scouts and spies, whose face was famously difficult to read, had forgotten himself so far as to allow a glint into his eye. "Just for that," Ahmad said to them both, "I should forbid you to ride anywhere but in the garden."

"You will not!" Owein said. "Tomorrow you will. But not today."

Ahmad cuffed him, for the principle, and swept him up and tossed him toward Mustafa. "Bring him back before dinner," he said.

Mustafa caught the solid weight and slung it onto his shoulder. Sioned, who had been maintaining a judicious silence while the men settled matters, blinked a little at the startling brightness of Mustafa's grin. Owein whooped as Mustafa deposited him firmly in the grey mare's saddle and took the rein of the bay that Hamid the stableman had wisely and presciently brought out for him.

Owein was a good horseman. He walked his new horse out of the yard, although Sioned was certain that the mare would be at the gallop as soon as she passed the castle's gate.

Ahmad sighed and shook his head. Sioned slid under his arm and settled in comfort against his side. "Do you think he's too young after all?" she asked.

"Not that one," said Ahmad. "He has sense, all things considered."

"He does, at that," she said. "Why the sigh, then?"

"Amazement," he said, "that he was born just yesterday, and he's so well grown already. I'll blink, and he'll be a man with sons of his own."

Sioned shivered lightly. She did not often remember that her husband was considerably older than she. With mages it mattered less; they lived longer than the run of men. Even so, he was mortal, and she could feel the awareness in him. He was not afraid, and not particularly sad. Death held no terrors for a mage of his power and skill.

She banished the thought and the chill it brought with it. Prescience was not her gift, but she knew in her heart that Ahmad was a long way yet from death. The shadow that had touched her was the old mindless fear of dissolution that every creature had. She opened her eyes to sunlight in her beloved castle of Montjoyeuse, and turned her back on the darkness.

They were back well before dinner, windblown and breathless and laughing at some jest such as boys loved. Mustafa was a man grown and a person of as much conse- quence as he would allow the king to bestow on him, but with Owein he let himself be a child again.

The guests had already begun to arrive. Owein had cho- sen them, with some advice from his father and mother, and they were a varied but peculiarly convivial gathering. Not many halls could have held both Knights Templar and emirs of Egypt and Syria, but Sioned was not surprised to see a pair of Owein's much older half-brothers conversing amicably with one of the Templars. Even more startling in its way was the Knight Hospitaller in stark black and white who stood with them; Hospitallers and Templars were even less friendly to one another than Templars and infidels. They were dis- cussing the relative merits of the Turkish bow and the Welsh longbow.

Richard was there. He had come in without fanfare, fresh from the hunt, and disappeared briefly, then reappeared in a cotte proper for a feast. His escort was small and his manner expansive. He did love, on occasion, to lay aside his crown and be a man among men.

Owein had a great many friends and well-wishers for a child so young. Sioned saw Master Judah and his wife Re- becca and the flock of their offspring, with half a dozen physicians from his hospital near the Tower of David in Jerusalem. Not far from them was Henry, the heir to Jerusalem, with a handful of barons and a prelate or two, none of whom frowned at the intermingling of Jews and Muslims with Christians and the very occasional pagan, of whom Sioned was one.

They greeted Owein's appearance with a roar of applause. He laughed and clapped his hands, and began a round of his guests that would not have shamed his grandfather, old King Henry himself.

Sioned's heart swelled with pride. Every child was perfect in his mother's eyes, but this one was honestly extraordinary. He danced through the hall, leaving a trail of smiles.

It was a grand feast. Blondel the singer sang for them, and there were dancers from Damascus and a troupe of acrobats from Cairo. Even while she shared in it, Sioned knew that she should commit it to memory, to bring out later and to cherish each separate moment.

The revelry ended at dusk. Owein would have preferred that it go on, but his mother was adamant. He was a young child, and he needed his sleep.

However rebellious he might be, he knew better than to defy his mother when she was in this mood. He said proper and respectful farewells, albeit with a hint of sulkiness, and let her lead him away.

He was nodding already as he walked, and when she took him in her arms, he barely protested. She climbed the stair to his tower with his head rolling on her shoulder; he was asleep with the suddenness of childhood, warm and heavy. She drew in the scent of him, which was still sweet, like an infant's.

His nurse was waiting to take him, but tonight Sioned was minded to look after him herself. She undressed him and washed him and laid him in bed, all without waking him.

It was terribly tempting to linger and watch him sleep, but she had guests and a husband, and a daughter who needed part of her, too. She withdrew reluctantly, leaving Atiyah to care for him as she had, admirably, since he was born.

Sioned started awake. Ahmad was sound asleep beside her. The twin gazehounds who guarded their door were snoring in a heap. Only the small brindled cat who always slept at her feet was awake as she was, eyes gleaming green by the night-lamp's flicker.

Sioned's heart was beating as if she had run a race. Yet she had no memory of nightmare. The castle was still. The hall full of their guests, the rooms in which Richard and Henry and the rest of the high ones were lodged, returned nothing to her senses but deep breathing and the occasional snort or snore. Even the guards on the walls were dozing at their posts. The wards were safe, the defenses intact. The jinn had gone away on some business of their own; there was nothing here to attract either their interest or their concern.

Still she could not slide back into sleep. She slipped out of bed, found her chemise and put it on, and with the cat padding softly after, followed her heart.

Teleri was asleep in her bed. Owein was not in his. Atiyah had fallen asleep in her corner, chin on breast.

Sioned resisted the urge to kick her awake. It was not difficult to tell where a child would go if he happened to rouse in the night and find everyone else asleep. Sioned borrowed Atiyah's mantle from its peg by the door and wrapped herself in it, padding down the winding stair to the inner courtyard and from there through the passage to the stable.

He was in the grey mare's stall, lying loose in the straw. The mare stood over him, nosing him gently. Her breath ruffled the curls on his neck.

Sioned would remember how soft those curls were, and how black against his white skin. He was very still.

There was no mark on him. No wound, no blood. Nothing was broken. And yet he was not breathing.

Her mind was perfectly clear. She never doubted the mare's innocence. No hoof had touched him, nor had the heavy body rolled on him in its sleep, crushing him. There was no reason at all why he should be lying there, motionless and empty.

The life was long gone from him. She had to bring it back. She was a physician. She healed the sick.

She could not bring the dead to life. Her magic was not enough for that. It needed a god or a saint, of which she was neither.

She took him in her arms. He was still warm, still supple. His eyes were open. There was something in them. Something . . .

Ahmad found her there, sitting still, but never as still as the child in her lap. He was growing cold.

"I can't find the reason," she said, "why—"

She watched the great cry well up in her husband. She was as empty as Owein. Her eyes were perfectly dry. When the cry escaped Ahmad, her ears rang. The horses screamed and battered the walls. The jinn came roaring from the quarters of heaven, and guests and servants from the earth below.

She was the stillness in their center. She felt nothing at all.

Not then. Not while the men ran wildly about, hunting a murderer, but finding nothing and no one. When they buried him in the earth outside of Montjoyeuse, on the hilltop where he had loved to sit and look out across the stark and beautiful country to Jerusalem, she watched dispassionately. Ahmad wept, deep racking sobs that would have rent her heart if she had had one. Teleri clung to him and wailed. Sioned stood apart. She knew as coldly as she knew everything else, that she would not weep again.

Of one thing she was certain. Whatever the evidence or lack thereof, Owein had not simply died. Something had taken him. Something subtle and secret. Something that could slip through wards and past guards and separate a soul from a body, and leave the body abandoned for its mother to find.

She would hunt that thing. When she could move again, she would track it to its lair and destroy it.

Ahmad left a month after Owein died. He would not have gone, but Sioned insisted. "You know you must," she said. "It's been too long since you saw to matters in Egypt. If you let it go, you'll lose it all."

"I can wait a little longer," he said.

She shook her head. "You know you can't. Your emirs will revolt. They need you there, with your hand on the rein."

"But you—"

"I have my work," she said. "I have our daughter. I'll be well enough."

He did not believe her, not honestly, but in the end she persuaded him. He never knew, or admitted to knowing, that she was glad to see him go. His presence demanded too much of her. It threatened to wake her again, and to set her heart to beating.

That must not happen. If it did, she would shatter.

She went on as she must. People learned to let her be, and that was well. She shut down Montjoyeuse, sent away the servants, locked and barred the gates and set a guard of jinn on them. The stable where he had died, she demolished. The grey mare she gave away. She kept nothing of Owein's, no token, not one thing that he had owned. She set aside even memory.

Her mind was a treacherous thing. It taunted her with dreams. In them she stayed with her son as she had persuaded herself not to do, and kept him from going out when he woke, and protected him against whatever had destroyed him. In dreams he lived. But even while she dreamed, she knew that when she woke, the part of the world that he had filled would be cold and empty. He was gone. No power in heaven or earth could bring him back again.

CHAPTER THREE

The King of Jerusalem was in a foul mood. He always was when he had a letter from his mother.

The sight of Mustafa improved his temper visibly, but he was still snarling and pacing like the lion he so vividly resembled.

He was aging well, Mustafa thought. The cares of kingship, for the most part, sat lightly on him. He had a gift, rare in princes, of finding people whom he could trust, who could carry part of the burden and not trouble him excessively with it. That left him free to do what he did best, which was to defend this perpetually embattled kingdom.

The person he trusted most in the world was also the one who drove him most nearly mad. "I had thought," he said with tightly controlled calm, "that she would settle matters for me in the west, and make such peace as could be made, and spare me the trouble of worrying about any of it. Now look. Look at this!"

Mustafa caught the sheet of parchment as he flung it. It was much creased and crumpled, and at one point it had been torn nearly in half. Mustafa had to guess at some of the words, but their meaning was clear.

Enough is long enough, Queen Eleanor had written from some cold castle in England.

> *I cannot keep your brother contained forever. He points out with all too cogent logic that you have not set foot west of Cyprus in over a dozen years. If you would continue to be either Duke of Normandy or King of England, you must come back to claim what is yours. You were not meant to die in Jerusalem. Let Henry have the office he's been waiting for with notorious patience, and come home where you belong.*

Richard paced to the wall, spun, stalked back. "Arrogant, high-handed, stubborn, obstinate, headstrong—" Words failed him. He sucked in a breath and began again with a fraction less heat. "Not God Himself can tell that woman what to do. A king is nothing to her."

"You're going back to England," Mustafa said.

Richard's eyes were bright blue, like the heart of a flame. "You always did cut to the chase. Yes, I'm going back. Damn her, she's right. This was supposed to be a fast war—get in, win, get out. Once I had the crown of Jerusalem, I told myself I'd stay a year, then I'd hand it over to young Henry and go back to the real world. Somehow that year stretched into a dozen. Am I really indispensable on this side of the sea?"

He was not asking for an answer, but Mustafa gave him one nonetheless. "You know you are. The fear of *Malik Ric* keeps Islam at bay. Egypt is yours in firm alliance, because its sultan is your sister's husband. Even the contentious Franks keep themselves more or less under control while you are here to restrain them."

"And to think," said Richard, "I used to have such a gift for making enemies."

"You still do," Mustafa assured him. "Only now they don't dare rebel against you."

"Henry's better at keeping the peace than I am," Richard said. "He's not so bad in war, either. He's ready—he has been for years. I won't be abandoning the kingdom."

"Henry is a good man," Mustafa said. "He'll be a capable king."

"You could be more lukewarm if you really tried," said Richard dryly. "Henry is not a weakling."

"He is not you."

Richard snorted. "And thank God for that! No, old friend—I have to go. England was mine first, and Normandy and Anjou have been in my family for years out of count. I'm a parvenu here. The west is home."

Mustafa bent his head in carefully calculated servility. "As you say, my lord."

Richard obviously did not believe that he had given in, but a servant came just then with a message that needed attending to directly. Mustafa had messages of his own to deliver, news and dispatches from Egypt, but they were not urgent. He slipped out while the king was occupied.

Preparations had already begun for the king's departure. He would leave at Pentecost; it was now just short of Easter.

Mustafa felt a strangeness in the kingdom, the sense that something powerful was ending. The court was already shifting, turning its focus toward the man who would take the crown when Richard relinquished it. Richard's most loyal servants saw their power weaken, and friends lose interest or become too busy to trouble themselves with allies whose day was past.

Not yet, Mustafa thought stubbornly. Not quite yet.

After he left the king, he went out into the city, listening in taverns as he had done so often in his years as Richard's eyes and ears in unusual places. As a Muslim he drank no wine or ale, but he could nurse a cup and catch the rumors that went flittering past.

Most of them had to do with Richard's leaving and Henry's taking the crown. A good number of rumors as well attached Ahmad's name among the Franks, Saphadin, to this story or that, and to stories of his sons and his nephew who was sultan in Damascus.

Mustafa recorded these in memory, although none was worth repeating to either of the men he served. But there were others that made him sharpen his ears.

"Masyaf," said a man in sergeant's gear with the white cross of the Hospitallers on the shoulder. He hissed the name, as men had done in this country since before Mustafa was born. "That cursed place. We thought we'd exorcised it when the Old Man went to hell where he belonged. But the dead won't stay dead. Shapes in white walk the passages at night. They're outside the walls, too, drifting by when you're on sentry-go. Sometimes they suck the blood from a goat or a sheep, and leave it by a gate."

"They say the Old Man himself is back," said the man beside him, likewise a soldier in the service of the Hospital. He drank deep of his mug of ale and blew the foam from his mustache. "People in the villages have taken to barring their doors at night. If they have a witch or a conjuror, they put up charms and protections."

"They'd do better to pray," the sergeant said, "if that's really the old devil himself. He's black, they say, and the only shape he has is the cowl he's draped in. He'll steal children if he can, lambs and kids if not, and they're never seen again."

"He's giving himself substance," said the other. That roused a rumble of incredulity. He spread his hands. "Now then. Now then! I asked a priest. He's a wise one, and knows about these things. He gave me a cross to wear and blessed it, and promised me that if I should happen to meet the specter, I'd be protected."

"A priest, well," said the sergeant. "Not all of them are as pure as the snow in dear lost Normandy, either. Did he keep his cowl over his face? Did his voice seem to come from underground?"

"He was a fine fair man with a great red face, as well fed and hearty as an abbot. If that's the form the old monster is wearing, I'd say he's dined on more than the blood of a lamb."

That won a round of laughter. Mustafa smiled thinly, but there was little mirth in him. If the Old Man of the Mountain was walking again, the precarious peace of this country would tumble into war. He had no reason to love the Kingdom of Jerusalem. Its king had struck a bargain with him and then destroyed him. Any man knew that when a spirit came back from the dead, it came to right a wrong.

Maybe Richard should leave this country after all. He was in deadly danger if he stayed.

"How likely is it?" Richard demanded. "Is it just rumor, or is it the truth?"

"I think there's truth in it," Mustafa said. He had considered leaving the king in ignorance, since Richard would be gone soon enough. But in all his years of serving the Lionheart, he had yet to withhold any scrap of knowledge that might be to Richard's advantage. Freed or no, he remained a loyal slave.

Richard was not a man to give way to blind alarm. "So the old snake's crawled back out of hell. You think he'll come for me?"

"It would stand to reason," Mustafa said. "You're his last memory of this life, and the reason for his leaving it."

Richard's lips pulled back from his teeth. "And a fine memory that is. If I'm known for nothing else after I've died, let men say that I sent the Old Man to hell."

"If he has come back," said Mustafa, "you can wager he means to send you in his place."

"That will be a fight worth fighting," said Richard.

They were on the walls of the Tower of David, looking out across the city to the golden flame of the Dome of the Rock. Richard loved to stand here, to know that he was in Jerusalem, and it was his. Now that he was close to leaving it, he spent as much time in this place as he could: held councils here, met with lords and emissaries, and shared privy conversation with the most trusted of his spies.

While they stood in companionable silence, a commotion brought them both about. One of the king's guards ran down along the wall, with a man in a clerk's gown panting behind him. "Sire!" the clerk gasped. "Sire, we—I—"

The guard caught the clerk before he could fall on his face, and bowed hastily to the king. "It's the treasury, sire," he said. "It's been invaded."

That caught Richard's attention as few things could. He set off without a word. The others followed as best they might.

The treasury lay in the heart of the Tower of David, behind doors of forged iron. More than human power guarded it. There were wards of ancient power and potency on that door and about the rooms behind it. None could pass but those whom the king had granted entry.

The doors were wrenched from their hinges. The rooms beyond were ransacked. Chests were flung open and their contents scattered on the floor. Coins and jewels and precious things were flung everywhere. Jars of unguents were shattered, filling the air with a cloying sweetness. Vessels of rare wines, oils of impossible rarity, boxes and packets of spices, lay as if blown by a whirlwind.

This was pure malice. Clerks were moving through it, lamenting the destruction, but even while they deplored it, they took inventory, item by item.

Richard called their chief to him. "What's been taken?" he asked.

"As far as we can determine, sire," said that harried and haggard man, "nothing."

Richard's brows rose. "Nothing?"

"Not a thing, sire," said the clerk. "Whatever it was, either it was hunting for one particular thing, or it simply came to wreak havoc."

"Which it has done," Richard said. "What was it? Or who?"

"We don't know, sire," said the clerk.

"Then find out!"

The clerk rocked under the force of Richard's temper, but he neither flinched nor retreated. "We will do that, sire. If you will allow us to summon those who might—"

"Do whatever you need to," Richard said. "But do it quickly."

Mustafa was already in motion. He did not wait for a dismissal, but ran where he knew Richard would want him to go.

Ahmad walked slowly through the tumbled rooms. His face was drawn and tired. He had seemed glad of Mustafa's coming, and even of his message. However difficult or puzzling the mystery which he had been brought to solve, it could only be an escape from the grief that filled his house still, even after a year. Mustafa had worried at first that he would be too exhausted to wield the power that was in him, but he seemed to gain strength as he took in the destruction.

He explored each room, moving softly around the guards and servants who had begun to restore order. There was nothing obvious about what he did. Mustafa could feel the subtle fire of magic on his skin, and see it flickering over the slender erect figure in its white turban. To eyes that had not the gift, he was simply taking stock of the damage, while Richard waited in waxing impatience.

At last he circled back through the rooms. His brows were knit. He barely seemed to notice how close Richard was to losing his temper. "Magic did this, yes," he said, "but it stole nothing."

"I already know that," Richard growled. "Tell me something new."

"Tell me where you keep that thing we do not name."

"That—" Richard's teeth clicked together. "Should I say it aloud? Especially here?"

"The hunter is gone," said Ahmad. "I'll raise stronger wards and more powerful protections, but for the moment this place is safe. Tell me."

Richard reached into his shirt and began to draw out a pendant on a chain. Ahmad stopped him before it came to light. "Good," he said. "Excellent. Be sure you keep it with you. It will guard you even while you protect it."

Richard sighed faintly and let the chain slip back into concealment. "You're sure this is what—whatever it was—was looking for?"

"Other things of power are here," Ahmad said, "and untaken if not untouched. The one you carry is greater than any of them."

"And if the Old Man has come back, he would come for the thing that was taken from him, that was the heart of his power." Richard laughed, as if startled into mirth. "Now there's a war for you, sultan of sorcerers: the living against the dead and damned."

"God help us all," Ahmad said.

CHAPTER FOUR

Sioned slept for a day and a night. When she woke, the knot of exhaustion had loosened. Her body, separated from the work that had kept it going day and night for months out of count, had begun to heal. Her mind and spirit . . .

Ahmad was gone from the house, but it was full of his presence. Teleri had been living for some weeks, the servants told her, in Master Judah's house. Sioned had not even noticed.

The pain of that was sudden and sharp. If she grieved—what of the others? What of Owein's father? His sister? She had been so wrapped in herself, so caught up in her own and singular sorrow, that she had given no thought to them at all.

She did not want to think or feel again, but there was no escaping it. The walls were down, cast in ruins. Ahmad had destroyed them. He had left her open to the wind.

She made herself get out of bed. She would, she must, do

something useful. The hospital, she thought, because people needed her there—and because it would give her time to think and plan. Somehow she must remember how to be a mother to the child she had left. Gods willing, Teleri would forgive the long neglect.

She bathed and dressed without the assistance of a maid. As she was plaiting her hair, one of the pages slipped timidly through the door. "Lady," he said. "There's someone—she insists—"

"A guest?" Sioned asked.

"Someone who says she has to see you," the child said.

"Tell her to wait," Sioned said with little patience.

She almost left the guest or petitioner to sit until she grew tired of waiting and left, but some remnant of conscience made Sioned go down as a gracious host should. She would stay a moment, then excuse herself, and courtesy would have been observed.

The visitor was sitting in the solar. A cup of wine and a plate of cakes lay untouched on the table beside her. Her hands were folded and her head bent as if in prayer.

Sioned realized that she was gaping. Queen Berengaria looked up just as Sioned shut her mouth, and gathered herself to rise.

"No," Sioned said. "No, lady. Sit." She went down in a curtsey and kissed the queen's hand. "This is an honor."

"I'm glad you think so," Berengaria said. She had been a sallow and nondescript creature when Richard married her, the year before he took Jerusalem. The years since had not been kind to her. Sioned would have expected that she would become plump, but she had lost weight and substance instead. Her skin had a distinct yellow cast, and her mouth was thin and tight. Unloved, unregarded, and for the most part forgotten, she was by no means a happy woman.

Sioned was as much at fault for that as anyone else. Everyone knew that Richard was not a man for women. The queen whom his mother had forced on him was still, as far as Sioned knew, a virgin. Berengaria lived in her own quarters, as cloistered as a nun. Once Eleanor had left for the west, Richard had stopped even pretending to keep her with him when he traveled through the kingdom. Sioned doubted that he ever troubled to think of her at all.

"Do you need my help?" Sioned asked as the silence stretched. "What may I do for you?"

The long pale fingers worked, tangling with one another. Berengaria's breath came hard. Her thin chest rose and fell.

At length the words found their way past the barrier of years and reticence. "Yes, I need you. But whether you can do it, or will . . ."

"I will if I can, lady," Sioned said.

"Will you?" Berengaria went still. "I come in all humility. I ask you, beg you, to consider what I ask. The world knows I am no queen to my king. I've endured that, and the neglect and insults that have gone with it, for the honor of my vows to him and for the vanishingly few concessions that he has ever granted me. Now he's leaving for England, and there's no mention of my leaving with him."

"You want me to persuade him?" Sioned asked. "I can try, but—"

"No," said Berengaria. "He can go. That matters nothing to me, and might actually better my position. I need another thing, a thing that may be impossible—but if anyone can accomplish it, it will be you. When he sails from Acre, let me be carrying his heir."

Sioned almost laughed. Did Berengaria even begin to recognize the irony of what she asked? For Sioned to work a spell that would get this bitter woman with child, after her own child had died and left her desolate . . .

She had been silent too long. Berengaria spoke again, the words almost tumbling over one another. "I've tried everything I can think of. I've asked every witch and charlatan and wandering saint who will come into my presence. Most of them have taken my money and given me some foolishness to say or do, then gone away and left me poorer and still childless. Now I am desperate, and he is going away and leaving me here. If I can provide him with an heir, however late, I will have worth in the world."

Sioned had felt nothing for so long that she came near to fainting from the power of the emotions that surged up in her. They seared like hot iron. Grief and pity, yes—those were laudable. But anger, too: red rage. How dare she? How dare she come to Sioned with this of all petitions?

"I can't," Sioned said. "I can't help you."

"Can't or won't?"

She met those narrowed dark eyes. "I can't," she said. "I do regret it. I wish there were a way. But not for me."

"Only tell me," said Berengaria. "Am I barren?"

"No," said Sioned, quite without thinking. "You are not."

"Then surely—"

"No," said Sioned. "I can't."

Berengaria rose. Twin spots of crimson stained her cheeks, but her voice was level, almost flat. "I thank you for such courtesy as you have shown me."

Berengaria left then. Almost Sioned called her back. But only almost. She could not face that particular bitterness. It was a pity, and a terrible one, but she could do nothing.

Sioned lingered for a while after Berengaria left, mustering her wits and trying to be strong. She made herself eat and drink from the dainties that Berengaria had not touched. They revived her well enough that she could think of getting up and going on.

Richard always entered a room like a blast of wind. He was a creature of great halls and palaces, or of battlefields. Small rooms crowded him.

This one barely contained him. Sioned regarded him in blank surprise. Either he was alone or he had left his escort outside. If he had passed Berengaria, he had not noticed. He looked as if he had been through a battle, though he was dressed for court, with no dust or blood to stain him.

He reached into his shirt and pulled out a thing that he cast in front of her. She stared blankly at the roundel of ancient pottery with its incised symbols. It seemed a trinket of little worth and no beauty, such as one might find in any bazaar.

It was one of the greatest instruments of power in a land overrun with them. Even as her eyes found it profoundly unimpressive, all the hackles of her magic had risen. The Seal of Solomon was a terrible and potent thing.

She had no desire to touch it. It was warded—she and Ahmad between them had laid on it the strongest shields they knew. No one outside of this room, even a great mage, could know that it was here.

"Someone tried to steal this," Richard said without greeting or preliminary. "Will you take it? Whoever it is will come after me next. We think—"

"You had better tell me," she said. She was suddenly weary beyond bearing, but for this she could not indulge in weakness.

He told her, succinctly. She heard him in silence. When he finished she said, "Where is Ahmad?"

"Assuring himself that nothing really was stolen. He sent me to you."

Richard was no one's errand boy. It was a measure of his dismay that he had let himself be sent away. Sioned drew a deep breath, hoping it would make her stronger. "*He* told you to give me this thing?"

"We agreed," said Richard. "It needs someone subtle, whose wards are strong."

"I am not—" She broke off. It was clear enough what they were doing. They were dragging her back to the world of the living.

She did not want to be dragged. But there was the Seal on the table, with the terrible weight of power and danger that was in it. She had stolen it from the Old Man. It was her fault that all this was beginning again.

Slowly she took up the Seal by the chain. It had been hung from a strip of leather cord when she stole it, but Richard had chained it with gold. She wrapped it in the napkin from her breakfast and slipped it into her purse.

Richard let out a breath. "Good," he said, "and thank God."

"It's no safer with me than with you," she said, "and I'm much less safe with it than without it."

"So hide it somewhere," he said. "Destroy it if you like. I've no love for it. It's a pernicious thing, and should never have been made."

"If I destroyed it now," she said, "it would take the city with it. It's too full of power."

Richard shrugged uncomfortably. "You know I hate magic. Just keep it, then. We'll lay a false trail away from you, with a tidy little trap at the end of it."

"More magic?"

He growled at her. She sighed. Once she would have laughed, but that was no longer in her. "I'll guard it," she said, "since you leave me no choice."

"Good," he said as he had before.

He left her not long after that, with his monstrous and burdensome gift on her purse, and the weight of living on her as it had not been since Owein died.

CHAPTER FIVE

Masyaf was empty.

Mustafa had gone there at Richard's bidding with a message for the commander of the garrison. The journey had taken longer than he expected: he met a party of raiders in the hills near the great fortress of Krak, and in eluding them had gone farther out of his way than he meant to. A riding of Hospitallers set him again on his way.

They rode back along his track, intending to deal with the raiders. Mustafa rode on through that bleak and tumbled country. Summer was coming; the heat was rising at midday, although the nights were still cold.

He had begun to feel uneasy even while he rode with the Hospitallers. The raiders had been ordinary enough, young Bedouin come in from the desert to rob travelers on the Damascus road. There was nothing magical or foreboding about them. And yet something about this country was not as it should be.

There were no birds. There should have been hawks and vultures circling, and lesser birds flitting through the thorny scrub. But the land was silent. He saw no thing that walked or flew or crawled, not even a snake or a lizard. If he had not had provisions from the Hospitallers' store, he would have been hard put to feed himself, with no hunting at all.

Masyaf stood on its steep crag. The banner of the Hospital flew from one of its towers, white cross on black. But there was no sign of life in or about it. No travelers on the road, no guards on the gate. The village at the castle's feet was silent.

Mustafa did not pause to search the houses. He rode up the narrow track toward the open gate. He already knew, when he had come to it, what he would find.

There was no one alive in that place, and no one dead, either. It was empty. The rooms were still furnished as he remembered, even the chapels gleaming with their golden crosses. There was food in the kitchens, bread set to rise and turned to a mass of mold, a flyblown ox spitted over a cold hearth. A thin film of dust had settled everywhere.

Mustafa the tracker found no tracks. Not one. There had been fifty knights in this garrison, a hundred squires, and an army of soldiers and servants. They were gone. No trace remained of any of them. They might have melted into air.

He barely remembered the ride back to Krak. He rode without fear, which was probably mad, but he could not find it in himself to be afraid. He had a thought that the garrison had been recalled so suddenly that there had been no time even to bake the bread, and that they had all passed while he was tracking down raiders in the hills. It was a foolish thought and he knew it, but he did not want to consider what else might have happened.

The knights in Krak did not believe him. If he had been any other infidel, they might have beaten him and thrown him out the gate. But he was the king's dog. Within an hour of his arrival, a company had ridden out at the gallop, aiming for Masyaf.

They did not come back, nor did they send a messenger. Mustafa would have gone to look for them, but the Master of Krak said, "No. I'm sending you back to Jerusalem, with escort. They are not your jailers. They are to see that you keep safe."

Mustafa bowed. "I understand," he said.

The Master eyed him doubtfully. Franks were never sure they understood a Muslim, even one whom the king famously trusted. This Frank at least was willing to let him go, instead of keeping him locked in a cell until the king came to let him out.

The king would happily have locked Mustafa's escort in a cell, the smaller the better, but Mustafa talked him out of it. They had brought him to Jerusalem both fast and safe, and in quite acceptable condition. They were even pleasant about it. The time was long past since Mustafa had been beaten and tortured for little more reason than that he was an infidel and the king trusted him.

Once Richard had heard what Mustafa had to tell, he sent a page to fetch the lord Saphadin. It was some while before he came, during which time Mustafa had a bath and a bit of dinner. When Saphadin passed the door of the king's privy chamber, Mustafa was just finishing his second cup of sherbet.

Ahmad accepted a cup for himself, and drank gratefully. The page had found him on the road to Jerusalem, riding from the direction of his wife's castle of Montjoyeuse. Mustafa could tell he had been there: the line between his brows was a little more pronounced, and his mouth was a shade tighter than usual.

Sioned would not even speak the name of the place where her son had died. Ahmad had not found the visit pleasant, either, from the look of him. He seemed almost relieved to hear ill news from another quarter.

"Fifty knights," he said. "That's a great blow to the strength of the kingdom."

"Fifty knights, a hundred squires." Richard was always calmest when he was closest to declaring war. "I didn't have you brought here to ask who did it. I don't think there can be any doubt of that. I need to know—are they lost? Or can we get them back?"

Ahmad laughed. It made Mustafa think of a sudden fall of rain in a desert, or a gust of cool wind in the noonday sun. "My lord," he said. "Oh, my lord! When I'm away, I forget how gloriously direct you can be. I can't answer your questions—yet. But I will try. Will you give me time?"

Richard started to snap a reply, but then he paused. It seemed he had remembered what they were, after all, and who Ahmad was. "This is yours to choose," he said. "You know that, I hope."

"I do know," Ahmad said, "and I thank you for thinking of it. Just as you know that when I come to Jerusalem as I have just now, I come as your kinsman and your sister's husband—not as the sultan in his glory. In Egypt I am what I am; in Damascus likewise. Here, I live a different life and serve another purpose. I am, to an extent, yours to command—until my other self calls me back again."

"How soon will that be?" Richard asked.

Ahmad shrugged slightly. "My sons are well disposed in Cairo. None of them is particularly eager to be rid of me, but they are pleased to have a freer hand, for a while."

"Good," said Richard with evident relief. "Good, then. I'll give you three days. Don't get yourself killed or worse, finding out. If we've lost them, we've lost them. I can't afford to lose you, too."

"I'll stay alive," Ahmad said rather grimly. "My wife will hound me through all the circles of your Christian hell, otherwise."

"She's not a Christian," Richard reminded him.

"Neither am I," said Ahmad. He drew a deep breath. "I'd best begin the hunt as soon as may be."

"Yes," Richard said. "Do it."

It was something to see a sultan bow to the bidding of the King of Jerusalem. How the world had changed, Mustafa thought. And yet there was nothing subservient about Ahmad's obedience. He did it because he chose. It was the concession of an ally, not the submission of a servant.

Ahmad was not in the best place for a great hunt. The power and holiness of Jerusalem reverberated through the planes of the worlds. It overwhelmed most workings of magic and blinded the eyes of foresight.

That was why Richard had been able to keep the Seal of Solomon here. It was safe inside these walls within walls, these magics piled on magics until there was no separating one from another.

Ahmad could go back to Montjoyeuse. For all the grief that was there, it was a clean place, well warded, and had been blessed before death came to take his son. But he could not face those memories again, not so soon.

Mustafa had followed him from his audience with the king. He had expected that. The king's Saracen was, in his way and within the limits of his various allegiances, as loyal a servant as Ahmad had. He always went where he was needed, or where he reckoned he could be of most use.

Mustafa fetched fresh horses, borrowing them from the

king's stable, while Ahmad gathered what he needed from his own house. Sioned was not there; she was at the hospital as always. It was as well. She would have insisted on coming, and she was too fragile yet for the kind of working that Ahmad had in mind.

Mustafa had brought the horses and was waiting in the courtyard. He had also thought to bring a mule burdened with food and drink for men and horses.

The mule slowed their pace, but Ahmad did not need to go far: only beyond the sphere of Jerusalem, into the hills. He stayed well away from Gehenna with its weight of dark memories, seeking out as clean a place as he could find in this ancient and haunted country.

It was nearly sunset before he had gone far enough. He left the road and went up into the trackless country, aiming to set a wall of stone between himself and city. As the sun touched the horizon, he stopped in a little dip of valley that looked and felt as if nothing human had walked in it since the prophet Jesus was alive.

Mustafa made camp quietly and with dispatch, and saw to the horses. Ahmad spread a small rug on the stony ground and said the evening prayer, matched by Mustafa on the other side of the camp's circle. When Ahmad was done, he remained kneeling, sitting on his heels, and lifted his eyes to the darkening sky.

The stars were coming out. The air beneath them was full of jinn and afarit and lesser spirits of air. Some hovered above him, curious. He greeted those he knew, gravely, and offered them respect. They swept great winged bows in return, with a sparkle of merriment that made him smile.

Their brightness of spirit made him stronger for the hunt. Mustafa tended a small fire with no fear of bandits—not with the jinn on guard. Its flames gave Ahmad a focus.

A handful of the jinn sailed with him through the winds of the worlds. A part of him was anchored by the fire, under the mortal stars. The rest rode on wide wings, soaring from current to current.

The earth below was a tapestry of light and darkness, an intricate weaving of magic and the mundane, inhabited by untold multitudes of spirits. Even a master of the Art could be dizzied and overwhelmed. Ahmad had to pause, to steady himself. There was order in that semblance of chaos, circles within circles within circles.

He veered away from the great pulsing brilliance that was Jerusalem, aiming northward. The way was not at all difficult. He simply looked for the deepest darkness, where all the light was not simply gone, it had been devoured.

All that Jerusalem was, this place was not. He hovered above it on the wings of the jinn, and sifted through the veils of worlds until he could see it in its mortal form.

The Hospitallers had strengthened the walls and built a new tower that looked toward Damascus. The Garden of Allah was gone. The part of it that had existed in this world was buried beneath the new tower, and the gate to the rest was shut and sealed with great wards.

The fortress was not empty. Men were coming to it in ones and twos and threes, most in robes of the desert and many in armor of Islam. All of them, once they had passed within, put aside their disguises and greeted one another in the white robes of the Assassins.

The Master had not yet come, but he was coming. Ahmad could feel him like the first breath of a storm in the desert.

Ahmad was not interested in him, not tonight. He wrapped himself in wards and descended toward the castle.

The taint of Christianity was not yet scrubbed from it. The Faithful had scoured the worst places: the chapels, the cells where the knights of the Hospital had slept, the kitchens that the cooks had fouled with the flesh of pigs. But the whole place reeked with the memory of them.

Ahmad slipped through those halls and passages, insubstantial as a shadow. Under the memory of the Franks were older, deeper memories, some good, some ill, but overlaid with a cold darkness.

The knights who had vanished must still be here, caught between worlds. There were ways, magics . . .

He had no warning at all. No flicker, no shift in the shadows. He had found a clearer trail, a more recent memory than the rest, and followed it to the tower. Just as he neared the gate, it struck.

The dark roared down. Instinct alone saved Ahmad. He flattened and slid, then with every muscle of his insubstantial body, he flung himself up and away.

The jinn caught him. They loathed and feared the place to which he had gone, but they had stayed for him, for love of his lady, whom they revered as a pure spirit. They snatched him away.

CHAPTER SIX

"You absolute, blazing fool."

Ahmad had no memory of leaving the hills or riding back to Jerusalem. From the number and placement of his bruises, he thought he must have traveled at least part of it face down over a saddle.

His first clear memory was of morning sun in the court of his own house, the deep green of the lemon tree in the corner, and his wife's face. She was stark white. He had fought wars out of count as both mage and fighting man, and even he flinched before the blaze of her eyes. She was in a high Angevin rage, and he was in no little danger of his life.

"If you kill me," he said reasonably, "you'll never be able to live with the guilt."

"I'll kill myself as soon as I know you're dead."

"Then we'll both be fools," he said, "and our daughter will never forgive us. Do you mind moving over? I think I need to sit down."

She got a grip on his coat and dragged him to the bench under the lemon tree, and dropped him painfully onto it. While he caught his breath, she said, "Next time you attempt suicide, at least tell me what you're up to."

He eased the barest fraction. She was still angry, but she had cooled somewhat—enough that she was unlikely just then to kill anything, even him. "I will if I can," he said.

"That's no promise."

"It's the best I can manage," he said. "This was necessary, beloved. Your brother—"

"I know what my brother did," she said through gritted teeth. "I'll deal with him next. As for the necessity, did you find anything you didn't expect? Do you know where the knights are?"

"No," he said unwillingly, "and no. But we do know for certain now: Masyaf is in the hands of the Assassins again. That means—"

"That means a hostile domain too near to Krak." She sighed and rubbed her temples as if they ached. "Damn you. Damn Richard."

He laid his hands softly on either side of her face. She did not fling him away, which encouraged him considerably. His powers were much depleted, but he had enough to soothe the pain.

She leaned against him for an instant. It was too short— she stiffened quickly and drew away—but it was more than she had given him in a year. He took great care not to draw attention to it, for fear she would bolt.

"You are sure it's the Old Man," she said.

"No doubt of it," said Ahmad.

"How?"

"His body was killed," Ahmad said. "We know that for certain. But a power as great as his, so strongly bound to the side of evil, would find ways to come back and take vengeance. It's not terribly uncommon, though ghosts and ill spirits are much more likely to empty a castle through fear than by causing the inhabitants to vanish. They must be hidden somewhere outside the world, but how or where or why . . . I don't know. I don't think I'm strong enough to discover it."

"Alone you are not," she said.

He set his lips together. Whatever he could say would not be diplomatic, and he was nothing if not a diplomat.

"You should have come to me," she said.

That too needed an answer he could not afford to give.

She hit him as if he had given it. It was not too hard a blow, but it rocked him. He had barely steadied himself before she was on him.

The rain of blows turned to a storm of tears, then after a long while to silence. He held her, stroking the hair that had escaped from its matronly veil, tangling his fingers in the tumble of curls. The bruises would heal. It mattered more that she was finally healing, finally breaking out of the shell in which she had lived since Owein died.

She did not thank him for it, nor did he expect her to. He lifted her, grunting a little for his strength was not what it should be, and carried her into the house.

Teleri watched them from a window that looked down on the fountain court. She felt odd, as if the world were shifting underfoot. She did not like it. It almost made her angry.

"Your mother hits like a boy," Benjamin said behind her.

They had been investigating the storeroom, looking for the wherewithal to work a certain spell. They had almost everything, and from the look of it, neither Teleri's mother nor her father would be taking inventory of the chests and boxes before the working was long over.

That was good, she told herself. Her mother never had time for her, or cared about her, but her father was different—and just now, she needed him to let her be. She had caused this trouble. She had to mend it. Then everything would be well again, or as well as it could ever be.

She turned away from the window. The last jar she opened held the last thing she needed. She tucked it in the bag with the rest.

Benjamin eyed her with deep suspicion. "You're going to do it now."

"Is there a better time?" Teleri asked him.

"You can't do it here. Your father will know."

"My father has been fighting demons," Teleri said. "He'll fall over and sleep for days, and my mother will be right beside him."

"Even so," said Benjamin, "I think we ought to ask someone else to help us. My father—"

Teleri ignored him. "We'll go up on the roof," she said. "No one will see us there. We can ward the door in case someone comes up. We'll be perfectly safe."

"But if we're alone, and it's too strong—"

She looked him straight in the face. "This is my fault. I have to fix it. If I can't, then I'll ask for help. But I have to try it myself first. You know that law, it's in every book of magic. If you make a bad spell, you're bound in honor to unmake it. Are you with me or not?"

Benjamin's eyes fell. "I'm with you," he said sullenly.

He was not completely convinced, she could tell. But once he had given his word, he would keep it. She decided to be satisfied.

The shadow-thing had gone away for a day, but then as Benjamin and Teleri were going about their business, they had felt it. It was very careful and very secretive, but Benjamin had a gift for sensing shadows. Once he let Teleri know of it, she could feel it, too. It was like a prickling in the skin, or cold fingers walking softly down the spine.

It did not do anything. It simply watched. But it was there, and little by little it was growing stronger. It warded itself from the jinn and disappeared completely when one of their fathers was near. It always came back when they were alone. Teleri would wake from a fitful sleep to find it watching from a dark corner, or Benjamin would be reading in his father's study while Master Judah was in his hospital, and would feel it hovering over him, watching, waiting.

They had to get rid of it. Teleri had not slept properly in a week, and Benjamin was looking hollow around the eyes.

"At least," he said as they prepared the circle on the roof, "I need to know what it wants."

"It wants our souls," Teleri said. "Isn't that obvious?"

"But why us?"

Teleri could not answer that, but it did not stop her from saying, "You know what Uncle Richard would say. Every man has enemies."

"I never did anyone any harm," Benjamin said, "except my brothers and sisters, sometimes, when they were asking for it. I can't imagine any of them setting a demon on us. And you—"

"You know what I've been thinking?" Teleri said. "I've been feeling it for a long time, but since we went to Gehenna, I'm almost sure of it. Owein didn't just die. I think something got him. He didn't feel magic the way you do, so he didn't know it was there. It hunted him and then it killed him. Now it's hunting us."

Benjamin shivered, though it was full daylight and sweatily warm. If Teleri had not been busy saving them from the gods knew what, she would have dropped what she was doing and run off to swim in the cistern.

They could do that later. The circle was done, the wards up, and the spell prepared. Benjamin had the book in which they had found it.

It was a strong spell. Even the act of making the circle had taken more strength than Teleri expected.

Benjamin had plenty to spare. He stood in the exact center of the circle and held up the book. As Teleri came to link arms with him, it fell open by itself. Benjamin dropped it, startled, but it did not fall; it hung in the air, pages flying as if blown in a wind. But the air was perfectly still.

The sounds of the city drifted up from below: people talking, a donkey braying, someone singing a naughty song off-key. There was a bird overhead, a vulture circling slowly. It must be watching something in someone's midden, or a beggar dead or dying in the street.

Teleri made herself shut it all out. That was the first lesson a mage learned: to focus. The words had risen from the page, the Hebrew letters still black but edged in fire.

Teleri's Hebrew was not bad—Master Judah had seen to that—but Benjamin's was better. His voice quavered at first, then steadied as the spell took hold of him. He let it do that. He had Teleri to keep him from losing himself in it.

"I call the powers of heaven and earth," he said, "the spirits of the elements, spirits of earth, spirits of air, spirits of fire, spirits of water. I call the light of sun and stars and moon. I call the morning; I call the blazing noon. I call the setting sun. Uncover this darkness. Give it its name. Be it opened to me. Be it revealed in the light. Be it made substance, that the light may search out all its secrets."

His voice had taken on a cadence as the spell unfolded, until it was a melodious chant. When it stopped, the melody seemed to go on for a while, as sound will linger in the string after the note is struck.

Teleri was dizzy; she felt sick. The light was too bright. The shadows were too dark. There was a ringing in her ears that went on and on.

With a clap like thunder, the book slammed shut and spun out of the circle. The wards broke. The circle collapsed.

Darkness stood on the other side of it. It had no face. The spell had revealed it but not named or bound it. It was too strong for that.

Teleri would not have said that she was afraid. Not exactly. She had been thinking that if she knew what it was, she could find a spell to get rid of it. She had not thought that the dark thing would confront her.

It had no face, but she could feel it laughing. Benjamin was right. It was too strong.

She had done exactly what it wanted. This time no one would come to drive it away. Her father was asleep, and her mother was beside him, just as she had known they would be. No one else in the house had the power to face this.

The dark thing raised the circle again, this time not to keep evil things out but to keep her in. It closed like a noose around her and the stiff and motionless Benjamin.

She pushed him as hard as she could, out and away. The circle held, flinging him back into her arms. Teleri spun away from him and leaped straight at the dark thing.

Its laughter was wilder than ever. It opened its arms and swept her in.

CHAPTER SEVEN

When Sioned woke after a long and blessedly dreamless time, Ahmad was still asleep. She brushed his lips with a kiss, at which he smiled but did not wake. She rose, wrapping herself in a robe, and padded barefoot to the latticed window.

They had slept from day until dark and around to dawn again. The light was pale, the air cool, although it would warm quickly when the sun came up. She stretched every muscle, like a cat, and yawned luxuriously. Ahmad's return had begun the healing, but yesterday had sped it remarkably. She felt almost herself again.

Her senses reached out as they used to do when all was well in the world. They touched each living thing in that house, taking count, finding it well. Except . . .

Teleri must be in Master Judah's house again. For all Sioned's recent and lofty intentions, she had taken no more notice of the child than she had since Owein died. Judah and Rebecca had been raising her, because Sioned would not.

That would end today. Sioned would go now, this morning, and thank those two dear friends for all they had done, and bring her daughter home where she belonged.

Sioned was preparing to go out when the servant announced that Master Judah had come to call on her. That was even more of an occasion than if the king had come. Judah never called on anyone; if he was not at home with his family, he was in his hospital, where everyone came to him.

Even before she could tell Ali to let him in, he thrust past the servant into her solar. He was in Frankish dress, looking like one of the knights who came and went all over the city: a big, wide-shouldered, strong-handed man with a black curling beard and eyes that, just then, made her heart constrict. "Benjamin is gone," he said. "Do you know where your daughter is?"

Sioned could barely open her throat to speak the words. "I thought she was with you."

Judah said none of the things he could well have said. That was one more debt she owed him, out of more than she could possibly count. "They came here yesterday," he said. "They were up to something—Leah tried to follow, but they put a binding on her that kept her silent until this morning."

"We were here," Sioned said, "from morning until—" She could not go on. They had been there, asleep as if drugged. Anything at all could have happened, and they would not have known it.

Just as she thought to send the servant for Ahmad, he came in, freshly bathed and wide awake, although his eyes were tired. They flicked from her face to Judah's.

She left Judah to explain. There was a glimmer on the edges of her awareness after all, a presence and then an absence, and a memory within a dream. Something had touched—something had come—

The roof was deceptively peaceful. The orange trees in their pots, the jasmine growing up over the arbor, were untouched. The remains of the circle of power, smudged but still comprehensible, were empty and silent. A book lay outside it, fallen on its face.

Judah moved past Sioned to take up the book. His hands flicked, warding it even as he lifted it. It was a powerful grimoire, far too powerful for children. Judah read the page to which it had fallen open, and handed it mutely to Sioned. Ahmad peered at it over her shoulder.

They both recognized the spell. It called up spirits out of the darkness, and made clear what was hidden.

Ahmad's face had gone grey. Without a glance at either of them, still less a pause to ask their leave, he flung a net of magic over the circle. It was a stronger spell than that in the grimoire, although he made it look simple.

Two child-shaped shadows appeared in the circle. Another, larger shadow took shape outside it. It seemed a hooded man, but there was a wrongness in it. It was not quite mortal, not quite demon, but strong—terribly strong.

"Allah," said Ahmad. *"Ya Allah."*

Judah said much the same, but in Hebrew rather than Arabic. Sioned could not find it in her to call on any of the gods of Gwynedd. They did not know this country or this thing that had taken her child.

Her voice was remarkably steady, all things considered. "So. Now we know what happened to the garrison at Masyaf."

Ahmad let the net of magic melt away into the sunlight. "I should have known," he said. "I should have recognized him. But I hadn't yet—I didn't think—"

"The leper in Gehenna," Judah said.

Ahmad nodded. "He was hunting them then. Or her. I don't think he meant to take Benjamin. This enemy is mine. We took his power from him. We all but led him to his death."

"Gehenna?" said Sioned. "What—"

"Later," Ahmad said. "I'll explain later."

"You will explain now."

He sighed faintly. "While you were otherwise occupied, our daughter was with Benjamin in Gehenna, looking for old treasure. Instead they stirred up something they should not have."

"Gods," said Sioned, moved at last to call on them. She scraped herself together. "I'm going to find them. You two go. Tell my brother. Tell anyone else who can help. I'll be—"

"You will not be running off alone," Ahmad said firmly, "not after what you said to me about doing the same. This we do together."

"Then hurry," said Sioned, "or I'll leave without you."

"Stop," Judah said, soft and yet with such power in it that they both went absolutely still. "It does no one any good to run about wildly. Whatever that one has done with our children, you can be sure he expects us to forget all common sense. Then he'll have us—and we'll be done for. This is part of a plan a dozen years in the making. You know as well as I, its real target must be the king."

"The king," said Ahmad, "and what he took from the Old Man."

Sioned's hand twitched. She could not let it slide toward the purse at her belt, where that deceptively simple and deadly thing was lying. Even in her confusion, she had never forgotten that Richard had entrusted it to her.

Above all she must not say any word of that, not here where the dark thing had been able to come. The children had called it, weakening the wards and the walls of protection on the city.

That weakness would not last long. There were mages enough to repair it; and so they would, as soon as might be. Sioned's mind turned from that to another and more pressing preoccupation. She would, she must find the children.

Ahmad's thoughts, as they often did, ran on the same path. He said aloud what she was thinking. "They won't be in Masyaf. The Old Man is too canny for that. Wherever they are, they'll be somewhere well hidden, and probably not in the world at all."

"If they live," Judah said in a moment of despair.

"They live," Sioned said fiercely. "By all the gods, they do live."

"What would it profit him to keep them alive?" Judah demanded. "Dead, they cause you more pain."

"Alive, they can suffer more pain," Sioned said. "And they can lure us to him. He wants that. He wants Richard stripped of his less worldly defenses. With Eleanor in England and us abandoning him for the hunt, he's vulnerable."

"Richard is leaving," Judah pointed out. "It would serve that one best to let him go, be rid of us, and move into the emptiness that we leave behind."

"No," said Ahmad slowly, as the thought took shape. "He wants Richard. Dead if necessary, but alive and enslaved would be far better. Imagine the King of Jerusalem in thrall to the Master of Assassins. The vanished knights are the beginning. Our children are a diversion, a ruse to be rid of us. Once Richard is stripped of his magical defenses and an apparent earthly war has begun, he'll be open to an attack he's in no way fit to face."

"I abandoned my daughter to wallow in grief for what was irretrievably gone," Sioned said. "Now, because I was a selfish fool, she too is lost to me—but by the gods, I will see that she is found. I care nothing for the cost."

"Not at random," Ahmad said. "Not without thought. He wants that. We must not give it to him."

"And if we delay," she said, "what of Teleri? What of Benjamin? What will be done to them?"

"What will be done to them, then to us, if we attack without forethought? We will attack, believe that. But if it kills us, then let us take him with us—forever this time; so utter and so complete that he can never again plague this earth."

Sioned was sick in her belly, where Teleri had been once, growing and dreaming, and now and then bruising a rib when she danced. Her whole heart and soul, and all of her guilt, rebelled against him. But her head was a colder thing. It knew he was right. However great the pain, however terrible the waiting, they should be wise. They should fight this war as great generals did, with patience as well as sudden force.

"At least," Sioned said, "let us be sure. If she's been cast somewhere in the world, or has escaped—"

"You know she has not." Ahmad rubbed his eyes and sighed. "Just as we both know she's alive. She's nowhere that we can easily reach."

Sioned knew. She could search the world around, and take until Lammas to do it, but Teleri was gone. That knowledge ran down to the bone. It was a gift and a curse, this magic of hers, and too often more curse than gift.

"What use, then?" she said. "Why trouble at all? Why not just fold our hands and wait until he comes for us?"

"If you want to be bait in a trap," Judah said, "then we'll

lay one. But first we should speak to your brother. I'm also thinking . . . in the war before, you two fought all but alone. He was mortal then. Now he'll be far stronger, and far less simple to defeat. He has the measure of you, and he knows what your brother is. He was a bad enemy then. He'll be much worse now."

"What, then?" said Ahmad. "For all the stories of guilds of mages, you know the truth as well as I do. We live alone, learn alone. We find each other by happenstance as often as by design. We're a solitary breed, and it's rather remarkable to see two together, let alone a whole family of us."

"That may be so," said Judah, "but some of the stories are true. Secrets can be breached and tales told out of turn. Your teacher in Egypt was the last of a great order, an alliance of mages as old as her country. Did she teach you that there were no others in this part of the world? That when she died, only you would be her heir, you and the children you had together?"

"I knew," said Ahmad, "that she was the last in Egypt, but that there were others far away in the world. In Chin, in India, in the land of snows—the east is full of them. On the edges of the world, in my lady's Gwynedd, in the isles by the cold ocean, the old and secret alliances still hold. But here, for what reason God only knows, no gathering has sustained itself for more than a generation. It's a curse, maybe, so ancient even its existence is forgotten."

"So it would seem," said Judah. "Go now, speak to the king. When he's done with you, come to my house. Come no later than sunset; we'll be shutting the doors then, and lighting the lamps. It would be an honor if you shared the evening meal with us."

Sioned glanced at Ahmad. It was all she could do not to summon the jinn and fly off to challenge the enemy to his face. Ahmad seemed as tightly drawn as she, but he was older and his magics were more firmly disciplined.

His strength made her very, very angry, but it also shamed her into sense. She nodded, bowing to Judah. "We'll come," she said. "We'll be honored."

Richard was not in Jerusalem on that day of all days. He had ridden out on one of his whims, taking a small company of knights and attendants, and gone hunting, no one knew exactly where. "Somewhere up around Nablus," said the chamberlain who seemed the least ignorant of the king's whereabouts, "or maybe down to Hebron. He was in one of his moods, lady. You know how he is then."

"I do indeed," Sioned said grimly. And how much had a certain undead enemy had to do with that too-sudden and too-vague impulse to be anywhere but where he should be?

He had left the day before. He was as long lost as Teleri, if never as completely. Mustafa had gone with him, which comforted Sioned a little. Mustafa could not work magic, but he could see it. If anything came to take the king, the king's dog would know.

And what could he do then? The king had surrendered the Seal that had protected him. Sioned had it. He was open to any power that came hunting.

Now if ever, an alliance of mages would have been a godsend. As it was, Ahmad's sons were scattered through the House of Islam, and Sioned's kin were at the far end of the world.

She did what she could. She sent a company of the jinn, strong spirits who served her of their own free will and altogether independent of the Seal. They would defend Richard as they might, and bring her word if he was in danger.

"I could go," Ahmad said as they left the Tower of David.

"I could travel by the secret ways and find him in an hour. Then—"

"No," she said. "You're all but empty. You'll kill yourself. We'll go to Judah. He's up to something, I can tell. We'll see what it is, and pray it helps us."

"And pray too that the king stays safe." Ahmad sighed. "I was a fool, lady. I never foresaw this. War, yes; confusion; disaster, maybe, once your brother leaves. But of this blow to our hearts and our house, I had no warning. None at all."

He was angry at himself, the anger of frustration. Sioned slipped her hand into his. She gave him such strength as she had, with the love of her heart to make it stronger.

He calmed somewhat, enough to go on. It was all either of them could hope for, just then.

CHAPTER EIGHT

It was nearly sunset after a long day of labor when Ahmad and Sioned came to Master Judah's house. The lamps were already lit in the gateway and in the passage just within.

Judah and his wife and children were in the dining hall of that house which had stood since before Rome came to seize this city. There were others with them, kinsmen who had come to keep Passover in Jerusalem and then stayed. It was a rather large gathering, more somber than the joy of their presence in Jerusalem called for, but none of them had given way to despair.

Sioned the Welsh pagan and Ahmad the man of Islam were welcomed with deep and honest gladness by all but one or two of the kinsmen. Those were young men who had not been away from England before, and who knew less of the world than they liked to imagine.

Places of honor had been kept for the guests. Rebecca and

her eldest daughter Leah brought water for them to wash their hands and faces. Mother and daughter were strikingly alike: small and round, with fair brown hair and soft green-brown eyes that made Sioned think of an English wood in summer.

She could not say anything of Benjamin yet, not in this rite of welcome, but she met Rebecca's eyes. They were dark with trouble, but she was not letting herself be overcome by it. There were six children still to look after, although the eldest had a son of his own, and her husband and her household and far too many duties to indulge herself in a paroxysm of fear and grief.

Sioned had much to learn from her.

This was a sacred hour, and it was not to be broken by the world's cares, however heavy they might be. In the light of candles, in the sound of ancient words and blessed songs, Sioned found a little peace. She ate with appetite, the first in time out of reckoning.

There was little laughter tonight in this family that lived by it, but Rebecca would not suffer any tears. Only when the table was cleared and the younger children sent to bed would she give way for a moment to the anxiety that was on them all. She had gone to fetch another jar of wine, and Sioned had followed her, drawn by some subtlety in the way she moved.

Sioned found her outside the storeroom by the kitchen, leaning against the wall. Her shoulders were rigid.

Gently Sioned took the jar from her stiff fingers. There were still servants in the kitchen, scouring pots and platters. Sioned took it on herself to send them away. "Rest a while," she said. "Come back later."

As they retreated, she coaxed Rebecca onto the bench by the hearth. The fire was banked already, and with the servants gone the room was quiet.

Rebecca's eyes were dry. She knotted her fingers tightly and clamped them between her knees, rocking back and forth. "Sorry," she said. "I am sorry. We can't give in. We shouldn't give in. It's only—"

"I know," said Sioned. "You're stronger than I ever was."

"I know he's alive," Rebecca said. "But what's being done to him—what's happening to him—sometimes I can't bear to think of it."

"He is a strong child," Sioned said as much to herself as to Rebecca, "and he has a great gift of magic, which has been well nurtured and well taught. We can hope that he and Teleri are together; if they are, they'll be so much the stronger. The Old Man knew little of women and less of children while he was alive. He can't be any wiser now. If he underestimates them enough, they'll escape on their own, even before we hunt them down."

"We can always pray," Rebecca said. She rose with an effort. "Come; the men are waiting. The Lord knows what they've decided without us."

"Nothing we can't undo," Sioned said.

They had in fact decided nothing. They were sitting in silence, with an edge to it that spoke of a quarrel barely averted. The cousins from England had somewhat to do with that, from the way the barbed glances were pointing.

Rebecca injected a note of determined good cheer, sweeping round with the wine and filling cups carefully: more for those who could be trusted to control themselves, less for the rest, and for Ahmad clean water made tart with citron, for as a Muslim he did not drink wine. While she did this, Sioned sat beside her husband and said, "Thank you for waiting for us. Now tell me: what shall we do?"

One or two of the young men opened their mouths as if

to speak, but Judah quelled them with a glare. "There are a number of possibilities," he said, "but excluding those that are deadly, impossible, or likely to ignite the whole of the east in a hundred years' war, we come to little of use. A long hunt that may find nothing, a confrontation that will get us all killed, or—"

"Or we can call on a greater Power."

Judah's brother Daniel was older, smaller, and less forbidding, but Sioned felt in him the same towering strength. He had come with the young hotheads from York in England, but he was far better traveled than they. She had met him years ago when he came with a caravan into the silk countries, and again when the caravan made its way back. He was a man of deep knowledge, a scholar to whom even Ahmad would bow in respect.

"There is that which, if we could find it," he said, "would give us the power to face the lords of darkest Gehenna."

"That was lost long ago," Judah said. "If the greatest scholars and magicians of the ages have failed to find it, what hope have we?"

"As much as they," said Daniel. "Maybe more, since we aren't looking to use it for mere gain."

"Will it think so?" Judah demanded. "It was deadly even to the priests who carried it. What might it do to us?"

"What will the undead one do to this kingdom?" Daniel spread his hands. "Listen to me, younger brother. I have a little sense for what will be, and this isn't a simple matter of two children lost. Fifty knights, I've heard, and a hundred squires are gone in the same way and, it would seem, by the same agency. This is only beginning. How far will it go? How much will it take and how much destroy? I think you know."

"I know," Ahmad said heavily. "Richard is its target. It's trying to remove us so that he's defenseless. Then it will do its utmost to destroy his kingdom. There will be more than fifty knights taken before the end, and more than one castle seized and occupied by means that no mortal can match."

Sioned's head was aching fit to burst. The Seal that she had hidden in her house was calling to her, ringing in her skull. It knew where Richard was; it would always know, because he had carried it for so long.

"Nablus," she said. And when they all stared at her: "Richard went to Nablus—without warning, without making it clear even to his chamberlain where he was going. Something is there. Something that called him. What if—"

"Then it may be over," said Judah's eldest son. "If he's been gone since yesterday, he's already enslaved to the undead."

"Not yet," Sioned said. "I sent forces to protect him. I would know if he were in danger."

"Of course you would," young Moishe said. "But shouldn't someone be fetching him back? He's not safe anywhere out of Jerusalem, not if what we think is true."

"Richard will never submit to confinement," said Sioned. "The best we can do is keep him under guard. And, I think, keep him on this side of the sea."

"That presents another question," said Daniel. "Might it not be best if he leaves immediately for England? The sooner he's on the sea, the faster he'll move out of reach."

"This power knows no constraint of distance," Ahmad said. "Wherever he goes, it will find him. He's safer here, where we are, than at the world's end. His mother will do her best to defend him—and hers is a very great power. But she doesn't have the power of Jerusalem, and she doesn't have us. She's as alone as we ever dreaded to be."

Judah nodded. "Yes. For once it's safer to be closer to the enemy than to be far away. And—"

"And," said Daniel, "it's time."

Sioned stilled inside. For all that they had said and done this long evening, none of it had been the reason why they were brought here. Now they would come to it.

Judah nodded. "It is time," he said. "Will you, or shall I?"

Daniel bowed, deferring to him.

Judah drew a breath. "Yes. Best I do it." He turned to Sioned and Ahmad. "You do guess, I suppose, what this is for—and what we are."

Ahmad inclined his head. Sioned said, "There is an order of mages in this part of the world after all."

"Not so much this part of the world," said Judah, "as in all places where our people are. This is our heart and center, although we've been banned from it, except for a very few with special dispensation, since the first Crusade took the city. My coming here in the king's following has brought certain matters to a head, and set certain others in train."

"There has been considerable debate," Daniel said with a glance at the young cousins from York, "as to whether we should speak of these things to anyone outside our circle. Time was when other orders knew of us and at times shared knowledge with us, or forged alliances against common enemies. This, I believe, is such a time. You, my lord, are the last of the great sorcerers of Egypt. You, lady, are the heir to the white enchantresses of old Britain. Both of your orders have allied with us before, though not in many a hundred years."

"Yes," Ahmad said. "It's written—there are accounts in the old texts. You are the priests of the fallen Temple?"

"In a manner of speaking," said Judah. "Our ancestors served in the place of the innermost secrets. Mortal histories say little of us, if at all. We were the last defenders of the Holy of Holies. We hid the great thing in the heart of it."

"So you know where it is," Sioned said. "You don't need to hunt for it at all."

"No," said Daniel. "We hid it, but then it was found. Its guardians were blinded or killed. It was taken from us."

"When?"

"Before Rome fell," Judah answered her, "and after Constantine was emperor."

"Christians," she said. "Christians took it."

"Maybe," he said. "Maybe not."

She looked at him in disbelief. "You really don't know where it is? You never looked?"

"We hunted," said Moishe, "and still do hunt, when time or inclination allow."

"When the children were in Gehenna," Ahmad said, "they were searching for the lost Ark. Benjamin knew of it. He told our daughter. Yes?"

Moishe flushed. He had his mother's cream-fair skin, and a boy's beard even yet, so that it was brightly obvious. "That is my fault. I let slip some things I shouldn't. Those young imps spied out the rest on their own."

"It seems to have been a pastime of theirs," Ahmad said. "They decided that the Temple was too obvious a place, and they had hunted everywhere in the city. Gehenna seemed logical—what better place to hide a thing of power than a place so cursed that it would overwhelm any higher magic that happened to be set in it?"

"And that was where the enemy found them," Rebecca said, breaking her silence with such a snap of authority that even the strongest of them, even Judah himself, sprang to attention. "I believe that heaven thrives on irony, and it is a great irony that the means to fight this enemy should be the very thing that brought our children within his reach. Hunting them will do us no good—we've all come to that conclusion, yes? Is there any reason to think that hunting the Ark will be any more fruitful? They've been lost a day. The Ark was lost close on two thousand years ago."

"It was hidden for a thousand years," Daniel said, "before it was lost."

"Ah," she said with a flick of the hand. "So much the better. Less than a thousand years, then. How very much simpler."

"We think we know where it is," said her second son. He was a quiet child, studious and gentle, but he had a quick mind and a remarkable level of ferocity in disputations of the Talmud.

He was the most like his mother of them all, and she looked on him in deep affection even while she said, "Then you are a greater mind than any of the multitudes before you."

"Oh, no," said Aaron seriously. "It's in the books. No one ever pursued it—mostly for lack of desire to challenge so great a force as the empire, but also because, you know, if you think about it, it's probably as safe there as anywhere."

"There?" Sioned demanded. "Where?"

"Why," he said, "Rome, of course. Next to Jerusalem, where else would you take a great relic? Well, maybe Constantinople, but Rome is older and stronger and its storehouses are deeper. It's somewhere in Rome, they say, though where, no one will admit to knowing."

"They say it's in many places," Moishe said. "We can't be sure that's where it is. For all we know, it's vanished from the world altogether."

"I don't think so," said Aaron, oblivious to his disbelief. "I did some hunting today. There's been endless nonsense written about finding the Ark, but in one or two books I found what I was looking for. First, that to the best of anyone's knowledge, the Ark is nowhere on this side of the sea. It was taken by sorcerers under the command of the Emperor Julian."

"Julian!" Sioned had not meant to interrupt, but her surprise was too great. "So it wasn't Christians at all."

"It would seem not," said Aaron. "If the chronicle is true, he sent a company of magicians to find the guardians, and through them the Ark. They seized it by some means not specified—most likely with loss of life, but that's not specified, either—and carried it back to Rome. The chronicle goes so far as to surmise that the Ark went because it wanted to. The time had come for it to move on to another master."

"But Julian failed," Sioned said. "Whatever he hoped to gain from it, he never got it. The Christians won."

"He was dead before it came to Rome," said Aaron. "When the empire had settled, the Ark was missing, and its discoverers with it. It wouldn't surprise me if their descendants were still hiding it somewhere in the city—in an archive or a treasury or a catacomb." He smiled the sweet and slightly dizzy smile of the scholar in his element. "I think it may be time again. I did the charts of the numbers and the stars. There are patterns coming together in this year, a shape of war and division. I thought it might be focused in Byzantium, but the thing that's risen in Masyaf has bent the currents of time and turned them toward us. Jerusalem is the center of the world, after all. It will draw everything to it sooner or later."

There was a silence. Sioned was thinking hard. The others seemed to have run out of words, until Judah said, "If the Ark is found and returned to Jerusalem, there will be such power here that no force of evil, be it an undead sorcerer or the Adversary himself, can stand against us."

"That then presents the question," Ahmad said, "of whether anyone can be trusted with such power."

"You trusted Richard with the Seal," Moishe pointed out.

"True," said Ahmad, "and that proved well enough in the doing. But this thing belongs to you from the old time. Would you trust the King of Jerusalem to become its master?"

Judah and his sons were still, but the visitors from England bristled. "It *is* ours," one of them said, all but spitting the words. "If we have it back, we will not surrender it to any Gentile, let alone that so-Christian king."

"Not so Christian here," Ahmad said mildly, "and much less so than he used to be. He has a surprisingly supple mind, does Richard, and at heart he's not the obedient son of the Church that he may choose to seem. We of Islam find him as congenial as a Frank can be. That he has a Jew for his most trusted physician—that tells me much, as well."

"He is still a Gentile," said the young hothead from York, "and the Ark is ours."

"So?" said Sioned. "Suppose we get it for you. What will you do with it?"

He sputtered in outrage, so that his cousin had to speak for him. That one was less intemperate though still none too friendly; he said, "It was made for the protection of our people. If we win it back, our kingdom will be born again. Jerusalem will be ours."

"Not without help," Moishe said, and this was clearly a contention they had shared before. "Like it or not, there's a Christian king on the throne, and a Muslim demon is aiming to take it from him if we're guessing right. We have no David or Solomon in this age of the world. There is no one who could incontestably take the title of king."

"*He* might," said the hotter-headed cousin, thrusting his chin toward Judah.

"No," Judah said. "Absolutely not. I don't want it and I won't take it. Neither does any of my sons. If Daniel wants it, then he can have it. The Lord knows, he won't keep it long. This may be the Ark's time, but it's not ours."

"You don't know that. You're simply afraid."

"I know as well as any man may know," Judah said levelly. "I can read the stars, too, and do the calculations. Everything centers on Jerusalem and on its king. He has the Seal. If the Ark is meant to come to him, it will."

"And if not? What then?"

"Then we'll be no worse off than we were before," said Judah.

His cousins subsided, growling. Judah ignored them. He turned his eyes on Ahmad and Sioned. "We believe," he said, "that the Ark is ready to be found. If it can be found and brought here, not only will there be a way to defeat your enemy; there will be a means to find our children."

"How?" Sioned demanded. "I read your Scripture. It kills men who come too close. I can see the use of it for protecting the city, but what can it do to bring back Teleri and Benjamin?"

"It is a great force for destruction," Judah said, "and a powerful weapon, but that arises out of what it is. It's a focus for magic—a burning glass if you will. Once brought within the circle and surrounded by wards, it can make any working immensely stronger. The histories tell of its use in war, but it had ample use in peace as well. The Seal was made through its power. Solomon ruled by the strength of it."

Sioned nodded slowly. She understood much that she had not before. "No wonder you want it. But you had better consider—if you're thinking of it, what's to prevent the enemy from doing the same?"

"Very little," Judah said, "except his own arrogance and obsession. He came back for vengeance. It may be a while before he remembers what else he wanted while he was alive.

I'm sure he wanted the Ark. He had the Seal; he would have known what made it. He would also know that if the Seal was intact, then the Ark was lost but not destroyed. If the Ark were broken, so would the Seal be."

"You never told us any of this," she said. "You let us take the Seal, and when we gave it to Richard, you never said a word. Weren't you the least bit afraid that we'd do something even you couldn't undo?"

"I knew you would do no such thing," Judah said. "Nor did you. Giving the Seal to Richard was not well regarded in our order, but events proved you wise. He's a better king than he promised to be when he was crowned. Jerusalem changed him. It made him stronger and gave him something more nearly resembling wisdom."

"He's still an impetuous fool," Sioned said. "He's just a slightly more restrained one." She drew a breath. "So then. What now? Who goes to Rome?"

"I was thinking you should."

That did not surprise her, but it did spark her temper. "What, after all the wailing and beating of breasts over our leaving Jerusalem defenseless, you'd send us away?"

"It's not defenseless," Judah said. "We're here. Nor will you hunt blindly through random roads of the world. You'll go straight to Rome and confine your hunt to that one city. Whether you succeed or fail, you'll come straight back here. You'll be protected throughout."

"But why us? Why not you?"

His mouth twisted. "Rome is not the most friendly place for one of us. Whereas you, sister of the great Crusader king, will be welcomed in the highest courts of the city."

"His emphatically non-Christian sister," she reminded him. "Wife of an infidel sultan. Persistent and incorrigible pagan."

"Rome will care little for that," Judah said, "as long as you shelter yourself in Richard's reputation."

"And if I'm in Rome and our children are in danger on this side of the sea? What then?"

"We will stand guard," Judah said. "This is far from the whole of our circle. All the rest that can are coming. We'll be gathered here, ready for the Ark when it comes. While we wait, we'll keep watch, and be ready to protect the children if they appear."

Sioned shook her head. "I won't leave. I can't. There must be another way, another weapon, a different rite—something."

"We can't think of any," said Aaron. He glanced at his father. "We'll look. We'll try. But, lady, I don't think—"

"Try," she said. "You say there are more of you coming. Maybe some of them will know what else we can do."

They clearly did not think so, but they were too polite to argue. The gathering ended on a note of respect and careful politeness, but with nothing resolved. Only one thing was certain: these were allies, if she would accept the task that they had given her. If she could agree to leave Jerusalem, to turn away from her child yet again—even if it was for that child's eventual salvation.

CHAPTER NINE

Richard had been feeling odd since he gave the Seal to Sioned. The impulse to hunt was nothing unusual—he did love a good chase—but to do it just then, abandon all his preparations for departure, and let the usual crowd of embassies and petitioners fend for themselves, was not the most reasonable thing he could have done. He was not the most reasonable of men, to be sure, but this was peculiar, as if someone else was doing his thinking for him.

At first, when he realized what was happening, he was not alarmed. That was part of the oddity, too. He should be disturbed, and he should be sending messengers to his sister, calling for her help. He could not bring himself to speak.

The hunting was bad. The gazelle were feeding far away from Nablus, and the wildfowl seemed to have gone elsewhere. He caught certain of his escort yawning with boredom, and there were mutters and grumblings. They would much rather have been in a city, taking their ease and hunting much sweeter quarry.

Worse yet, he was not sure exactly where he was, or exactly when he had got lost. He was somewhere near Nablus, he hoped, but this wilderness of rock and thorns could have been anywhere between Ascalon and Damascus.

Mustafa was no help. He had ridden out with them, but at some point on the first day he had disappeared. He often did that; he was a scout by nature and preference, and he went where his instincts took him. Those had kept him away for two days now. There was no one else that Richard could trust to discover where they had been led—for it was that, he was sure.

Toward evening of the third day, Richard was riding somewhat ahead of the rest, looking for a place to camp. As he came round an outcropping of rock, he found a tiny oasis. There was an oak tree, ancient and near dead but still holding out a handful of green branches, a minute patch of grass, and a spring that trickled into a small but surprisingly deep pool.

Richard approached it warily, but he did not get the prickle in his nape that warned of danger. It was an honest place, as far as he could tell. The water was cold and pure. His horse, golden Fauvel whom he had won from the King of Cyprus before he took Jerusalem, was glad of the grass.

Richard looked back, meaning to call to the rest and tell them to hurry—here was water, grazing, room to stop for the night.

His escort had disappeared. So had the track he had been following. The grass spread out into a bit of meadow surrounded by sheer rock walls. He thought he could see a gap in them, but he did not trust his eyes.

He turned around slowly. The tree was still there, but it was very much alive, spreading a canopy of leaves overhead. The grass went on for a little distance beyond it, then thinned until it vanished in sand and stones.

A shadow darkened the sun. He looked up. Something large and winged was circling overhead. It did not look like a hawk or a vulture. It looked, in fact—he squinted under his hand—like a gigantic, bat-winged, fanged and taloned man.

Someone was standing in its shadow, holding the rein of an elegant bay mare. Richard grunted in relief. "Mustafa! What is this? What—"

The winged thing dropped down out of the sky, landing lightly just behind Mustafa. Its eyes were round and yellow like a cat's; its voice recalled the deepest chords of an organ. "We are safe," it said in unaccented French, "for the moment. But how long we can—"

"It will have to be long enough," Mustafa said to the creature.

With a subtle shock, Richard realized who and what the winged thing must be. He had heard of his sister's army of jinn that her husband had won for her in a wager with the Old Man of the Mountain, but he belonged to the mortal world. He did not see spirits, and he was perfectly happy with that deficiency.

Now it seemed he had been given the gift of sight. Unless of course he was dead and on his way to hell, and this was the gatekeeper.

The jinni was speaking to him. The words crept through the fog of preoccupation. "There is a little time to rest and eat, but then, king of mortals, be ready to ride."

"Why?" said Richard. "Where? What—"

"Back to Jerusalem," Mustafa said.

Richard scowled at him. He did not like what he was see-ing. Mustafa had changed little since he first came to Richard as a deserter from the army of Saladin. He was a little taller, a little broader, and his beard was thicker, but he was still the hawk of the desert, with a beauty that had never been in the pale and cold-blooded north.

He was, at the moment, still beautiful, but his face was drawn and his eyes were sunk in his skull. He looked as if he had traveled a long road and a hard one, and no end to it that he could see.

"Where are my men?" Richard demanded. "What is this place? Why am I here?"

"Your men are taken," Mustafa said. "They rode through a rift in the world. So did you—but this prince of jinn was able to catch you and send you here."

"Which is where?" Richard said through clenched teeth.

Mustafa paled a fraction further. "I think it's in Persia. It doesn't matter. We'll take you back through the gate into Jerusalem."

"My men? I'm just going to abandon them?"

"I'm sure they're not alone," Mustafa said. "They're with the knights of Masyaf, wherever that is."

Richard swept out his sword and whirled, as if somewhere in this place he could find the power that had done this. But there was only Mustafa, and the jinni rearing up over him, mantling like a hawk as Richard's blade sang past its face.

"You should know," Mustafa said, "that he's taken Teleri, and Master Judah's son Benjamin."

"God's bones," said Richard. "When? How?"

"At the same time you left on this hunt," Mustafa said. "The jinni told me. It was all part of the same trap. Please, my lord. Come. If you're going to mount a rescue, it should be from Jerusalem. You are not safe here."

"I wasn't safe in the desert, either," Richard muttered. "That was a spell, wasn't it? He almost had me. That easily— that fast."

Mustafa bent his head.

Richard lowered his sword's point to the ground and drew a shuddering sigh. "This isn't my world. My world is

armies and marches and castles that I can lay siege to, and res-
cues that are simple and straightforward and usually involve
ransom. I hate this world. I hoped I'd never be caught in it."

"You've been part of it all your life," Mustafa said,
"through the blood that is in you and the powers that you refuse to acknowledge. When you let your sister give you the
Seal that she had taken from the Old Man, you accepted this,
little though you may have wanted it."

"I don't have it any more," Richard said. "I gave it up."

"Yes, and that left you vulnerable—just when its old master came back to take revenge on you for his death." Mustafa
retrieved Fauvel, who had been grazing calmly through all of
this, and held him for Richard to mount.

But Richard could not make himself move, not quite yet.
"This is not my kind of war."

"Nor mine," Mustafa said, "but it's the one we're being
forced into. Your people are being taken away. You nearly
were. Come, please, my lord. Please come to your own city."

"Is it my city?" Richard said, but he took the rein and set
his foot in the stirrup. "Take me back there, then. And God
help us all."

This must be how the jinn traveled. The walls of the oasis
opened like a vast stony gate. A road led down from it into a
blur of distance. It was like fog, that blur, but it did not clear
as they rode closer.

Richard would have slowed, but Mustafa beside him and the
jinni flying overhead drew Fauvel inexorably forward. The fog
closed about him. It had no taste, no feel. It was nothingness.

Just when he touched the edge of panic, it was gone.
Mortal sun beat down on his head. The walls of Jerusalem
rose in front of him, blindingly bright in what must be morning light.

It had been late afternoon when he rode to the oasis, not an hour before. Somehow a night had gone past and the sun come up again, as if he had been trapped in a hollow hill in the ghost-ridden isle of Britain.

He shuddered. In the stories, it was always more than a night. It was a lifetime, or a hundred years, or a thousand. If he had been away that long, and his kingdom was lost—

The guards at David's Gate wore the livery of Jerusalem, the golden crosses superimposed with the leopards of the Plantagenets. Their faces were familiar. They greeted him with evident gladness, bowing him within. The jinni had vanished, or else in this world Richard still lacked the power to see it.

The tension in Richard's shoulders eased slowly as he rode into the shadow of the gate. This was his city, heart of his kingdom. If anywhere in the world was home, then that place was Jerusalem.

It was dark under the arch of the gate. Good place for an ambush, he thought with a small prickle in the nape of his neck. The light was straight ahead, his own courtyard and his servants waiting. He urged Fauvel forward.

They must have been clinging like spiders to the upper reaches of the arch, though how the guards had failed to see them, still less to be alarmed, Richard was not pleased to contemplate. *Magic*, he thought sourly. They dropped down on him in a blur of white, clawed with steel. They dropped down on him in a blur of white, clawed with steel.

He was ready for them. A great happiness unfolded inside him. Surprise attacks and sudden knives—those he knew. Those were his world.

He caught the first with a broadside sweep of the sword. Even as it bit flesh, he ducked the slash from the second. Fauvel wheeled and lashed out with both hind feet. Richard hacked the head from the Assassin's shoulders.

Blood-spattered and grinning like a fiend, Richard rode into the light. Two heads swung from his saddlebow. Fauvel snorted at the stink of blood and voided entrails, but he was long accustomed to this sport. He halted in the courtyard and tossed his mane, and snapped lightly, playfully, at the groom who came to take his bridle.

A good war would do them all good, Richard thought—a real war, with armies and marches and battles. To the Devil with armies of jinn and undead sorcerers. He wanted—he needed—an honest enemy.

"I can't give you that," Sioned said. Richard had left the Assassins' heads still bleeding in the hall, propped on spears, and gone up for a bath and a bite of supper, breakfast, whatever he wanted to call it. She came while he was eating, although he had not called for her. Obviously she had been waiting for him.

"I'm not a sorcerer," Richard said, "and I refuse to be tricked into becoming one. These kidnappings and disappearances are out of my province. But Masyaf in hostile hands, and Assassins in my own gate—those I can deal with."

"Masyaf is in sorcerous hands," she said. "If you try to invade it with an army, your men will go the same way as everyone else who has tried it. Where, I should point out, you would have gone if my prince of jinn had not been watching out for you."

"And I do thank him," said Richard, "and you. Now tell me how I can turn this into an earthly war—a war that I can win."

"There may be no way," she said. "The enemy is making sure of that."

"So stop him," Richard said.

"Believe me," said Sioned, "if there's any way in the world I can do that, I will."

CHAPTER TEN

Berengaria did not remember exactly when the shadow came. It was after Richard took Jerusalem and installed her in Saladin's old harem in the Tower of David, but she could not reckon the count of days or months. Time was a blur when one had nothing of consequence to do and no one of consequence with whom to share it.

In the early days, when she first understood that her marriage was a sham and her husband a lover of men who would never respond to her with anything but revulsion, she had faced a choice. She could throw herself into the petty follies of the court, she could retreat into religion, or she could find some diversion that would let her forget her troubles.

She chose the third. She came upon it partly by accident, in pursuit of something interesting to read, and partly by design, as she recalled that Richard had an honest hatred of all things magical. With no teaching but that of books that she had hunted down in secret, and no master but her own

heart's desire, she had become a fair-to-middling decent sorceress.

It was a great pleasure to know that, and to know also
that no one suspected. Maids were not too difficult to dismiss, and less so as she learned arts and sleights to elude
them. Guards stood on the other side of doors, keeping invaders out but seldom troubling themselves with what went
on within. The great and terrible Eleanor herself never
stopped to wonder if another queen, imprisoned by her husband's neglect and hatred, might have taken the same road
that she had. Even she looked down on the wife she had
forced on her son, and despised her for failing so signally to
provide him with an heir.

The day the shadow came, Berengaria had been reading
from a new book that she had found in the Temple's library.
Some of the books had been there since before the first Crusade, locked away in dusty chests, abandoned and forgotten
as she herself most often was. The first few had been in Arabic, which she did not read, but then she found the poems in
Greek, and beneath them, wrapped in faded silk, books also
in Greek that would not have been suffered to exist if the
knights of God had known what they were.

They were books of magic. Most of it was harmless
enough, but those on the bottom, wrapped most securely,
looked toward the darker realms. The new book was very
dark indeed. Dark as old blood. Dark as her mood when she
read it after yet another rebuff from her husband and yet another round of sneers from his courtiers. The Shadow Queen,
they called her. She had nothing of her husband but the title.
All the love he had to give was given to his mother and to the
beautiful young men who were always about him.

She did not at first intend to work the spells in the book,
but the temptation was irresistible. She chose a simple one

that needed only her own blood and nothing too terrible by way of lesser elements: dust from a grave, a little powdered bone. It was a spell of foreseeing, of opening the veil between time now and time to come. The dead to whom all time was one were best suited for such a spell.

She took care to protect herself with strong wards before she began. She drew the circle in graveyard dust, hoping that what she had gathered would be enough. It was, just. Then she brought out the finger bone from the same grave, gritting her teeth against a shudder, and ground it in the mortar that she had bought new that morning. It was stubborn, being bone, but she persisted. After a while, and after her arm and shoulder had begun to ache, it gave way suddenly and puffed into powder.

She felt a moment's chill, but it passed. She pricked her finger with the silver knife, also bought new and blessed with oil from the lamp that had burned in the crypt. The blood welled, bright scarlet and unexpectedly beautiful. She dripped seven drops into the mortar, no more and no less.

She could feel the power sparking as each drop fell onto the crushed bone. That was a new sensation, startling but not unpleasant. It made her skin tingle.

There were words to speak in the language of magic, words that were power without sense. She spoke them quickly as she mixed blood and bone. Fear was dangerous; she must not show it or give way to it. But there was something about the way the shadows shifted, and the way the silence became suddenly very deep.

Darkness coalesced above the mortar. She backed away to the limit of the circle. Only instinct kept her from stepping through it and breaking it.

The crypt from which she had taken the dust and the bone had belonged to an old queen of Jerusalem. She had

had some vague thought of finding sympathy there, an ear to listen and a mind to understand the loneliness she suffered.

This was no queen, no woman, and no mortal. It was shapeless, faceless, but the darkness in it was as real as the pestle still gripped in her fingers. Blood had called it. Death bound it, but her words, babbled too quickly and perhaps not precisely enough, had set it free.

"I owe you great thanks," it said. It had a man's voice, and she could sense clearly that in the flesh it had been male.

Of course, she thought sourly.

The dark thing bowed before her. "For the blessing of freedom, I will serve you with such power as I have. I have but one requirement—if you will."

She eyed the shadow in mistrust.

"Blood," he said. "Blood gives me strength. Feed me and I will do your bidding."

"How much—"

"Only a little," he said, "now."

She chose not to hear that last word. A little blood from her finger, or a mouse, or a fowl from the kitchen, and she would have a servant who was wholly hers: a secret, a magical servant. "What will you do for me?" she said, trying not to sound too eager.

"What will you ask?"

It was just like the stories in the bazaar. She narrowed her eyes. "There's no limit, is there? I won't make my third wish and then you'll tell me I've spent them all?"

"No limit but your own will," said the shadow.

"Well then," she said. "Take me back to Navarre."

The shadow bowed. She liked the way it did that, curling like smoke, with a scent about it that was purely submission. Even as it uncurled, the walls of her chamber melted away. She stood in a courtyard of her father's palace, between an orange tree and the stone image of a knight on horseback. The slant of the sun, the heat that was not quite the same as the heat of Outremer, the smell and taste of the air, made tears spring to her eyes.

"Inside," she said to the shadow, which though invisible was palpably there. "Take me to my father."

He had grown old. He was sitting on his throne, cheek resting on hand, watching his courtiers trace the figures of a dance, and his expression was unrelentingly sour. He had a new queen—again. This one, the third or perhaps the fourth, looked all of twelve years old, but her belly was already rounded with his child. It would be another daughter, Berengaria knew without knowing how. He was cursed with daughters. There would be no son to rule after him.

He did not see her. She was standing by the door, and she was dressed like a servant. She could have demanded that her new servant equip her with fine clothes, jewels, and a handsome escort, so that she could announce her return in proper royal fashion. But she did not say the words. The happiness that had filled her when she first appeared in this country was gone.

She was not home. It was familiar as any memory of childhood was, and that familiarity had deceived her, briefly, into thinking she had ever been happy here. But looking at her father's lined and discontented face, she remembered the reality. She had been glad to leave, glad to follow the redoubtable Eleanor on Crusade, even glad to contemplate marriage to a man who had barely exchanged two words with her.

As miserable as she had been in Jerusalem, she at least had a life of her own, after a fashion. In Navarre she had been smothered with nurses and governesses and duennas. A father who despised her as simply the first of a long and bitter succession of female offspring, a mother who had died bearing the third—or was it the fourth?—of those daughters, a court that found her plain, dull, and resolutely unfashionable: a return here was a return to an even less appealing prison. These devout Christians would never tolerate the arts that she was learning to practice.

"Shadow," she said, not caring who heard. "Take me to Jerusalem." And she was there, in her familiar room that until now she had thought she hated. "Shadow," she said again with beating heart, "set his child in my belly. Make me an heir for my husband."

But the shadow said, "Alas, lady, that is the work of the Lord of Life. It is not permitted to us who have passed out of the world."

The anger that rose in her was enormous, far out of proportion to the refusal. She swept up her hand to cast the shadow back out of the world, with all its lies and its worthless promises.

But just as she shaped the word of dismissal, the shadow said, "Lady, I cannot give you the heir of your king that you desire so strongly, but I can give you riches, pleasure, even respect. I might even, given sufficient time, lead you to one who can grant you your wish."

"Respect?" said Berengaria. "You can gain me that?"

"In time," said the shadow, "all the world shall bow to your name."

Berengaria considered that, and the half-promise of a child someday, and made her decision. "You may serve me," she said.

The shadow needed more blood the longer he served her. She could not supply enough even at the beginning. Mice, then rats, then the cats and dogs of Jerusalem fell prey to him. Berengaria would lure them in with a spell, and he would feed. Each time he fed, he was a little stronger.

It was slow, the work of years, but there was no denying it. He was gaining substance with each drop of blood.

The time came, close on a decade after he began, when beasts were not enough, when he needed more. He needed the blood of men. Strong men, sturdy men. Men who served the kingdom as the shadow served Berengaria, with perfectly selfish devotion.

At first she refused, and her horror was real. She would not turn murderer on behalf of a servant. But little by little her resolve weakened. She was a queen, after all. Queens and kings ruled the lives of their subjects. Her husband took immoderate delight in hunting Turks and taking their heads. How was this different? Blood was blood. Her servant needed it in order to be strong.

She let him hunt as long as he did it judiciously. Raiders and footpads took lives enough in this world. What was another one or two or three in a month, or in time a fortnight, and then a week?

The shadow was taking on substance. His voice lost the odd, echoing quality of words formed out of pure air. When he came at her summons, she heard the soft pad or slide of feet.

Then one day not long before Richard was to sail to England, the shadow said, "Lady, I have somewhat to ask of you. It is not so very great a thing, but it requires the strength of immortal soul in mortal flesh. A thing was taken from me when I died in the body. I have been given the gift of taking it back again, if only I may work the spell in its proper form and ritual."

"What sort of spell?" she asked warily.

"It is simple enough," the shadow answered. "To open a gate."

"That is simple," she said. "Why do you need a living being to open it for you?"

Was the shadow the faintest bit impatient? He still had no face to betray his emotions, but she could sense how he stiffened ever so slightly. "Some spells," he said in his soft purr of a voice, "need living flesh and mortal will. This is one. I will give you the words and the rite. You have only to perform it as you have performed spells so often before: with care, precision, and a gift of native magic."

Berengaria was immune to flattery. No one ever meant it, and by now no one bothered. But she was raw in her heart. She had gone to the king's sister that morning, in a moment of desperation, and begged her for what the shadow had never managed to produce. The king's sister had cast her off. She had had to face a fact that she had been evading for far too long: that there would be no heir of Richard's making, by magical means or otherwise. As for an heir of someone else's making . . .

She could not think that thought quite yet. Later, maybe. But for the moment she would keep on hoping, however fruitlessly, for an honest and legal heir.

In the meantime she would divert herself with magic. Someday, some part of it would give her what she wanted. She made that a vow to herself, even as she said, "Very well. For your good service, and for the pleasure of the deed, I'll raise your gate."

It was as simple as he had promised. It needed blood—all spells of this rite did—but the beggar whom the shadow brought was already unconscious, and never felt the prick of the knife. She caught his blood in a tall jar that once had held wine.

While she prepared the circle, the shadow disposed of the carrion. She suppressed the last, barely perceptible stab of guilt and read from the parchment he had given her. The words were difficult to pronounce, and it was vital that she pronounce them properly.

In the other gate-spells that she had studied, the gate grew out of the blood, drawing it up and consuming it. This one seemed at first to do the same, but it was a much larger gate than she had seen before, with blood-red pillars and a lintel of fire. It hung in space, visible within the room but present at some untold distance. She saw the teeth of mountains, and a tumbled, twilit sky.

The gate came to rest over a shape that after a moment she recognized. It was a castle, built on a crag as they so often were. Banners flew from it, but in that strange light she could not see what device was on them. The gate was vast: it enclosed the whole of the castle. Small dark flecks streamed toward it. They looked like insects, each with a spark in its belly, but some of those sparks were struggling. In those struggles she saw the shapes of men and heard their cries, faint and shrill like crickets chirping far away.

On the other side of the gate crouched a shape of darkness. Its jaws gaped open, sucking in blood and souls.

That was not her servant. Surely it could not be. And yet . . .

The last soul was gone. The beast had swallowed it. The castle was empty.

The shadow stepped through the gate onto the roof of the nearest tower. He was as solid there as any man in a dark mantle, standing on booted feet, taking in his newly won domain.

She still could not see his face. The depths of his hood concealed it. But she saw his hands, gaunt but strong, reaching in a mingling of joy and raw greed, as if he would clasp the whole of that place to his newly substantial breast.

She called him back. And he came, for his old oaths

bound him. He stood in front of her, hooded head bowed, and waited upon her will.

Once she had him, she was content, for a while. "Go," she said. "Take your pleasure. I'll summon you when I need you."

He left at her will, just as, when it pleased her, he would come back. She smiled as she opened a new grimoire that he had brought just the other day. His wages were high, but he was a good servant. Certainly she had none better.

CHAPTER ELEVEN

Henry, once of Champagne, now heir to the throne of Jerusalem, brought his horse to a halt just below a hilltop. His escort halted behind him. He tossed the rein to his squire, signaled his men to wait where they were but beckoned their sergeant to follow, and climbed the rest of the way on foot. He kept to the concealment of tumbled rocks at the summit, looking down into the wadi.

"There they are," the sergeant said beside him.

He nodded. The raiding party was riding up the dry riverbed in the early-morning light. Already the leaders were almost directly below him. They had looted a village within the borders of Henry's demesne, and carried their prizes with them: bundles and bales on the backs of mules that looked suspiciously like refugees from the king's army, a small herd of rather weedy horses, and at least a dozen women and young boys trussed and slung over saddles.

These were not the usual Bedouin in dusty robes of the

desert. They wore Turkish mail and turbaned helmets, and they were well armed. From the look of them, they were out on a lark—most were young and some looked as if they had indulged in the wine that was supposedly forbidden in their religion. Young hellions from Homs or Hama, Henry guessed, raiding rather deep into Frankish territory, and breaking a number of treaties while they did it.

Henry exchanged glances with his sergeant. Tariq raised a brow. Henry nodded. They left the summit together, slipping back down toward the waiting troops.

They were ready and eager. It had been a while since they had had a decent battle. Peace was all very well, and the Church claimed to love it and hailed the king whose rule had brought it, but it made for lean pickings for a soldier.

This promised to be a good fight, with ample reward for the victors. The raiders somewhat outnumbered Henry's scouting party, but his men were even better armed, and they were awake, sober, and thirsty for blood. These boys had tired themselves out already with raiding the village, but they looked fit enough and keen enough to put up a fight.

Henry reclaimed his horse from the squire, put on his helm, and lowered his lance. With a long, low roar like the surge of the sea, they swept up and over the hilltop and down upon the Turks.

Henry was the point of the spear, driving his heavier, stronger force into the light Turkish cavalry. Mules and loose horses scattered. Henry's lance caught a Turk in the throat and sent him tumbling to the ground.

He had broken through the thin line. His horse was well trained to charges; he slowed even before Henry touched the rein, and began to turn.

Turks were closing in on him. He dropped his lance and drew his sword. He was aware as commanders must be, not only of his own small portion of the fight but of the whole battle. His charge had broken the line of march. Men were engaging one on one and two on two. Neither side was stronger yet, but his men still held a slight advantage.

The Turks had recovered quickly from the shock of surprise. They were drawing apart, leaving a gap in the center. That was an old trap, and could be deadly. Henry called out a warning. His men withdrew somewhat, moving toward him.

They had avoided that trap, but the prickle of warning did not grow less. Something was not as it should be. Something—

He snatched his hunting horn from his saddlebag and blew a sudden blast. It was not exactly the call to retreat, but close enough.

It came too late. The army that swarmed down into the wadi far outnumbered Henry's fifty men. They were shrilling the name of Allah. In the same moment, the bundles and bales burst, disgorging armed men, and the women and boys threw off their ragged robes and whirled to the attack, wielding daggers with deadly precision. They knew exactly where to strike through chinks in armor.

Henry wasted no time in despair. He called his troops in as close as they could come. Only half could obey; the rest were down or locked in combat.

He did what he could. Those who still had lances, he bade face outward with lances lowered. Those with bows shot over their heads. Turkish arrows fell in a black rain, rattling off armor. Too often they found flesh, usually horseflesh, and bit deep. Horses screamed. Men shouted and cursed. Someone was singing a loud, monotonous song.

Henry's lance was gone, fallen somewhere on the field, and he had not brought a bow. He unlimbered the mace from its bindings on his saddle and swung it gently, reminding himself of the feel of it, taking some small comfort in its weight. The pathetically small circle was holding its own, for the moment. He kicked his horse into motion, aiming toward a battling knot of Turks with a pair of his men in the center.

The heavy, spiked club crushed helmets even through turbans, and shattered bone. An attacker's yelling face blew apart in a spray of blood. Henry swept his rescued men with them and aimed for the next, hewing his way through massed bodies. There should not be so many in this place. There could not be—

Part of him stood to the side, remote and calm. It observed that this ambush was far larger than it needed to be, and that if he was to continue as heir of Jerusalem, he had to survive it.

None of the enemy seemed to be striking at him in particular. They never had been able to tell armored knights apart. Was that why there were so many here? Enough to crush each knight, and hope that one ranked high enough to deal a blow to the kingdom? Did they know that Henry was here?

All the while his mind wandered, his body, trained and honed, fought for its life and the lives of his men. He had gathered a handful, but the rest kept eluding him. The enemy surged between again and again. One by one they were falling. His arm was beyond ache. His lungs burned. His horse was wheezing; its legs were shaking with charge after charge.

A horse loomed up beside him. He nearly smote its rider down until he recognized his sergeant. Tariq sprang from the saddle.

Henry's charger fell rather abruptly to its knees, then groaned and rolled. Henry sprang free, staggering in his heavy mail. His men had beaten the enemy back, for a while. It was almost quiet here in the center of the circle.

Tariq flung the rein of his horse into Henry's hand. "Get on," he said. "Get out of here. We'll guard your back."

"I can't abandon you," Henry said.

"May I be damned," said Tariq, "to the bosom of Iblis, if I let my king be killed in this miserable sandpit. Take this horse and go. We'll follow if we can. If not, we'll see you in Paradise. I'll be the one with the seventy-two virgins, and every one more beautiful than the last."

"I won't," said Henry. "I can't. Even to save my life. Even to be king. The dishonor—"

Tariq threw himself against Henry. Two more of Henry's men abetted him, leaving the fight to wrestle their liege lord down and fling him into the saddle like a sack of barley. While he reeled with the breath struck out of him, one of them smote the gelding across the rump with the flat of his sword. The beast squealed and bolted.

The battle closed over Henry's men like water over the head of a drowning man. The bay gelding, mad with pain and shock, clamped the bit in his teeth.

Henry's hands would not grip the reins. He was dizzy with want of air and, he realized dazedly, loss of blood. He had not even known he was wounded. He clung to the saddle as best he could and gave up his resistance. The gelding carried him away.

Two days later, Henry rode into Jerusalem. Eleven men rode with him: ten men-at-arms from his castle of Baalbek, and one in the livery of the Hospitallers.

He had not stopped or slept since Tariq's gelding carried him away from the battle. He had let a physician in Baalbek bandage the worst of his wounds while he waited for his escort to arm and mount.

The Hospitaller had caught him on the road, bearing

messages from Krak. Richard needed to hear what the man had to say; Henry bade him follow.

Richard was in Jerusalem, which Henry had not been sure of. It was close to the time when he should be moving to Acre with the final preparations for his voyage to England. Even without that, he usually left Jerusalem after Easter Court and began the yearly round of his kingdom.

But he was still there, and there was no sign of imminent departure. His chamberlain escorted Henry to the solar. On the way they passed through the hall, where a pair of grisly trophies grinned from the heads of spears. Both heads were wrapped in turbans, and the severed necks were wound about with white.

The things had not yet begun to stink, which at this time of year meant that they were at most a day old. Henry nodded to himself, grimly. A pattern was coming together. He did not like it at all, but it was difficult to mistake.

A council of sorts was sitting in the solar. Richard was there, and Hubert Walter who had become Patriarch of Jerusalem some ten years past, and the sultan Saphadin. Richard's sister Sioned was sitting with her husband, looking more honestly alive than she had in a year. Beside her was someone a little surprising: the king's physician, Judah bar Samuel.

Henry bowed to them all, taking care not to topple onto his face with the sudden rush of exhaustion. Firm hands caught hold of him and eased him to a chair. "He's wounded," Judah said to the others. And to Henry: "Do you remember when last you ate?"

Henry dared not shake his head: he was too dizzy.

"Bring him a posset," Judah said to someone, most probably a page. "Warm milk, honey, a very little wine. Bread soaked in it with nutmeg and a grain or two of pepper. Bring it quickly."

While they waited for the page, Judah proceeded calmly, with Sioned's assistance, to strip Henry of his armor and bandages and investigate his wounds. In very short order they had sent a servant for hot water, soap, and cloths, and a box of medicines. These came quicker than the posset, which suited Judah well enough. Henry submitted to being scrubbed, salved, and bandaged anew, then wrapped in a robe that must be Richard's: it was embroidered with the golden crosses of Jerusalem.

While they did that, Richard listened to the tale that the messenger from Krak had to tell. "Krak is besieged," he said. "An army has grown up out of the earth and surrounded the crag. We count ten thousand, and more every morning. Where they come from, how they get there, none of us knows. They're simply there."

Richard frowned as he always did when he heard mention of magic. It made his head hurt, Henry thought in sympathy. "What manner of men? Weapons? Engines?"

"They look ordinary enough," the Hospitaller said: "Seljuk Turks, mostly, and Bedouin, and troops in Persian armor. Their commanders are dressed all in white. Those are Persians and Arabs no Turks."

That was odd. Turks led armies in this part of the world. "No Kurds, either?" Richard asked.

"Not a one," said the Hospitaller.

Richard nodded. The people of Saladin and his brothers and heirs were firmly allied with the Kingdom of Jerusalem. These new enemies were the conquerors, now conquered; their rebellion was no great surprise.

"They're well armed," the messenger said: "weapons not always new but well cared for. They have Turkish bows and a few crossbows. Their siege-engines are strong."

"So is Krak," Richard said. "There's none stronger."

"Anything can break, if you pound it enough," Sioned said from Henry's side, "and there will be more than stones coming over those walls. They should be warded, and soon— if it's not too late already."

The messenger crossed himself. "Lady, with respect, you know how the Church looks on those arts."

"I do," she said, "and if you don't want to lose the heart and center of your order, you'll set aside your fears and defend yourselves in the one way that may be of use."

Her husband fixed her with a quelling stare, which she ignored. The Hospitaller, mercifully, was not as hot-headed as most of his kind. He nodded and said, "Lady, you are wise, but it may take more persuasion than there is time or space for."

"I would call a siege persuasion," Sioned said.

"There is that," he conceded.

Richard rose from his chair and started to pace. That silenced everyone, as it always did. Richard in motion was impossible to avoid. He was big, he knew how to loom, and he completely ignored everyone else in the room except to sidestep any who might be in his way.

Hubert Walter drew back out of his path. Sioned stayed in it. She was not much more than half his size, dark to his fading red, cream to his sunburned crimson, but then one could see that they were bred of the same fierce-tempered line. "Krak is going to fall if it tries to defend itself the mortal way. You'll fall, too, if you go to the rescue with an ordinary army."

Richard stopped short and glared down at her. "What, are you going to insist on flying to Krak and saving it?"

"No," she said, "but I know others who will—if you ask. And if you can pay their price."

"No blood," he said promptly. "No souls. No—"

"I would think," she said, "that it would more likely be

the freedom of their people to come and go in Jerusalem, and to live in it as freely as any other."

Judah was just finishing Henry's bandages. He stopped with the last one half-bound. Henry heard the breath hiss between his teeth. He was watching the king and his sister with sudden, ferocious intensity.

"Your spirits want to live here?" Richard asked, puzzled. "Don't they already fly wherever they please?"

"Not spirits," Sioned said. "Men. Women, too, and children. They're strong, and their powers are old and well practiced. They can keep Krak safe from magic while your armies contend with the siege."

"You do not have authority—" said Judah even as Richard said, "What? More Saracens? They're already as free in this city as—"

Sioned ignored Judah and answered Richard. "Jews," she said. "They built this city. Their power is sunk in its stones. They can defend it as no one else can. And maybe, for its sake, they will agree to protect Krak, which is your strongest defense in the north of the kingdom."

"Jews?" Richard rubbed his jaw under the greying red beard. His eyes slid past her to Judah. "You?"

Judah bound off the last and somewhat delayed bandage. "She is not delegated to speak for us," he said, "but yes. You must swear, all of you, that you will not speak to anyone outside this circle of what is said here."

He was not looking at Richard then, but at Hubert Walter. The Patriarch bowed as low as his girth and his seat would allow. "I will take that vow," he said, "by my king's leave."

"There's a price for this, isn't there?" Richard said. "There's always a price."

"She stated it," said Judah. "To live in our city again, free as we were when it was truly ours."

"Not to rule it? Not to depose me and set up your own king?"

"Not in this age of the world," Judah said. "I've served you loyally since you took the crown. I'll continue to do so. If you grant what your sister demanded on our behalf, you'll have the service of my kinsmen and my allies, and such defenses as all of us together can raise."

"Magical defenses," Richard said with a sour face.

"That is what you need now," Judah said, "sire."

Richard looked as if he had swallowed a lemon whole, but he spread his hands. "Very well. We'll keep your secret. Tell me what you're offering, and I'll tell you if I can take it."

"We offer protection," said Judah, "and such assistance as you need or will accept."

"And 'we' are?"

"The priests of the inner sanctum in the First Temple," said Judah, and he did not say it easily. Long habits of secrecy were difficult to break. "We are their descendants—in learning and power as well as in blood. All or even most of us will not ask to live here. We will not overwhelm you with numbers. We only ask for a share in this city that was ours."

Henry's mind had focused remarkably, assisted by the arrival at long last of the posset that Judah had ordered. This was a very great thing that Judah was asking, greater maybe than the Church could endure. He glanced at the Patriarch. Hubert Walter did not look appalled, at least, although his brows were knit.

Richard did not seem to be thinking of the Church at all. "You must all swear fealty to the crown of Jerusalem. Not to me, mind you. To the office, and whoever holds it, for as long as such a pact will endure. Can you do that?"

"I'll have to ask the others," Judah said, "but for myself,

yes, I can. The only condition being that if either side breaks the pact, all obligations of loyalty and service will cease."

"That should go without saying," said Richard.

"Still," said Judah, "it needs to be said. Your people and your Church have a long history of bad faith toward us. You have persecuted us, tortured us, slaughtered us on a whim. You borrow our gold, pay it back in part or not at all, and murder us when we ask for what is ours. Your priests thunder denunciations against us, calling us Christ-killers. We were cast out of this city and banned from our holiest places. A cross crowns the dome of Islam that rises over our fallen Temple. Can you throw yourself in the face of all of this, in order to win this war?"

Richard looked him steadily in the face. "Are you going to ask for your Temple back?"

"We might," said Judah.

"That won't be as easy as the rest of it," Richard said.

"We won't insist on it," Judah said, "for the time being. The rest will be enough."

Richard nodded. If it had been anyone but Judah, Henry thought, the king would be in a right rage. But it was a man he trusted as he trusted few others, and with reason. If Judah asked this, Richard would give it. He would not even think of the battles he would have to fight in court and council, or of the screaming outrage in the Church. He needed this, he needed it now, and he would take it. The rest would take care of itself.

"If you can get men through to Krak," he said, "I'll send someone with them who can beat some sense into the Grand Master. We'd best do it fast. I'll get an army together as soon as may be, but Krak will have to hold on until I can get my men mustered and on the road."

Judah bowed in deep respect.

"Go," Richard said. "Get to it. I'll send my man to you in an hour."

Judah was already at the door. "Old friend," Richard said, which made him pause, "God go with you."

After that, Henry's news was a distinct anticlimax. But Richard did not seem to think the less of it. "He tried to kill you," he said. "He tried to kill me. He's taken my sister's child—and Judah's youngest son with her, if you're wondering why we're suddenly receiving the help of these secret priests. He took my garrison out of Masyaf and he's laid siege to my strongest castle. Do you think we can call this a declaration of war?"

"That might be a safe assumption," Henry said.

He shifted in his seat, unable quite to hold back a groan. They all looked ready to leap to his aid, especially Sioned. He shook them off. "I'm well enough. I'm stiff, that's all. Sire, I need to sleep, but when I get up, I'll be ready to ride."

Sioned looked as if she would have argued with that, but she held her tongue. For that he was grateful.

Richard was already in motion. A war, even one as sudden and immediately devastating as this, delighted him to no end. Henry would enjoy it himself, once his eyelids stopped dropping shut.

No one, he noticed, had asked Richard what he meant to do about his voyage to England. Henry did not see fit to ask him, either. First things first. War, then the rest of the world.

Chapter Twelve

Sioned managed to escape Richard's solar on pretext of seeing that Henry was settled and properly medicated. That was not a ruse, not exactly. She did as she had said she would. But when she was done, instead of going back to the room where Ahmad and Richard were planning this sudden war, she went up to the roof.

It was still daylight, rather to her surprise. The prince of jinn had been hovering. He came down before she needed to call, and stood in one of his more human forms. He looked like a larger, redder, fanged and clawed version of her brother. "My friend," she said, "will you carry me where I need to go?"

The jinni's round yellow eyes were keen. He knew her well—too well, maybe, but this was a gamble she must take. "Not unarmed, dear lady," he said, "and not unprepared."

She bowed to the wisdom of that. "To my house first, then," she said. "And then—"

"Then will come when it comes," said the jinni, swelling into a much larger and more terrifying shape. It was the first he had taken in front of her, and she found it familiar, even comforting, to look up four times the height of a man and see great batwings stretched out against the sky.

She stepped into the outstretched hand and held on easily as he shifted her to his shoulders. Even as she settled, he took to the air.

She fetched what she needed, quickly, without disturbing the servants. With bag in hand and cloak over arm, she returned to the roof and the jinni.

He knew where she was going, but he was not afraid. The one thing in any world that he feared was wrapped in silk and hidden in the heart of her house. No other power on this earth or from the realms below could touch him.

They rose into the sky, concealed from mortal sight by the jinni's wards and magic. He circled above Jerusalem, hovered briefly over the golden flame of the Dome of the Rock, and turned northward.

He outflew the wind. Her eyes blurred; she wrapped her mantle about her, for the air at this height and at this speed was chill. If she had not been so sick with worry for her daughter, she would have given herself up to the exhilaration of flight.

She could not believe as Ahmad did that the enemy had simply removed his captives from the world and was holding them for ransom. Teleri was alive, she would swear to that, but for how long, she did not know. Sioned had read too much of the darker magics. She knew how the undead sustained themselves among the living. They needed the living—blood and souls, to give them substance and make them strong. The blood of two young mages, both of ancient and magical blood, would swell his power enormously.

She must not think of that. She must be calm. All fear, all confusion must vanish. She must be cold and still, as hard and impermeable as glass, and as strong as steel.

Armored in magic, she sat upright on the jinni's shoulders as he spiraled above the battlements of Masyaf. There were strong wards on the castle, and waves of power lapping toward the borders of the old domain of the Assassins.

No banner flew from the tower that the Hospitallers had added to the rest. There were men on the walls, small figures in white. They were mortal men, unmagical, but lit with a fire of fanaticism. They or their fathers before them had served the Old Man when he was living, and never known what he was. That was all the more true now that he was dead. They were enspelled, bound to him in blind devotion.

He was in the castle. She could smell him, like dust and old graves. A faint charnel stink hung about him, and infused the air above his stronghold.

The jinni set her down on the roof. Even as she found her feet, he shrank, taking the shape of a big ruddy man in armor of the Franks. It was a great defiance in this fanatically Muslim place, from a creature who could take any semblance he chose.

With him as her guardsman, she made her way down from the roof. People tried to stop her. Some had knives, and one had a spear. Her jinni disposed of the weapons with cool dispatch. She felt nothing. No fear.

She caught one of the would-be defenders as he bolted, and said, "Take me to the lord of this place."

He squealed and struggled, but she was stronger than she looked. The jinni, moving in behind him, swung him up by the scruff of his neck. "Obey," he said in his deep melodious voice.

That was no human voice, and even one of the Old Man's

ensorcelled servants could perceive it. The man blanched. The jinni dropped him; he fell on his face, then sprang up. "This—this way," he babbled. "Come. Come this way."

He led them well, and he did not try to trick them. He was an honest Assassin.

Masyaf still held traces of the Franks who had ruled it for a dozen years: tapestries and furnishings in the style of the west, walls painted with images of saints, racks of weapons fitted to the larger, coarser hands of Christian knights. There was not a cross to be seen, and images of the Christ were hacked and disfigured. And everywhere were soft-footed men in white.

They stared at the woman walking calmly through the realm of men with her strange guard at her back. Some saw the magic in her and bowed. Others ventured to stop her, and stopped short at the gleam of the guard's great Frankish sword.

The Old Man was waiting. He had no fear of her, and no dread of what she could do. The manner of her coming was a flag of truce, her wards and protections turned carefully inward. She carried no weapon, offered no hostility. She came as an envoy to a parley.

Envoys could die, and often had, but she did not expect that. Not until he had spoken with her. She could feel him; the stench of death was stronger, the air growing dark even as she walked through the sunlight of an open court.

Her skin pebbled along her arms and down her spine, but her heart was quiet, empty of horror. Death did not frighten her. She was a physician; she had seen disease, decay, dissolution of body and mind. She had seen all the faces of death, from the spirit's first passing to the polished skull.

He sat in a windowless room, with no light upon him but a faint corpse-light; but she had eyes to see in the dark. She saw the robe that wrapped him, and the shape beneath: more bone than flesh, but it was flesh. How much blood had gone to clothe those bones, she did not want to think.

He was the blackest of black things, come out of the Pit to take revenge on those who killed him. "Suppose we dispense with the amenities," she said, "and get to the point. Where is my daughter?"

"I would hardly be wise to tell you that," he said.

"I will find her, if I have to harrow heaven and hell," said Sioned. "If you let her go now, I may consider mercy when it comes time to expunge you from the worlds."

"That is tempting," said the dark thing that had been a man, "although the mercy of a Frank leaves much to be desired. Let me counter with an offer somewhat more generous. A certain thing of mine is in your hands. Return it to me, and I will give you your daughter."

"Free? Whole? Unharmed?"

"Altogether unharmed," he said.

However cold, however remote she tried to be, she could not face that without a quiver in the heart. "The Seal of Solomon," she said, "in return for the child of my body— and, I would hope, the child you stole with her, who is an innocent. That is a powerful bargain."

"Is it not?" said the dark thing.

"Surely," she said, "in your current state, you have little need for the Seal. Your power is enormous. Your magic is as potent as I have ever seen. What can the Seal do that your triumph over death has not done?"

"Call it a whim," said the dark thing. "It was mine, and was stolen. I want it back again."

Sioned set her lips together. The Seal was no whim. He needed it badly enough to exchange Teleri for it. Therefore it must be of vital importance. If he took it, and the power that went with it—

Deep within the armor of her heart, she wept as she said, "And you in turn stole it from its guardians. Should they come back from the dead as well, and lay their own claim?"

"That will not happen," he said in a dangerous purr. "Do we have a bargain?"

Oh, he was desperate, to press so hard and so soon. "Tell me where my daughter is," she said.

"Ah, no," he said. "You will not refuse me and then, with its power, snatch her away. I will keep her—alive while it suits me—until you return what is mine."

"If you kill her," she said, "you will never have the Seal. Not in this world or any other."

"Then we are at an impasse," he said. "The solution of course is simple. The Seal for the child."

"Children," she said.

"Children," he agreed after a brief pause.

"I must ponder it," she said. "The Seal is not mine to give away. It belongs to my brother. He may accept or refuse. I cannot do it for him."

"You have nine days," the dark thing said.

"My brother takes poorly to this kind of force," she said. "Give us until the new moon. Nine days, times three. If I can't persuade him by then, I never will."

She held her breath. The dark thing did not answer at once, but just as she began to grow dizzy, he said, "You will not find them in nine days or ninety. But I am inclined to be indulgent. Until the new moon. Then, the Seal, or your daughter is mine for eternity."

Sioned shuddered. It took all the strength she had to say, "Eternity is not part of this bargain."

"It is if I choose to make it so," the dark thing said. "But I too can be merciful. I will surrender the body of the other. But the child of two great mages, daughter of two worlds—

that one I keep. Every scrap of her, both soul and body. Unless, of course, you return my Seal."

It would be useless to curse him. He was a living curse. She turned on her heel.

He did not try to prevent her from leaving his castle. That was the cat's pleasure, letting the mouse run free for a little while before he caught and devoured it.

So little a while. She had been a fool, thrice and nine times fool. If she had let be, time would be short, but there might at least be more of it. Time for him to come for the Seal, and fight for it—weeks, months even, with the help of Judah and his kin.

Now she had just under a month. Unless she could delay him. Unless—

The jinni carried her back to Jerusalem in silence that grew great enough to swallow her. If it had been only her own life that she had bargained away, she would not have been afraid. But Teleri, and Benjamin who should have had no part in this . . .

Ahmad did not roar at her. He never roared. Richard would, but that was for later. It would be much less painful than her husband's quiet words. "It seems I recall a time not more than a few days ago, when you upbraided me for running off alone on errands that could be the death of me. What were you thinking?"

She flushed at the rebuke, which she had to admit was well deserved, but she answered him steadily enough. "I was thinking that if I forced his hand while he was still short of full strength, I might give us an advantage—and possibly discover where the children are."

"Did we gain an advantage?"

She was still his pupil in many ways, but she resisted the compulsion to hang her head like a guilty child. "I would say that we did not. Unless . . . is there a spell that will cling to him and follow him, and when he comes to them, return to us with their whereabouts?"

"That would require that someone go back to his lair," Ahmad said. "If so, it will not be you."

She opened her mouth to protest, but thought better of it. "So it can be done? Someone can do it?"

"It is possible," he said. "Whether it can actually be accomplished . . . I doubt it."

"Even a little hope is better than none."

He did not answer that. There was no answer that he could sensibly give.

CHAPTER THIRTEEN

"We need the Ark," Judah said.

He did not roar, either, but his long, dark stare was even more devastating than Ahmad's soft and mild rebuke. It was all he did or said to reproach Sioned for her folly. She caught herself shifting on the bench in his workroom, wishing she could escape and go back to her work in the hospital. But there was no escape from this.

"There is a spell," he said, "to spy on such a power, but to conceal it and to place it will require more strength than any one of us has. It needs a burning glass, a focus of power—in a word, the Ark. It's the only thing greater than the Seal. Which we must defend, because he will come for it. Of that we can be certain."

"The Ark is in Rome," Sioned said. "Or so you believe. If we can get there—if the secret roads are not blocked—we still have to find it. Legions of scholars and treasure hunters have been there before us. And we have twenty-six days."

"Nearly twenty-seven," said Judah. It was as close to humor as he ever came, and it was as black as humor could be. "You have two things the others never had. You have us. And you have the Seal."

"I can't take it," said Sioned. "The power of the city conceals it. If it leaves these walls—"

"If you travel by the hidden ways," Judah said, "under such wards as we can raise, direct from Jerusalem to Rome, from power to power, he may not detect it."

"Rome has its own magic," said Ahmad. "It's younger than Jerusalem, and less holy. Still, it's full of old gods and ancient powers. They'll shield our magic just as it is shielded here, and some may even be of use—since neither of us is Christian, and the yoke of the Church has been so heavy for so long."

While Ahmad spoke, Judah was watching her keenly. "You're afraid of Rome," he said.

Her temper flared, but she kept it—barely—in hand. This was her penance as the Christians would say, for being nine different kinds of idiot, and for placing them all in even worse danger than before. "I have never been there," she said, "and never wanted to go. It's a city of ghosts and ruins, with the Pope squatting atop them, declaring himself lord of the world."

"Well then," said Judah, "he's a fine match for the monster in Masyaf. And somewhere in his throne of rubble is the thing we need to win this war."

"Do you really need it?" she demanded. "Or is this your excuse to get back what was yours?"

She never had been able to ruffle Judah's feathers. He raised a sardonic brow and said, "So: you *are* afraid. It's only a city after all, and in most ways it's less horrifying than Jerusalem. It's younger and its history is slightly less

bloody. If it's the Pope who's been haunting your childhood nightmares, what better way to banish them than by
discovering that under the triple tiara he's as mortal as
you?"

"Which is more than can be said of the thing in Masyaf,"
Ahmad observed.

"You are insisting that I go," she said. "Why? Prescience
has never been my gift. It's even less so now."

Judah shrugged. Ahmad sighed. "Foresight fails us all,"
her husband said. "If you truly refuse, I'll go alone. But I
would rather have you with me."

"We're done with running off alone," she said with ill
grace. "I'll go. We've wasted hours as it is. How soon can you
be ready?"

"As soon as we've seen Richard," he said, "we'll go."

"God's teeth," said Richard. They had dispensed with
mortal amenities and gone direct to his bedchamber, where
he had gone to snatch a few hours' sleep amid his preparations for war. He was just lying down when they stepped out
of air. He leaped up, snatching the first weapon that came to
hand, which happened to be the bolster of his bed.

"We're going to Rome," Sioned said. "We haven't come
to ask your leave, but your blessing would be welcome."

His jaw had dropped. He shut his mouth with a sharp
click. "Now? You're leaving now? Have you gone mad?"

"Probably," she said. "Judah will be protecting the city."

"By the time you get back," Richard said, "the war will be
over, one way or another. It will probably be over before you
even get to Italy."

"Not unless it ends tonight," she said.

He widened his eyes.

"We're searching for a weapon," she said, "by other

means than the ordinary. We may be back before you march on Krak."

"Not unless you're back within the week," he said.

"We could be," she said.

"God's teeth," he said again. "I hate magic."

"It may save you," she said.

"That doesn't mean I have to like it." He pulled on a shirt and groaned, running his hands through his hair and rubbing his cheeks. "Christ, it makes me itch. A week from now, we march. I'm sending scouts ahead. If you look for me again, you'll find me at Krak, or on the road there."

"We'll find you," she said. "May we have your blessing?"

He did not ask her why. That was more perceptive of him than she might have expected; or else he was simply too sleepy to trouble himself. He laid his hands on her head and said, "Go with the blessing of all good things."

She looked up startled. That was more than perceptive. It was almost . . .

He was no more magical than ever, but no less. He was, when it came to it, the king.

Then at last there was no avoiding it. They gathered together such things as they would need: clothing, a purse of gold, a little bag of jewels. Only enough food and water for a short day's ride. Ahmad would put aside his turban for this and pretend to be a Frank. It was safest and most unobtrusive.

They meant to take no servant, but when they went for the horses, they found three saddled and Mustafa holding the reins of them all. "My lord sent me," he said.

"You can't come," Sioned said. "He needs you."

"He thinks you need me more. He has an army of sorcerous Jews, he says, and enough knights and men-at-arms to keep him in mischief for a while. You need someone who can look after you while you hunt for whatever it is you're hunting for."

That was Richard's very voice. Mustafa was his gift, and it was a gift of no little value.

There was a great deal more to Mustafa than one might think. Dressed as a Frank, as he was now, he looked like a man of Provence, or a Gascon. He could assume the accent and the manner of moving and speaking, so cleverly and with such verisimilitude that a man of Bayonne or Toulouse would take that Berber of Morocco for one of his own.

Nor was that his only talent. He could not work magic, but he could see it. He could hunt as well as she or Ahmad could, when she stopped to think. And yet—

Ahmad had already mounted. That was his answer, clearly enough. Mustafa was holding her mare's stirrup. She opened her mouth, closed it, shook her head. With her lips tight shut, she settled into the saddle. Even as she took up the reins, Mustafa was on his own mare's back, waiting for the others to lead him.

She rode past them to the front. To mortal eyes they stood in the fountain court of her house in Jerusalem, but she could see the roads leading from it, the paths of power that wove and tangled throughout Jerusalem. This was a nexus, and she had chosen the house because of it. She had not known then how it would serve her.

There in the court, where the fountain mingled water and air and light, a gate waited to open. She spoke a single Word on three ascending notes. On the third, the water leaped upward and divided. Through the posts and beneath the lintel of the door, she looked into infinity.

She must not falter. Ahmad's presence at her back, and somewhat to her surprise Mustafa's, steadied her. Behind them she felt the great shape of the jinni, with his wide wings folded and his talons sheathed.

They were an army. However few they were, however odd an assemblage, they were strong. They could only pray that they would be strong enough—and fast enough to find what had been lost for so many hundred years.

CHAPTER FOURTEEN

E ven strong mages walked these roads rarely. It did not take great power to walk them, but it took great strength of will to come direct to one's destination. The roads branched and branched again, weaving through infinite worlds and countless possibilities. A mage could be lost forever, wandering wherever his whim and the roads took him.

Tonight there was no temptation. Both Sioned and Ahmad focused on the straight track, the clear line from Jerusalem to Rome. There was none straighter, none clearer.

That made it dangerous. The jinni moved smoothly ahead of them. Mustafa took station behind. They raised wards with all the strength that they could spare. Of all the powers that haunted these ways, spying on those who passed, none must know who they were or where they went.

Sioned kept her head down. This mode of travel played havoc with her senses. Her stomach heaved and her head spun. Ahmad claimed that he felt no such distress. She would never call him a liar, but if it was true, she could be tempted to strangle him.

She fixed her eyes on the high pommel of her saddle, and on her hands clinging white-knuckled to it. She refused to see how the road shifted and swirled beneath her mare's feet like oil on heaving waves, or how the sky overhead surged from bright to dark and thence to bright again. She thought of Rome and only Rome, of the old imperial city now fallen to grass and ruins.

Jerusalem was burning gold, a scent of hot metal, a blinding brightness through the multitude of worlds. Rome was cold iron and forged steel, the tramp of legionaries' boots, the ringing of bells in its thousand churches and chapels. The scent of Jerusalem was blood and dust. That of Rome was incense and blood.

They passed through a grove of shadowy trees. Eyes watched them through the branches. Strange shapes floated overhead, like fish swimming in the air. The iron tang of Rome was stronger. The trees blurred and shifted. Sometimes they seemed to be a grove of spears, and each tipped with ancient blood.

The jinni had drawn his wings in tight lest he brush those edged branches. The horses plodded calmly as their kind always did on these roads. Whatever they saw or felt, it roused in them no fear.

Sioned took her lesson from them. She slowed and deepened her breathing and willed her stomach to settle. It almost succeeded. She did not fall over retching, although she still could not look down at the shimmer of the road.

Rome was close. It both drew and repelled them. All roads led there, but as the travelers came to it, the roads warped and bent and slid aside. There were great walls of power about it, and potent defenses.

The jinni halted. The wood of spears drew in perilously close.

Ahmad spoke the Word that opened the way to the mortal world. The roads resisted. The power rose like shields of iron.

Two Muslims, a pagan, and a spirit of fire did not please these guardians in the slightest. Sioned began to regret that they had not brought a Christian. The water of baptism held great power.

Almost on a whim, she sang the same triune note that had opened the way in Jerusalem. The shields ground to a halt, then retreated. The wood of spears melted away. They stood on a road of closely set stones, much worn and somewhat overgrown, but there was no mistaking the paving of a Roman road. There before them was the city, walls somewhat less worn than the road, much patched and built over, and a gate opening into that strange, half-thriving, half-crumbling city.

Ahmad had a map and such wisdom as Judah and his kin had been able to offer. They knew every city, even this one. A Christian might take refuge in the guesthouse of a monastery, but none of them was minded to carry the pretense that far.

There was a house known to the brotherhood of magic and of trade. It had been a great mansion once, indeed a palace, but it had fallen on hard times. Now it was an inn for travelers of quality. It stood on a hillside overlooking the Tiber, and resembled nothing so much as a farmstead in the odder parts of Britain. A sizable kitchen garden surrounded it, and an olive grove was planted behind it. And yet it was within a few furlongs of a crowded and tumultuous bit of city.

Even in her dark mood, Sioned found it delightful. The innkeeper was a large but agile woman of no age in particu-

lar, with a brisk manner and an air of indefatigable energy. She
bade them call her Domna Maria. Having judged them with
a swift glance, she gave them a suite of rooms on the upper
floor, with a staircase to the roof. From there they could look
down to the river and out across a landscape of ruined splendor, malarial marsh, and clusters of houses huddling about
churches.

Some of those were magnificent. Sioned did not need to
ask which one held the Pope. She could feel him, all cold iron
and fiery sanctity.

Closer in were a few other manors like Domna Maria's.
The closest stood somewhat farther up the hill, and was
walled like a castle. It had a gate with a portcullis, and a tower
surmounted by a cross. It made her think of Templars and
Hospitallers, although those orders had no such house in
Rome, that she knew of.

That first night, they rested. The rooms were clean and
the beds comfortable. They were fed well—with nothing set
before them that might cause a Muslim to transgress. Domna
Maria had not asked, but at the mention of Daniel and Judah
bar Samuel, she had arched a brow slightly and drawn a clear
conclusion.

Both Ahmad and Mustafa chose not to disillusion her.
Muslim or Jew, *halal* or kosher, they were people of the Book,
and their laws of the table were like enough to make no matter. She asked for no names, either, although Sioned was
ready with expedients if they should be needed. They were
safely and comfortably anonymous, with nothing between
them and their landlady but a handful of gold bezants.

The men prayed at sunset in the privacy of their rooms.
So did the jinni, whose semblance was the most human he
had ever shown. He was the very image of Richard in his

younger days. Only his eyes betrayed him. They were golden like a hawk's, and in the heart of them was a flicker of flame.

While they prayed, Sioned went up on the roof to watch the sun go down. It was warm here, but never as warm as in Jerusalem. The mists were rising with the night, cloaking the river and creeping up the hill. Insects buzzed but did not sting; her wards were up, driving them off.

It was still faintly light when Ahmad came to stand beside her, with a thin curve of moon resting above the hill to the westward. He stood close but did not offer to touch her. She slipped her arm about his waist and leaned against him, a little stiffly. With a faint sigh he drew her in.

She felt his breath on her hair, and the brush of his lips. She had not wanted him or any man in longer than she cared to think, but tonight she turned on him with fierce and sudden heat. He froze for an instant in startlement, but then his eagerness rose to match hers. He swept her off her feet and laid her down in a nest of silken softness that had not been there a moment before.

She laughed softly. Magic could be a great burden and terrible danger, but once in a great while it had its advantages.

He set hand to her lacings, but she could not wait for that. She tugged urgently at his drawers. He shed them and thrust up her skirts and took her by storm. She met him midway.

It was nothing like their usual long, slow, delicious dances of love. This was swift and fiery-sweet, the release so strong that she cried out as if in pain.

He sank down beside her, arms still about her, holding her safe. Her body was ringing like a bell after it is struck, the note going on and on, pulsing slowly into silence.

When the last of it was gone, she drew a shuddering breath. He was lying on his side watching her, his eyes dark and soft, his face seeming years younger. The lines had smoothed away, except for the creases of his smile.

She touched him gently, tracing the curve of his lips. "It's been too long," she said. "Don't let it be this long again."

"Not unless you wish it," he said.

"I won't." She meant it, not only for now but for as far as she could see. "I'm sorry," she said.

"Don't be."

"I need to be." Her eyes were spilling over. For once she did not try to stop them. "Everything I've done, I've done badly. I'm a disgrace to my teacher."

"Not altogether," he said.

"I should be stronger. I have to be. I won't lose my daughter as I lost—as I lost my son."

Her voice had caught, but she had got the words out. He kissed the tears from her cheeks. "Beloved," he said, "we will do this. Or we'll die and meet in Paradise. We'll not fail in the end, whatever falls between."

"Sometimes," she said, "I envy you your faith."

"It is a great comfort," he granted her. He kissed her again, softly, on the lips. "Beloved infidel. There is no other like you."

"And thank God for it, as my brother would say." She moved against him. She knew as a physician that men of his age were not the eager lovers that they had been in youth, but there again it was an advantage to be a mage. She needed to remember that; to remember the joy that had been in magic, before magic took her life's joy away.

CHAPTER FIFTEEN

Teleri had been floating in a long dream. She remembered clearly the darkness that had taken her and snatched away Benjamin, but once they were swallowed up, there was nothing. Truly nothingness: no touch, no sight, no sound or smell or taste. She was pure spirit, and pure consciousness.

Slowly her body came back to her. First there was discomfort, not quite enough to be pain, and a sour taste in her mouth. Then there was sweet scent blowing across her, and after it the soft rippling sound of water falling, and last of all, a dawning of light.

She was lying on mown grass in a garden. A fountain was playing just out of reach. Great strange trumpets of blooms hung over her, wafting forth sweetness. She ached in every bone.

She sat up carefully, wincing at the many twinges and the small stabbing pains of a body flung down hard and left untended for too long. Her hand found Benjamin before her eyes did: he was lying behind her, sprawled on his face, with his black curls in a hopeless tangle.

Her heart beat so fast she was dizzy. She pulled him onto his back. He looked dead: his face was white, his eyes rolled up in his head. Just as she was sure of it, he gasped for breath and choked and coughed, and doubled up in a fit of simply being alive.

She fetched him water in the cup of a leaf, and poured it into him until he stopped choking, then dashed the rest on his face. He was awake by then, spluttering and glaring. "Are you trying to kill me?"

"*I'm* not," she said.

He held his head in his hands as if it hurt him. "That wasn't a dream, was it? The leper came and took us away."

"That's what I remember," she said. "Can you tell where we are?"

"Not with this headache," he said.

She had one, too, but either it was not as bad or she was tougher to begin with. She drank some of the water from the fountain, with a moment's thought that it might not be a wise thing to do, but she was thirsty and the water seemed clean. It was cold and pure, bubbling from a deep spring into the carved stone of the upper basin, filling it, then streaming down to the bowl below.

She washed her face and hands, welcoming the shock of icy water on her skin. She was more awake when she turned back to Benjamin. "I'm going to look for a way out," she said.

He scrambled to his feet. He was not a coward and she would never accuse him of it, but he had a great dislike of sudden changes and unexpected adventures. He stayed close as she walked away from the fountain through a grove of trees with long glossy leaves and flowers as white as wax. Their fragrance was like honey and wine.

The paths seemed straight, but after a long while it dawned on her that they curved invisibly. They led in circles, twisting through a maze of hedges and woven branches, so intricate that she never passed the same way twice. Sometimes she thought she heard the fountain, but she did not see it.

Just when she was ready to fall down on the strange soft grass and scream to let out her frustration, the maze opened in front of her. There was a long sward of green and a table laid in the middle of it, with white cloths and silver plates and cups and bowls, like a king's feast.

The smell of it was intoxicating. There were roast meats and honeyed fruits and new bread and cakes and candies in royal profusion, all fresh, all steaming if they were supposed to be hot and glistening with frost if they should be cold. There were mounds of ices and sherbets in every flavor imaginable, and nectar of fruits and honey and spices, and whole edifices of spun sugar. There was even something dark and sweet that she had never seen before, that smelled like the Muslims' Paradise.

Teleri's stomach growled audibly. This was pure temptation. She did not even think before she leaped toward it— until Benjamin caught her arm and brought her up short. "Haven't you ever listened to stories?" he said. "You know what sorcerous banquets mean. They're a trap. If you eat anything on that table, you'll be bound here forever."

"I hate you," Teleri said without force. She let him pull her back off the grass. Her mouth was watering so hard that she had to keep swallowing. Her stomach echoed, it was so empty.

"We are going to have to eat before too long," she said. "Unless we're supposed to starve here."

"We don't dare touch anything," said Benjamin. "It's too dangerous."

"Maybe," Teleri said. "Maybe not."

She raised the hand he was not holding, and shaped a sign in the air. It hung, burning, singing faintly. "What is foul, make vanish. What is fair, bring to light."

The table shimmered like a mirage. The towers of sugar and sweetness melted away, and the ices and sherbets faded into mist. So did most of the more savory things. But some stayed: a dish as big as a shield, full of rice and spiced lamb, and most of the bread and some of the cakes, and a basket of perfectly ordinary and earthly fruit, oranges and apples and pomegranates, figs and dates and fruit of paradise.

Benjamin was still suspicious. He worked his own spell of warding and detection. The pomegranates puffed into ash, but the rest stayed as it was, as safe as their magic could make it.

"It's always pomegranates," Benjamin said, approaching the table warily and taking a handful of lamb and rice. He screwed up his face and popped it into his mouth, chewed and swallowed, and paused.

Nothing happened. He did not fall down in an enchanted sleep, or turn into a lizard, or sprout fangs. He took another bite, then moved on to the bread and the fruit and the one remaining frosted jar, which proved to be full of sherbet.

Teleri followed him. She ate as carefully as he did, not afraid of poison but too well aware that if she ate too much after a fast, she could make herself sick. She stopped when her stomach was full, and resisted the urge to gorge, especially on the sweets.

Then she could think about going on. There was a way out. It was probably magical. If she looked long enough, she would find it.

She turned to Benjamin, meaning to tell him what she was

thinking, but he was staring at something behind her. His face was perfectly blank.

If they had not worked spells of true seeing, they would have seen a kindly old man in white, smiling at them from a gate in the hedge. Teleri saw the shadow of the spell, like a reflection in a dark glass, but behind it was the truth.

She shuddered. This was worse than a leper. It was a dead man walking, a shape of bones and tattered flesh, with a corpse-light in the hollow sockets of the skull, and a rictus grin. The voice came echoing out of its hollow chest. "Welcome to my garden," said the dead thing.

Neither of them spoke. Benjamin looked as if he might be thinking of it, but Teleri trampled his foot and he changed his mind.

"My name is Sinan," the thing said. "I hope your dinner was to your liking."

Teleri thought quickly. The thing seemed not to realize that they could see it as it was. She deliberately made her eyes see the way it wanted her to see. She saw the old man with the gentle smile and the deep eyes, and imagined that she heard his low melodious voice. "It was very good," she said to that image, although Benjamin shot her a sulfurous glance. "We thank you. Can we go home now?"

The shadow-man smiled while he shook his head, but the thing behind the shadow stiffened in contempt. "I had thought you would like to stay," he said. "This is the most beautiful garden in the world, and the most wonderful. Anything that you wish, it will grant you. Only tell it what you would like."

"To go home," said Teleri.

"Not yet," said Sinan. "But anything else, ask the garden, and it is yours."

"No, thank you," Teleri said politely. "Maybe another time."

"Then I shall wish for you," said Sinan. He raised his hand—odd to see the shadow of the living hand over the bare and gleaming bone—and gestured grandly, as the ignorant must think sorcerers did. "A palace for their pleasure," he said, "with all comforts, and their every desire."

A palace took shape out of air. It looked as if it was made of spun sugar, and once the wonder of it had passed, it was not so very large. Her father's summer house in Damascus was bigger. It had a garden inside the garden, and a fountain court, and another court with a pool in it that reflected the shifting colors of the sky, and rooms full of games and toys, and one whole room for the table that had held the feast.

It was all a shadow. Even the beautiful silvery horses in the stableyard, with their long waving manes and their big soft eyes, were creatures of the Old Man's magic. Teleri was sorry for that. She did love horses, and she loved to ride.

She did not let him know that she could tell what was real and what was not. She clapped her hands and was delightedly amazed. So, very convincingly, was Benjamin. She sighed inside at that. She had been afraid that he would not understand the game, and would refuse to play it.

She need not have worried. He ran with her through the little palace, ducking in and out of rooms, and exclaimed over the marvels in each, and danced and laughed as if the spell had taken him completely.

The Old Man followed them at a dignified pace. The smile on his shadow-face was indulgent. The one on his true face was smug—there was no other word for it. He thought he had them trapped, wound in his spell.

After a while he left them alone. He was called away: Teleri saw the force that reached from beyond the garden's wards and pulled him out. She started to leap for it, but restrained herself. He would catch her if she tried to escape now. She studied it instead, and remembered what she saw.

Benjamin sat with her on the rim of the pool in the shadowy palace. There were things in the water, not quite fish. They were not evil: they did not make her skin crawl. They were merely strange.

"He wants to corrupt us," Benjamin said.

She nodded. "We have a lot of power between us, and more coming when we're older. And we're a weapon against our families."

"If we don't pretend, he'll kill us. Or worse."

"Probably worse," she said. She was afraid, in a dim and foggy way. Mostly she was determined to get out.

"What's worse than death?"

"You saw that thing, and you need to ask?"

He shuddered. "He'll make us like him?"

"He might. Or he'll enslave us, and make us do all the things he can't do because he's not alive any more."

"We can't stay here," he said. His voice was calm, but his eyes had gone wild. "We have to get out."

"We will," she said. She hoped she meant it. "Meanwhile we pretend. We let him think we're stupid children."

"There are no books here at all," Benjamin said. "How am I going to live without books?"

He was falling apart. She took hold of his shoulders and shook him until his teeth rattled. "Think of getting back to your books," she said fiercely. "Think of being strong enough to last until we can escape."

"I'm not weak."

"No, you're not," she said. "Just remember that."

He swallowed and nodded.

"If you heave," she said without much sympathy, "don't foul the water."

The rush of temper stiffened his spine. It kept his dinner down, too. He squared his shoulders and looked a little less green. "So where do we begin?"

"We rest," she said. "Then we keep hunting for ways out. There has to be one that won't have that thing's watchdogs on the other side."

"Every castle has a postern," said Benjamin, "and every battle an opening for retreat."

"Ah," she said. "You've been listening to my father."

"And the king," said Benjamin. "Rest, then. Maybe we'll dream a way out."

"Maybe," Teleri said.

CHAPTER SIXTEEN

Mustafa had expected to find himself in the most absolutely Christian city of all. To his astonishment,
Rome was no such thing. There were churches
enough, and a priest or monk or nun at every turn, but their
feet trod on earth far older than their faith, soaked with blood
and power.

The earth that had welcomed worshippers of every god
and demon in any pantheon did not revolt at the presence of
a Muslim. He walked it in his Frankish clothes, which by now
were familiar enough for comfort, and it accepted him as it
had so many others. Roma Mater was mother to them all.

While the lord Saphadin and his lady searched in their
way, he hunted as a scout did: on foot, walking through the
streets and among the barren places. The jinni chose to walk
with him and not to stay with the mages. The great creature
looked so much like Richard that Mustafa almost could not
bear it, but in time he persuaded himself to find it reassuring.

The first day of searching, as they walked down from the hill on which the villa stood, Mustafa said, "Great lord, if I don't trespass, and please forgive me if I do, have you a name by which I may call you?"

The jinni smiled, which was not a comfortable sight: his teeth were much too numerous and much too sharp. "Call me Hamad," he said. "We are allies, yes?"

"It seems so, my lord," Mustafa said.

Hamad bowed to his courtesy. "We hunt," he said.

"We hunt," Mustafa agreed.

They hunted down toward the river and back up along the hills. Once or twice Mustafa was aware that they were hunted themselves. Footpads followed them for a while, but then went in search of easier and less well-armed prey.

At midday they paused. They had worked their way back toward the villa and the castle above it. There was a bit of town there, a village of sorts, with a market square and a handful of taverns and a clump of houses.

Hamad did not eat in the mortal fashion. He wandered through the market while Mustafa found the tavern that did not reek of pork. The serving-girl fetched him bread and cheese and olives and a mug of barley water, although she eyed him oddly when he asked for that. His smile made her blush; she brought him the mug surprisingly quickly, with a little bowl of pickled onions that he had not asked for. "Compliments of the house," she said.

He thanked her politely, at which she blushed even more. Women did that when he smiled. He never intended it, but he could not help it. Richard said he was too pretty for his own good, and that was all too true.

This woman would have been pleased to offer more than a meal and a smile. Mustafa judged it wise to pretend that he did not see. Franks grew strange and sometimes violent when he confessed that he was not a man for women.

While he ate, he watched the jinni move round the far edge of the market square. At the same time he was aware of what passed closer in: people eating, drinking, walking, haggling with the merchants in the stalls.

Mustafa's eye took in nothing in particular. People here were quite similar to people in the east: small for the most part, dark, sharp-featured. Now and then someone taller and fairer happened past, though none as tall or ruddy as Hamad. Mustafa fit well here, was even on the tall side, which was a novelty. He was long accustomed to being towered over by big blond Franks.

There was no one suspicious here, apart from the pickpocket over by the greengrocer's stall. Most of the marketgoers were women with baskets on their heads or over their arms. The men were either idling in the taverns or hanging about the smithy across the square.

One drew Mustafa's eye: a young man who stood watching the smith turn an iron bar into a set of tongs. He was plainly dressed but his clothes were of fine quality, and they were clean. He was younger than Mustafa, no longer a boy but not yet come to man's years; his cheeks were shaven clean in the Frankish fashion, but the beard even so young was a strong and vigorous thing. So too his hair, thick and glossy black and curling, curls that owed nothing to the barber's art. They were all his own.

He was a glorious creature, with a face out of the old marbles, broad clear brow and long straight nose and firmly rounded chin; his mouth was full but strong, his eyes wide and dark and thickly fringed with lashes under level black brows. But most wonderful to Mustafa's eyes was the shim-

mer of magic in him, like moonlight on deep water. It was evident even in the bright sun. In twilight or in darkness he
would shine like the moon.

Mustafa drew a long sigh. Beauty and magic both. He
knew just then how Ahmad had felt the first time he saw
Sioned.

There were no coincidences: that was an article of
Mustafa's faith. He left the tavern and made his way toward
the smithy. His gait was easy, his air casual. He kept his hand
well away from the small dagger at his belt. No one need
know how many other weapons were arranged about his person.

He stood near the beautiful young man, but not too near.
The smith's hammer clanged on iron and anvil. As the blood-
red metal cooled, the hammer shaped it, drawing it out, giving it roundness.

People were talking over the clangor, idle chatter in the
dialect of Rome. Mustafa's ear recorded it, noted its distinc-
tions from other dialects of the Italies, and remembered each
of them. That was his gift, as close to magic as made no matter.

The smith finished shaping and hammering the iron, and
plunged it into a vat of water in a great hissing and cloud of
steam. The young man turned as if to wander off, but his eye
caught Mustafa's. It widened.

Mustafa knew that swift assessment, and after it the slow
softening. Deep within him, a knot of tension eased. This was
not a man for women, either, then, praise to Allah, the Merciful and Compassionate.

He lowered his eyes before they gave away too much, and
kept them focused on his feet even as the young man's
shadow fell across his. "Greetings, stranger," the Roman said
in a slightly different dialect than Mustafa had been hearing.

It was closer to the Latin, crisper and clearer: a nobleman's accent, with the precision of books behind it.

"Greetings," Mustafa said. He had meant to sound like a Gascon, but in his confusion he spoke in his native accent, like a Berber who had learned Italian well but not perfectly.

"Are you new come to Rome?" the young nobleman asked. Then he laughed at himself and said, "You seem very much at ease here, but I haven't seen you before. And—"

"And I sound somewhat foreign." Mustafa raised his eyes. "I come from Jerusalem."

The young man's face lit with pure delight. "Jerusalem! What joy! You were in the Crusade?"

Mustafa inclined his head.

The young man applauded like a happy child, hooked an arm through his and drew him away from the smithy. "Come, you must tell me—I dream of Jerusalem, I pray to walk there before I grow old. I was too young for the Crusade, you see, and no one here had a part in it, and my father—my family—" He broke off. "Never mind. Here you are a stranger, and I'm vexing you with trifles. I am Giuliano; Giuliano Tiresi."

Mustafa had a choice to make. It might be a poor one, but he could not lie to this beautiful young creature. "My name is Mustafa," he said.

Giuliano's face did not fall, nor did he turn on Mustafa in sudden rage. "Mus—are you—"

"I am a Berber of Africa," Mustafa said, "and I serve the King of Jerusalem."

"Then you are an infidel." Still Giuliano was not appalled, only fascinated. "Why, that is wonderful! I don't suppose you were ever moved—to—"

"I remain unregenerate," said Mustafa, "and will to my grave. But I am loyal to my king."

"Loyalty is the best of virtues," said Giuliano. He drank

Mustafa in as if he had been a draft of good wine. "An infidel. And from Jerusalem. That is a marvel. You were in the Crusade? But no, you must have been too young. Unless—"

Mustafa laughed. He could not help it. "I was old enough. I thank you for the compliment, and yes, I fought in the battles."

"For the Lionheart?"

"For the Lionheart," Mustafa said.

Giuliano sighed in a mingling of envy and bliss. Suddenly his eyes widened. "You are—are you—you're the king's dog!"

"I am," said Mustafa, surprised. "How did you—"

Giuliano regarded him in awe. "You are a legend. I've heard all the stories, sung all the songs. How you were a slave of Saladin, and you saw the king and knew you were meant to serve him, and you escaped to him, and he set you free. You were at Acre and Arsuf and Ascalon. You were at the taking of Jerusalem. You—"

"Please," Mustafa said. "I'm not—"

"Oh," said Giuliano, abashed. "I cry your pardon. I babble; it's a terrible fault. Please, I didn't mean to offend."

"No," said Mustafa. "No, I'm not offended. I didn't know there were stories. Or that they had traveled so far."

"Everything about the Lionheart is a story," said Giuliano, "and everyone about him, too. You and Blondel the singer and the young lord Henry and the terrible queen and—" He stopped. "*Dio.* I'll stop babbling now."

"It's rather charming," Mustafa said. "And disconcerting."

"Here," said Giuliano. "Let me atone for it. Come home with me. Our cook will make you something that a man of your faith can drink. And I'll teach my tongue to behave itself."

Mustafa was swept in his wake, borne by the strength of

his spirit, but one thing made him dig in his heels. "Hamad," he said. "I can't forget—"

Giuliano's eyes were starting out of his head. Hamad had not been there an instant before. Now he was, looming over them, bowing low. "I will continue," he said. "You go as you will."

"My lord," said Mustafa.

Hamad bent his great ruddy head and turned away.

Giuliano's teeth rattled together. "Was that—how could—"

"No," Mustafa said a little regretfully. "That wasn't Richard."

"Ah," said Giuliano, half relieved, half disappointed. "I thought—" He blinked and shook his head. "So many wonders. And the day was so ordinary before I came to the market."

Giuliano lived in the castle on the hill above the inn. It truly was a castle, with walls and dry moat, but in the heart of it, instead of a bleak stone keep, was a villa of rather remarkable size and elegance. The guards at the gates wore a device of birds in flight, silver on blue.

The walls were visible and tangible wards. Mustafa had all he could do not to stagger when he passed within them. This place tapped a deep well of power, and every creature in it was ashimmer with it.

Whatever this was, even if it had nothing to do with the Ark, it was a mighty thing. Mustafa the king's servant, the skilled spy, was greatly pleased. Mustafa who had seen a beautiful man in the market knew the stabbing of unaccustomed guilt.

He had no need for that. He had told Giuliano the truth of himself. When the time was suitable, he would tell more. Maybe all of it, if Giuliano could help him. The boy was a mage; he had lived in Rome all his life. He might know where to find the Ark.

All this raced through his head between stride and stride as he passed the first gate. He had mastered himself by the second. Giuliano had not noticed anything. He was pulling Mustafa down a passageway, calling to a servant: "Marco! Tell Messire Galoubet that we're invading."

Marco ducked in a bow and ran.

"Your cook?" said Mustafa, and as Giuliano nodded: "He's French."

"From Provence," Giuliano said. "He was an undercook for the Queen of England when he was young. He tells wonderful stories. Come, we'll see what he can do for you."

Messire Galoubet was younger than Mustafa had expected, and stronger. He did not have the softness of a man who lived forever indoors; he looked like a fighting man, but his field was the kitchen and his armies were the cooks and scullions.

"Messire," said Giuliano, "this man drinks no wine or ale. What can you give him that will delight him?"

The cook's bright black eyes looked Mustafa up and down. "You are far from home," he said. "Go on, sit. Out of my way. I have an art to practice."

He practiced it with both skill and dispatch, creating a sherbet out of essentially nothing. It was cold and sour-sweet, with the faint wild taste of snow beneath the sugar and citron. Mustafa bowed low to the art and the artist, and murmured a compliment in Provençal.

Messire Galoubet's brows rose. He said in the same language, "You have been in Provence?"

"Not yet, messire," said Mustafa, "but there are many of your countrymen beyond the sea."

"He's from Jerusalem," Giuliano said. "He serves the king." He turned to Mustafa. "Are you hungry? We could—"

"I've eaten well enough," Mustafa said, "but I thank you."

"Then come," Giuliano said eagerly. "I should like to hear stories of the Crusade. You must have new ones that we in the outlands have never heard."

"Rome is hardly the outland," Mustafa said.

"Jerusalem is the heart of the world," said Giuliano. He paused. "You don't mind? You don't—"

For you, Mustafa wanted to say, *I would do anything.* But he could hardly do that in front of all the cooks. He said instead, "I'll be pleased."

Giuliano started to rise, but Messire Galoubet said, "Stay. We do like a bit of taletelling while we work."

Mustafa did not mind. It seemed Giuliano did not, either. He stayed in that surprisingly cool corner of the kitchen, lit by a door into the kitchen garden, and told tales of Outremer until the light shifted visibly westward.

CHAPTER SEVENTEEN

Sioned cooled her heels for three days in the antechamber of the first rank of papal secretaries before she allowed herself to face the fact that a letter from the King of Jerusalem would not bring her direct to the Pope. Her rank did not impress these servants of the Christian God, and she had not come with a royal escort. A lone woman, plainly and sensibly dressed, won veiled sneers and no visible respect. Even when the jinni came with her, the fourth day after she began, and stood formidably at her back, they only rolled their eyes.

Ahmad was having no better fortune. Rome was as difficult a city as Jerusalem for a mage to hunt. There was so much magic, so much power, and so much faith all tangled together. So many skeins to unravel, and so little time.

The morning of the fourth day, with the jinni at her back, Sioned resolved to force the issue. She did not know what she would do, but she was sure it would come to her as she rode from the inn to the palace of the Lateran.

She was admitted as before, directed to the same musty anteroom and directed to sit on the same hard stone bench. The same petitioners were there who had been there every day. Maybe half a dozen had been allowed to go forward since the first day she came there. There were a score or more ahead of her, and all with the air of people who had waited a long while to be heard. They cultivated patience. Some dozed, others stared blankly into space.

Sioned reflected on possibilities. She was wasting time here. Even if the Pope knew where the Ark was, or would tell her, she was unlikely to reach him before it was too late.

If it was here in this palace, she could not sense it. The place reeked of incense and old bones. It was a prison for parchment, a realm of clerks and secretaries, ruling the world through the Word.

She rose from the bench. A few of the others regarded her without expression. She eyed the inner door, and considered breaking it down. But there was only another antechamber beyond that. Instead she went out the way she had come, with the jinni looming silent behind her.

The palace of the Lateran, like many of the great houses in Rome, had been a nobleman's villa when it began. It had grown over the centuries until it was a maze of halls and courts and chambers of many sizes, committed to countless uses. It went deep and rose high, and all of it bowed to the basilica that stood beside it, the first of all the churches of Christendom, of which the Pope was bishop and shepherd.

Sioned found herself in the basilica in the soft glow of the sun through windows of alabaster, a hushed light and deliberately holy. She was alone; her jinni had not followed her.

As she paused halfway down the apse, she caught herself missing the groves and springs of her own religion. This was a faith of walls and restraint, a closing of the spirit to any thought but what the priests bade their faithful to think.

She passed by pilgrims, some standing, some kneeling, some prostrate on the floor. Vendors were selling relics and tokens and, near the door and out on the steps, sausages and sweets, and trinkets marked with symbols of Rome and the papacy. She fended off a persistent person who insisted that he had scraps from the Virgin's veil. They were common blue-dyed wool to her eye, much faded and soiled. They had been a lady's garment once, perhaps, but had served as dust rags and ended in a midden, from the look of them.

She paused near the front of the basilica, not far from the great altar. The air hummed with ages of belief. She sank down dizzily, sitting on her heels. Watchers might think she prayed.

If she could master this, if she could steady herself, she could use this mingled magic and soaring faith. She could follow the lines of power through the inextricable tangle that was Rome.

She drew herself in toward her center. The world retreated. She was aware of cool stone under her and human bodies about her, until she dismissed them with the rest. Only the jinni remained clear in her awareness, a beacon set to guard her. He had not entered the basilica; he would not subject himself to that much Christian holiness. But he was present and aware of her. For a moment she felt his hand in hers, his strength that had sustained her since he struck a bargain with Ahmad before the taking of Jerusalem. *Great lady*, he said in her heart. *Pure spirit.*

Purity of spirit was a great virtue among the jinn, and all but unheard of among mortals. Sometimes Sioned called it pure stubbornness. She was certainly not sinless in the Christian sense.

She thrust those thoughts away. She must be empty of the chatter that vexed a mortal mind incessantly. She was as clear, as transparent as a pure spring.

Through that spring ran the skeins of magic that were in Rome. Slowly, with care, she sought out the differences in them. This was old Rome, this Rome of the emperors. That, Christianity before it rose to rule; that great blazing knot of power, the faith that had held this city for nigh a thousand years.

Once she had those, she could set them aside and seek out the lesser skeins, powers that might not be smaller in themselves but were buried beneath the shimmering tangle of Christianity. One by one she found and committed them to memory. Later she would put her mind to them. Now she was only recording them, as a clerk would write down words that his lord spoke. She was a conduit, a passage from the mind to the hand.

"Lady." The jinni's voice was like a chord on a great organ.

Sioned spun back into the confines of her body. She was lying on the floor. The jinni had braved the stench of Christianity to kneel beside her, to bring her back among the living.

"Lady," he said. "You must not forget to breathe. Your magic needs your body to contain it."

He rose, drawing her with him. She was stiff and weak in the knees, but she was certainly alive. After a few staggering steps she could walk on her own. He continued to support her down the length of the basilica and out into a day that was nearly done. The sun hung low over the hills of the city.

It was a long empty way back to the inn, but she was safe with the jinni at her back. The sun set while she rode; it was dark when she came to the inn. But the landlady's hulking son was waiting at the gate, fawning like a great hairy dog as he let her in and took her horse. She thanked him with a smile, and would have given him a silver penny, but he would not hear of it.

She sighed faintly. He was in love, poor thing. She pressed the penny on him until he would take it, and smiled again to soothe his pride. She could feel his eyes on her as she walked through the court and up the stair to her rooms.

Ahmad was bent over a scroll that looked as old as Rome. He looked up blinking. She sat across the table from him and covered her face with her hands.

"Domna Maria kept dinner for you," Ahmad said. "She'll send it up now you're here."

"I don't know if I'm hungry," said Sioned. "I just want to sleep."

"You should eat," he said.

She rubbed her eyes. He rose and came round the table to stand behind her, and rubbed her neck and shoulders. She groaned as his fingers worked out the knots of tension.

More might have come of that, even as tired as she was, if Domna Maria had not chosen that moment to bring in Sioned's dinner. She was a generous woman and kind to a fault, but she did love to chatter. It seemed hours before they were able to bid her goodnight.

By then Sioned was falling asleep where she sat, but Ahmad stood over her until she had eaten and drunk enough to satisfy him. It was much more than she wanted, but she knew better than to refuse. Her body needed to replenish itself.

She barely remembered finishing her dinner, and did not remember going to bed at all. When she woke it was daylight and Ahmad was gone. She could feel him close by, shimmering faintly as he always did when he was deep in study. The jinni was not there, nor Mustafa.

She had not seen Mustafa since shortly after they arrived in Rome, but she would not worry yet. Mustafa was a prince of spies. He went where he pleased; he might disappear for days or weeks. She would know if he was in trouble. Maybe he was having better luck in the hunt than she or Ahmad. That would be a fine thing.

She rose and dressed and ate the bread and cheese that were set aside for her, with a jar of ale to wash it down. Her head ached somewhat from a full day of hard magic, but thanks to Ahmad she was otherwise well.

She had no intention of going back to the Lateran. But when she tried to reach the skeins of magic from the inn, they were blurred and indecipherable. The basilica was like a crystal, bringing them clearly into focus.

She had to go back, to finish what she had begun. Her first impulse was to go alone, but a belated attack of good sense forestalled her.

She found her husband on the roof, engrossed in the same scroll as before. "Ahmad," she said. "Come hunt with me."

She waited while he extricated himself from the depths of the scroll. He was frowning slightly. "I am hunting," he said.

"I need your help," she said.

He sighed a very little, but he was an obedient husband. He rolled up the scroll with care and slipped it into its case.

Hulking Carlo had their horses saddled and ready. They mounted and rode through the empty places, on the road that Sioned's mare knew well enough by now to follow on her own with little guidance.

Ahmad was scrupulously silent. If she wanted to tell him what she was up to, his manner said, she would. He would not beg.

She preferred to show him. She did not expect him to be surprised as they came in sight of the city of the Lateran, set as far as it was outside the most numerously inhabited portion of Rome, and indeed he was not. His lips tightened at the sheer Christianity of the place, but then so did hers. He could bear it. He had to see what she had seen.

There was one disadvantage that she had not foreseen in having as little to do as possible with Christian rites. She would have noticed if it was a Sunday, but the many feasts and saints' days were inclined to pass her by.

So would this one have done if she had not planned a great magical working in the basilica of the Lateran. As she rode nearer to the papal city, the road grew thick with pilgrims. That was not unusual, but they did seem more numerous than they had on previous days. They were milling about in the square within the walls and streaming into the basilica.

Sioned, intent on her purpose, only noticed them insofar as they blocked her way to the place where she had been yesterday. Human nature served her: people were slowest to occupy the front, but kept to the back as much as they could. She was able to kneel in the same place, and Ahmad beside her, following her lead in silence that made her fall in love with him all over again. Whatever he might be thinking or feeling, he trusted her.

She slipped her hand into his. The skeins of power were just within reach, just as she had left them. She could feel him reaching with her, studying them, waking to understanding of what they meant. His eyes had widened. He bowed to her in deep and honest respect.

Within the interweavings of magic, something shifted. In the same instant, voices rose, bell-clear and heavenly sweet. The choir of the Lateran had begun to sing.

Sioned balanced precariously between the worlds. Except for Ahmad she could not have done it. He was her rock as always—here, in a way she had not known before. Her faith was a faith of living things and open sky. His was a faith of the Book, as was the faith celebrated in this place. He understood the Book and venerated its prophets, among whom was the prophet Isa, the Christ of the Christians.

Whatever feast this was, it called for a high and sacred rite, with choir and incense, grand processional, and the Pope himself at the altar. She saw him as the nexus, the center of the power that was in this place. When he was not there, the nexus remained, but in his presence it woke to the fullness of its power.

She forced herself to stand briefly in the mortal world, to see what mortals saw: the glitter of gold and jewels, the prelates, the lesser luminaries, the attendants and the acolytes. Before them all stood the man in the towering tiara, in his vestments of white and gold.

He was young—not a boy by any means, for he must be past forty, but as prelates went, he was a stripling. He was one of the taller, fairer Italians, with a long oval face and heavy-lidded eyes. He might have seemed lazy, even unintelligent, but those eyes beneath the lids were fiercely bright. This man was not only intelligent, he was brilliant—and dangerous, because he knew his own strength.

He was not a mage. Sioned had not expected that he would be. He was something more perilous. He was a devout believer in the dogmas of his faith. She saw the suppleness of the theologian in him, like an image in miniature of the skeins of Christianity that emanated from this place. It was flexible, pliable—but only in bending the world to its will. It would never shift its roots, nor would it endure another faith to thrive under its power.

His kind preached Crusades. Richard's kind, who fought them, often thought like soldiers, of enemies and allies rather than evildoers and servants of the god. Allies could become enemies, enemies transform into allies, but to the righteous there was only one good and only one evil. Good was what one believed in, to the letter. Evil was all else.

She contemplated him in a kind of despair. He must abhor the King of Jerusalem, who infamously fought with the sultans of Cairo and Damascus against their enemies of Islam; whose court was full of infidels, whose own sister was wife to one of the allied sultans. So far his communications with Richard had stopped short of anathema, but in the last year or two they had been growing sharper. Seeing him now, Sioned saw the Crusade that he was dreaming of: to take back Jerusalem yet again, this time from the Crusade that had won it before.

Only one thing held him back. She saw it within him like a talisman, as strong in its way as the Seal of Solomon. It was an image, tiny and complete, of an old woman dressed in black.

Sioned bit her tongue until it bled. She dared not laugh in this place. Queen Eleanor was a dread power, and little enough of that was of the light, but even she did not bear the horns and scales of a dragon.

The Pope of Rome was afraid of her. Sioned doubted that he suffered that weakness before any other creature of earth. Whatever Eleanor had done to keep him off Richard's back, it had kept him in check for six years. That was a notable feat.

Deliberately Sioned closed him out. He was a distraction. Her magic had realized, while she indulged in it, that this Mass he sang was a great working. The words, the cadences, the movements of the ritual, were older than most priests would wish to know. In this place, where nine hundred years of faith had focused like a burning glass, it made the mingled magics of Rome, for this hour, immeasurably more powerful.

She felt Ahmad's excitement, the high scholar's glee. He had ridden quietly in the back of her thoughts, venturing only to be amused when she reflected on the Pope of Rome and the sultan of Cairo—it would indeed be fascinating to see the Pope's face if he knew that one of the massed, alleged faithful was that son of Satan himself. He had called Ahmad that in more than one letter, and been in other ways uncomplimentary.

His fingers wove with hers, just as his magic sustained hers. She would lead here, and he would follow. It would take most of the rite to make a beginning, but now that she knew, with the gods' favor she could do it again.

This morning she closed off the blinding wall of Christian power, contained it within its own ritual, and rode on the notes of its chant to the older roots below. Those that she had marked already were waiting. She shifted them carefully aside, taking note of the place where each had been. They were as layered, as intricate as living roots in a plot of earth, but like living roots, each had its proper source.

The deeper she went, the more complex they became. The new world forced simplicity on the human spirit; and it was growing narrower as the years passed. The older world had been markedly wider.

Still, however many and tangled the threads, they were finite. She could touch them and know in which of the categories they were, or whether they were new or altered or reborn. There was a convoluted beauty in them, as her power consigned to each a color—for her magic was Sight, as Ahmad's was the Art and the book.

His awareness touched hers, so soft it did not disturb her seeking, but clear in its warning. The rite had reached its crescendo. The bread and wine had passed. In very little time, it would be over.

She hated to let go, even more than before, but he was waiting, ready to be firm if she refused. He reached out a hand for her to clasp. Reluctantly she took it. She withdrew, skein by skein, swiftly and smoothly through the aid of their conjoined power.

Just before she disengaged, in the instant before she allowed a breath of relief and a glimmer of satisfaction, she thought she sensed something. An eye, an ear. An awareness that had awakened and noticed that she was there. Whether it meant her good or ill she did not know. Only that it existed.

She shot out a tendril to catch it, but it was gone. Maybe it was only a ghost or a memory of herself from times before or since. She would watch for it again, but for the moment there was no trace of it.

CHAPTER EIGHTEEN

Giuliano knew every blessed inch of Rome from the Vatican in the far northwest to the Lateran in the far southeast. He had been born and raised in it, and he had indulged his lively mind and keen sense of mischief by exploring it from end to end and from top to bottom.

He was delighted to share what he knew with Mustafa. Mustafa was careful to return to the inn each night, although he did not see Ahmad or Sioned and he did not seek them out, but in the mornings he would meet Giuliano in some place agreed upon, and they would discover a new portion of that peculiar city.

There were an uncommon number of churches and monasteries and houses of religion great and small, with hospitals and hospices and guesthouses sprawling out from them like roots from a thicket. Mustafa considered hunting there—where better to conceal a thing of divine power than in a place full of its like?—but the prickle in the base of his spine said no,

not there. That might be his natural reluctance to have anything to do with Christian worship, but he had learned to
trust that prickle. It was close cousin to the gift that allowed
him to see magic.

Wherever the Ark was, if it was in Rome at all, it was not
in a church. That left a dizzying number of ruins, open fields,
and wilderness, interspersed with thickly inhabited patches of
city. Nor was Rome entirely on the surface. There was a maze
of sewers and catacombs below, in which a man could wander
for years and never find the end of them.

More than once Mustafa came within a breath of con-
fessing his mission to Giuliano. The boy never asked why he
was here, or seemed in any way suspicious, but Mustafa had
not been an innocent since he was old enough to walk. He
trusted very few creatures in this world, and Giuliano had yet
to become one of them.

On the fourth day after their meeting, Giuliano could not
meet him in the morning as usual. It was a festival day, and he
was expected to accompany his family to church. "Then," he
had said with a wry shrug, "I have the family duty to do. But
if you want to come to the house in the evening, I'll find a
way to get free."

"I might do that," Mustafa said.

And so he still might, he thought as he waited in the shrub-
bery outside Castel Tiresi. He had tried to tell himself that it
was foolish to follow this boy and his family, whom Mustafa had
not yet met, to a ritual he would have preferred to ignore. But
he was a spy, and spies thrived on instinct. Instinct told him that
he wanted to see Giuliano's kinsmen, and that he wanted to be
within sight while they performed whatever duty their family
owed to the powers of Rome. If it turned out to be futile, he
promised himself, he would turn his back on that too-beautiful
boy and find other places to hunt for the salvation of Jerusalem.

He could wait in hiding for days if he must. For this he waited an hour by the sun, which was threatening to withdraw behind a veil of cloud when the gate opened and the procession emerged.

There were nearly a hundred of them. The armored guards had the same features as the rest, blunter and less perfect variations on Giuliano's carved antique profile. Those who were on horseback must be the high ones of the house. Most were older. The rest went afoot, with the same upright carriage and light, catlike gait. They had a look about them that Mustafa recognized. Desert tribesmen had it. They were fighters, born and bred.

They were all men. And they were all mages. Every one had at least some small spark of power.

Mustafa knew a fair few tribes of the magical sort. In every one, most of them had little of the gift, and many had none. Those to whom it was given in greater measure were rare. Even when they were bred for it, that was so. It had been a great thing that one of Sioned's children was strongly gifted. Of the rest of Ahmad's offspring—and he had a respectable number, as a sultan should—half a dozen at most had the power, and only one had it in his father's measure. The same was true of Judah's family, and the devil-children of the Plantagenets. Of all the issue of King Henry of England and the dread Queen Eleanor, only one had had the gift, and not in great measure. He had died young. The rest were as mortal as anyone else, although Mustafa had his doubts of Richard. Richard was not quite like the rest of the world, in his family or out of it.

This family was magical to the youngest child, the small page who waited on a grey-bearded elder. They cast a shimmer on the ground as they walked and rode down the hill toward the river. Mustafa could not have kept himself from following if he had tried. He was drawn like a moth to a flame.

They attended Mass in one of the churches down by the Tiber. Mustafa kept to the shadows by the door and forbore to enter. If he had to, he would, but he was simply here to watch.

They came out as they had come in, in an easy flow that belied the ordered nature of their passage. They did not all return to the castle; the younger ones in particular wandered off, some in the company of other young Romans. They seemed a convivial family, and well respected about the neighborhood.

And yet there was that shimmer of magic, and that prickle in Mustafa's spine. Beneath the smile and the air of noble ease lay a secret.

Giuliano had been with them throughout, of course. Mustafa had been deliberately not thinking of him, of how he wanted to move in toward him, speak to him, touch him if he could. Giuliano was one of the armored guards, straight and strong and oddly elegant in coat of mail and blue-and-silver surcoat. He had left his weapons and helmet at the door of the church with the rest, and claimed them as he came out walking arm in arm with two who must be brothers or close cousins, so closely did they resemble him. They belted their swords on one another, tossed their helmets like balls, shouldered their blue-tasseled spears, and strode laughing down the street.

Mustafa followed them. There were six of them; once they had had their amusement, they put on their helmets and fell into marching order. The streets of inhabited Rome were as crowded and raucous as any in the east, and its people were as headstrong as any Mustafa had seen. A cardinal could advance with his entourage and be stopped short by a donkey collapsed under its load, and either the cardinal found another way or he waited until the drover was ready to open the street. Mere worldly noblemen won no more respect than passing paupers, and considerably less than the mule-drivers or the carters.

When Giuliano's kinsmen swung down the street at a brisk pace, the crowds parted. There was nothing obvious about it. No one spoke of it. They simply cleared the way.

It was not only magic. People knew the device on their coats. No Roman would ever admit to fear, let alone awe, but Mustafa saw how eyes rolled and bodies slid aside. Not even a Roman would challenge a troop of Tiresi.

That was very interesting indeed. Mustafa kept them in sight down along the Tiber, then back up toward the hills. Houses and churches clustered thickly here; the city that had taken root by the river was strong, and it was growing. New banks of houses were going up, and of course a new church and a stone box of a monastery. The work was halted for the feast day, the skeletons of stone and the scaffolding deserted except for the cats and the occasional urchin sunning themselves on the heights.

The Tiresi continued past the half-built walls. The hill rose abruptly there into a wall of its own, overhung with greenery. A path wound up it. It was a broad thoroughfare for a goat; for a man it was a brisk climb, not too well trodden, but to Mustafa that felt odd. Someone did not want the world to know that this way was used often—not perhaps every day, but regularly enough to have set into the bones of the hill.

It was harder to pass unseen here, but Mustafa had been tracking wary prey in the desert since he was a child. He ghosted from shadow to stone to thicket, keeping the blue-

and-silver backs in sight. They went without apparent concern for secrecy; a shimmer had fallen over them, distinct
from their native magic.

Mustafa knew a spell of not-seeing when he saw one. It
was his gift, to see the unseen. The six men would be invisible to mortal eyes; at most, to the keenest, they were a flicker
in the air.

He smiled. This was becoming very interesting indeed.

Not far from the summit of the hill, they turned aside on
a path that must be invisible to mortals: they walked through
what appeared to be a solid thicket of brambles. It melted like
mist around Mustafa as he passed it, a judicious few moments
after.

They went only a little distance along this path. Then, indeed, they vanished.

Mustafa had been staring directly at them. One moment
they were there, walking in file on the narrow path; the next,
they were gone. There was no shimmer, no flicker in the air.
Nothing at all.

He waited, perfectly motionless, for them to reappear, or
something else to change along the hillside. Nothing did, not
even a whisper of wind. He glided forward, alert to every shift
of the air.

Their tracks came to the point at which he had last seen
the armored knights, and disappeared. He knelt there and
peered closely.

It was a very good illusion. If Mustafa had not been looking for it, even he would have walked on past it. To the eye it
was a thicket of brambles under an overhang of the steep hillside. To Mustafa's hand it was a cool emptiness.

The illusion made him think of a veil of water. It was
stronger and more solid than the last, more clearly perceptible as he slipped through it. On the other side was the mouth

of a cavern, an opening in the hillside. The vines and brambles that overhung it were real, turning the light in the entrance faintly green. That light faded quickly as the cavern deepened.

Mustafa squatted on his haunches just where the faint light turned to darkness, chin on fists, thinking on what he should do. He had a lamp and a little bottle of oil, enough to light him for an hour or two. But if he went on, having lost his prey, he risked losing himself in the earth.

He needed the jinni, or he needed the mages. He did not like to abandon a pursuit without discovering where it led, but he would be a fool to do otherwise.

He drew back out of the cave and beyond the curtain of illusion. It seemed as solid as it had before, once he was outside it.

He could have left then, but he chose to return to hiding and to wait. If nothing came out of the cave by an hour before sunset, he would leave.

They came out just as he was drawing himself together to rise. It seemed they appeared out of air, shimmering in their armor and their magic. The shimmer was much brighter than Mustafa remembered; his eyes narrowed against it.

Wherever they had been, it had fed their magic to gleaming satiety. Mustafa made himself as small and as invisible as he could. They passed him coming down the track, walking one by one, their faces still, exalted.

None of them saw him or seemed to sense him, although as Giuliano strode past, his head turned slightly and his nostrils flared as if at a familiar scent. But he did not stop or slow his pace.

Mustafa did not move until they were long out of sight. Even then he advanced warily. If they had dropped into hiding to surprise him, Allah willing, he would sense them before they saw him.

There was no ambush. The men were gone, vanished into the city. Mustafa made his way back to the inn alone, and reached it just before nightfall. He was glad to see it, which surprised him a little. It had become home, after a fashion: the place where he looked for friends and sustenance, and where he could sleep in peace.

CHAPTER NINETEEN

"One more time," Sioned said when she had made her way back with Ahmad to the inn. "If we go back once more, I'll have it all. Especially if we're there during another Mass. The Pope made it stronger, but any priest would do. It's the rite that focuses the power."

Ahmad was as deeply excited as she was by what she had found, but he was surprisingly reluctant to hunt in that place again. "It's too dangerous," he said. And before she could object: "No, not because you're too weak to protect yourself. Because a working of that magnitude in that of all places lays you open to discovery. You've passed for a pilgrim in a trance twice. I won't trust fate to keep you in luck a third time."

"Why not? You'll be there. So will the jinni, if it pleases him. If I fall over frothing at the mouth, you can tell the priests I'm in a holy ecstasy. If they do take me away, it will be to crown me a saint."

Ahmad had no humor in matters of war. "No. It's been too easy. There should be wards and protections, but there appear to be none. I can't believe the powers of Rome are such innocents that they leave the roots of their magic altogether undefended. You're being allowed to hunt, but until we know why and by whom, I trust nothing in this city, either mortal or otherwise."

"That's wise," she said equably, "but since we're on guard, and since I'm not creeping off to do this alone, what greater harm can there be than there has been already in hunting from the Lateran?"

"Maybe none," he conceded, "but maybe a great deal. There are far safer places to continue."

"It's faster there. That's the power's center. The farther we are from it, the less penetrable it becomes. I'm nearly done with it. If I can manage just one more hour—"

Ahmad's face had closed. She knew that look, and it raised her temper. "Why are you afraid?" she demanded. "You forced me to come here. Now I'm here and the hunt is getting somewhere, you want to stop. I know what I was afraid of. What has sucked the courage out of you?"

"Prescience," said Ahmad. "We won't go back to the Lateran. If we can't hunt from here, we'll find another and safer place."

For all the Sight that was born and bred in her, of foresight she had next to nothing. He knew it. It was maddening of him to say what he had said.

Even if it was true.

She challenged him with a hard stare. "What do you see? How much protection will I need?"

"More than we can muster here," he said.

She opened her mouth to press him again to tell her his foreboding, but before she could begin, Mustafa slipped through the door into the room.

That was the first they had seen of him since they arrived in Rome. Sioned almost forgot her fit of temper. He was holding something inside him like a pearl of light. She had never seen anything quite like it.

It was the working she had been doing. It had altered her sight. Was this what Mustafa saw when he saw magic?

It was part of the power of Rome. She had marked it, could remember the intensity and the placing of it. If she could perform one more working, she would know what it was and where, and who had wrought it.

Or she could simply wait for Mustafa to tell her.

She was losing herself in complexity if she could not see the simplest solution in front of her face. Gods forbid she tell Ahmad he was right, but maybe she had gone a little too deep.

"My lord," Mustafa said, "my lady."

Ahmad set the remnants of their dinner in front of him— a feast in itself, for Domna Maria believed in feeding her guests. Mustafa reached for bread and cheese and roast mutton, folded them together, and ate them so carefully that Sioned knew he was ravenous.

They let him take the edge off his hunger before Sioned said, just ahead of Ahmad, "You have news."

He nodded. "I don't know what it means, but you may. Listen and I will tell you."

He told of watching the family from the castle above the inn, and of seeing its procession to the church.

"They are all mages?" Ahmad said. "Every one of them?"

"Every single one," said Mustafa. "They aren't all great mages. Most would be village witches at most, if they were anywhere but here. But they all have magic."

"Of what kind? Can you tell?"

"Mostly foresight, I think," said Mustafa.

"Tiresi," Sioned muttered. "Teiresias? The old seer? The one who was a man and then a woman and then a man again? Which incarnation are they descended from?"

They were both staring at her, Ahmad with amusement, Mustafa with the confusion of a teller startled out of his tale. She lowered her eyes and tried not to flush.

"Foresight," said Mustafa after a pause, "and illusion, and wards."

"Obviously wards," Ahmad said. "I had not the faintest inkling that there were a hundred mages within a bowshot of this room."

"They hide very well," said Mustafa, "but Romans know what they are. Wherever they go, the crowds part. Even the Pope has to work for that."

"What are they?"

"Guards," Mustafa said. He told them of his pursuit along the Tiber and up the hill, and of the cave. "Maybe I should have followed them. But I was alone, and no one knew where I was. I did wait; an hour ago they came out. Their magic was stronger than ever. They looked as if they had bathed in the source of it."

Sioned's eyes went wide. So had Ahmad's when she turned to him. "Do you think—" they said, both at once.

"I don't know if it is what we're hunting," said Mustafa. "It could be any number of things. They go back to Rome and Greece, not to Jerusalem. And—"

"Magicians under the command of Julian the Apostate stole the Ark from Israel," Sioned said, remembering the story as Aaron bar Judah had told it. "These magicians? Is fate that kind?"

"Fate can be as kind or as cruel as it pleases." Ahmad steepled his fingers as he did when he served as judge before his people. "Obviously we must pursue this. Sioned, is it any of the threads that you've found?"

"Yes." She frowned as she turned her focus inward. Mustafa's pearl of light was woven through the fabric of Rome from the beginning. At a certain point, its power deepened. It was subtle, veiled in wards and illusion, but what had been a thin strong thread became a cord of pure power.

Ahmad's awareness was like a hand slipping into hers, stopping her before she fell any deeper. He drew her out to the light, and the cord with her, so that they both could examine it.

Ahmad closed himself to it first, shaking his head. "I can't tell what it is," he said. "It has no feel of Israel. It's a Greek thing, then a Roman one. It's Christian, too, but that's as thin as paint on glass."

"They are protecting something," said Sioned, "and it's underground, whatever it is. I wonder why they can't simply go down to it from their castle? Or why didn't they build the castle over it?"

"Because a castle in a city is impossible to miss," Mustafa said. "If I were hiding something very powerful and very secret, I would live at a distance from it. But I'd dig a tunnel to it, and not risk betraying its whereabouts to a spy in the street."

"Maybe they've been so secure for so long that they can't believe a spy would dare to follow them," Sioned said.

"Or maybe there was a reason why they went over earth instead of under earth on this particular morning," said Ahmad. "A gate that needed securing, a rite that needed celebrants to come from above and go below. You haven't seen them go out before, have you? And you didn't see any change in the guard. If they are guards, they'll be guarding the treasure night and day, and changing with every watch."

"We have to find out if they're guarding the Ark," Sioned said. "If they're not, well and good. We'll let them be. But if they are . . ."

"If they aren't," said Ahmad, "then I owe a camel's weight of gold to my brother's mosque in Cairo." He arched a brow at her scowl. "It's not a wager I intend to lose."

"We have to be right. The Ark has to be there. We don't have time to be wrong." Sioned squeezed her eyes shut. They were aching as they often did after a hard working. "In the morning?"

"At least," Ahmad said. "Mustafa, will you be ready to spy out the castle by then?"

Mustafa bent his head. "I only need a little sleep. Will you wait to act until I come back?"

"We will wait," said Ahmad.

"Take the jinni with you," Sioned said. "If he can pass through their magical walls, that will tell us a great deal about them."

"I had thought of that," said Mustafa. "By your leave I'll ask him to come." He regarded her with narrowed eyes. "You won't do anything until I'm done?"

"We will not," Ahmad said before she could open her mouth. "But do be done quickly."

"You tied our hands," Sioned said when Mustafa had gone to bed. "Is this your way of enforcing caution?"

Ahmad paused in rolling up the carpet on which he had said the last of his daily prayers. "This is my way of planning the war. We can't rush in blind."

"There are things we can do from here," she said.

"What, use the Seal?"

"You yourself said—"

"Yes, I said that we cannot risk unveiling it until we have

the Ark in our hands, for fear that the enemy will be aware of us." He finished rolling the carpet and laid it away in its bag, then sighed and stretched.

He took his time, stretching each muscle. He was still a lithe and supple creature, a dancer, a rider, and a swordsman. Beside him, the larger, more massive Franks lumbered like bears.

She would take full advantage of that suppleness of his, but first she would settle this matter between them. "I was thinking of finishing what I began in the Lateran. I can do that, surely. I'll even agree not to do it there, now I know there's a focus so much closer."

"That can wait," he said. "If you betray yourself to these mages, you endanger Mustafa. Whatever study this needs, and whatever action, will come soon enough. First let him work in peace."

She did not want to hear it. "This is—"

He caught her hands, which had clenched into fists, and kissed them. "When was the last time you contemplated a day without work or royal obligations or plain and inescapable duty? When did you last simply play?"

Her teeth had clenched as he spoke. "We don't have time," she said. "Even while we dally here, Teleri may be— Richard—Jerusalem—"

"We do not dally," he said gently. "Mustafa is continuing the hunt while we, like good generals, wait. I believe we should wait in as pleasant a manner as possible. In the morning therefore, my lady, we shall be properly agog at all the marvels and the fabled sights of Rome."

"I don't want to—"

"I don't care." He swept her up and dropped her onto the bed. "Now then. Will you undress yourself, or shall I?"

"I don't—"

He smiled sweetly and set hand to her lacings. She made a show of fighting him off, but she was defeated for the moment. He was in one of his antic moods, when he could do anything that came into his head; better he be here, making mischief with her, than gods knew where.

She let him infect her with his wild humor. Why not? There was nothing else she could do, for the moment. Surling and growling would not bring Teleri back any faster.

CHAPTER TWENTY

Mustafa lay in his bed in Domna Maria's house, wide and painfully awake. What he was contemplating might be a terrible betrayal of a new friend, but much older friends needed it for their lives and safety. And who knew? Giuliano was a great lover of Richard's Crusade. Maybe he would prove to be an ally.

Whatever the truth of that might be, Mustafa knew that he needed to sleep. That, first and foremost. He could force it if he tried: it was an art he had learned in a lifetime of war. He could not keep the dreams entirely at bay, but they were only phantoms. In among them, he snatched what rest he could.

Morning came all too soon, and yet not soon enough. He rose and dressed and prayed, and prepared carefully for a foray into unknown territory.

He had decided, wisely or unwisely, on direct assault. Not long after sunup, replete with Domna Maria's good breakfast and carrying a basket over his arm, he presented himself at the gate of Castel Tiresi and said brightly, "I come to visit the lord Giuliano. Would he be at home?"

The guards had the same air of ease as the rest of that family. They glanced at each other and shrugged, peered beneath the napkin and found a basketful of savory cakes made with rosemary and bay and sharp cheese, and were happy to share a handful each, with honey from the pot and pepper from the tiny and precious trove, before passing Mustafa within.

He still had a reasonable number of cakes, and was blessing Domna Maria's generous nature, when he reached the innermost hall. There he found Giuliano, just out of bed, sharing wine and cheese with a troop of his kinsmen. He greeted Mustafa with delight and swept him toward the table, where he found himself plied with wine and cheese and onions and dried figs and loaves of coarse brown bread.

His offering of cakes was most kindly received. Giuliano had not named him, he noticed; he was simply "my friend from down the hill." No doubt they knew all about him; although if so, they did not find him worthy of a stare or a murmur.

They were all as convivial as Giuliano, with the same wicked humor. It was odd to see them so light-hearted, and yet to know that they protected some great secret. It had been a part of them for so long, he supposed, that it was nothing so very momentous; it was simply the family duty, present and inescapable, which one did when one's turn came round, and otherwise did not pause to think of.

Mustafa noticed as he watched them and pretended to eat, that just as on the foray to the church, every soul in the hall was male. The servants and pages were men and boys; the diners were all men. There was not a woman to be seen, nor any sound of her voice.

Giuliano tired soon enough of showing off his friend. "Come with me," he said abruptly. "I need a bath, and then I've the morning to use as I will. You can eat in the bath if you like. Messire Galoubet likes you. He'll send you anything you ask for."

"More sherbet, then," Mustafa said. His heart was beating harder than it strictly needed to. He had by no means come here for a seduction, but if one presented itself . . .

He put that thought out of his mind. Giuliano led him through a maze of halls and passages, up and down flights of stairs, until even his keen sense of direction was blunted. The baths were, in the end, down a flight of very old, very beautiful stairs, ornamented with mosaics in black and white and now and then a spark of red or gold.

The chamber to which they led was a bath in the old Roman style. It bore a close resemblance to the Muslim *hammam*, and no doubt was its parent. It had a room to undress in and wash down and scrape off the worst of one's ills, and a hot pool and a cold one and, great luxury, a warm one between; then at the end, a room for dressing and for idling while one recovered from one's bath.

Giuliano did not insist that Mustafa do anything but keep him company. The sherbet was waiting in the undressing room, crowned with mint and tasting wonderfully tart and sweet. Mustafa sipped it, then made his choice. He dropped his clothes, all but the drawers.

Giuliano was naked as Franks loved to be. After a long moment's thought, Mustafa let fall his drawers as well.

The boy stared at him with honest curiosity. "So many scars," he said. "And all from battle?"

"Not all," Mustafa said. He never had tried to hide the stripes on his back. It was no secret that he had got them from the Duke of Burgundy's torturer through the jealousy of the singer Blondel. That bitterness was long set aside, though never forgotten.

Giuliano was kind enough not to press him for the story. He was staring now at another thing, as unabashed as a child. "I've never seen one so close before. May I—"

A circumcised member, he meant. Mustafa did not mean to blush, but he was a Muslim. He was modest. He could not help it.

Giuliano blushed in turn, sensitive as always to subtle shifts in his companion's mood. "I'm sorry. I didn't mean to—"

"No," said Mustafa at the same time. "Oh, no. I—"

They stopped, then laughed. It was all very silly and very awkward. Giuliano snatched up a sponge and pulled Mustafa over to the small washing-pool and set to scrubbing him with more enthusiasm than finesse.

Mustafa had to fight back or have the skin scrubbed off him. He had a defter hand, and a quieter way about him. It quelled Giuliano, which was well for the safety of Mustafa's skin. They were both tingling clean.

The hot pool was just short of scalding. The cold pool seemed born of melted snow. Mustafa would have lingered in the warm pool between, but Giuliano was restless. In the small warm room after the cold pool, where more of the lovely sherbet was waiting, he dropped onto the silk-cushioned couch and sighed gustily.

Mustafa knelt beside the couch and laid his hand lightly, daringly on Giuliano's forehead. "Are you ill?" he asked.

Giuliano shook his head under Mustafa's hand. "No, of course not. I'm never ill."

Mustafa smoothed the thick damp curls. Giuliano's eyes had fallen shut. His lashes were long and curling and very thick, like his hair. As they lay on his brown cheek, they were altogether irresistible.

Mustafa had spent his life resisting. What he wanted, or had wanted until now, had never been his to take. Richard might have let him have it for an hour or a day or a year, but in the end it would fade. Mustafa had never taken it, or even asked for it. He would rather be the king's dog for his life long than his lover for a season—and then be cast aside.

He did not want to resist this. Fate had set it in his path. It would end; it must. He was here as a spy, and Giuliano would hate him for it before it was over.

But for this little while, this day or week, maybe there could be something other than hate.

He had never seized the moment before. It was a dizzy sensation, like leaping from a high cliff into deep water. He brushed his finger across Giuliano's eyelids.

They quivered; the dark eyes opened. Giuliano smiled. Quite without warning, he drew Mustafa down in a long, giddy kiss.

This man lived to seize the moment. Mustafa's hesitation and slow ponderings were alien to him. And yet he surprised Mustafa with gentleness. He was eager, but he waited; he let Mustafa tell him when to move and when to be still. That was his pleasure, to give even while he took.

Mustafa was in love. It was dangerous; he did not care. He did not care for anything, not in that moment, that long blessed morning in the scent of herbs and sweet oils and clean young bodies. They needed a bath again when they were done, and swam in the warm pool, playing like dolphins, until a languid voice above them said, "Giulio, you'll be late."

They were wound together in the water then, lost in the last of many kisses. Mustafa froze.

Giuliano took his time in freeing himself, and grinned up at the brother or cousin who stood by the pool. "Gianni, I have all the time I need. What is it really? Do you want the bath to yourself? Do you have a sweet friend?"

"If I do," said Gianni, "she will present herself in the evening like a proper paramour, and leave me the morning."

"Some of us prefer the morning," Giuliano said. He lifted himself out of the pool into a breathtaking handstand, dropped, rolled, and came up dancing, holding out his hand for Mustafa.

Mustafa had caught the contagion of his mood. He somersaulted out of the water, launched himself with hands from the pool's rim, and landed lightly on his feet.

Even Gianni applauded him. Giuliano kissed him for good measure. Mustafa hardly knew where to look. Never among Franks, not even in Richard's most private gatherings, had he ever seen—had he even imagined—

"Mustafa is modest," Giuliano explained. He produced a towel from, it seemed, the air, and wrapped Mustafa in it, taking advantage of the opportunity for embraces and kisses.

"Giulio," said Gianni. "Truly, it is late, and you know Grandmother—"

"I know Grandmother," Giuliano said, sighing. He turned to Mustafa. "My love, I would stay with you all day and all night, and every night forever, but our grandmother needs us for a little while. Will you stay here? Will you wait until I'm done?"

Everything about this man was a gift. Mustafa bowed. "I can wait," he said.

Giuliano was already in motion, running toward clothes and decorum and duty. "Gianni," he said over his shoulder, "spare a moment. See what Mustafa wants, and see that he gets it."

When Giuliano was gone, it was as if a whirlwind had blown through the room. Mustafa met Gianni's eye. "There's no need to trouble yourself," he said. "If you have a library, I can wait happily until your brother is done."

He had guessed the relation rightly: Gianni did not correct him. "You read?" Gianni seemed surprised, although he caught himself quickly. "I didn't mean—I know you must read Arabic, for your scriptures. We do have books in Arabic. But—"

"I read other languages as well," Mustafa said.

Gianni examined him with the same frankness that Mustafa had come to love in his brother. "There's more to you than meets the eye. At first I took you for some eastern prince's plaything—nothing with a brain could be so beautiful. But you're no one's toy. Are you?"

"They call me a king's dog," Mustafa said with a faint shrug.

"You're not that, either," Gianni said with conviction. "I don't know if I like you, Saracen. But my brother does, and I love my brother. Be careful of his heart. If you break it, it may be your neck I break."

Mustafa smiled in true and luminous bliss. "I don't like you, either, signore. But I think I love you. I would happily submit my neck for your breaking, if I ever harm your brother."

"Good," said Gianni. "Go, dress. I'll take you to the library."

Mustafa did not have to dress under those cool, measuring eyes: Gianni excused himself from the room. When Mustafa was done, Gianni was waiting in the hallway outside. He raised a brow at Mustafa's perfectly ordinary cotte and hose. "No turban?"

"In Rome?" said Mustafa. "No."

"I do see your point," said Gianni.

The library was glorious. It was the largest Mustafa had seen outside of Alexandria, and the treasures in it—Allah! The lord Saphadin would be beside himself if he could see them.

Mustafa had not, all appearances to the contrary, forgotten why he was in this place. Gianni left him in the library with no guard on him, either visible or invisible.

There were wards here. Most of the books were only lightly protected; some few were so rare and so precious that they lived in sealed boxes under spells of preservation and protection. But one corner, up in the second level, was more strongly guarded.

Mustafa was not interested in books of magic. Those were for either Saphadin or Sioned to explore. He was looking for a much more mundane treasure.

He found it among the household accounts, rolls and records going back so far that they were dated in consulships rather than *anno Domini*. The most recent were not there; those, he presumed, must be in the castellan's care, elsewhere in the castle. But he did not need to know last year's outlay for wine, grain, and oil. What he needed was the place where these were stored—and where every other room was, and what was in it. He needed a map of the castle.

There was one from the reign of Charlemagne, and one from the consulship of Julius Caesar. He spent a happy hour with the two side by side, learning how the villa of Teiresias had grown into Castel Tiresi.

Then he went exploring. If he guessed rightly, no one would find it particularly odd that Giuliano's new friend was wandering through the castle. He went openly, he bowed and smiled when he met Giuliano's kinsmen, and he did not, that day, explore anywhere that might arouse suspicion. He found out that yes, this family bred daughters, and he discovered where they were. Those that were not practicing with swords and bows in one of the courts were pursuing occupations equally intriguing in their own wing of the castle. He would examine that more closely later.

He ended in the kitchen, telling tales in return for dainties from Messire Galoubet's private store. Giuliano found him there, greeted him as if they had been apart for days and not hours, and kissed until he saw stars.

"No one minds," Mustafa said. Giuliano had all but dragged him to a room along the upper gallery, the purpose of which was obvious. They pursued that purpose until Mustafa was wrung to a rag, and even Giuliano looked somewhat blunted in his enthusiasm. Then they lay in one another's arms, with the occasional wandering kiss, and Mustafa gave himself up to the wonder of it all. "No one cares that you—that we—"

"Why would they care?" said Giuliano. "Are you ashamed of me?"

"No!" Mustafa tried to pull away, but Giuliano laughed and held him until he stopped struggling.

"Our family was in Greece before it came to Rome," Giuliano said. "We never let the world taint us any more than it had to. We value love in all its forms, and love of a man for a beautiful and fascinating man, that is one of the noblest."

"You should not exist in this place, in this age of the world."

Giuliano laughed so hard he tumbled out of bed and rolled across the tiled floor. He was still laughing, crumpled in a heap against the wall. Mustafa had to shake him to make him stop.

He wiped his streaming eyes and quelled the hiccoughs and said, "Beloved! You look terrified. Really, I haven't gone mad. It's that . . . most of the papal curia would agree with you, but it has a distressing inability to take action."

"Why? Is your family so old?"

Giuliano pulled him down the wall until they were sitting side by side. The floor and wall were cool against Mustafa's bare backside. Giuliano's arm was warm about his shoulders. "Old," Giuliano said, "and other things. The Roman Republic brought us here, not particularly willingly, for reasons that seemed sufficient to it. When those reasons were gone, whatever they were—no one is certain after so long—we stayed because there were other reasons. Now we're one of the oldest Roman families, if we aren't in fact the oldest of all. We're as much a part of Rome now as that great monstrosity of a Colosseum. Fit for tribes of cats and for lovers' trysts—that's our family. But we remember what we were."

"Is that why your women live apart?"

Giuliano seemed surprised. "What? Oh. No. I suppose. I never thought about it. They rule themselves, mostly. Once in a great while they condescend to rule us. They say we're noisy, boisterous, and excessively distracting. Therefore they keep to themselves."

"Teiresias," Mustafa said suddenly. "He was a woman first. Wasn't he?"

"Yes," said Giuliano. "The story changed later, when the Greeks got hold of it, but she was born a great seer and priestess of the old Mother Goddess. Then she was cursed to be a man, and in the end she earned the right to be a woman again. Her descendants never forget. They'd have their own city and keep us for stud, if they were minded. For some reason they like to be here."

"Maybe this is their fate," Mustafa said.

"That's what they say." Giuliano rolled his curly head on Mustafa's shoulder and let his hand slide down until it rested ever so casually on Mustafa's thigh. "They pity us. A man has no stamina, whereas a woman is always ready for love."

"Have you ever loved a woman?"

Giuliano tilted his face upward. "A time or two. Are you jealous?"

"No," Mustafa said. "I only wondered."

"And you?"

Mustafa shook his head.

"Never?"

"I am not made that way," Mustafa said. It sounded stiff, but it was the best he could do.

"A man, then. Have you had many lovers? You must. A man so beautiful—"

"Never," said Mustafa. "Only you."

Giuliano's eyes went wide. "No."

"Yes," said Mustafa. "I was a slave, you see, and men used me, but that was their right; they were free and I was not. I never had anyone of my own. Then I saw the king, the great golden lion, and I knew I would follow him until I died. With him . . . it would have ruined what we had. I never saw anyone else. Until I sat in a market square in Rome, and saw a man standing in a smithy. And I knew."

"That you loved me?"

"That the Lionheart could have a rival."

Giuliano drew a sharp breath. "He can't. Not even me."

"I won't ask you to lead a Crusade," Mustafa said. "Only to love me."

"Only that? It's too easy."

"I could make it difficult."

Mustafa meant it. Giuliano shook his head firmly. "No. No, I don't want you to break my heart. Promise you won't do that."

"I already promised Gianni."

"Then you're sworn for life."

"I rather thought so," Mustafa said.

Chapter Twenty-One

Sioned contemplated the wall of brambles that seemed to hang down from the steep slope of the hill. It was a very clever illusion, and very old.

The day had begun frivolously, with a long lazy breakfast and a leisurely morning of loving. When she went out with Ahmad, she went to play: to watch singers and players and jugglers in the market, to wander through the sights, and to be for a little while an innocent visitor to this holy city.

But Ahmad had no more restraint than she. When they found themselves in a particular market, looking up at a particular hill, they did not need to exchange glances. They abandoned their pretense of play and set off up the hill.

Sioned knew better than to hope that this was the end of the hunt. The best that it could be was a beginning.

"We should wait to see what Mustafa finds," she said.

"We should," he agreed. He stepped toward the brambles and vanished. His voice came out of air, as clear as ever, unmuffled by any obstacle. "I don't sense any danger here. Whatever they're guarding, it's deep in."

She passed the illusion with a faint shiver as it dissolved about her. Ahmad was already on the far side of the cave. He had lit a magelight, very carefully shielded. She made certain to ward herself, so that any mage who came here after would not know that strangers had trespassed.

The cave ended in a tunnel. Parts of it had the look of nature; the rest were cut and chiseled by human hands. A worn flight of steps descended into the earth. It was steep and much smoothed by the passage of feet; someone not too long ago had bolted rings to the wall and strung a rope through them. She was glad of it in places, where the steps were so worn she could barely keep her footing.

A good castellan would repair the steps. A good general left them as they were: they were a surprisingly effective defense. No one without wings could descend this stair at a pace faster than a shuffle.

The stair ended none too soon. They were well below the level of the hillside, and might be as low as the Tiber, although there was no dampness in the walls, only the chill of earth and old stone. The tunnel continued, shored with bricks of the Roman fashion, broad and flat, and held up with plain stone pillars.

At first she thought she had imagined it. Ahmad's magelight could leave odd reflections, and this was an odd place. The corner of her eye persisted in seeing what at first seemed to be streamers of light. Gradually she saw them as an interweaving of cords in colors that—

In colors that she had given them. The skeins of magic were running through this passage. There were never as many as in the Lateran, but here Christianity had barely penetrated. These were older powers, some very old indeed.

The passage widened. To earth and stone her nostrils added a very faint charnel reek, and the sharp, dusty smell of old bones. They had come into a catacomb through a side way that, she realized as she looked back, was rather well hidden. The entrance was indistinguishable from any other shadow along the wall.

Most of those shadows were niches—tombs. They had come into an ossuary. Whose bones those were, or what gods they had worshipped, she could not tell. There was no cross on the wall and no stench of Christianity in the air.

Beyond the ossuary they passed through a region of colonnades marching through dark waters. The stink was long gone, but the imperial sewers still underlay the ancient city. Sioned had begun to wonder if they had been led astray, but the skeins of power ran on without breaking.

"We're going back toward the inn," Ahmad said softly, lest he wake the echoes. "They must have had a reason for coming in from here."

"Securing the postern gate?" Sioned asked. He had paused at the end of a gallery, casting carefully with his power as a hound might course for a scent.

"Definitely a postern," he said. "The wards here feel as if they were badly worn and have been patched just lately—maybe yesterday."

"They aren't keeping us out," Sioned observed.

"Maybe," he said. "And maybe whatever they protect is anywhere but where we are. We could have passed it a dozen times in this maze, and never known."

"I think it's still ahead," she said. "Can you feel it? The lines of power are converging."

"Be careful," he said, as if he were not in just as much danger as she was. "If we discover where it is, that will be enough. There's time to discover what it is."

"I think I know," she said.

He raised a brow. "You know?"

"I feel something," she said. "If this is not what we're hunting, then it's not in Rome."

"It's calling you."

"Maybe," she said.

"Then," he said, "we stop now. We need wards, we need protections. We need strength."

"We have those. We've had them since we came to Rome."

"More than that," he said. "If you are certain, without going farther and without seeing it for yourself, that this is the thing we came for, then we're done with hunting like innocents. We go on battle footing."

"We don't know that's necessary. The keepers might be willing to relinquish it, for the saving of Jerusalem."

"It was taken by priests of the old gods. If those still exist and still guard it, Jerusalem is nothing to them."

"We can't know until we ask."

"We can't ask until we know what we face."

They were at impasse. Ahmad was ready to turn back. But Sioned said, "Wards, then, and caution. We see if we're hunting what we think we are."

He accepted the compromise. The wards were the matter of a moment; Sioned had a gift for them, and he had the skill to make them strong. So shielded, they advanced more slowly, casting as little magelight as possible, alert to any misstep that would rouse the guardians.

The sewers gave way to another catacomb, another ossuary, and another dim subterranean hall. Halfway across that, Sioned slowed to a stop. The lines of power came to this point and suddenly vanished.

Just so had the brambles concealed the mouth of the cave.

It was an illusion, even stronger than the one on the entrance. To the eye, the foot, every sense of the body, the hall went on into featureless gloom. She could even see how it ended in a line of arches and columns and, one would suppose, another passageway.

But the power gathered precisely here. She could feel the newness in the working that concealed it, the lines of greater strength and fresher power. This was the working that had absorbed Mustafa's quarry yesterday. She would lay wagers on it.

She reached back blindly. Ahmad's hand slipped into hers. She laced her fingers tightly with his, focused on the power, and let it draw her forward and down.

This stair was in much better repair than the other. Whatever passed the protections above knew what lay below. Concealment was no longer necessary.

She could feel it then, the thing that had been calling her so subtly from behind such powerful wards. It had allowed her to penetrate them. It was calling to the thing that she carried now in a silken bag about her neck, hanging between her breasts.

If she had been wise, she would have turned back the moment she was certain. But the Seal had been wrought by the power of the Ark. They were drawn to one another. And she wanted to see. She wanted to be absolutely, mortally certain.

She was under the spell of one or both of them. She knew that, but she also knew that as long as she held the Seal, the powers here could not touch her.

The passage was smooth and open. Lamps rested in niches. The first score were dark, but then as she approached them they lit themselves, burning with a soft, steady light. She advanced even more carefully, still hand in hand with Ahmad.

One final stair led to a broad landing. Water lapped at the

edge on the left hand. The right was a blank stone wall. Ahead was another, but in that one a door. A knight stood on either side of it, a dark young man in blue and silver, armed with sword and spear.

Both were mages, masters of wards. But the Seal was beyond any mortal power. Both she and Ahmad were invisible to them, imperceptible, passing more softly than a whisper of air.

The door melted before them, then formed again when they had passed. They stood side by side in a circle of stone, a hall of pillars upholding low arches and a shallow dome. How it was upheld beneath the weight of earth was a mystery of its magic.

The floor was a pavement of mosaics, a pattern that after a moment Sioned recognized as the skeins of power in gold and silver, red and saffron and green and blue. They curved and coiled about one another, but always leading toward the center, where stood a long, squat pedestal like an altar. On the altar, beneath a heavy cloth of silk not unlike that in which she had sewn the Seal, was the great singing thing to which the Seal had been calling.

It had been singing in its sleep. In the Seal's presence it began to wake.

Ahmad's arms clasped about her. She felt the opening of the way, and no care on his part for either subtlety or concealment. Even as the air parted, he flung them both out of that seductive and deadly place.

Chapter Twenty-two

The army of Jerusalem was nearly mustered and ready to march into the north. Richard had bidden his vassals to gather at Beit Nuba where once he had camped just out of the sight of the city, and where now was a newly built castle with a raw but thriving town and a shrine of Saint George of England.

In the morning they would begin the march. Tonight he was in Jerusalem, seeing to the last small particulars of the kingdom and standing host to the High Court in the hall of David.

He had not, of course, invited his queen to preside over the court. Nevertheless she was entitled to be there. Even he could hardly forbid her if she took her proper place.

She prepared herself carefully. Beauty would never be her province, but she could strive for dignity. She brought with her a gift that she had made, a surcoat embroidered with the leopards of the Plantagenets. The leopards' eyes were jeweled, their coats picked out in golden thread.

She had not faced the court in longer than she could re-member. The banks of lamps and candles seemed unbearably bright. The crowd of lords and ladies, maids, squires, ser-vants, sycophants, and hangers-on took her aback with the sheer mass of their presence. So many people, so many eyes, looking her up and down, judging her, whispering and titter-ing as they told tales of the forgotten queen.

Not for much longer, she thought behind the mask of her face. They would remember her soon, and never forget her again.

Richard greeted her with a bare semblance of courtesy. But he did not order her out. That was a victory in itself. Nor did he ask why she had come out now of all times. She doubted very much that he cared.

It was not so difficult once she had set herself to do it. She had nothing to do but go where she was led, sit where she was placed, and pretend to eat what was set in front of her.

She was not expected to speak. It was a great shock there-fore when, in a lull in the festivities, she rose and bowed in front of the king and said as clearly as she could, "My lord, my prayers as always go with you to battle, but I beg of you to accept a gift."

Richard had been sharing some obviously delightful jest with Henry and the Patriarch and one or two other great lords. He might not have noticed Berengaria at all, if Henry had not touched his arm and cocked his head and said, "Richard."

The king frowned, puzzled and a little annoyed at the in-terruption. Then he followed Henry's gaze. The puzzlement abated somewhat, but the annoyance deepened.

He managed a polite expression, at least, and a stiff incli-nation of the head. "Lady. Is there something you need?"

"Your indulgence, sire," she said. She brought out the

package on which she had been sitting, which the guards had taken for a somewhat stiff, oblong cushion. She stripped off its wrappings, trying not to fumble, and shook out the surcoat.

Richard's indrawn breath was as gratifying as she could have hoped. Indeed it was a beautiful thing, tightly woven of white silk, strong and light and cool in the heat. The leopards gleamed with silver and gold and the blood-red gems of the eyes.

"A gift," she said, "from a queen to her king. My prayers are woven in it. May it bring you good fortune in your endeavor."

She held her breath. Richard stretched out a hand. Whatever he thought of her, her work was good, and she knew it—more than he could imagine.

"It's splendid," he said. "Truly fine." He took it up. She could see how it captivated him; how it held him rapt. "You have my thanks, lady, and my honest gratitude. I'll think of you when I wear it."

Berengaria did not believe that, but it did not matter. The gift was given. The spell had taken hold. She could breathe again. She allowed herself a smile, and let him kiss her hand.

She did not stay long after that, nor did anyone expect her to. They never even noticed that the queen was missing. When she looked back, there was a knight in her place, leaning on Richard's shoulder, taking liberties that made her lips tighten.

Once she was out of sight, if anyone had cared to notice, she picked up her skirts and ran up the stair to her rooms. She was breathing hard when she bolted the door behind her, stripped off her unwieldy court dress, and put on a simple chemise and a plain woolen gown with a skirt cut for riding.

Her new servant was waiting for her. It, or he, had come

to her a few days ago with the silk and the threads and nee-
dles and the jewels for the leopards' eyes, and instructed her
in how she was to create a great work of magic to ensorcel the
king. He and it were a gift, he said, from the one who had
been her servant.

The creature looked like a Saracen page. His hands were
clever, with long supple fingers, and his eyes were large and
bright. He was a pretty thing, and perfectly charming, and utterly evil.

He put away her court dress while she finished preparing
the rest. She had fashioned an image of potter's clay, and
dressed it in her own garments. It only needed to be brought
to life. She cut a lock of her hair, murmuring the words of the
spell in precise cadences. She secured the lock to the crown of
the image's head, stabbing it through with a silver pin.

That same pin had pierced her finger. She traced a Sign in
blood on the still-damp clay of the forehead, and let the rest
bleed into the lank dark hair.

Her skin shuddered. The image blurred and reshaped itself. She looked into her own face, plain and sallow, and her
own flat dark eyes.

She surprised herself with the intensity of her dislike.
Small wonder no one cared to notice this unprepossessing
creature. When the war was won, she would give herself
beauty and charm—not too much, not to excess, but just
enough that men would find her appealing to look at.

For the moment, the more nondescript she was, the better. The image would sit as she sat, eat and sleep when she was
accustomed to do those things, and speak when spoken to.
Since that was seldom, there would be no great tax on Berengaria's magic to sustain the illusion.

The image sat by the window and opened a book and pretended to read by the light of the lamp. Berengaria looked

away from it, shuddering faintly. One last thing she would do; then she was ready to go.

Her latest purchase and most enthralling treasure was lying on the wine-table, wrapped in dark silk. She uncovered it carefully. The servant hissed and threw up a hand. The light of the crystal was bright in this dim place, casting sparks of many colors on the walls and on her face. She narrowed her eyes against it and spoke a Word. The light dimmed.

She peered into the crystal. At first she despaired: she saw only shifting colors and a reflection of the earthen image on the other side of the room. But as her eyes focused, so did the crystal. She was seeing from an odd angle, not quite upright, not quite tilted; then as she got the measure of it, it straightened. She was looking out across the hall that she had lately left.

A slow smile curved her lips. It was better than she had hoped. Richard had put on the surcoat. The crystal in the eye of the topmost leopard saw whatever he saw, from whatever angle he chose to sit or recline. He must have been sprawled across a chair as he liked to do, then sat up to answer some sally from the man whose face moved in eerily close.

She did not attempt to wake the spell of listening that was bound within the scrying-spell. It was there, it was ready. That for the moment was enough. She had to be in Beit Nuba before morning, before the king came there to lead the army northward.

Her servant was waiting. The image seemed absorbed in the book, if one did not happen to notice that it had not turned a page since it began. She turned her back on it, wrapped herself in mantle and hood, and slipped out of the room.

Whatever was guarding Jerusalem took no notice of Berengaria. It was not trying to keep anyone within from leaving, only to prevent invasion from without. Such lack of forethought would cost it dearly.

She had not sat on a horse in years. When she traveled, which was seldom, she rode in a cushioned litter, or in a carriage. She had grown soft in body if not in mind. Within an hour of dragging herself into the saddle, she was in rather exquisite pain.

She set her teeth and endured. Her servant was not a creature to invite confidences. If she told him she hurt, no doubt he would laugh and find ways to torment her even further.

The town of Beit Nuba was a fair-sized city now, swelled by the camps of Richard's forces. Berengaria had been instructed in the import of the various banners. Henry's men were there, of course; Hospitallers and Templars; the Patriarch's picked troops; levies from the demesnes of the kingdom, from Dan to Beersheba as the Bible would say, from Shaubak to Tripoli.

They were not the full count of his army. These had been in the region or were close enough to muster within a week. Others would join him as he marched northward.

They were a respectable force. She could not help a small surge of pride in her kingdom. In haste, against an enemy mostly unknown, ten thousand men had mustered—and left that number again to guard the kingdom behind them.

Richard's realm was strong. He ruled it well, in defiance of doomsayers who had given him at best five years before he was either brought down or hounded back to England. It had been more than twice that now, and although he intended to leave, it was by his own will, for his own sake, and not because he had been driven out.

Yet, thought Berengaria as she contemplated the campfires of his army. She did not go down among them. She was here to watch, and to wait.

Her servant had vanished. She quelled the brief rush of panic. He would return before the sun came up. She was safe meanwhile, if not exactly comfortable, settled with the horses in a fold of the hillside. No one could find her unless she wished it.

Toward dawn, hooves clattered on the road below. The great ones were coming from Jerusalem. Richard glimmered in the lead, wearing the surcoat that she had made.

The spell had held. The trap was sprung. Through that glittering thing she, and her ally if he chose, could see all that Richard saw.

Her servant came back just before the sun came up. He did not tell her where he had been, but he was licking his lips with a long, unnaturally thin tongue. He smiled charmingly at her and held her horse for her to mount.

She suppressed a groan. The sooner the ordeal was begun, the sooner it would be over.

Her purpose in these first days was to do nothing but follow, and to watch when she could. She did not expect her ally to speak with her. That would come when the army reached Krak.

The summoning seized her on the second day. Fortunately the army had paused to welcome a deputation from the castles nearby. She was hidden in a thicket of thorns, warded against the stinging flies.

The force of the spell flung her headlong. She twisted among the rocks and the thorns. The bruises and the sharp stabbing pains brought her out of shock and into something resembling consciousness. She flung up such protections as she could, so that the blast of magic turned into coherent thought.

Her ally hovered above her in a globe of darkness. The light was painful to him in this undead state. It was one of the short-comings that he hoped to overcome as he fed on the blood and souls of living men.

He was sorely pressed if he would appear to her in daylight. She drew herself to her feet and faced him. "Ah. My servant. What troubles you?"

He gave her no title, nor did he bow to her as a servant should. "Have you seen the Sultan of Egypt? Do you know the whereabouts of his wife?"

That, she had not expected. "What, are they not in Jerusalem? She has estates outside the city. Maybe—"

"They are not in Jerusalem," he said. "They are nowhere that I can see. What guards the city now is new to us and this age, but not at all to the city. The Jews are in Jerusalem. But the king's sister is not. Nor is her husband."

"Did he go back to Egypt? Has he gone to Damascus?"

"In either place, or anywhere else in the House of Islam, if he were there, I could find him. I cannot find him."

Berengaria labored to be courteous, but she could not lie to him. "I fail to see why that is a matter of such dire urgency."

"It is dire," said the dark thing with studied patience, "because I owe my state to them."

"But I had thought—"

"The king of Franks killed my body. The sultan and his wife stole the heart of my power and left me at his mercy. They are the enemy. They above all have earned my hatred."

"But this war—" Berengaria began.

"They are part of it. Wherever they are, you can be certain that it bodes no good for me, or for you."

"You want me to find them." Berengaria's voice was flat. "I can't both do that and carry on here."

"The imp of Iblis will spy on the army for a little while. Find the enemy before the king comes to Krak. Do not try to stop them. Send me a summoning, and I will do what must be done."

Berengaria set her lips together. These were orders, as if she and not he were the servant. She considered a reprimand, but years of hiding and deception had taught her caution. She knew too well that he was a greater sorcerer than she could hope to be. If she was to oppose him, she must do it wisely and with careful preparation.

She would not force a confrontation, not yet. She bowed her head, which he could take as acquiescence if he chose. It seemed he did. He vanished as abruptly as he had appeared, if somewhat less explosively.

She spent some time in removing thorns from her person, a time she spent in reflection, and in making choices. As she finished, her servant eeled into the thicket, grinning. His teeth were numerous and very sharp.

"You will spy on the army," she said to him, "but not until tonight. Darkness is better for what I have in mind, and they will camp, which makes matters simpler for both of us. Today you will guard me and keep me hidden."

The servant bowed to the ground. Thorns did not seem to trouble him. She caught herself wishing for a hide as impervious as his, as she extricated herself from the thicket.

Richard's army camped long before nightfall. In this country, armies marched from well to well, and only fools risked being caught in the waterless hills. Richard was in haste to come to Krak, but he would not destroy his army before it could come there.

Constantly while the army marched, and all night long when it camped, messengers and scouts came and went. It was a simple enough matter for Berengaria to enter the camp, riding as swiftly as her aching body would allow. The guards saw what they expected to see: a courier in the king's service, dusty and travelworn, on one of the royal remounts. They passed her with a cursory glance.

She had not walked free in a military camp before. Always when she was present as the queen, she had had her own camp, her own guards, or had shared them with the rest of the queens: Eleanor who was now in England and Joanna who had taken the regency of Normandy. Queens were never alone. They went nowhere without escort, and never set foot on ground that had not been smoothed before them.

This was a different world. It was rough, but there was a perceptible order in it. Men went where they were entitled to go. Ranks and orders kept their places. The different nations and domains had their allotted portions of the camp.

There was magic here. It was subtle; she could barely perceive it even from within. But once she had recognized it, she saw it as a banked fire, embers buried in ash, which at need could spring into flame.

Its source was diffuse. More than one mage had ridden with the army, and they were scattered through the camp. There was one near the king's tent in the center, the light of him breathing in the slow rhythm of sleep.

There was another near the tent she had been looking for. She shielded herself with even more care than before. The mages did not appear to be looking for a single intruder; their wards spread like a net through the camp, set to catch some great power or a sudden invasion.

The dark thing could not have entered. Berengaria, bound to the king and otherwise forgotten, slipped unnoticed through the net.

The lord Henry was in his tent. His squires were asleep across the door, his servant snoring in an alcove. Berengaria cast them into an even deeper sleep.

Their master lay on the border between waking and dream. His body was at ease, his face calm except for a slight furrow between his brows. Berengaria paused for the simple pleasure of looking at him. He was a handsome man, was Henry of Champagne, the heir of Jerusalem. His wife had no complaints of him. He saw her often in her castle of Banias, and there were children: six of them, Berengaria recalled, or seven. Most of them were sons.

Berengaria's heart was beating hard. Years of solitary discipline kept her calm and kept her thinking clearly. This was her decision and hers alone: to be here, to do what she would do. The spells were ready. She had only to speak the words.

The first cast him into the dream. The second made her part of it. She wore the face of his wife, the princess Isabella, who was in every way the opposite of Berengaria. She was tall, fair, a famous beauty; she lived in the light, and ruled over the court in fact as well as in name. She was renowned for her brilliance and wit. It was a peculiar sensation to wear her body, to move with her grace; to look down into Henry's eyes, and to see gladness there, and the softness of a man who had learned to love his wife.

There had been no love or even much liking when they began. Berengaria had been there; she remembered. All of that had changed with time and proximity. They had made children together; when Richard left at last, they expected to rule as king and queen. It was by Isabella's right that Henry would rule, for she was the true heir of Jerusalem. Richard ruled because she did not, indeed could not, prevent him.

All of this shaped the dream in which Berengaria walked. She made no effort to create a palace. It was enough that Henry saw his own tent and his own men asleep; but when he looked for warmth, he found it in the image of his lady.

Berengaria knew what to do. She had studied; she had observed. It was still a shock, first in what her own body persisted in doing and feeling, then in the mingling of pain and pleasure. She nearly lost her grip on her magic, and nearly betrayed herself, but somehow she held on.

When he was done, she lay in his arms while he kissed her softly and whispered endearments. He would sleep soon, unless she prevented him.

She filled his ears and mind with a murmur of enchantment. In the midst of it she slid the question that her erstwhile servant had asked: "The Sultan of Egypt; the king's sister. Where have they gone?"

Henry stirred. Even through the layers of spells, suspicion had roused. He was not fighting her, not yet, but the thought was there.

She soothed him with a crooning song. "Where? Where have they gone?"

He struggled, but her song lulled him into placidity. "Gone," he said. "Away."

"Where?" she sang in his ear.

"Hunting," he said.

"Hunting where?"

"Away."

She must not give way to frustration. He was stronger in resistance than she had expected, and closer to waking than she liked. Short of drugging him, which would render him unconscious, she could do no more than she had done. "Where away?" she asked him, softer and sweeter than ever.

"Hunting," he said. "Hunting destruction. To destroy— to win—"

"To what country have they gone? Are they in Egypt? France? England?"

"No," he said, a long sigh.

That was the best he would give her. He was struggling

harder, fighting against the bonds of her magic. She drew away in body and spirit before he woke and saw her true face. When she was on her feet, she cast him from dream into deep sleep.

She hoped as he sank into the dark water that he would let go a bubble of knowledge, the answer she was seeking. But he gave her nothing.

Her hand went to her middle. He had given her what she came for. There would be other ways to find the dark one's enemies.

She wrapped herself in her mantle and her cloak of spells. It was nearly dawn, but there was a little time still for sleep, once she had escaped the camp. She slipped out as she had come in, unnoticed and, as ever, forgotten.

CHAPTER TWENTY-THREE

Sioned tumbled with Ahmad onto a hard and bruising floor. She lay winded and half stunned, rousing slowly to the fact that he had brought them to their rooms in Domna Maria's inn.

That was a relief. As desperate as he had been, he could have taken them anywhere: Cairo, Damascus, Jerusalem. He had kept his wits better than she had. She had simply shut down her rational faculties and fled.

She sat up painfully. Ahmad was just coming to himself, holding his head in his hands, staring at something behind her. His expression was perfectly blank.

Her spine prickled. She turned with great care, wishing she had a weapon to hand.

A very old woman sat in the chair Ahmad favored for his studies. She was wrapped in black, like enough to a nun's habit that one might have mistaken her for a servant of God, but that had never been this woman's weakness. For all her appearance of great age, she had the strength of pressed steel.

"What," said Sioned, "are you doing in Rome?"

"A fair greeting to you also," said the Queen of the English. "Would you rather I had let you whirl yourselves away to the stream of Ocean?"

"How—why—"

Eleanor filled two cups from a jar on the table. It proved to be sherbert. There was no poison or potion in it that Sioned could detect.

Ahmad had risen, bowed to the queen without falling over, and sat at the table with his cup of sherbert. Sioned decided to follow suit as far as sitting and drinking the sherbert, but she did not bow to the sorceress who had allied herself with the Old Man in the Crusade and set them all on the course to this time and place. Eleanor had done it for her son's sake, but her ill judgment might yet destroy him.

"You brought me here," said the queen. "Rather abruptly, I might add, and somewhat painfully."

"We did not," Sioned said. "We would not have dreamed of it."

"You tore the fabric of creation," Eleanor said, "and knit it up again. The cause for which you did it, and the thing of power with which you wrought it, caught me as I was performing a rite of my own. I had cast a wishing on my son's behalf. It caught your working and cast me in this place."

"Then you may cast yourself back," Sioned said. She was too tired and her head was aching too badly for politeness. "England needs you. We do not."

"I believe you do," Eleanor said imperturbably. She folded her long white hands and regarded Sioned under heavy eyelids. "England is secure for the moment. I had made sure of it before I began the working. As to why that working was necessary, tell me now. What has happened in Jerusalem?"

"You don't know?" Sioned was honestly surprised.

"Letters are slow," said Eleanor, "and my son has a strong dislike of magical means. I expect there will be a letter, and it will explain adequately, but in the meantime all the aethers are most strangely disturbed. Now I find myself in Rome with the two of you and a certain great thing of power, and more that I have yet to understand. You had better tell me why you, my lord, sent out a cry of pure need, and why that cry determined that I was its target."

"That I cannot answer," Ahmad said. "We were endangered. We escaped as best we could."

"Tell me," said Eleanor.

Sioned exchanged glances with Ahmad. He bent his head and spread his hands. She could tell it, if she would.

She tried to make it brief: the disappearances at Masyaf, the Old Man's return, the threat to Jerusalem, Richard's march on Krak. She hesitated before she told the rest. She did not trust the queen; she had every reason to regard Eleanor as the enemy.

But the magic had brought her here, and there could be no doubt that everything she did, she did for Richard. Sioned drew a shuddering breath and told the rest: the circle of mages, Teleri's abduction, the search for the Ark.

After she had finished, Eleanor was silent for a long while. It was a great deal to ponder, and some of it must have been thoroughly unexpected.

At length the queen said, "This is dire. I had not known how much so. There was no warning at all—no foretelling, no sign or omen."

"He concealed himself well," said Ahmad. "Even in Egypt

we heard nothing, and our magic has great power among the dead."

"Nevertheless," said Eleanor, "it has happened, and my son takes the brunt of it. I see now why I'm here. Your Jews will do well in defending the kingdom. But you will need the Ark if you are to destroy this enemy for all of time."

"We found it," Sioned said. "We were escaping its protections when you were drawn into the spell. Now we have to find a way to remove it from its guardians."

"In a word, to steal it," said Eleanor.

"Is it theft to return a stolen treasure to its owners?"

"After nigh a thousand years," Eleanor said, "it might be seen as such. You did badly to leave it where it was and run. You should have taken it while you still could. The wards will be all the stronger now, and the guardians have been warned."

"But we know where it is," said Sioned, "and we have the means to master it. The guardians have nothing but the fact of intrusion. They know nothing of us, nor will they."

"Perhaps they should," said Eleanor. "Have you considered asking them for the thing they guard?"

"Now that we know what it is," Ahmad said, "we may try. They may refuse. Then we'll be forced to steal it outright." He paused. "Are you thinking to prevent us?"

"That would be foolish," she said. "To have found that of all things of power, after it was lost for so long . . . I applaud you. Your skills as a hunter are extraordinary."

"Not mine," he said gently, "but my lady wife's. With assistance."

"Of course," said Eleanor. "I shall require a room and a maid. May I impose upon you to obtain them? The resources of England are at your disposal."

"That is generous," Sioned said, and it was honestly meant.

"Certainly you have the sense to use them wisely," said Eleanor.

Wisely and immediately, she meant. Sioned's only desire was to fall into bed and sleep until night fell again, but that would have to wait. She went in search of Domna Maria.

Domna Maria raised a brow at the sudden and solitary appearance of Sioned's aged kinswoman, but she had both a room and a maid: her youngest daughter, who had been a maid in the inn since she was small. What she lacked in noble airs, she made up for in skill. She knew how to wait on a patron.

Eleanor professed herself satisfied with both the room and the servant. Then Sioned should have been able to sleep, but she found herself lying awake while Ahmad slept peacefully beside her. She was thinking not of Eleanor but of the Ark.

It was calling her. Even with the Seal in a locked chest at the bed's foot, doubly and trebly warded, she could hear the voice of the great working of the Jews. She was no kin to it or its makers, and yet it resonated in her. Its power somehow was bound to hers.

She clung to Ahmad as to a rock in a gale. The temptation was overpowering to open the walls of the world again, to go back into that chamber and mingle her magic with the power of the Ark.

Ahmad shielded her somewhat. The call did not touch him. His magic was of another kind, and his defenses were notably stronger. Even in sleep he protected her.

She could rest a little in his calm. Sleep came slowly, but once it came, it gripped her fast. She sank into the depths of it.

Chapter Twenty-four

Mustafa had not meant to fall asleep. There was dinner in the hall, which Giuliano insisted that he share, and after it the room in the gallery again. When Giuliano slept, Mustafa had intended to slip away to the inn.

But sleep took him, and when he woke he was alone. He performed the morning prayer, still half asleep, then walked out barefoot to the gallery. Sunlight slanted into the hall from above. It was midmorning—he had slept unconscionably long.

He looked down into the hall. It was full of people. Many were men in the livery of the house. There were a few women, most of those in livery as well, and on the dais at the end of the hall, a great lady and her attendants.

Only after some moments did Mustafa realize that this must be the grandmother. In spite of her title, she could not be older than middle years. Her thick black hair was lightly shot with grey, but her face was as ivory-smooth as a young woman's. From where he stood he saw her in profile, flawless and cleanly carved like an image of Hera from a pagan temple.

It was a quiet gathering, but Mustafa's hackles had risen. There was an undercurrent like a long, low growl. As calm as those faces were, as unperturbed as they seemed to be, something was deeply wrong.

"We have been found," the lady said from the dais. Her voice was quiet, but Mustafa heard each word distinctly. It was a subtle magic, performed with ease that won his respect. "The shrine has been invaded, its sanctity violated. Whatever, whoever did this had great power and unassailable wards. It came upon us without warning. It escaped before any of us could muster force to stop it."

Mustafa stood very still. There was no question in his mind as to who had done this. Royal they might be, but he would give them the honed edge of his tongue. If they could have waited a single day, instead of crashing in without knowledge or sense . . .

He understood another thing as he stood there. It was a profoundly simple matter for a mage to cast his unsuspecting lover into sleep. Whatever uproar had shaken this castle earlier, Mustafa had been oblivious.

Maybe he had not been meant to wake as soon as he had. This had the feel of the last council before battle, the exhortation of the troops as they prepared to fight.

"We will find the enemy," said the lady of the Tiresi. "We will capture it. We will discover what it is and what it intends. Hunt with all your skill, my children. Wield magic at need, but bring out the hounds and dispatch the spies as well. Mortal means have won wars before."

The growl had risen to the threshold of audibility.

Mustafa withdrew into the room and dressed as quickly and quietly as he could. His clothes were neatly folded on the stool by the bed: not his doing, and he was sure they had been searched thoroughly. He was also sure he carried nothing that would betray his purpose here.

When he was dressed he paused, listening with more than ears. The haze of magic was so thick in this place that he could barely distinguish the separate mages or the spells they worked. It made spying difficult, but it also concealed him. As far as he could tell, no one yet suspected him.

He slipped out under cover of the general exodus. The hunt was up. Most of the hunters had gone below, but many hunted the streets and the wild places. Still others must be searching as Sioned had been doing, through the currents of magic in and about the city.

They were not searching outside of Rome. That might be significant, but Mustafa was not mage enough to judge.

He took a roundabout way to the inn, but not too roundabout. Time, his bones told him, was short. He had to pray that the lord and lady were in the inn, although it would be far wiser of them to have taken themselves back to Jerusalem.

It was near noon when he paused at the gate of Domna Maria's vineyard. It was not the most direct way to the inn, but he was feeling very indirect at the moment. More by habit than by any expectation of trouble, he sharpened his senses.

Something was behind him. It was well hidden, but the spark of magic betrayed it.

He opened the gate with careful lack of concern and walked through it into the vineyard. The spark hovered behind him: still following, then. He set off down a row of young vines being trained to poles. At the end, he slipped aside. Keeping low, running silent in his light shoes, he ran back through the concealment of the vines.

Giuliano was standing where Mustafa had been a few moments before. His face was blank: searching as mages did,
with the eyes of the mind.

Mustafa took him from behind. He was down and bound
with his own belt before he emerged from the seeker's trance.
The search had succeeded: he opened his eyes to Mustafa's
face.

Mustafa smiled a little sadly. "Mages can be surprisingly
vulnerable," he said.

"But you are not—" Giuliano stopped. He sighed. "It
doesn't matter, does it? Serving the king you serve, how
could you not know magic?"

"Fairly easily, actually," Mustafa said. "Richard detests it.
But his court is infested with magic as he often says, and his
family even more so."

Giuliano frowned. "You couldn't have done it. When it
happened, you were with me. But you know something."

"I may," said Mustafa. He had been considering alternatives while they spoke. The one he chose might be the most
dangerous, but in the end he could not do otherwise.

He lifted Giuliano and set him on his feet. It was somewhat of an effort: Giuliano was a solid weight. "Come with
me," he said.

Giuliano shrugged. He had no choice, the gesture said,
but he had no particular objection, either. He was not afraid.
He even smiled.

Beautiful, sheltered child. For all his fine armor and his
bright fire of magic, he had never met a challenge to his
guardianship. He had not even engaged in a fight, except in
practice or in play. He was the purest of maiden warriors.

Mustafa was dangerously besotted. But he was Richard's
man before all else, and even for love, he would not betray his
king.

"On your word of honor," he said, releasing Giuliano's bonds.

"By my honor," said Giuliano. He was brightly curious and all too willing to follow Mustafa to Allah knew what.

For the moment, his innocence was useful. Mustafa led him through the vineyard to the rear gate of the inn proper, and from there through the stableyard and up a stair.

The lord and lady were in the room. There was another with them. Mustafa snapped erect at the sight of her and dropped his hand to his dagger.

To be sure, no one seemed to be holding anyone else hostage. There were books and scrolls on the table, open and marked, and the air held a hint of thunder. If Mustafa were to wager, he would suppose that they had been debating strategies, and had not yet come to an agreement.

His arrival seemed a reprieve for them all. He bowed low to each, and named each: "My lord of Egypt. My lady Sioned. Your majesty." He was aware of Giuliano's wide eyes as he realized who these people were, sitting together in this none too luxurious room in an inn a stone's throw from his own house.

Mustafa extended the bow with practiced grace and gestured toward his captive. "Giuliano Tiresi." He bent his glance toward Sioned, whom he would crown the ringleader of anything outrageous. "I believe you raided his family's treasury."

"We were not raiding," Sioned said with dignity. "We were spying."

Mustafa was very careful not to express his opinion of her skill. She took his point: her cheeks flushed faintly.

"I think," Mustafa said after a moment, "that we should

tell Giuliano why we came here. They all know that the Ark has been found. They're hunting you—us—now."

"Are you asking us to trust this man?" Queen Eleanor inquired.

The sight of her set Mustafa's teeth on edge. He would get an explanation later, he was sure. For the moment he chose to answer her honestly. "I think we have no choice."

"You're here to take back what we guard," Giuliano said, looking from face to face. "There's a strong king in Jerusalem again. He wants to secure his power beyond any threat of resistance. Naturally he's thought of the great lost treasure."

"In a manner of speaking," the lord Saphadin said, reducing Giuliano to goggle-eyed silence. "The kingdom is threatened by an old enemy, a creature of great power and terror. Jerusalem is beset. Knights have vanished and men-at-arms been lost. Children are taken and their whereabouts unknown. Masyaf of the Assassins has fallen and Krak of the Hospitallers is under siege. The king rides to war, but this will not be resolved by simple steel. We fight an enemy who has died and returned. Even strong magic may not be enough to destroy him."

"If he is strong enough to alarm you, great lord," Giuliano said, shaking with the splendor of speaking to a legend, "then he must be terrible indeed."

"He ruled once through the Seal of Solomon," Sioned said. "We took that from him, and Richard destroyed his body. He has good reason to pursue us from beyond the grave."

"And so you need what we guard." Giuliano had lost none of his bright edge, but his face had gone somber. This touched what he had been born for. "You should know that your spying is punishable by death. No one is ever to find the thing of power. It must be kept hidden for all of time."

"Why?" Sioned demanded. She had the black temper of the lords of Anjou, and it was rising now.

"I think," said Giuliano with unusual diffidence, "you should speak to our grandmother."

"Then let us do that," Sioned said, standing and shaking out her skirts.

"Not," said the lord Saphadin, "without assurances that once we go in, we can come out again—alive and with all our limbs intact."

"I can give you safe-conduct," Giuliano said, "with myself as surety."

"You'd trust us that far?" said Sioned.

He blinked as if the question startled him. "You are who you are, lady. You've done what you've done, too, but I'm sure your reasons seem sufficient to you. I'll trust you not to sacrifice me unless there is no other choice."

The boy was not so innocent after all, Mustafa thought. He knew what he was promising. Death was real to him, although he had never seen it on a battlefield.

The lord Saphadin had risen. "Guide us," he said to Giuliano.

Mustafa was less than delighted to return to Castel Tiresi so soon after he had left it. But there was no stopping the others. Even the queen had come, walking far more briskly than one might have expected of one so old.

He followed in silence. Giuliano was almost subdued, and yet Mustafa could see in him a deep excitement. This was a dream he was living, like a song or a story.

Mustafa, who had lived in songs since he was a beardless boy, seldom saw the charm in it, but through those eyes he almost did.

They were admitted into the women's wing of the castle

with grave courtesy and a hint of a smile for Mustafa. For some reason, people here liked him. Maybe they were smitten with his face.

The room in which they waited was pleasant enough, well lit, and the guards were not obtrusive. Mustafa's companions sat perfectly still, not speaking. He slipped into the shadows and wandered a little, exploring nooks and corners, looking for another way out. There were only two doors, the inner and the outer. The windows were high and narrow and latticed with lead.

As he circled back to the others, the inner door opened. A woman in a blue gown beckoned them to follow her.

The women's solar was wide and unexpectedly airy. Its floor was a jeweled pavement. The paintings on the walls must have been made when Rome was yet an empire. Mustafa recognized Diana the huntress taking aim at a stag, grey-eyed Athena with her helmet and shield, and Hera the queen on a peacock throne. But they did not hold the highest place. That was held by a goddess whom Mustafa had not seen before—until he remembered the Christians' scriptures: a woman clothed in the sun, crowned with stars, with the moon beneath her feet.

It seemed she was older than the faith that claimed her. Even painted on a wall, she had great power. Her eyes reminded him rather forcibly, not of Eleanor's as Mustafa might have expected, but of Sioned's. They had the same expression, half fierce, half gentle. If he had not been a good Muslim, this was a goddess he could pray to. She seemed a sensible sort, as goddesses went; her glory was oddly practical, her gifts such things as a man would need: light, warmth, a world to stand on.

He brought his mind back with an effort to the mortal world. They were all staring at him. He looked about for a place to hide, but the room was too full of light.

The grandmother, the matriarch of the Tiresi, was sitting in a rather ordinary wooden chair in front of the painted goddess. She was quite mortal, and yet in her he could see the living face of divinity.

"I see you understand Her," the lady said. "That's rare in a man."

Mustafa shrugged in desperate discomfort. He could not think of any word to say in any language that he knew.

"Grandmother," Giuliano said, coming to Mustafa's rescue, "I think they all understand. These are the great ones of the east. They are—"

"I know who they are," she said gently. She bent her eyes on Sioned. "You were never baptized," she said.

"Only one of us was," said Sioned. "No more were you, lady, although your men show the signs. Is it that they matter less, and if they're baptized as infants, the intrusion on their magery is insignificant?"

"We do what we must for safety's sake," the lady said. "This world requires certain things of our sons. It pays us women little mind, except to preach sermons against the evil of our nature."

Sioned nodded. "A priest's world is a terribly narrow place. There's no room in it for the likes of me."

"Many would call us antiquated, if not outright heretical." The lady shook her head at the folly of the age. "Now then. Your visit has a purpose, I'm sure."

"It does," said Sioned. "I hear you've been hunting us."

The lady's brows rose. She must not be surprised; surely she had understood what these foreigners were doing in her hall. But Sioned's directness could be disconcerting. "It was you," she said. It was not a question.

"We were hunting," Sioned said, "and we found our quarry."

"It was not yours to find," said the lady.

"One might argue," said Sioned in the mildest of tones, "that it is not yours to keep. An apostate emperor entrusted it to you close upon a thousand years ago. The descendants of those who made it have need of it again, and sent us to find it."

"I see no Jew here," the lady said. "I see a pagan and an infidel, and a Christian queen from the far ends of the world. If they are so desperate to have it back again, could they not be troubled to fetch it themselves?"

"We're better hunters," Sioned said. "They're guarding Jerusalem."

"Even so," said the lady. "If the need were great enough, they would come for it. They sent a deputation of Gentiles. Whatever they may tell you, to us that is damning."

"A deputation of royal Gentiles," Eleanor said.

"You think they care for that? Their memories are long and their hatreds deep. They serve no kings but their own."

"They serve Jerusalem," said the lord Saphadin. "For Jerusalem they will do what they would do for no mortal, even one of their own."

"Jerusalem is endangered," Sioned said. She had a quick eye; she must see that her husband's words had swayed the matriarch ever so slightly. "A monster of magic threatens it. Lesser magics are of no use against that one. The great work of power, the heart of the people, that gave the city its strength, must come back to the city. Rome is an empire no longer. The Church rejoices in its hegemony. It is time to let the Ark go."

The lady shook her head. She was as stubborn as Sioned, and unlike King Richard's sister, she felt herself to be on unassailable ground. "We were given this charge for all of time. Our orders were simple, and strict. To guard it with all our strength, to protect it with our lives and souls, and never again to bring it into the light of day. It is too great a power, too deadly dangerous, to let fall into the hands of any other guardians. We were bred and trained for this."

"We would hardly object to an escort of your people," the lord Saphadin said. "Indeed, from what I've seen of them, they would be deeply welcome. Knights of prowess are always sorely needed in the Kingdom of Jerusalem."

"I cannot let it go," the lady said. "Not for Constantine, not for Julian himself, would I do it. We must not unleash this power on the world."

"What of Solomon?" Sioned demanded. "Would you do it for him?"

"Not in this age of the world," said the lady of the Tiresi.

CHAPTER TWENTY-FIVE

"So much for diplomacy," Sioned said. They had been dismissed—with great courtesy, but it was a dismissal nonetheless. The Ark was not to be given for any compassion, and certainly not for any sense of obligation to the people who had made it.

"There is one who might persuade them," Eleanor said when they had returned to Domna Maria's house.

"What, the Pope?" Sioned shook her head. "We tried that. We couldn't get near enough to him to say a word."

"Then you were not trying hard enough," said Eleanor, "and you did not have me."

"Are you sure you aren't needed in England?" said Sioned.

Eleanor arched a brow. "What, tired of me already? England is secure for the moment. Strong guardians protect it—of whom your mother is one. So would you be, if you were mindful of your inheritance."

Sioned was not to be cowed by guilt. "I am where my destiny has sent me. And how is my brother John?"

Eleanor's eyes did not so much as flicker. "Comfortable," she said, "in a tower in Rouen. He'll be let out if his brother fails to appear within the year. I was forced to come to that agreement with the English barons. They want a king, they need a king. If Richard won't come back to them, I'll give them another of the same breeding. Richard he is not, and that festers in him, but he has a decent intelligence in spite of it all. Something may yet be made of him."

"I don't suppose he's been studying sorcery in that tower," Sioned said with deceptive casualness.

"I have made sure that he has not," said Eleanor. Her calm was just as deceptive. "Your brother is as harmless as a Plantagenet can be."

"As harmless as a snake, then," said Sioned. "A fact of which Richard is well aware. He was nearly ready to take ship when the dead rose and threatened Jerusalem. The sooner he settles this, the sooner England gets him back."

"England will get him back," Eleanor said with certainty so perfect that there was nothing to say either for or against it. "I will do everything in my power to assure it."

Mustafa left Giuliano behind in Castel Tiresi. He did not say goodbye; he did not look back. He expected nothing and asked for nothing. It was clear that the truth must divide them irremediably.

The great ones went direct to the inn. Mustafa wandered for a while, not caring where he went. Somewhere along the Trastevere, in a deserted alley overhung by trees, he heard soft footsteps stalking him. He was ready for the attack, but it came a little quicker than he expected. The footpad fell on him, knife out, ready to slash his throat.

He whirled in pure bloody glee and ripped the fool from chin to navel. The man's expression as he died was utter, blank astonishment.

Mustafa cleaned his blade on the dead man's shirt. Whatever he might be carrying, Mustafa did not want it. He left the body where it lay.

As he straightened, he looked into Giuliano's eyes. The boy was standing in a slant of sunlight. He looked as if he had taken shape there, like some spirit of old Rome.

Mustafa turned his back, but Giuliano was in front of him. He stopped. "A curse upon mages and all their tricks," he said mildly.

"You think I hate you," said Giuliano.

"No," said Mustafa. "I think you have a family, and I came to take its greatest treasure. I won't ask you to choose between us."

"You don't have to," Giuliano said. "I'm doing it for myself."

"Understand," said Mustafa. "Whatever you have to do for your family's honor, I will never hate you."

"Nor I you," said Giuliano. He hesitated. Then he said, "I need to know. Tell me why you need this thing. Not the little you told my grandmother. The deeper reasons, if you know them."

"I will tell you," said Mustafa, "but not here. Will you come back to the inn? I promise I won't hold you prisoner this time."

Giuliano dipped his head. They turned and walked together in silence that was surprisingly companionable.

Mustafa had his own room in the inn. He had protested at first, calling it excessive, but he had come to be glad of it. It was a much smaller room than the others had, but clean and airy. One wall was nearly all window. He had come and gone by it more than once, rather than contend with the stares and questions of people below.

Giuliano did not blink at the journey up the vine-covered wall. He had to tilt somewhat—his shoulders were broad—but he slipped neatly through the window and landed on his feet, light as a cat.

There was little to offer by way of hospitality, but Mustafa had kept a napkinful of raisin cakes from breakfast, and a jar of juice from Domna Maria's grapes, sweetened with honey and touched with spices. Giuliano professed it better than wine.

"You're being polite," Mustafa said.

"Oh no," said Giuliano. "It is wonderful. Though I should be unhappy to forswear wine."

"I've never tasted it," said Mustafa. "It smells strong."

"It can be." Giuliano reached for another cake, his third. "I saw you praying last night."

"I thought you were asleep," said Mustafa.

"I woke up," Giuliano said, "and you were there in the lamplight, you and your God. Did you know you shine when you pray?"

"You have a mage's eyes," Mustafa said.

"No," said Giuliano. "You have magic—you don't know it, but it's very strong. When your spirit is exalted, you're brighter than the lamps."

"I have no magic," said Mustafa. "I can see it and feel it, but there's none in me."

"You only think so," Giuliano said.

Mustafa shrugged. He was not going to fight over it. Whatever he had, he could not work spells. That he knew for certain.

Giuliano ate the last of the cakes, after a glance at Mustafa to be sure he did not want them. Mustafa's throat had closed on the first bite. He was in love, he knew that all too well, but he must not let it cloud his mind.

No use. The sight of that beautiful creature in his own room, however seldom he occupied it, made his heart beat fast and hard.

After this day Giuliano might never come near him again. That would be right and proper. Giuliano was guardian by blood of the Ark of the Jews. Mustafa had come to take the Ark from him. What hope could there be for the two of them, with such a thing between them?

"Tell me," said Giuliano, "why you need it so badly."

"The lord of Egypt told the truth," Mustafa said. "Jerusalem is threatened. The Old Man of the Mountain has come back from the dead to take revenge on those who destroyed him. The lord Saphadin and his lady took from him the Seal of Solomon and gave it to Richard. Richard seemed to enter into a bargain with the Old Man, but as soon as he fulfilled his half of the bargain, Richard killed him."

"Through the power of the Seal?"

"Through the power of cold iron and a lion's heart. Richard uses magic as little as he can."

"The Lionheart is afraid of magic?" Giuliano was incredulous.

"Not afraid," said Mustafa. "Determined to have nothing to do with it. Now it's struck at the heart of his kingdom over the sea."

"The Ark," said Giuliano. "Why does he need that?"

"Against what has risen to destroy him, no ordinary power is enough. The Ark is bound into the very roots of Jerusalem. Its absence weakens the city. Its presence, if it can be returned, will make it and the powers within it strong— enough, maybe, to overcome the enemy."

"He is that strong?"

"He died; he clawed his way back from hell. He feeds on blood. His existence is the blackest of black magic."

Giuliano nodded slowly. He was thinking hard. "And you need the whitest of white magic to oppose him."

"To us of my faith," Mustafa said, "the world is twofold. One part is the House of Islam. The other is the House of War. Islam enters the House of War and conquers it, and makes it one with Islam.

"Now imagine," he said, "that Jerusalem was taken; that darkness ruled in the heart of the world. The darkness is of Islam: a corrupted Islam in service to Iblis—whom you would call Sathanas. The whole world would be the House of War. There would be no peace. Light would be overwhelmed; darkness would rule. Mankind would be enslaved to the undead."

Giuliano shuddered. The sun was warm, the air sweet, but Mustafa knew how bleak his words were. To a mage of Giuliano's strength, they would be devastating. He could see what Mustafa spoke of: it was in his eyes. "Why didn't you say this to my grandmother?"

"She knew," Mustafa said. "She still refused. Maybe she thinks that Rome can be safe."

"It is far across the sea," said Giuliano, "and the undead was an infidel fanatic before he died. He'll look to destroy Jerusalem, then turn eastward."

"Then after the east falls, he'll turn west."

"You have to understand," Giuliano said. "We were given this charge so long ago that it's become a part of what we are. It feeds our power. Every child born within its sphere is gifted with magic. We guard it and keep it hidden. In return it gives us whatever our hearts desire. If we give it back, all that will be gone. We'll be mortal again."

"I doubt that you were mortal even before you stole the magic of the Jews," Mustafa said. "You were the keepers of Rome's magic. Won't that still be yours, even with the Ark gone?"

"We have no way of knowing that," said Giuliano. "If the Ark goes, all our power may go with it."

"What," said Mustafa, "if it went with a deputation of your brothers? What if you continued to guard it, but under the Jews rather than the Pope?"

"Is that possible?"

"I don't know. Is it?"

"I don't know, either," said Giuliano. "If it were . . ."

"Would your grandmother agree to it?"

"No," Giuliano said. He did not say it gladly at all. Neither did he hesitate. "She will not leave Rome or allow the treasure to be taken. Not for any reason."

"Then you know we have no choice," said Mustafa. "Nor do you."

"I don't believe that." Giuliano reached across the table and pulled Mustafa toward him. "If it is goodbye after this, let's have something to remember."

CHAPTER TWENTY-SIX

Eleanor was not to be hurried. "I have preparations," she said. "Go, rest yourselves. Desist from hunting until I summon you."

"Time is getting short," said Sioned. "We can't just—"

"The moon is at the full," Eleanor said. "There is ample time before it dies again." She raised a hand in a gesture all too familiar. "Will you go? Or shall I encourage you?"

Sioned preferred not to be encouraged. She retreated, not too rapidly, but quickly enough to avoid the blast of magefire.

Eleanor made them wait four days. The first two, Sioned thought, were necessary; she was preparing for what she must do. The rest were pure malice.

Sioned was tempted to take matters into her own hands, but when she tried to think about it, the headache and confusion warned her that Eleanor had anticipated that. She had perforce to rest, read, and play the pilgrim in the city of a religion that had nothing to do with her or her husband.

There was of course one thing that one could do with one's husband, if one were inclined. Sioned was, more strongly than she might have expected. There were magics that she had been studying, arts of the east, which were best explored with a lover and a degree of leisure. That, for the moment, she certainly had.

On the morning of the fifth day, she knew that even love would not keep her from breaking loose, shattering the spell, and doing whatever came into her head. Ahmad was sleeping, happily worn out with the night's exertions. She was a jangle of nerves.

She started as one of the shadows moved. It was the jinni, who had not been in evidence since before Eleanor appeared in Rome. She examined him closely, but he seemed much as always: wearing his human form, standing like a guard, unmoved by her nakedness or the evidence of what she had been doing.

"Jinni," she said softly lest she wake Ahmad. "Is there news?"

He bent his big ruddy head. "Time flies," he said. "The Ark is guarded."

"Do you trust the queen?" she asked him.

"Today," he said, "I do."

It was a perfectly sensible answer, if one were a jinni. "Have you been hunting?"

"Watching," he said. "If you want the Ark now, you'll face an army. There are a thousand of them."

Sioned's heart had gone cold. She tried to speak lightly. "That many? Women, too? Children? Infants in arms?"

"Men in mail," said the jinni, "and mages. They speak of moving it, of concealing it beyond any discovery, mortal or otherwise."

"Gods," said Sioned. "If they spirit it away now—"

"I will go," the jinni said, "and go on watching. My brothers will help me."

"Stop it if you can," she said, "but don't endanger yourself."

"All magic is dangerous," said the jinni. He bowed low. Even as he straightened, he melted into air.

"Now," said Eleanor.

She had had the courtesy to wait until Ahmad and Sioned were eating their breakfast before appearing at the door, fully clothed and ready to travel. There was a horse-litter waiting below that looked as if it had been borrowed from a noblewoman, and their horses were saddled and ready to ride.

Mustafa was there already. He had an odd look to him, half dreamily happy, half hollow-eyed and haunted.

Sioned would ask what troubled him, but not now. They were Eleanor's escort, and she was in no mood for casual chatter. Nor was she about to tell them how she intended to penetrate the walls of the Lateran. They were to be silent and follow. More than that, they need not know.

She did it with arrogance and the power of names. She knew whom to ask for and how. When she met opposition, her voice lowered and she whispered in the clerk's ear. He blanched, bowed, babbled, and passed them on hastily.

Ahmad's brows rose a fraction more with each wall that they passed. He was a famous envoy and diplomat, but even he could find her skill impressive. He was a master; she was a master of masters.

Even she however came at last to an impasse. The man was a cardinal, too lofty to grovel before a mere queen. "You must understand," he said with well-trained patience, "that even the great cannot simply appear before the Holy Father and demand his attention. If you would but hint to me of your message, then I may—"

"My message is for the Holy Father alone," Eleanor said with an air of sweet reason. "With all due respect, of course, your eminence."

The cardinal smiled tightly. "He has requested, lady, that he not be disturbed with trivialities. Not to imply that you would vex him with such, but he has also requested that we, his servants, determine which petitions are most worthy of his attention."

"You may be sure," Eleanor said with dangerous softness, "that I would not travel all the way from England at my age and with such small escort if it were not a matter of the highest importance."

"Lady," said the cardinal, "you are as ageless as the spring."

"I'm as old as the hills," she said with a sudden lash of sharpness, "and I'm tired. Will you let me pass or must I cause a disturbance? For I will not hesitate, as you know full well, who first encountered my temper when you were a young and feckless page in Cardinal Moltisanti's train. You wet yourself then. Have you discovered the virtue of continence in the years since?"

For a stretching moment Sioned was certain that Eleanor had miscalculated. The cardinal's glare was pure poison. Eleanor met it blandly, with a complete absence of fear.

He gave way before her. She had not made a friend, but friendship was not her purpose here.

He was not the last wall, or even the next to last. There was still the Pope's own line of defense, his clerks and secretaries, each less easily cowed than the last. The day was winding toward sunset. They had not eaten since their interrupted breakfast, nor drunk so much as a sip of water. The hospitality of the Lateran left much to be desired.

If they must fast, then they must fast. The men uttered no word of complaint. They had taken what opportunity they could to pray, once in a clerk's cluttered office, once in a cloister where a battalion of monks paused to stare. None seemed to know what he was seeing, only to find it strange.

Sioned began to think that either they would camp in a cloister or they would have to leave, then begin again in the morning. They could be here for an infinity of days.

Teleri did not have infinity. She had until the new moon.

Desperation helped nothing. Sioned had already made matters worse, and worse again. She had to trust this woman whom she had grown up mistrusting, and for most excellent reason.

It was nearly the hour for the daymeal. The Pope was in the great dining hall, the hall of his predecessor Leo, with its mosaics of the great Pope and the Emperor Charlemagne. The walls gleamed with jeweled tesserae, the figures stiff and yet oddly supple, movement arrested but promising to begin again if the eye slid aside.

Eleanor walked through the door with the air of one who had done so more than once before. The hall was full of priests and prelates, monks and abbots. There were no women. Today there were no secular guests at all.

The Pope sat at the center of the uppermost table under a canopy of gold. His robes were white and gold. His face was a blur amid the splendor, but his dark eyes were sharply clear.

He recognized Eleanor. The emotions Sioned read in him were almost unbearably complex. Respect and fear, hatred, awe, admiration, loathing—and that was only the surface.

"Lothario Conti," said the queen, "I request an audience."

"His Holiness' secretary—" one of the cardinals nearest him began.

"I have had enough of secretaries," Eleanor said. "I will wait, my lord, until you dine, but I have no intention of leaving until I have spoken with you."

The Pope's lips were a thin line. He raised a finger. Almost at once, servants appeared, coaxing the Pope's uninvited guests to a table not excessively far down the hall—though far enough to be construed as an insult to Eleanor—and serving them with the rest.

Sioned had no objection to wine or roast pork, but she saw how Ahmad and Mustafa exchanged wry glances. Fortunately there was fish and beef and roast fowl as well, and they need not be obvious about declining certain of the numerous dishes. They had had some little practice in it, especially Mustafa, having lived among Franks so long.

However lukewarm the welcome, the food was plentiful, and it was good. When the last of it had gone round, a soft-footed priest came to fetch them.

He brought them to a chamber nearly identical to every other anteroom they had been in since this hunt began. Sioned looked for Eleanor to rise up in outrage, but she sat in the chair to which she was escorted, and seemed to have surrendered the fight.

A servant, this time a monk in a black habit, lit the lamps in the slowly gathering dusk. The men watched for the moment of twilight, when it would be time again to pray.

Just after that moment, the summons came at last. The messenger had to wait. However great the Pope of Rome might be, he was as nothing to the power of Allah.

Innocent, third of that name, already reckoned one of the great Popes of the age, who had been born Lothario Conti, did not like to be kept waiting. His religion might preach the virtue of humility, but he did not indulge in it himself. He was brilliant and he knew it, just as he knew the magnitude of his own importance.

He had put aside his court robes in favor of a simple white habit and cowl. There was a burly priest at his back, guarding him, and a clerk in a corner to record whatever was said. Otherwise he was alone.

It was not trust. It was arrogance. He knew with sublime certainty that no one would dare to harm him. Not in his own palace in his own city, in the heart of the Christian world.

It was a pity his guests were honorable infidels. Sioned had taken an instant dislike to this man. It had nothing to do with reason or sense; it was a perfect antipathy, as if they were natural enemies. Cat for dog, bird for snake, pagan for fanatic Christian.

Eleanor bent her knee in front of him and kissed his ring. The others bowed in their fashion but offered no extraordinary reverence.

That piqued him, the more so for that Eleanor did not name them to him. She disregarded them as if they had been servants, and yet he could see that they were rather more than that.

"Your holiness," Eleanor said, "we need your help."

Innocent made no secret of his surprise, or of the fact that it shaded toward skepticism. "I gather it's urgent, lady, for you to have demanded this audience so peremptorily."

"Lives and souls depend on it," said Eleanor. "Jerusalem is endangered. The armies of hell have risen against it."

"Indeed?" said Innocent. "How did the King of Jerusalem raise them?"

He walked a thin edge. He knew it: Sioned saw how he watched Eleanor.

But Eleanor was older than any of them, and wilier. If she was disturbed by the thinly veiled slur against her son, she betrayed none of it. "He killed the Old Man of the Mountain," she answered coolly, "and broke the Assassins' power in Syria. Unfortunately the Old Man was sorcerer enough to find death a mere inconvenience. He clawed his way back to life. The blood of Christian men has fed him: Knights of the Hospital of Saint John in Jerusalem, and soldiers of the Crusade. He is now a great power, and he has no love for the knights of Christ."

"A Crusade?" asked Innocent. "You ask me to preach a Crusade?"

"No," she said. "Maybe in time, but this threat is too urgent. By the day of the new moon, he must be overcome, or he will rule us all."

"The new moon? That's only—"

"Yes," said Eleanor. "We need something of you now; tonight if possible, tomorrow at latest. There is a thing in Rome that can destroy this enemy and close the gates of hell. We have come to find that thing and bring it back to Jerusalem."

"You? All of you?" Innocent looked hard into her escort's faces. His finger stabbed at Ahmad, and then at Mustafa. "These are not Christian men. They touched no wine or pork. They were seen prostrating themselves and muttering what my servants took for spells, but no doubt were prayers."

"We were praying," Ahmad said, as cool as the queen and no less haughty. He bowed with the grace of his people, beautiful and utterly foreign in this place. "I am al-Malik al-Adil Saif al-Din, and I am sultan in Egypt and close ally and kin to the King of Jerusalem. This is my wife, Sioned, daughter of King Henry of England and lady of Montjoyeuse in the Kingdom of Jerusalem, and this, the king's most trusted servant, his friend and ally, Mustafa ibn Mursalah. We are not Christian men, but we also are people of the Book, and Jerusalem is our holy city as well. We have long been enemies of the Master of Assassins."

The Pope's eyes had gone wide at that recitation of names. He was human after all, and not immune to awe—although it gave way all too quickly to suspicion. "Indeed," he said, "I do not question the truth of that. But why and how would a sultan of the infidels appear in my palace, playing servant to the Queen of the English? Are you her prisoner? Is the Crusade at last and truly won?"

"I am her ally," Ahmad said, no less cool than before. "I come of my free will. This thing is enemy to us all, and will destroy us all."

"I do not know him," said the Pope.

"You will," said Eleanor, "unless we stop him. For that we need your help. You know where the Ark of the Jews is hidden."

Innocent went still, within as without. Sioned felt that stillness in herself. "Even if I knew that great secret," he said, "I would not be at liberty to divulge it."

"We know where it is," said Eleanor. "It is the only weapon that can prevail against the enemy of Jerusalem. Its guardians have refused to let it go. Even to save the Holy City, they will not do it."

"Their guardianship is very old," Innocent said.

He might have said more, but she spoke first. "They were given the task by an apostate emperor, in aid of his war against the Christian empire. They serve the old gods of Rome, not the new God of the world."

"They serve the Church now," said the Pope.

"Do they?"

If she had sown a seed of doubt, it was slow to grow. "They have been ours for years out of count. What they do, they do with our blessing."

"Good," said Eleanor. "With your blessing, they will let it go."

"You are aware," he said, "if you have spoken to them, of the great power and danger of what they protect."

"I am also aware," said the queen, "of the great power and danger of the thing that threatens Jerusalem. The guardians may accompany it—we have no objection to that. But if we are to save the city, we must have that one of all weapons."

"Must you? Who will wield it? You? These followers of Mahomet?"

Eleanor hesitated very slightly. "The sons of Levi have returned to their own city."

The Pope's nostrils thinned. "Jews? You would give that mighty weapon to Jews?"

"It was theirs for a thousand years," she said. "They made it. They know better than anyone how to use it."

"Jews," said the Pope, as if the word had an ill taste. "What, so that they can take back their kingdom? So that they can mock us all?"

Sioned had been silent long enough. "They serve the King of Jerusalem both willingly and loyally. This is not a conquest; this is an alliance of faiths. The Jews know best how to wield their own weapon. The king knows best how to conduct a war. Jerusalem will stay in Christian hands, if he wins. If he loses, what rules it will partake of nothing holy."

"I will give no power to the Jews," said the Pope with a twist of pure hatred: "the Christ-killers, the enemies of our faith. Bad enough that infidels should come to me to ask this thing. That they should surrender the great weapon to Jews . . . no. It shall not be."

"You should have lied," Sioned said. "Or at the very least, omitted a part of the truth."

Eleanor looked like a hunched and ancient bird, sitting in the lamplight in Domna Maria's inn. That they had been let go at all was testimony to the strength of her will and the power she still held over the Pope.

Pity that it had not only failed to overwhelm him, it had turned him against them. Eleanor had miscalculated at the last, badly. Innocent had begun in suspicion and ended in active hostility. He was blindly irrational in his hatred of the Jews. It had no reason, no sense; it was set as deep in him as the faith by which he lived. No persuasion, earthly or otherwise, could touch him.

If it had not been for Richard, Sioned would have been certain that Eleanor had failed deliberately. But if Richard was in danger, his mother would fight to the death to protect him. She had erred, that was all. She had misjudged a man's fears and his bone-deep hatred of a people who had never, that Sioned could tell, done him harm.

"We'll have to fight for it," Ahmad said. He sounded tired but not particularly discouraged. "A thousand knights, each armed with magic as well as steel . . . what is that to the likes of us?"

"Our need is greater than theirs," said Eleanor. "It will find us a way."

"You had better hope so," Sioned said grimly, "or we're all done for—even your fool of a Pope."

CHAPTER TWENTY-SEVEN

The armies of Jerusalem marched for three days with little opposition. As they passed Nablus, a little more than a dozen leagues from the holy city, the attacks began. Little by little, in brief raids and sudden forays, bands of Turks and Bedouin fell on the column as it marched and on the camp at night.

Berengaria had made herself a part of the baggage train. There were women enough there, camp followers and servants, brewers of beer and ale, bakers of bread and sellers of necessities and lesser luxuries to the soldiers of the king. None of them cared what she did or how she did it.

Her imp of a servant saw that she had food, drink, a tent to sleep in. Within those narrow leather walls, she spied on the king through her crystal. She heard his councils; she watched his drinking bouts and his rounds of gaming. She never saw him locked in embrace with any of his squires, which rather surprised her. In her head she had no desire to see such a thing, but her heart confessed to a guilty curiosity.

They were drawing near to Damascus. She heard the debates among the war council as to whether they should stop there and call on the sultan's oaths of alliance. Nothing had yet been decided, but tempers were rising high on both sides.

She had a little to do with that. It was a simple working, and useful.

On the night of the full moon, she worked a greater spell—as great as her strength could sustain. The moon's power fed hers: she was bound to it as all women were, but more so now that the flow of her monthly blood was stopped. There was a life growing inside her. It made her stronger than she had expected.

She mustered the powers of air. Icy cold from the peaks of mountains, mist and fog from the sea, fiery heat from the deserts of Egypt and Arabia: she cast them into the cauldron of her magic and stirred them with a harlot's thighbone. So were the elements mingled and bound to inconstancy.

They strained at the bonds she set on them. She held on grimly. The moon crawled up the sky. The camp sank into its nightly silence. The only sounds were the tramp of sentries, the snorting and stamping of horses on the lines, the groan of a camel, and softer than any, the whisper of wind.

Just as the moon touched the zenith, the spell wrenched free. It caught the wind and bound itself to it.

Berengaria sank down, drained all but dry. The wind played lightly round the tent, brushing the walls, tugging at the flap. She should dismiss it, but she was empty of power.

The tent breathed like a great beast. Its walls sucked inward. She gasped, but there was no air.

The walls billowed outward. Berengaria gulped air. She could feel the spell swirling overhead. Clouds had begun to gather, wind to blow. It was slow yet, but that was well. She had hoped for slow.

The morning was grey and blustery—unheard of for summer in Syria. The newest recruits from England and Normandy found it a welcome breath of home. The veterans rolled their eyes at the strangeness.

Richard had them up and on the road as always. "If it rains," he said, "then more power to it. Meanwhile it's cooler than it's been in months—prime marching weather. Let's march!"

The storm broke near noon. The clouds had thickened through the morning; the wind was blowing strong, stirring up clouds of dust. The army marched in a deepening haze.

There were no raids today. Turks and tribesmen of the desert knew better than to brave such a storm as was brewing. Franks should have known better, but they were blinded and befuddled. Richard would not listen to the mages who had come with the army. The men knew them as physicians and surgeons in the hospital tents. They raised what protections they could, but this spell was stronger than they. It was stronger than anything mortal.

It smote like the hand of God. The wind roared down. The lightning cracked. Hail pounded unprotected flesh. Horses screamed and bolted. Their riders were thrown off or carried far away.

Richard tried to rally them. Drums and trumpets were barely audible over the howl of the wind. He set his personal guard to riding back along the line, relaying his orders to the captains one by one. He did the same from the center to the van, beating against the wind.

The van had had the sense to stop and raise such shelter

as they could: shields, cloaks, the bodies of camels and horses. The ranks behind had begun to slow. On Richard's orders they halted and dug in.

Men and animals were down, battered by the hail. The surgeons made their way toward them, warding themselves with shields.

The hail died away. There was a lull. Richard had reached the van. Berengaria huddled under an overturned wagon, wrapped completely in her cloak, peering into her crystal.

They had raised a roof of shields. She saw the Grand Master of the Hospitallers, who led the vanguard, and beside him—with an unexpected flutter in the belly—the lord Henry. His face was bruised, his cheek split.

They were saying nothing unusual. The only sensible course was to stop, make what camp they could, and wait out the storm.

"We need to post guards," Henry said. "No sane infidel will travel in this, but once it lets up, they can be on us while we're still reckoning the damage."

"This is not a natural storm," the Grand Master said. "Who knows when it will stop?"

"When it suits the enemy." Richard's voice was grim. "We'll need more than steel, if that's the case. Hold fast here; be on guard. Whatever comes, don't let it through."

"We understand," Henry said. "We'll hold on."

Richard took a moment to steel himself and to brace the shield above his head before he forayed out into the storm. The lull took him by surprise. He lowered his shield, peering at the sky. The clouds boiled. There were faces in them. Eyes. Shapes that twisted and writhed, coiling upon one another.

He shuddered and raised his shield, just as the rain began to fall. It was a hard, drenching rain, as strong almost as the hail. It turned the dust to mire and the fallen hail to a sheet of melting ice. He slipped and skidded and sometimes fell, but he persevered.

The master physician had had the same thought as the commander of the baggage train: he had upended the wagons to shelter the wounded and the sick. He was setting a broken arm when Richard found him, working by lamplight and by feel. Berengaria could barely see him in the crystal; he was a shape of shadow touched with fugitive glints of light.

"Yes," he said before Richard could speak. "It's a mage's work."

"I knew that," Richard said. "I want to know why now, why here, and what can we do about it?"

"I don't know," said Judah. He finished splinting the arm and said to the man-at-arms, "Rest here a while, and drink what you're given. Then you can go."

The simmer of Richard's temper was perceptible through the crystal. Once the wounded man was settled, he said tightly, "What do you mean, you don't know? Can't you tell?"

"I've been busy," Judah said. "Ask the boys—they've more time to spare than I do, and they're better hunters and spies, too. If you want a guess, I'd say it's the enemy you would expect. We're two days from Damascus at normal marching speed, Krak is not so far away now, and he's been letting us come on blithely as if we had nothing to fear. Now the war begins."

"I can't fight sorcery," Richard said. "I don't want to fight sorcery. Can't you do anything to get rid of it?"

"Talk to Moishe and Aaron," said Judah.

Richard growled so low in his chest that the crystal shook, then whirled and stalked out from under the wagon.

*   *   *

Berengaria swayed. The crystal blurred. She had over-strained herself.

She could not stop now. She must know what Richard said to the young Jews. They were the mages she had sensed throughout—that was evident. She had not thought that they would be Judah and his sons; when she had thought at all, it had been of the Christian clerks and physicians, or the Welsh witch Sioned.

Sioned was not here. Berengaria had hunted for her, but she was nowhere to be found. It was as the dark thing had said: she was gone. And maybe Richard would say something to Moishe and Aaron that would hint at where she was.

She stopped to shake her head, as much to clear it as to respond to the thought that was in it. Jewish mages in Richard's service. Muslims she would have expected; he had numerous allies on that side of the war. But Jews—that changed things. How much or how far, she did not yet know, but she could feel the shift in her own skin.

She could not make the crystal come clear. Her magic was drained dry. She had to eat, sleep, give it time to restore itself. No amount of frustration could force it.

In a perfect world she would have had a room to herself and solicitous servants and whatever comfort she could have desired. In the world she had made, she had a corner under an upended wagon and a restless, fitful sleep, broken by gusts of wind and the hammering of rain.

She could feel the dark thing trying to come in. Its patience was wearing thin. Her storm was very satisfying but rather overwrought, and she had not discovered what he wanted most to know. She retreated deep inside herself, too deep even for dreams.

She could never retreat deep enough to escape the undead. He appeared in the innermost chambers of her spirit, wearing a cloak of flesh: an old man, gaunt but strong, dressed all in white. He seemed altogether human, except for his eyes. There was nothing in them but darkness.

"Lady," he said in a soft purring voice. "Are you well rested? May we begin again?"

"I am not rested," she said with as much civility as she could muster. "Give me until morning. I'll search out the truth you're looking for then, and do my best to find it."

"How frail is flesh," said the dark thing, "and a woman's frailer than any." He sighed, which was a great performance: the dead did not breathe. "Very well. Tomorrow. But do beware. Not all of my servants are easily mastered, and some will destroy anything in their path. If you can withdraw from this camp, you will be wise to do so before morning."

She bowed. "I understand," she said.

The dark thing slipped out of her dream. She held still for a long while, until it was truly and absolutely gone. Then slowly she unfolded, swimming up through the levels of her consciousness, until she hovered just below the threshold of sleep.

She could not sleep long, but what little she could manage, she must. There would be rest enough after it was over.

CHAPTER TWENTY-EIGHT

The storm raged for two nights and a day. Men and horses drowned in it, and a whirlwind destroyed a great portion of the baggage train. When at last the clouds parted, the sun rose over a field of devastation. The earth was turned to mud. Everything that had been green was battered or gone.

Men crept out from their shelters: wagons, a few hastily battened tents, and around Richard a fortress of shields. Mounds of mud stirred and groaned and lurched to their feet. Nearly all the camels were safe.

The same could not be said of the mules and the horses. The worst blow was to the knights. Their heavy destriers, brought from the west at great cost—for this country would not sustain such a mass of horseflesh; the great beasts died or bred down to the little light horses of Arabia—had not weathered the storm well at all. Those that had not drowned or gone mad with the pounding of rain and hail were standing with heads low, too battered and bruised to care what went on around them.

"God's feet," Richard said as he reckoned the cost of the storm. He set men to salvaging what they could of both beasts and baggage. The rest he put to work breaking camp.

They were going to march that day, whatever it took to get them moving. They needed to move; they needed clean rations and a dry place to sleep. Damascus was not so far away now.

"If we can reach that," he said to Henry after they had helped to haul a wagon out of the mud, "we can regroup before we move on Krak."

"We'll have to do something," Henry said. "We're damned near shattered as it is."

"Maybe we should do it here," said the Grand Master of the Templars. He had come up while they were speaking, grim as always, although his scowl was visibly blacker as he looked out across the wrack of the storm. "I don't know that I trust al-Afdal. His father—"

"His father was my most honorable enemy," Richard said. "The enemy we fight now was his father's murderer. He'll honor the alliance."

"Are you sure of that?" the Templar said. "I trust nothing in this strange war—not allies, not enemics. The House of War, they call this country. I call it the House of Treachery."

"Al-Afdal is still with us," Richard said imperturbably. "We'll make for Damascus. My lord, will you take the van and send out scouts? Even if the sultan is loyal, God knows how many of his alleged subjects won't be."

That mollified the Templar somewhat. This he could accept. He had orders and the prospect of a fight.

"I'm thinking," said Henry, "that if I were a sorcerer who had raised a storm to flatten an army, I would send my earthly armies against it before it could haul itself back out of the mud."

"Yes," Richard said, "I had thought of that. We'll move as fast as we can, and set as many men on watch as we can spare. The sooner we're in reach of Damascus, the better we'll be."

Berengaria watched and listened from a much drier and cleaner vantage than she had slept in the night before last. The village had been deserted when she came to it, but she had found its storehouses. She was well provided with food and warmth and whatever else she might need. The house of the *rais*, the headman, was comfortable enough. And best of all, it was out of the path of the war.

Her strength was still somewhat frail, but it was enough to scry and search. Once she had a sense of what Richard intended, she directed the crystal elsewhere.

She had not tried this working before. It was more difficult than she had expected to turn the crystal away from the jewels on Richard's surcoat and focus it on the thing that she had enchanted before she withdrew from the camp. She appreciated the irony of it: it was a talisman of the Jews, hung in the young mages' tent. There had been a spell of protection on it. There still was, but her scrying spell was woven inextricably through it.

The young Jews were in the tent, rolling up blankets and packing away belongings. Theirs was one of the few intact tents that the army had left, and Berengaria had no doubt as to why.

She loosed the bonds of hearing as well as sight, in time to hear one of the young men say, "I don't like it. It's too quiet."

"The wards are out," the other said. He was older and

seemed calmer. "We'll move as soon as we can. We're ready for whatever comes."

Berengaria set her teeth. What she had in mind was new, and she was not sure that she could do it. But she had to try.

She turned the spell carefully inside out. The eye that had looked inward became a burning glass, a focus for her will. She turned it on the younger of the two men. He was only a boy, wobbly-kneed as a foal, and although his magic was considerable, it was as yet imperfectly contained.

She worked her way through the cracks and crevices of it, to rest within his shields. They were elegant in their structure, but they were still more promise than fulfillment, like the boy to whom they belonged.

What he might know, she could not tell, but she had wagered her life and more on the attempt. She set in him a wishing, the hint of a word, a niggle in the back of his mind. Part of it was the name and face of the king's bastard sister, and part was the Egyptian sultan.

He knew them both. His start of recognition nearly flung her out of the working. He was seeing—remembering—

"Aaron!"

His brother's cry was as high and fierce as a hawk's. An instant later a different cry rang out: the battle-cry of the Saracens, a shrill ululation that contained within it the name of their god. The attack had come, and Aaron forgot all else.

Berengaria came to herself on the carpeted floor of the *rais'* dining room. She was alone. Her head ached abominably. She had a hint, a suggestion of an answer, but that would not be enough. The dark thing wanted more. He was no longer even pretending to be her servant—and she had to face the reality of her position. She truly was not strong enough to defy him.

She gathered such necessities as she could. Her second alleged servant was nowhere in evidence, but she managed somehow to saddle and bridle her horse, and to mount and ride.

The track of the storm was clearly marked. The great part of the Syrian desert was its wonted summer self, bone-dry except in the oases and around the wells and cisterns of the towns and castles. But a narrow swath not far from Damascus had turned to mire. Green things were budding already, as hopeful as the desert could be when granted the blessing of water, but the rest was mud and wind-ravaged emptiness.

Richard's army struggled in the heart of it. Raiders had struck from all sides. The camp was nearly ready to move—he bellowed at them to leave what they could not carry, to get up, move, escape. "Damascus! Make for Damascus!"

The enemy knew where he was going. He faced a wall of armed men on fresh and well-fed horses. Half his knights were on foot, half the rest were mounted on horses that would not sustain more than a charge or two. His troops were slipping and staggering in mud, and sweltering already in the heat of the summer sun.

He flung back his head and roared with laughter. Even as he laughed, he gathered his forces with a sweep of the glance and a singing of trumpets. *"Now!"* he bellowed.

They must have heard him in Jerusalem, so powerful was that cry. The knights surged into motion. Archers and crossbowmen covered them with a hail of arrows. The infantry pressed behind, both the footsoldiers by trade and the knights and sergeants who had lost their horses.

They broke through the line. They had learned in years of battle against the lighter, faster, more agile infidels to protect their sides and rear and not to let any part of their army be cut off from the rest. The knights were the head of the spear. The rest of the army drove them inseparably from behind.

Turks died for their unholy war. They died gladly: they had been promised a supernal reward. Their master had not been precise in his promise; he had not told them that their blood and souls would feed his power. Their recompense was to make their master stronger, but to lose their souls and selves.

Richard was happily unaware that in killing Turks, he fed the enemy who had set them on him. He broke their army and scattered it, and rode the tide of his elation toward Damascus.

Berengaria laid her snare beyond the wrack of the storm, where the road was dry and the going much easier. Small parties of knights and lesser fighters pursued the Turks, but most of the army had fallen into a column. Men wandered aside from it often enough, to relieve themselves or to go after birds or small game for the pot.

The mages rode together. They dressed like knights and squires when they marched; they wore mail and carried weapons. It was not obvious what they were.

Her quarry liked to ride with his brother somewhat ahead of the others. The brother was a hunter; he had a small bow, with which he shot wildfowl. Aaron trailed after him, lost in reflection as often as not, or with his knee hooked over the pommel and a book resting on it—as perilous as that could be while riding with an army. He was skilled in the working of wards, so much so that Berengaria drew back in sudden caution.

He was not aware of her, although she was nearly as close as his shadow. His protections were armed against Assassins and their master. He was not looking for a Christian woman with a gift for sorcery.

She called doves out of air and cast them in front of the brothers. They had wandered almost out of sight of the column—idiocy, if they had not been what they were. They were safe from raiders; those had retreated into the hills to lick their wounds and prepare the next attack.

Berengaria's doves swirled in the air. She watched from an outcropping of stone. The elder brother strung his bow quickly and set an arrow to the string. Berengaria sent the doves over the hill in a sudden flurry.

As she had hoped, the elder brother galloped after them, but the younger hung back, dallying in the sunlight. He reached into his saddlebag and brought out a book, opened it and began to read. His horse, accustomed to his habit, wandered until it found a bit of grass, then lowered its head to graze.

She snared him with a net of sunlight and spun malice, and held him with a Word. He stared at her without recognition. Without the state robes and the crown that she could wear only when Richard ordered it to be brought out of the treasury, she was as nondescript as a woman could be.

That served her now, even as it fed the resentment that, in turn, fed her magic. She pitched her voice to bind the spell tighter. "Speak and be not silent. Tell me what I wish to know. The king's sister—where may she be?"

"Why," he said, "in Normandy. Doesn't everyone know that?"

Berengaria ground her teeth. "Not Joanna. The old king's bastard—the Welsh witch. Where is she?"

He said nothing. His eyes were wide. His mind and will were perfectly blank.

She pressed the spell harder. "Tell me. Where is the witch?"

It was as if he had turned to glass. He was smooth, translucent. She could get no grip on him. She could not penetrate his shields.

She shifted the spell, twisting and transforming it until his eyes reflected, not her plain and sallow face, but an ebony-and-ivory beauty with eyes the color of wood violets. Berengaria had always hated Sioned for that beauty, and even more for that she seemed not to notice it at all.

Aaron softened in front of it, as men invariably did. "Sioned? But you're—"

He broke off. Berengaria gasped. He had wrenched himself away from her spell. He saw her and not the illusion.

He snatched rein and kicked at his horse's sides. The beast, startled, threw up its tail and bolted. Still with the book in his hand, he bent over the long brown neck and urged it to even greater speed.

She had no strength to stop it. But one thing she could do. She had set a wishing in him, a barely visible spark of will. It might be futile, but she had to try. If he turned his thought toward Sioned, if he lowered his guard even for an instant, she would know.

It was the best that she could do. Her erstwhile servant would not be pleased, but he would not exact the price quite yet. She was still more useful to him alive than dead.

CHAPTER TWENTY-NINE

Benjamin found the window in the hedge.

Teleri had been hunting for something like it for as long as they had been trapped in the Old Man's pretty prison. It was even prettier now, and even more alluring if one were the kind of idiot that he seemed to think she was. Voices whispered constantly, trying to corrupt her with lies and twisted truth.

The dark thing did not pay as much attention to Benjamin. It was Teleri he wanted, and Teleri took the brunt of his attacks. Benjamin could slip away unnoticed and find things that Teleri was too busy fighting to even look for.

Sometimes the dark thing went away. The voices went on, but they were not as insistent. She had a little peace then. Her head stopped aching quite as badly, and she could let herself think thoughts that she did not want the dark thing to know.

She pretended to be weakening. It was not as hard as she would have liked. It was tempting to live in a palace, waited on by invisible servants who catered to her every whim. The things the voices showed her were magical and wonderful, and if she had not been who she was, she might not have seen the darkness in their hearts.

But she was heir to the magics of both Gwynedd and Egypt, and she had grown up knowing what was light and what was dark. Sometimes they looked exactly alike. But the feel and smell were different.

Everything here smelled rotten underneath. She tried not to get used to the faint stink, even to start thinking it was right and good, but it was hard. She could use magic whenever and however she liked, the voices whispered, and no one would stop her or tell her to be careful. "Darkness is freedom," they whispered. "Darkness is joy. In darkness you can be and do whatever you please."

She knew that was not true. Her bones were sure of it. But her head ached so much when she resisted.

She had lost count of the days, if there were days to count, by the time Benjamin found the window. The dark thing had gone away. He was far too busy to pay attention to his prisoners. She was important, but she was safe, locked away in his garden. He did not have to think about her until he had a moment to spare.

She had been trying to sleep, as she did whenever the voices retreated. Benjamin woke her with a touch on her shoulder and a whisper in her ear. "Wake up. You have to come."

She did not want to wake up; she wanted to sleep. But he insisted. Before he could drag her out, she kicked him off and stumbled to her feet. Her hair was snarled out of its braid. She pushed it back behind her ears.

Benjamin caught her by the hand and pulled her with him out of the room. He was almost running.

She dug in her heels. "Stop! Wait. Can't we—"

"No," said Benjamin, breathless. "It might not stay. You have to see. Come on!"

She gave in and let him tug her back into a run.

The garden changed whenever it pleased. New parts added themselves, old ones disappeared. The roses that bloomed white in the morning might be blood-red by evening, or would have turned into jasmine or honeysuckle or beautiful, poisonous oleander.

This hedge had been there from the beginning. It divided a grassy meadow with a fishpond in it from a grove of oranges and lemons. The window had appeared halfway down along it, a circular opening that looked as if it had been cut in the green branches. From the side with the grove, it should have looked out on the fishpond. Instead it showed a sky full of stars.

Before Teleri could ask questions, Benjamin made her go around to the other side, where instead of a line of orange trees, she saw a steep ravine and a wooded gorge, and far below, a silver ribbon of river.

"It changes," Benjamin said. "That was an island in the sea when I went to find you, and before that it was a bazaar in a city I didn't recognize." He gripped her arm so tight his fingers would leave bruises. "You know what this means. If we can climb through it—"

"I wouldn't want to do that now," Teleri said. Her stomach was a little fluttery from looking down from so great a height.

He waved that away. "Of course you don't want to go just anywhere. But I was thinking, if we can catch it when it's open on somewhere familiar, or better yet, if we can tell it what to look at—"

"How do you propose to do that?"

"When we scry, we guide the magic. If I can adapt the spell, we can use it here. If the window stays open. If it's not just another temptation. If—"

"Stop it," said Teleri. "You're dithering. This is real. I don't think it's a temptation. Did you try a working? Maybe a seeing spell?"

He started to shake his head, but then he stopped. "I tried to see where we are. The spell didn't work, and I tried it days ago. I don't think—"

"It might have taken that long to work its way through all the magics that are on this place. Then it had to convince them it's not enemy magic, even if it is good magic and the rest is bad. Can't you feel it? It's like a hole in the middle of everything."

"It could get bigger," Benjamin said, "and eventually swallow everything here. Including us. Does it seem to be getting bigger?"

"Not that I can see," Teleri said. "Can you get it to show us somewhere we know? Not Jerusalem. We don't want to be obvious. Do you know Damascus?"

"A little," said Benjamin. "I remember the orchards outside the city. There's a place where you can stand and see—"

"Do it," she said.

He rolled his eyes at her, which should have been her signal to offer to do it instead, but she did not dare. The dark thing was in her, trying to corrupt her. If he got hold of her while she was helping Benjamin to escape, she was afraid of what she might do. Death was not the worst thing that could happen to Benjamin.

While she waited for him to start the working, she worked a magic that she hoped would not be spoiled if the dark thing got his claws on it. If he looked in, he would see Teleri asleep in her room and Benjamin playing at knucklebones in his, one hand against the other.

"Knucklebones!" Benjamin looked ready to spit. "I haven't played that silly game since I was five years old."

"Chess, then," Teleri said. "I don't care. There's no book for you to read, and that's what you'd really be doing anyway. Are you going to get to it or aren't you? He'll be back all too soon. If we're still at this when he gets here, we'll never get out at all."

That got him moving. He was annoyed with her, but he did not let that taint his working. It was a simple matter of words and will: the words spoken just so, the will focused to a single, powerful point. He was better at that than most mages she had seen, except her father. She had not realized just how good he was getting.

She was careful not to let herself be impressed where the dark thing could see. As far as he knew, she was asleep and dreaming of being a great and powerful sorceress, the greatest in the world.

Benjamin leaned toward the window. Without thinking, Teleri got a grip on him before he fell in. It was still showing the cliff and the gorge. Then, like smoke swirling in a gust of wind, it melted away. In its place was a grove of oranges. For an instant she was ready to groan in disappointment—but that was not the grove in this garden. The walls beyond the trees were familiar, the clutter of roofs and towers beyond them, and the slender spires of minarets.

The spell had worked. They were looking through the orchards of Damascus to the city.

Benjamin was grinning like an idiot. Teleri supposed she was, too. "Now," she said, "can you get through?"

His grin faded a bit. "I think so. I'm not sure . . ."

"Try."

His grin disappeared completely. "I don't think—"

Benjamin was not a coward, but he could dribble and dither with the worst of them. Teleri shifted her grip on him and pitched him toward the window.

He fell forward with a squawk. The window opened like a mouth. Teleri had a moment of absolute horror, in which she knew that it had all been a trap—then he had fallen through. He stood in the grove outside of Damascus, reeling dizzily. As she watched, he fell down.

He was not unconscious, just confused. He picked himself up soon enough and looked around wildly. He stared straight at her, but he did not seem to see her. His lips moved. She recognized the shape of her name.

She gathered herself to follow him. But just as she was ready to jump, all her wards went off at once.

The dark thing was coming. She shut the window without even thinking and ran as fast she could, back to her room and her bed and her illusion of a dream.

When he came, she was dreaming that she ruled the world: sitting on a throne with crown and scepter, wrapped in an enormous mantle of ermine and purple. Wherever she looked, people fell flat on their faces. When she lifted her hand, the earth shook.

The dark thing did not seem to notice that Benjamin was gone. She made sure that he went on not noticing, by waking slowly and letting the dream drift with her. It had been a black-hearted dream, the perfect dream for this place. She buried the truth deep, and hid it thoroughly.

CHAPTER THIRTY

The second attack on Richard's army came outside of Damascus, within sight of the orchards and vineyards. It came from the city, or so it seemed: a massed army of infidels under banners that Richard all too easily recognized. As far as he could tell while he disposed his troops to deal with attacks from all sides, the sultan in Damascus had cast his lot with the dead thing from Masyaf.

Richard could not make himself believe it. Not al-Afdal. The Old Man had killed his father. He would never forget that, nor ally himself with the one who had done it.

Still, Richard was facing men under Damascene banners, Kurds as well as Turks, in numbers that made his heart sink. They were behind him and all around him, and the strongest force of them was in front, between his army and the city.

That was odd, if they wanted to herd him into the gardens and hunt him to his death. He would have done that, if he had been in the Old Man's place. Instead he was barred even more from going forward than from falling back.

He gathered all the knights who were still mounted and whose horses could manage a charge. There were enough of them to make a difference, if a small one.

The enemy were expecting the charge down the center: they had drawn together there. He nodded to Henry, who was in command of the knights. He put on his own helm, settling it securely, and firmed his grip on his lance. Henry's hand slashed down. The trumpets rang, deafening in the metal prison of the helm.

Richard's destrier had leaped into motion even before he clapped spurs to the golden sides. He rocked, caught somewhat off guard, but the high saddle held him in place. His lance swung down.

They struck the enemy sidewise, a long, glancing blow along the edges of the line, driving deep into the flank. The line was thin there; it broke in confusion.

A destrier in motion was not an easy object to turn, but it could be done. The charge swung round in a long arc, curving back toward the rear of the enemy's line.

The enemy who had surrounded Richard's army now found himself outflanked. But victory was far from certain. Richard needed the full force of armored knights, and he had less than half. His infantry were already exhausted from days of storm, then a hard fight. The enemy were fresh, well armed, well mounted. They barely noticed the bite of wounds. Spellwork, he supposed. This whole war reeked of magic.

He was gambling on a feeling in his gut. If Damascus had turned against him, he was as good as dead. But if it had not . . .

His men had their orders. They ignored the forces behind

and to the side, except to defend themselves against attack. Their charges focused again and again on the armies in front, between them and the city. They pressed as hard as they could.

They were starting to drive the enemy back, but whoever the enemy's commander was, he was no fool. He saw what Richard was doing. He shifted his line, spread it wide, and dug it in.

One wing of it swung round to cut off Richard's knights. Their horses were flagging, but he hurled them against the enemy once again, a short charge in constricted space. The Franks' heavier horses set chests and shoulders to the enemy's much lighter mounts and drove them bodily back.

The fighting had taken Richard's knights into the orchards. He could not see the whole of his army, although he could follow it in the calls of horns and trumpets. The left and center were holding. The right was hard pressed.

An eddy of the battle swirled him round so that even as he clove a shrieking Turk from brow to breastbone, he looked up toward the walls of Damascus. Was there movement there? Did he catch a flash of sunlight off a Saracen helmet?

He swung almost absently at an enemy who tried to take advantage of his distraction. The man's sword grazed his arm, but glanced off the closely woven mail. He hacked the head from its shoulders and swung his horse away from the gout of blood, into a knot of Turks.

Their commander kept eluding him. He thought he saw the man—a turbaned infidel in white—but each time it was in a different place. One thing only he was sure of: the commander was not the Old Man. He was alive and apparently mortal.

He was not al-Afdal. Richard knew Saladin's son well, and this was an older, taller, thicker man. Al-Afdal, please God, was still in Damascus.

The shrilling of pipes and the clatter of nakers brought Richard's head about sharply. Drums beat in a swift and unmistakable rhythm. The battle music of the Saracens rang from the walls and the gate, signaling a new and deadly charge.

The gate of Damascus had opened. An army poured out. The sultan led them in golden armor, astride a tall halfbred charger that Richard had given him. Any man could ride under a royal banner, but there was no mistaking the stallion's shimmering coat.

The enemy had paused as Richard had, to stare. That told him everything he needed to know. He snatched the trumpet from his trumpeter and blew a blast that made up in volume for its lack of melody. "Hold on!" he roared. "Keep the line! Help is coming!"

Not all of his men believed him, but they had the sense to obey an order. Captains and commanders relayed his words along the scattered line, even to the struggling right.

Al-Afdal was aiming for them—to help them, Richard was sure; not to destroy them. He trusted in faith, and in the sudden crumbling of the enemy's ranks. That was not a ruse or a trap set to suck Richard in. Something had gone wrong, some spell or treachery meant to keep the sultan inside his walls. They had not been expecting this attack.

Richard's lips drew back from his teeth. He fell on the enemy with renewed vigor.

The king of Jerusalem and the sultan of Syria came face to face in a long avenue of dark-green glossy trees. Their men, together and separately, were driving the enemy in retreat, doing as much damage as they could.

Al-Malik al-Afdal, whose father had been Richard's great opponent in the taking of Jerusalem, had grown well into his

position. He looked a great deal like his father, or so people said
who had met the great sultan: the same fine-drawn features, the
same deceptive air of gentleness. Richard would not have
known for himself. In all his battles and his great war, he had
never once met Saladin. All his dealings had been with captains
and lieutenants, and with the sultan's brother Saphadin.

He could not say the same of al-Afdal. Saladin's heir had
been Richard's prisoner and eventual guest, once Jerusalem
was taken. They had taken to one another, each in his way.

"Well," said Richard, grinning at his ally.

"Well indeed," said the sultan in not too badly accented
French. "I do beg your pardon for the slowness of my assistance. I had a slight difference of opinion with certain of my
emirs, which took some time to resolve."

That was an understatement, Richard was sure. "I can see
where that might have been a difficulty," he said blandly.

The sultan dismissed it with a graceful flick of the hand.
"No matter. It's done. When we've cleared the field, will you
be my guest in my city?"

"Gladly," said Richard, and he meant it.

All of the dead and wounded that they found were their
own. Of the enemy there was no sign. Even the dead were
gone, leaving nothing behind, not even a stray weapon or a
loose horse. For all anyone could tell, they had melted into
the air.

"I'm wondering if they even existed," Henry said. He had
greeted al-Afdal with delight: they were friends from the beginning, and frequent guests in one another's houses. Now,
as they shared the feast in the palace of Damascus, Henry
pondered what he had seen, frowning and rubbing his jaw
where a spear-butt had clipped it. "God knows they felt real
enough, but real men don't turn to mist and melt away."

"They do if they're enspelled," al-Afdal said. He was not a mage as his uncle Ahmad and certain of his cousins were, but he saw clearer than most. "They're taking a heavy toll, whatever they are."

"The storm took more," said Richard, "but the raids have eaten away at us. We'll be lucky to make Krak at three-quarter strength. Half will be more like it."

Al-Afdal raised his brows. "You are determined to break the siege at Krak?"

"It's a direct threat," Richard said. "Krak is the greatest of our castles. If he takes it, we lose most of the knights of the Hospital—and we can't afford that."

"Can you afford to lose Jerusalem?"

"Jerusalem is safe," Richard said. "It's guarded. There's the whole length of the kingdom for a shield."

"Not to a sorcerer," al-Afdal said. "You've been lured away from it. Its strongest defenders are with you or else-where. It's ripe for the plucking."

Richard clenched his fist before he closed it about the sultan's throat. "What? How do you know that?"

"Common sense," said al-Afdal. "I've been watching; I've seen the pattern. I remember what he did before. He wants Jerusalem—he wanted it even while he was alive. Now he'll want it more, because it's yours, and you killed him."

"Not to mention," said Henry, "that there's power enough there to feed him for a long age. It does make sense, uncle. Krak is a long way from Jerusalem, and a siege can delay us for weeks, even months—while he slips in behind us and takes the real prize."

"You're forgetting," Richard said, "that I've fortified the kingdom behind me."

"He's an undead sorcerer," Henry said. "Do you think he needs to travel the roads like a living man? I'll wager he can swim through the earth like a great blindworm, or pass through the planes of the world the way your sister can. While we're slogging on foot through the length of Syria, his armies can be appearing out of air in front of David's Gate."

"One can assume that he knows you well," al-Afdal said. "He'll lure you with a war you can fight, and keep you happily occupied while he snatches your kingdom from beneath you."

"Are you trying to make me throttle you?" Richard asked.

Al-Afdal shrugged, smiled. Just then he looked a great deal like his uncle Ahmad, who also could drive Richard to distraction. "You were never afraid of the truth, *Malik Ric.*"

"The truth doesn't usually have anything to do with magic."

"You were born to it," al-Afdal said, "however little you may like it. It's in you and around you. It comes to you."

Richard growled wordlessly.

"You know," said Henry, "if you win this war, it's likely you can go back to the life of an ordinary, earthly king."

"I have to win it first," muttered Richard. "God's feet. I wanted an honest fight. I get armies of shadows. If you two are right, and this is a diversion—"

"You have mages with you, yes?" said al-Afdal. "Why not ask them if our guesses are true?"

"You have them," Henry said. "You might as well use them."

"I have been using them," Richard said. "I hate what they do, but I'm not blind. I'm not a complete fool, either."

That silenced them. They glanced at each other, but neither ventured to provoke Richard further.

They let him finish his dinner in peace. He could put magic out of his mind for that hour at least.

CHAPTER THIRTY-ONE

Benjamin wandered for hours, maybe days, in a state of confusion. He knew where he was. He was outside of Damascus. There was fruit to eat and water to drink. They should not have been enough to satisfy his hunger, but they were.

He thought he might not be entirely in the world. He saw the armed men gathering. He watched the battle from high up in a tree, where no one seemed to see him and no stray arrow touched him. Of course the Lionheart won, and the sultan came from Damascus to help him do it.

Battle was much bloodier and uglier than he had imagined. He was no stranger to either blood or mutilation—he was a physician's son, and would be one himself when he was older—but there was something uniquely ugly about war. It was the fact of conflict: the hate, the antipathy that could not be settled except in blood and death.

For some while after the battle ended, he stayed in his

tree. He saw the enemy's dead and wounded melt into the earth, and the living vanish into air. The men of Jerusalem and Damascus cleared away the debris of the fight. He saw his father and brothers among the physicians, tending the wounded and the dying.

He could not bring himself to go to them. As the sun sank lower, they went away into Damascus.

Just before the gate closed for the night, he slipped in behind the last of the fighting men. He felt a little more real now, a little more firmly anchored to earth, but he was still not quite himself. The path his feet chose was nowhere near his father. He found himself slipping through the streets, in among the evening crowds, making for the sultan's palace.

Its gates were open, although they would close soon. He made his way in in the middle of a motley gathering of slaves, servants, guards, and entertainers for the feast. They thought him a Muslim, because he was wearing clothes from the Old Man's gilded prison. That served him well enough.

The sultan was celebrating the victory with the King of Jerusalem. Richard would stay in the palace tonight. It was easy enough to find out where, and even easier to walk in as if he were one of a legion of servants. He found a corner and curled in it, and settled to wait.

Richard did not stay overlong at the feast. The infidels set a fine table, if overmuch given to sweets and spices, but there was no substitute for good wine. Sherbet palled after a while, and *kaffé* was stimulating but overwhelming in quantity.

With a full belly but a sense of faint dissatisfaction, which was not uncommon after a Saracen dinner, Richard made his way up to the rooms that had been prepared for him. He meant to rest a while, then go back to his army where it was camped outside the walls. His men needed to see him, and he needed to see them.

He might never have noticed the small huddled figure in the corner, if he had not been too restless to lie down. He prowled the rooms, trailed by a servant or two. His squires and pages knew better than to trouble him when he was in this mood, but the sultan's people were as attentive as good Muslim servants could be.

He nearly fell over the intruder, pacing widening circles as his mood grew more agitated rather than less. The boy scrambled up against the wall, pressed tight to the corner, eyes rolling wild.

Richard had a gift that was a great advantage in kings: he never forgot a face. He kept his eyes on it, even as he said to whoever was hovering behind him, "Fetch Master Judah. Now."

The sultan's servant asked no questions. He turned and ran.

Benjamin's fingers scrabbled at the wall. His breath came fast and hard. "You're not real," he said. "You can't be—"

"Benjamin," said Richard.

"No," said Benjamin. "No, no. I'm dreaming this. It's an illusion. He wants me to see—he needs me to find out—"

Richard moved slowly closer. Benjamin went still. Richard caught him before he could duck and bolt, and held him while he struggled. He was all bones and thin skin like a bird, but he was surprisingly strong. Richard grunted as a knee caught him in the gut—and thank God it was not a handspan farther down. He clipped the boy's ear with calculated force, just enough to take the edge off him, and got him out of the corner.

When Judah finally appeared, Benjamin had gone quiet. He was neither asleep nor unconscious, although his eyes were shut. His breathing was a little rapid, a little shallow.

Judah barely spared Richard a glance. He went direct to the bed in which Richard had laid the boy, and bent over him. He laid a hand on the damp forehead.

Benjamin went perfectly still. Something in him changed profoundly. Richard would have said that a darkness went out of him, or a light came in. He drew a deep breath, then another. His head tossed under his father's hand.

He opened his eyes. They were sane; the wildness had left them. He looked into Judah's face. He did not burst into tears as Richard might have expected, but said, "You shouldn't be here. The real war is in Jerusalem."

He might never understand why Richard laughed—though maybe he did not hear it at all. He was intensely focused on his father. "Don't tell me," he said, "where Lady Sioned is. Promise me."

"I promise," Judah said—no question, no argument. "Teleri—is she—"

Benjamin's face twisted. "She pushed me out, and then she was gone. I tried not to leave her. I tried—"

"Hush," said Judah.

"I can't," Benjamin said. "I can't be quiet. She's still there. She's in the garden. He didn't care for me, I wasn't even supposed to be there. It's her he wants. He's pushing at her, pushing and pushing. He wants her power. He wants who she is and what she is. He wants all of her. She's fighting, but without me there, I'm afraid—I'm so afraid—"

"That's enough," Judah said, quiet but so firm that Benjamin's mouth snapped shut. "I can give you something to calm you down, but it will be better if you do it for yourself. There are questions we must ask, and knowledge we must have, before we can let you sleep. You have to be strong."

Benjamin swallowed hard. Richard, whose father had been formidable and whose mother was no less so, could well understand what the boy was feeling. But it was necessary. Benjamin knew it: he brought himself visibly to order, a feat that would not have shamed a man of three times his years, and said with remarkable steadiness, "Yes, Father. I'll answer whatever I can."

"Good," said Judah. As brusque as his tone was, he had his son's hand in his, and held it even when it gripped so tightly it must have bruised.

He glanced at Richard. "Will you begin? Or shall I?"

"I'm not sure I know what to ask," said Richard.

Richard found a stool and set it by the bed, then sat on it. Judah did not at once pelt Benjamin with questions, but let the boy rest for a bit, even become a little drowsy, before he said, "Can you tell us where you were?"

Benjamin started into full alertness. He had been braced for that question, Richard could tell. "We were not in the world," he said. "I don't know if I could find my way back there, though I could try. I have to. Teleri is still there."

"How did you get out?"

"A gap opened in the world," Benjamin said: "a window. We worked a spell, and it let me through. But she didn't—she couldn't—follow."

"Is she in danger?" Judah asked him.

He nodded miserably. "Great danger. But I don't think she'll be killed quite yet. He wants her on his side. She's been pretending to give in. If she can keep pretending, he'll keep her alive. Maybe she can escape. She knows the way, if it's still open."

"That's a deadly game," Richard said, "even for a child of that breeding."

"I know," said Benjamin. "My lord, I wish she hadn't stayed. I'm afraid I was let go. If I'm some sort of spy unawares—"

"We're on guard," his father said. "We'll catch anything that tries to use you against us."

Benjamin did not seem altogether reassured, but he let it go. "I did find out some things. This is old revenge—as old as the dark thing's death. It started a while ago. He took Owein. I saw in a pool of clear water how he did it. He sucked the soul out of him. It was so strong that it lifted him out of hell. He's been feeding on blood and souls ever since."

Richard nodded slowly. He was not surprised, not after everything he had seen since the Old Man rose again. "So," he said. "Is it true? We're galloping off on a diversion?"

"As soon as you're dug in at Krak, the strongest part of his army is set to launch on Jerusalem. They'll take roads he's been building for a long time, over hill and under stone. I saw something about lines of power, how they all go toward Jerusalem."

"To it and from it," Judah said. "The sultan is right. If you go to save Krak, you'll lose Jerusalem."

"Not if I can help it," Richard said.

"There is something else," Benjamin said hesitantly. "I could feel it everywhere when he was there. He's lost Teleri's mother and father. He can't find them anywhere. He's desperate to know where they are and what they're doing. I think he's had a foreseeing."

"Good," said Judah with a bloodthirsty edge. "He's tormented us enough. It's time he suffered a little torment of his own."

"We can use that," Richard said. "I don't know how, but—"

Before he could go on, a small commotion brought him about. Benjamin's two elder brothers who had ridden with the army, Moishe and Aaron, came in with some semblance of dignity, but there was a windblown and scattered look to both of them.

Aaron in particular seemed ready to leap out of his skin.

Richard did not like the look in his eye. Young soldiers with that look had been known go wild and attack their fellows.

· He got a grip on the boy's shoulders and sat him down on the stool. Aaron was crackling with sparks like a cat in a sandstorm. He stared at Benjamin as if he had had no inkling that his brother was here. "Is that—how—"

"Later," said Judah. "Is this something that can wait, or should we know it now?"

"I think you had better know it now," Moishe said. He was much less flustered than Aaron—which he explained as he said, "It's nothing to do with me. Aaron, can you tell it, or do I have to?"

"I—" said Aaron. His voice cracked.

"I'll do it," Moishe said. He addressed his father, with frequent glances at Benjamin. "There's a spy in the army. She caught Aaron while we were hunting yesterday, after the storm and before we came to Damascus."

"She?" said Richard.

Aaron nodded. "She was very plain and ordinary—dressed in black. But her magic was strong. She set a spell in me. I can't name it. I can't go near it. If I touch it, it springs the trap."

"A woman," Richard said. "Now that's odd."

"He has allied himself with a woman before," Judah said.

"With my mother," Richard said. The taste of that was sour in his mouth. "Aaron. Was it a Christian woman? Could you tell?"

"The water of baptism leaves a trace," Aaron said. "She had it."

"One of ours, then," Richard said. "Can you remember—"

"Plain," said Aaron. "Dark—eyes, hair. Sallow skin. Not young. Not old, either, not terribly, but bitter. She stank of loneliness."

"We'll find her," Moishe said. "As for the rest—"

Richard would have been happy enough to forget the spell, but he knew too well that it meant something. Probably a great deal, since this whole war was about magic.

"It's like a worm in my brain," Aaron said, holding his head in his hands as if it hurt him. "It burns. It wants me to think about—I can't let myself—"

"I tried to get it out," Moishe said to his father. "I only made it worse."

Judah's expression did not change. It was always dour; even his youngest son's return had not altered that. "Let me see," he said.

Moishe moved aside. Benjamin was staring, but he was calm, as if he had seen this sort of thing before. Richard thought of disappearing, but there was too much still unsaid.

He expected to see nothing. He was slightly appalled therefore, as Judah sat Aaron down on the chest that stood at the bed's foot, to look into the boy's face and see something like a spark and something like a candle-flame in a windless room. It was eating away at him. He could even see what it was trying to find. It wanted Sioned, or knowledge of her.

Judah went in with magic as keen as a scalpel, moving with utmost delicacy. If he slipped, he would maim his son's mind, perhaps beyond repair. The spark or worm or whatever it was did not become aware of him until he was almost on it. Then it tried to flare and consume its host.

Richard did not know what he did. He was not a sorcerer—by God, he was not. But he had held the Seal of Solomon for a dozen years, and something of it must have rubbed off. He acted as if the Seal had still been with him, to quell the spark and collapse it on itself. An instant later, Judah had it, extracting it as neatly as a sliver of glass from a fleshly wound.

By the time it emerged from Aaron's spirit, it was dead. It crumbled into ash and scattered with a breath.

Judah knelt with head bowed, as if exhausted. Richard was not tired; in fact he felt intensely alive, as if he had just fought a rousing skirmish. Aaron's eyes were on him. "Sire—" he began.

"No," Richard said.

Aaron seemed to understand. He looked rebellious, but he kept quiet. Nobody else was paying attention. Benjamin's eyes had fallen shut.

Judah drew a shuddering sigh and straightened. "It was a seeking spell," he said to Aaron. "You were strong, to hold it off this long."

"I was desperate," Aaron said. "The enemy suspects something, if he's hunting for her in so many places—even using a spy."

"Then he must not find her," Richard said. "You can make sure of it, I hope?"

"We've had warning," Judah said. "We'll act on it."

"I'll do what I can to find the spy," Richard said. "If it's a woman, and she's hiding with the army, she won't be as hard to find as if she were dug in elsewhere."

"Moishe will help you," Judah said. "I'll keep Aaron and Benjamin close by me. Will you be needing me for the war council?"

Richard's brows rose. He had said nothing of any council, but of course there must be one. "That depends on whether you need to hear what we decide."

"I'll know," Judah said.

"Then go," said Richard.

Judah bowed without irony and lifted his youngest son in his arms. With Aaron trailing behind, still faintly dazed, he left Richard to contend with the shambles of his lovely war.

CHAPTER THIRTY-TWO

Sioned woke the morning after their failure with the Pope, and knew absolutely and beyond question what she was going to do. "You can help me or not," she said to Ahmad and Eleanor over breakfast, "but I am going to do this. If it kills me, well and good. If it works, we're back in Jerusalem, we have what we came for, and gods willing, we'll win this war and get our daughter back."

Ahmad had a haggard look to him, as if he had not slept in days. He had had the same dream she had, then, and seen what she saw: Teleri in the greatest danger she had yet been in, beset from all sides, and fighting alone.

He went on eating as if she had not spoken. It was Eleanor who said, "Don't be a fool. This is no time to be rash."

"I am anything but rash," Sioned said. "Time has run out. There is one thing I can do, and I am going to do it. If you are wise, you will go back to England and forget that you were ever dragged into this."

"Too late," said the queen with a wry twist. "I'm as much a part of it as you are. So—the child has done something to provoke her captor. I applaud her; but she has made matters difficult for the rest of us."

"Maybe not," said Sioned. "Gods know, if I could find her as well as dream about her, I'd snatch her away and give us more time. But that gift hasn't been given me. I'll have to do it all at once. I do mean it. Leave; let us do this without interference. It's probably going to be the death of us, and England needs you."

"England needs Richard," Eleanor said. "It can dispense with me if it must. Now tell me what you have in mind."

"You haven't guessed?"

"I do not play games," the queen said with a distinct chill.

Just as Sioned opened her mouth to begin, the door opened, and Mustafa slipped in. He looked even more hag-ridden than Ahmad. Still, his eyes though sunken were clear, and he sat to his breakfast with reasonable steadiness.

"Ah," said Eleanor. "Mustafa. Where is your friend?"

Mustafa flushed ever faintly, then paled. "I suppose he is at home," he said.

The queen frowned just enough to be alarming. "Pity," she said. "We could have used him. That is a dreamer and a lover of legends. He might be induced to—"

"I will not ask," Mustafa said. He was a gentle creature, but like any beast of the desert, he had a core of pure wildness. Nothing could touch that, not even the Queen of the English.

She did not press the point, although Sioned hoped Mustafa was prepared to be tracked down and cornered later.

If there was a later. Sioned knew perfectly well what she was about to do. If she did it alone, she would certainly die. If she did it with help—the help she had here, all of it, jinni and mortal—her death might be a little slower.

It would not matter if only, before she died, she sent the Ark to Jerusalem. She let Mustafa eat a little before she said, "There is a way to take the Ark. It will get me in, and if I reckon it rightly, a door will open to get me out—all before the guardians can muster their forces."

"The Seal," Ahmad said.

She nodded. "It's bound to the Ark. The Ark's power made it. Now it's bound to me in its way. I've done nothing to foster this, but if I do—if I act as soon as the bond is secure—I can do what needs to be done."

"It will kill you," Ahmad said flatly. "Two such powers brought together, with the guardians' power between . . . it doesn't need an alchemist to predict what will come of that."

"Maybe," she said, "but it may also serve as a catapult, to break the Ark free of its protections and fling it toward the center of its old power. It's one of the laws of magic, which you know as well as I: that power of it by nature will seek the place where it was made. If I'm right, and if the Ark finds its way home, it won't need me. The sons of Levi will know what to do."

"It's mad," said Eleanor reflectively, "but it could work. You Celts never die in any event—you simply shift worlds. If that happens—if you can work this even from the other side—"

"There are too many *ifs*," Ahmad said. He was diplomat enough not to remark on the sheer coldness of Eleanor's reckoning.

"There's nothing else we can do," said Sioned. "We can't win the Ark by force of arms, even if we had them. Neither the chief of its guardians nor the Pope will give it to us freely. This is all that's left. I recognize the risk; I accept it. We—"

"I do not accept it," he said with banked heat, "and if that sets me in defiance of fate, then so be it. If it is written, I wish it unwritten. There must be another way."

"I don't see any," she said as gently as she could. "Nor do you, or you would have told us of it. We've racked our brains for days, weeks. We've tried everything even remotely reasonable. Reason is not in force here. We have to do something so wild, so mad, that it's altogether unexpected. They don't know we have the Seal. Nor will they look for a sacrifice."

"There is not going to be a sacrifice," Ahmad said grimly. "I will not—"

"It's not for you to say," she said. She met his glare. "If you try to stop me, I will use the Seal."

"You would not dare."

"For this I would."

"Even if it costs you all that was between us?"

"Even so," she said, although her heart had begun to weep. She wanted to plead, to beg and explain, but she could not. She must not weaken. It was not only for Teleri that she did this. She did it for Owein, too. And for Richard. And for Jerusalem, and for all that would fall if the city fell.

Ahmad was not angry because she was wrong, but because she was right. He was so wise and so calm in so many things that even she could forget that he was, after all, a man. Once in a great while his discipline faltered.

Now was not the time for him to let go. She drew the Seal from her purse, still in its silken wrappings. They shielded it from any who might be seeking it, but she could sense the power there, thrumming under her skin.

"No," he said, but he could not touch her. She shook loose the golden chain that Richard had had made, and hung the Seal about her neck. It burned between her breasts. So close to the Ark from which it was made, it was stronger than ever.

She was as ready as she was going to be. If she waited, she would lose her courage and her focus. "Are you with me?" she asked the others.

Ahmad rose, with Mustafa half a breath behind him. "You've gone mad," her husband said, "but I'll stand at your back."

She nodded. She did not intend to wait for Eleanor. Yet as she set hand to the silk that warded the Seal, the queen stood. "You need someone of both sanity and experience," Eleanor said. "I'll go. Most likely it will be the death of us all. Let it be a good death."

Sioned neither liked nor trusted Eleanor, but in this fight, she was more than glad to have the Queen of the English on her side.

Sioned unwrapped the silk, and with it the wards that bound the Seal. It was as relentlessly plain as ever, but the power that roared from it made her sway where she stood. It was like a beacon in the darkness, a mighty flame leaping up to heaven. Every power that was awake or aware could not help but know that it was there.

It was hers to master—just. She bade it take her to the Ark.

The others caught hold of her just as she was whirled away, and streamed behind her like a comet's tail.

She had precious little time to do what she must do. The Seal opened the way to the Ark. She must direct it, then when she had come there, gather the great thing of power and send it home.

The jinn were all about her, riding the winds between the worlds as easily as they flew through the mortal sky. She had not seen so many of them since they first came flocking to her, fulfilling a wager that Ahmad had made with their prince.

There were dozens, scores of them—hundreds. They swirled together like great birds.

The Ark was a terrible presence before her. There were others, some nearly as terrible, drawn by the magics that she had raised. One of them must be the enemy, but she could not let herself be distracted by the search for him. She must focus on the Ark. She must bring herself to it, then become it—then unleash it.

The wards about it were densely woven and strong. A thousand fires of magery sustained them and defended the thing within. They buffeted her, flinging her back.

Her jinn descended from the world between to the world below, armed with fangs and talons and armored in power. She had never forced the Seal upon them, never broken their will with it, and for that they served her.

They waged war with the children of Teiresias. She heard the clash of swords and the shouts of men and jinn. When men were wounded, blood sprang forth. Jinn bled essential fire.

She thrust against the walls, holding up the Seal before her. It was barely enough.

As she began to falter, strength bolstered strength behind her. Ahmad and Eleanor joined hands and power and poured their magic into her. The Seal began to sing.

The Ark sang the descant. When their notes met, the power would be complete.

The clangor of weapons jarred them into discord. Sioned held to the harmony, though it tore deep at the roots of her magic. She could feel Ahmad within her, and Eleanor with breathtaking strength.

She pressed harder. The wall began to crack.

Power roared up from below, power of moon and tides—power of the women of the Tiresi. Their men were but fireflies. These were the living stars.

The Seal strained. The Ark cried like a woman. The men fought with renewed vigor.

Mustafa left magic to mages. He was there to be strong if they needed strength, and to see what he could see. Sight was his gift.

He was aware of the battle that raged in more worlds than the one he lived in. Much of it surpassed mortal understanding. To the eyes of the body, they burst out of air into the chamber of the Ark, face to face with a wall of blue-and-silver shields. The room was far larger than he remembered, as wide as a battlefield, and the army of jinn fought the army of the Tiresi across the breadth of it. Behind the jinn, the queen and the sultan and the lady from Gwynedd wielded weapons of magic, battering against the Ark's protections.

The spirits of fire were stronger fighters than he could hope to be. He slipped away from the mages, loosening his sword in its sheath and resting his hand on the hilt, but forbearing to draw it. The light was strange here: sudden flashes like lightning, then sudden dimness, with crowding shadows. The shadows concealed him. He made himself part of them.

The Tiresi were as like to one another as mortals could be: a thousand men equally tall, equally broad, with the same swift strength and light grace, and the same dark eyes between helmet and shield. And yet Mustafa knew which of them was Giuliano. It was a surety of the heart, a calling of body and spirit to the one of them all who belonged to him.

Giuliano was fighting only to defend himself. His strokes were swift and sure, but he was not striking to wound.

His heart was not in it. Mustafa was not going to exult, not yet, but he measured distances and considered possibilities. After a while he saw his opening.

The battle had a pattern to it of eddies and swirls. Some-

times Giuliano was hard beset; others, he could pause, lower
his sword, rest with his brothers while the fight raged elsewhere. Mustafa could not see that either side was gaining the
advantage. They seemed perfectly matched.

During a lull, he slipped through shadows until he was
within reach of Giuliano. He knew nothing better to do than
will Giuliano to see him.

At first he was sure that he had failed. Just as he moved to
show himself, Giuliano drew a shadow to him and made himself a part of it. Behind him, the gap closed of itself. None of
his brothers seemed to notice that he was gone.

Mustafa never saw the attack until he was flat against the
wall with Giuliano's hand locked over his throat. He could
breathe, just. Giuliano's face in the helmet was stark white, his
eyes blazing.

Mustafa did not beg for mercy. He waited for Giuliano to
tire of grinding his teeth and, Allah willing, come somewhat
to his senses.

It seemed an endless time before the iron fingers slack-
ened. Giuliano sagged. Mustafa caught him before he sank to
his knees. "Damn you," he said. "Damn you to your own
hell."

Mustafa held his tongue. This was Giuliano's fight, as desperate as any in that place. He could feel the battle hanging
on it, balanced on the point of one man's choice. Any word
Mustafa spoke, any move he made, could shift that balance
against him.

Giuliano's weight grew too great for Mustafa to sustain.
He let it sink down slowly. Giuliano was weeping in silence.

Suddenly he gripped Mustafa's wrists. Mustafa set his
teeth as bone ground on bone.

"You never scream," said Giuliano. "Do you? Not for anything. Or anyone."

"It's a flaw in my character," Mustafa said, rather lightly in the circumstances.

"Tell me what to do," Giuliano said. "Tell me how to do this. You did it. You left everything—your whole world. You betrayed your faith, your god, your holy war—and all for love."

"In the end I betrayed nothing," said Mustafa.

"Will I do that? Can I? All that I was born for, I look at it and I see : . . I see that I cannot. I was born to guard, but against what? I can't guard against you. It isn't in me."

"You can save Jerusalem," Mustafa said. "You can do that."

"I can—" Giuliano caught his breath. "I want to save Jerusalem."

Mustafa was silent.

At last Giuliano let go Mustafa's wrists, lurching to his feet with none of his accustomed grace. "Help me," he said.

Mustafa clasped his hand, strong but not strong enough for pain. A shudder ran through him. He turned, with Mustafa still gripping his hand, and let his shield slip to the floor. The power was rising in him. It was born of the Ark, fed by it. Mustafa saw how he lived in a net of wards and discipline, woven to contain a magic so strong, so beautiful and so terrible, that mortal flesh would char to ash if it were set free.

One by one he let go the wards. Mustafa's heart constricted. This was deadly dangerous to soul as well as body— and he was caught in it. He was part of it. Giuliano was wielding him, using his peculiar power or lack thereof, to protect himself and to arm them both against the Tiresi.

It was as beautiful as it was ruthless. Mustafa felt power drawn out of him that he had never known he had, and workings made of it that he could never have wrought for himself.

This was the other half of his power. This was the part of him that had been lacking.

One man could not overcome a thousand by brute force. But as any footpad knew, it was not strength that mattered; it was knowing where to strike, and how to thrust the blade home. Giuliano found the center of the magic that warded this place. Mustafa was the dagger that slipped beneath the breastbone and pierced the beating heart.

Sioned felt the stroke, knew the moment when the wards began to fall. She raised the power of the Seal and struck with all her force.

Power called to power. The Ark cried out to its child. The Seal shattered the wavering wards and bound itself to the thing from which it was made.

But the Tiresi were no weaklings, and their magic was ancient and strong. They called up power from the earth below, from the deep roots of creation. The Ark began to hum a sweet, deadly song. It was drawing power to itself—all power. When it had filled itself, it would erupt in a blast of pure and killing magic, the fire from heaven of the old scriptures.

They would all die. The invaders, the defenders—every one. The Ark itself would burst asunder. What the loosing of so much magic would do in a place of so much power . . .

Sioned struggled against the whirlwind. The gate was opening as she had intended, the window upon Jerusalem: the Ark's native earth calling it home. Ahmad's strength bolstered her, then another, new and strange and quite wonderful, which seemed to be Mustafa, but was something greater than he had ever been. Yet even that was not enough. She was losing ground. The earth of Rome was sucking her down.

"Go." Eleanor's voice was calm and clear, as if she spoke in perfect silence. "Go on. Leave this to me."

"You'll die," Sioned said equally clearly. "You can't—"

"Go while you can," Eleanor said, as dispassionate as ever. "Don't make me die for nothing."

"You are not going to—"

"Go!" The word was a spell, driving Sioned away from the queen, toward the gate and Jerusalem. The Ark, the Seal, her allies, were all bound together, all flung with sudden, blinding force, through the gate and away.

CHAPTER THIRTY-THREE

The silence was immense. The gate was shut. Eleanor was gone—body and soul—in the freeing of the Ark and the closing of the gate.

Sioned surprised herself with grief. She had hated that terrible woman her life long, but Eleanor had offered a sacrifice of rare and splendid courage.

Slowly Sioned called her senses to order. It was dark. She sneezed at the scent of dust and old stone. Wherever she was, she was below the earth, in a chamber that had been closed, from the feel and smell of it, at least since the Ark was lost.

Close by her, someone stirred and groaned. She risked a spark of magelight.

Ahmad blinked at her, still half unconscious. Mustafa was crouched beyond him, bent over a figure in blue-and-silver armor.

Something loomed over them all. The oblong shape in its

heavy veil of silk had gone quiescent, but once she was aware of it, she sensed the depth of its power.

Wherever they were—and she could devoutly hope they were in Jerusalem—the Ark had come with them.

She staggered to her feet, then reached down and pulled Ahmad up with her. The knight of the Tiresi was coming to his senses. Sioned knew an instant of blind panic. The enemy had followed them—the battle would go on—they had won nothing but a moment's respite.

Her wits recovered soon enough. She saw how they were, he and Mustafa. This was the mage who had broken the shield-wall—and there could be little doubt as to why he had done it. They all owed him their lives and souls, and their magic, too.

He pulled off his helmet and let it fall. He was as pale as they all must be, but his eyes were clear. He kindled his own spark of light and let it grow until it encompassed the shape of the chamber.

It was remarkably similar to the one they had lately left: low arch of vaulting, stone pillars. It was much older than the other, and much plainer. The lines of magic that ran through it were altogether different from those of Rome.

"Jerusalem," Giuliano said as if he could read her thought. It was a long sigh, half sad, half exultant. "We did it. We won the battle."

"So we did," Ahmad said. "It seems we've found our way to the foundations of the Temple. If that's so, then the Dome of the Rock is over us. We have but to find a passage that leads us up and out."

"And leave this thing here?" Sioned did not like to say it, but it had to be said.

"It will be safe."

The voice was like the deep chord of an organ. The prince of jinn stood where a moment before had been nothing but shadow. He bowed low, even to the paving. She could sense his satisfaction. He had fought well, he and his people.

"We will guard it," he said. "No power of heaven or earth will touch it."

"We owe you a great debt," she said, and she spoke from the heart.

"Pure spirit," said the jinni, "you are all our recompense. This is our pleasure."

She bowed in her turn, as low as he would allow. As she straightened, fantastic shapes appeared out of air. The jinni's kin had come. Some were limping, some bleeding thin trails of fire, but they had all come back alive from Rome.

That road was shut and barred. Sioned could not even sense the gate. Eleanor had closed it with her death. There would be no returning by that way.

Ahmad was circling the room, keen as a hound on a scent. "The wards," he said. "They came with us. Between Rome and this place, we rent the fabric of creation—there can't have been a mage alive who didn't sense us. But we're hidden here. I don't think . . ."

"It's the old spell," Giuliano said. "When my ancestors took the Ark away, they blurred understanding and concealed power. Any who hunted, hunted far afield. It's quite likely whoever goes looking will look in Damascus. Or," he said with a flicker of wickedness, "Masyaf."

"Masyaf?" Ahmad laughed, less for mirth than for release of tension. "Was that your inspiration?"

Giuliano shrugged. "Maybe Mustafa's. The enemy will be hunting ghosts and shadows in his own castle."

"That won't hold him long," Sioned said. "He's no fool. He'll recognize the ruse, and know where we must be."

"Then we'd best move fast," Ahmad said, "before the enemy's wrath descends upon us all."

Sioned glanced at the jinni. He inclined his head. She nodded briskly and turned until her bones told her there was a door. It opened; it was not overly willing, but her magic was stronger than its weight of age and rust and settled stone. With the others behind her, she left the sphere of the wards and entered the Jerusalem that she knew.

Judah's house was quiet. It was early morning; the servants were up, the day's bread baked and cooling on the hearth. Rebecca came out of the kitchen as Sioned and the others were let into the house, brushing flour from her hands and greeting them with such quiet joy that Sioned's eyes pricked with tears.

"So," she said. "That was you, in the night."

Sioned nodded. "How obvious was it?"

"A bit like a splitting headache," said Rebecca, "and somewhat like a dream that slips from the memory."

She drew Sioned into a quick but heartfelt embrace, then Ahmad and Mustafa, and after a measuring pause, a rather flustered Giuliano. That boy had a proper awe of women.

"Come now," said Rebecca. "Time is short, yes? But you look as if you need rest, and surely you must be starving. While you eat, I'll send for Daniel."

"Judah's not here?" asked Sioned.

"He went with the king," Rebecca said. "Daniel will tell you everything. Come."

Daniel found them somewhat after they had taken the edge off a sudden and ravenous hunger. He was fully dressed and all in order, and looked as if he had had no more sleep than they had. He greeted them with the same restraint Rebecca had shown, and the same deep relief. "God be thanked," he said, "that you are safe. And . . . it?"

"You can't feel it?" Sioned asked.

"I feel . . ." Daniel's eyes narrowed. He had gone within as a mage could, delving deep. She knew when he found it: the look of incredulous joy was unmistakable. "It is here. And yet I hardly knew—I thought I dreamed—what—"

"Wards and protections," she said.

"They won't last long," said Ahmad. "The enemy knows we've wrought a great working, though he may not know yet what exactly we've done. He'll press the attack as soon as he can." He met Daniel's stare. "Tell us what we need to know."

"I had word from Judah last night," Daniel said. "The army is in Damascus. There was a battle, which Richard won, with the sultan's help. They believe now that the siege of Krak is a ruse—that the enemy will pass by all other targets and attack Jerusalem. And," he said, "Benjamin has been found."

Sioned's heart stopped. "Benjamin— Teleri?"

"Only Benjamin," Daniel said with honest regret. "That was all that was in the message: that he had come back."

"It is something," she said as strongly as she could. "Can you call your people together and tell them the time has come? I have another errand. Who is in command of the city in my brother's absence?"

"The Patriarch, lady," said Daniel.

She nodded. "Good. I'll speak to him."

"You trust him?"

"He may be a Christian priest," she said, "but he's a good man, and loyal to the king. He will help us."

"Let us hope so," said Daniel. Then after a moment: "Do you think we might see it?"

"Soon," she said. "First, we need a plan. The enemy will come here. With Judah gone, and Richard, we're not at full strength. We must be as strong as we can be before the attack begins."

She left them to settle matters of the city's magical defense, and set out for the Patriarch's house. Mustafa followed her with the young Roman. It might have been wiser if they had stayed for the council of mages, but she was not inclined to stop them. She was glad to have them at her back, even in her own city.

It had not changed since she walked there last, not to the eye of the body. But to the eye of the spirit, something had shifted deep in the heart of it. The Ark, even shielded, altered the magic of Jerusalem. All that it had been for twice a thousand years was focused and centered in the great work of power. As deep as it had been rooted for so long, now it ran to the core of the earth.

Something was waking. It was slow and barely to be sensed, and yet it was there. As she walked, she felt the strangeness.

She struggled to focus herself. There would be time later for magical battles. For this one hour, she had a quite earthly one to face. In spite of what she had said to Daniel, she was not at all certain that Hubert Walter would agree to fight in this particular way or with these particular allies.

Her time in Rome had made her as skittish as a whipped pup. She stiffened her spine and willed herself to remember who she was and what power she had. This was her city, the home of her heart, as was no other city in the world.

The Patriarch of Jerusalem, unlike the Pope of Rome, threw up no walls against Sioned's coming. His clerks knew her; his privy secretary came to her often for this ailment or that. They greeted Mustafa with respect and often liking, and eyed his somewhat wayworn but still resplendent companion with appreciation.

Gerard the secretary was delighted to see her. "Lady! I missed you in the hospital a day or two ago. See, I have a canker, it troubles me sorely, if you might offer some small assistance . . ."

"If you will send a clerk for my medicines, which are in the hospital—ask for Lucas; he knows where they are—then I will see what I can do," Sioned said. "In the meantime, would you be so kind as to tell the lord Patriarch that I've come? If he can speak with me soon, that would be well."

"Of course," said Gerard. "Of course, lady. Here, sit. I'll be back directly."

They sat where he directed, on stools and a bench in his workroom, amid a pleasant clutter of books and parchments. Sioned did not expect the wait to be long, but even that was long enough for her to slide perilously close to sleep. Mustafa had given up even trying to fight it. He propped himself in a corner, closed his eyes, and let nature take its course.

Giuliano, like Sioned, struggled to stay awake. He was wide-eyed at everything he had seen, from the lower reaches of the old Temple and the passage that led to a hidden postern near the Wailing Wall, to the ways of the city that they had crossed and crossed again, first to Judah's house, then to the palace of the Patriarch. She had barely noticed the sights, but he had drunk them in with a pilgrim's zeal.

He prowled the room as they waited. Odo the clerk had brought wine and sugared almonds, for which Sioned had no appetite, but Giuliano being a young thing was glad to have them. He drank half a cup of wine and ate the bowl of almonds, and was licking his fingers when Gerard came bustling back.

"Lady!" said the Patriarch's secretary. "Lady, my lord begs your pardon for the length of the delay. He'll see you now."

Sioned bit back a smile. After days of cooling her heels in the Pope's anterooms, she could hardly begrudge an hour here—with food and wine, no less, and a warm welcome.

Mustafa had roused swiftly and completely, and was on his feet. The three of them followed Gerard down a passage to the Patriarch's own workroom.

It was a mark of their importance that he did not receive them in his solar, surrounded by guards and clerks and secretaries. He was alone in a room even smaller and more cluttered than the one they had left, dressed in a monk's habit, with his tonsured head bare, and no ornament but the ruby on his finger.

Sioned did not kiss that, although Giuliano did. Hubert Walter raised a brow at him.

"Giuliano Tiresi," Sioned said, "a knight of Rome and a faithful ally of the Kingdom of Jerusalem."

"You are most welcome in our city," Hubert Walter said.

Giuliano bowed, too awed or too polite to speak. The Patriarch blessed him, but turned then to Sioned.

"We have it," she said before he could ask. "It's hidden for the moment. The sons of Levi will be tending it, once we've all settled on a plan of battle. The enemy can't but know we've raised something powerful. He'll be here within days, if not hours."

"Even through all the kingdom's defenses?" Hubert Walter asked.

"No mortal walls or armies can stop this," said Sioned. "He'll come here and he'll come fast. We can take measures to slow him, but we don't want to stop him. We've chosen the battlefield. He'll come to it, and us."

The Patriarch nodded. There was no resentment, no anger that she could see. "That's reasonable enough. What of the king? Is he safely out of the way, or do we need him here?"

"We'll get him here if we can," she said. "I came to be sure that you are with us. We will not be giving the Ark to the Church, my lord. It's going into the hands of those whose forefathers made it. That was the bargain, and that is the wisest course. Their power is woven with the power of the Ark, and their arts are shaped by and for it."

"That too is reasonable," Hubert Walter said. He frowned slightly. "You expected me to argue otherwise?"

"Your Holy Father did," said Sioned, "vehemently. It seems he found it unbearable and unconscionable that we should entrust this thing to the murderers of Christ."

Hubert Walter nodded slowly. "Ah," he said. "I see." He sighed. "That is a great man, a devoted servant of God. He loves the Church as a son loves his mother, with a fierce intensity. Too fierce perhaps in this world we live in. He knows Rome and Italy, the rest to him are dreams and stories. Jews, Muslims, unbelievers of any and all faiths, are not real to him; he knows nothing of them."

"He hates them," Sioned said flatly. "My lord, there is something else you should know. The Queen of the English came to help us. She won through to the Pope and spoke to him of our need and urgency. He refused even her, because the compact requires that the Jews take the Ark for themselves. We did not part amicably. There will be a price, my lord, and perhaps a high one, if we win this war."

"So I see," said the Patriarch. "Where is the queen? Has she come here? Or has she remained in Rome? Will she return to England?"

"The queen is dead," Sioned said. She knew no better way to say it.

Hubert Walter's breath hissed. He crossed himself. "Dear God in heaven. Does the king know?"

"Not yet," Sioned said. "She's not been dead a day. She

died for the Ark, to free it from its guardians in Rome. If we win the war, it will be because of her."

The Patriarch bowed his head in a murmur of Latin. It was a prayer for a soul that, Sioned had reason to suspect, was nowhere in the vicinity of the Christian heaven.

"My lord," Sioned said with the hint of a snap. It brought his head up and focused his eyes on her. "This venture will probably be excoriated in Rome, once the Pope hears of it. Are you still willing to be a part of it?"

"My lady," said the Patriarch, "as a good Christian of the West, I should acknowledge the supremacy of the Bishop of Rome. As Patriarch of Jerusalem, I reflect that in the east he is regarded as *primus inter pares*—first among equals. He may ask a thing of me, but he may not command it. I live in this city; the safety of its souls is entrusted to me. Whatever I can do to protect them, I will do."

"Even if you must ally yourself with Jews?"

"Even then," said the Patriarch. His voice was steady. She had to trust that he was telling the truth.

CHAPTER THIRTY-FOUR

Berengaria started out of a fitful sleep. Her imp of a servant had found her a place to lodge in Damascus, a house for noble travelers, in which she could have a room to herself.

She had taken advantage of the sudden comfort after so many days on the road and let go for a night her spying and watching. Richard would not leave that night or the day after. A battle, even a victory, needed time to recover. Nor did she expect to be troubled by the dark one for a while. He would be thoroughly preoccupied with the consequences of his defeat.

She had had a bath in the Muslim manner, and a dinner that had tempted her appetite for the first time in days—and better yet, it had stayed down once she ate it. She should have slept deeply and well, but once she had lain down, her contentment unraveled. Her sleep was restless, full of strange dreams and half-formed visions. The peace she had looked for was nowhere to be found. In its place was a gnawing unease.

She woke abruptly with a sense that the earth had shifted. Something weighty, something terrible, had come. She cast about for it blindly, hardly knowing she did it.

"Jerusalem." She sat bolt upright. "It's in Jerusalem."

With it were the two whom the Old Man had been seeking so desperately. The sultan and the Welsh witch had come back from wherever they had been. She could feel them like twin cankers in her spirit.

She did not waste time in calling for her servant. She gathered her belongings into some sort of order and summoned the innkeeper.

He was an old man; he had seen all the whims and follies that a traveler could succumb to. It was hardly worth a raised brow that the utterly ordinary woman in the dark mantle insisted on riding out alone in the dark before dawn.

The Old Man found her at midmorning. Damascus was still in clear sight, an oasis of jeweled green under the teeth of mountains. She had paused to rest and to water her horse at a travelers' well beside the road. Riding was still an unpleasant ordeal; riding at speed was somewhat beyond her, even without the heat of the Syrian desert in midsummer. She was regretting the impulse that had sent her out of Damascus in the morning; she would have done better to wait until the cool of evening.

She sat on the well's rim in the shade of a tree that had been planted there long ago and was now wide and tall. A faint wind played among its dusty leaves. She sipped water from her cup and closed her eyes. She would have to mount again soon. It would be days at this pace before she reached Jerusalem, and the urgency in her was rising.

A blast of wind flung her to the ground. She lay gasping for air, caught in sudden darkness. The wave of wrath broke over her.

She held on grimly until it passed, then counted a hundred breaths before she ventured to lift her head.

The dark one had made himself part of the tree, or else the tree had swallowed him. He shifted within the confines of trunk and branches, roiling with rage. "You! You have failed me."

Berengaria had gone rigid with fear. There was death here, of the soul as well as the body.

She was a king's daughter and a king's wife. This thing had bound himself to her as a servant. She stood erect, although the force of his anger rocked her. "In what way have I failed? I've found the king's sister for you. She's in Jerusalem."

The dark one hissed like a snake. "She was not in Jerusalem yesterday. Where was she then? What was she doing? What has she brought that shakes the earth with such power? Can you tell me that?"

"Not today," said Berengaria, "but when I come to the city, I can and will."

"When you come to the city? How long have you been dallying about on this road? The war will be over before you pass Nablus."

"Not if you assist me," she said levelly. "If you need me there sooner, take me there."

The dark one was coming to his senses. She regretted that a little. If he had killed her, she would have been free of him and his ever-increasing demands. He growled, a deep rumble in her bones, but he said reasonably enough, "I cannot take you into the city. It is barred to me. I must leave you outside the walls."

"I believe I can pass the gate," she said dryly.

"See that you do," the dark one said, "and see that you open the way for me from within."

She set her lips together. The dark one did not see, or else chose not to trouble himself. He knew as well as she that she had no strength to fight him. She was an apprentice; he was a master. If she would not consent freely to do what he asked, he would compel her.

She had fallen into an ancient trap: the demon that began as a servant had became the master. But she was not a complete fool, or completely without resources, either.

For the moment she kept silent, made no promises she could not keep, and let him think she had yielded to his will.

"Throw yourself into the well," the dark one said.

She stared at him. "What?"

"That is the gate," he said.

Her eyes narrowed. "Indeed? And what of the horse?"

"Leave it," he said.

She shrugged. If he lied, and she drowned, what did it matter? She would be free.

She took a moment to take off the horse's bridle and saddle. The beast trotted off a few steps and stopped, nosing about for such bits of forage as it could find. It would have a new master by nightfall, she was sure.

She left most of her belongings with the saddle, only taking the water bottle and a bag filled with the necessities of her magic. The dark one was waiting in sorely strained patience. She walked toward the well and knelt on the rim. She could see the gleam of water far below. A breath of earthy coolness wafted over her face. She shut her eyes and let herself fall.

Teleri was not going to last much longer. She had kept the Old Man from noticing that Benjamin was gone, with bits of spells and workings, but sooner or later he would look aside from his own troubles for long enough to see that she had been deceiving him.

The voices were back, pushing harder than ever. Without Benjamin to help her focus, she found it harder and harder to shut them out. The Old Man wanted her—needed her. He was going to take her soon, strip her power and enslave her will, unless she did something—anything—to stop him.

There was not much time. She had to open the gate again and try to work the spell as Benjamin had. If she failed, she might die—but that would be better than what the Old Man wanted for her.

Before she did it, she tried to rest. It was just for a little while, to be sure she was strong enough.

She fell deeper into sleep than she meant to. When the worlds shifted, she was almost too far down. She fought her way toward the light.

It was a long, long fight. Everything was shaking, as if something vast were rising up from below, thrusting aside earth and stone, crushing any bold or reckless spirit that tried to stop it. Teleri looked down into the abyss, and saw it coming up toward her.

Strangely, she was not afraid. It was a great, a terrible thing, but it had not come to harm her.

She thought fast. She could keep on struggling back to the garden, try to open the gate, and hope it opened and let her through before she was caught. Or she could let go and fall.

The vast thing was suddenly very close. She could almost see it. It was walled in wards and shields, protected more strongly than anything she had ever seen. What was inside . . .

Light. Pure light. So pure it was beyond human comprehension. Even magic could not grasp it.

It was a part of her somehow—as if her magic were related to it, or made in the same way. What she was as a mage, it was as a work of power. It rang on the same note, although hers was much, much smaller.

It swept on and upward, surging past her like some great beast swimming through the sea. She cast herself loose in its wake.

Berengaria stood on a narrow rocky track in the middle of a bleak and stony valley. She remembered vaguely how she had got there: darkness, deep water, the surety that she was drowning.

Her clothes and hair were dry. She sucked in a lungful of hot, dusty air.

She must be somewhere near Jerusalem—please God, no more than a day's walk, or two at the most. She could make her water last. She only needed to know in which direction to walk.

She turned slowly. Her mind was muddled, her magic confused, as if the greater part of it had lagged behind. She closed her eyes and took deep breaths. Little by little some of her focus came back.

She was closer to the city than she had thought. This was the valley of Gehenna: there was no mistaking the darkness that ran beneath, or the faint stink of old death that hung about it.

It was rough going, and slow. She picked her way down off the hill to an approximation of a road. Just when she was sure that she had somehow managed to take a wrong turning, she came round a jut of rock onto a much broader, better-traveled road. Under the dust and the wearing of years, she could see the remnants of Roman paving.

The shadows were lengthening. She could not walk any faster. If night caught her in this cursed valley, so be it.

She kept her head down, setting foot in front of foot. No pilgrims crowded here. No one walked in Gehenna if he could avoid it. All the seekers after sanctity were on the Mount of Olives or crowding the shrines of the city.

She would come there soon enough. Then it would all end, one way or another.

Teleri fell hard and rolled, fetching up against something large and shrouded in softness. The softness was silk. The thing it covered was the thing that had brought her here. She could feel the wards about it, but she had somehow got inside them. The thing they warded was thrumming with power. It made her think of lightning and the fierce heat of the sun, and something else. Something like . . . Benjamin?

By that, she knew what it was. After all her hunting, she had not found the Ark—the Ark had found her.

She opened her eyes. It made little difference. She was in the dark.

She made a light. It came up quickly, dazzling her. She damped it until her eyes could stand it. Then she could see the shape of the Ark in its shroud, and the room it was in, and the door that had been opened not long ago: the dust was scuffed away there.

It was very quiet: unnaturally so. There were protections, and protectors. The latter felt very familiar indeed. She would know the scent and sense of the jinn wherever she found herself; they were as much a part of her as her mother or father.

They could not see her within the wards. She had come through the Ark, not against it. Their vigilance was directed outward.

That could be a mistake. She would tell them later, after she had found her way out and discovered where she was.

If she had been a tracker like Mustafa, she would have known what those prints were that led from the Ark to the door and out into a crumbling passageway. She followed them because it seemed the best thing to do.

As soon as the door shut behind her, she knew she was in

Jerusalem. Her knees almost let go. She stiffened them and stumbled on. One more passage and a door and a stair, and then a very long passage, led her out into the brilliance of daylight and the clamor of the city. She could hear the pilgrims wailing at the wall of the old and fallen Temple.

Benjamin had been right after all. The Ark was in the Temple. And yet she knew it had not been there when they had that argument. It had been somewhere else. If she had been a Muslim like her father, she would have fallen down and given thanks to Allah.

She settled for a tear or two, which was pure indulgence, then a long and determined stride toward her own house.

CHAPTER THIRTY-FIVE

Richard was awake deep in the night, pondering alternatives in this cursed mess of a war, when he felt it. It was like a knife thrust in his belly and twisted. He groaned. "Mother!"

God knew where that came from. Before he could think too hard on it, the world changed. He had been drinking nothing stronger than ale, and yet all at once he felt as if he had downed a vat of strong wine: light-headed, dizzy, strangely exultant. He had been tired, frustrated, baffled by this war. Now that was gone. He looked down, somewhat surprised that he was not dressed in full armor, with a sword at his side and a lance near to hand.

He sprang up. Never mind the hour; he bellowed for squires, servants, and as many clerks as could be found outside of the army's camp.

They all came at the run, with what seemed to be half the inhabitants of the palace, and the sultan in their midst.

Richard disposed them rapidly. Only when they had run to do his bidding did he say to al-Afdal, "By your leave, of course."

"Of course," the sultan said with a crooked smile. "I take it you felt it, too?"

"God knows what I think of magic," Richard said, "and God knows I could be wrong, but I think our kinsfolk's hunt is over. They've found what they were looking for. And if you felt it, then I'll wager so did every waking soul from here to Baghdad."

"And, one would suppose, one lord of the undead."

"I can't imagine he missed this," said Richard. "I've got to get to Jerusalem. If you don't mind, I'll leave most of my army with Henry in command, and send them on to Krak. I'll take a small force and ride for Jerusalem."

"If I may suggest," said al-Afdal with eastern tact, "there is another way."

Richard's mind was blank. "What—"

"You have mages, as do I. Since all time for secrets is or soon will be past, let them raise a gate and send you through. Your whole army can go, and you can hope to reach the city before the enemy resorts to the same expedient."

"That's what it comes to, doesn't it?" Richard said. "I have to use the weapons he chooses—the ones I would never, of my own will, even think of touching."

"Isn't that always so in war?" said al-Afdal.

"After this," Richard said, "I'm going to pray for a common, ordinary, blood-and-guts war with a human enemy."

"Maybe you will get it," the sultan said. "Until then, allow me to offer you five thousand of my own troops, and myself in command of them. We will attend to Krak for you while you ride to Jerusalem."

"That is generous," said Richard.

"Certainly," the sultan said, "and expedient, too. Krak is

some fair distance closer to my city than to Jerusalem. I would rather have allies in it, even allies who are Christian, than the spawn of Iblis."

"I can see how that might occur to you," Richard said. "I'll take your offer, my brother, and be glad of it. But this gate spell—"

"How long will it take you to march to Jerusalem? A week? And that supposes the enemy doesn't raise any barriers to stop you. Even if you take your hundred men and ride at courier's pace, that's still days you can't spare—not against an enemy who can and will travel by the roads of sorcery."

"Damn you for making sense," Richard said. "Somehow I don't think the enemy is reckoning on our alliance holding as well as it does."

"And maybe it would not," said al-Afdal with a flash of teeth, "if he were not my father's murderer."

Richard grinned as ferally as he. "We'll sort it out after we're dead."

"You in your heaven with the sexless angels, I with my houris in Paradise."

"Ah," said Richard with a wave of the hand. "I'll be in hell with all the rest of the people who are worth talking to." He gathered his wits to face what he must face. "Well enough, then. I'll summon my sorcerers, if yours will help them."

"Most certainly," said al-Afdal.

Richard's army would follow him to hell if he asked them. This was as near as made no matter. He mustered them by torchlight, ordered them to break camp, and in the dark before dawn drew them up in ranks before the Jerusalem Gate. It had seemed most apt, and it did look toward the southward road.

The sultan's magicians had formed their own rank of

white turbans and, mostly, white beards. Richard's Jews could not come near their numbers, and most of them were still so young that their beards grew in patches. Still, they seemed amicable, and Richard thought he saw one of the grey wise men bow to Aaron in visible respect.

He had been given to understand that this was a working of great power and complexity—not a common or everyday bit of spellcasting at all. It needed every one of them, and all the powers they could call up. The sultan's mages would build and arm the catapult, as it were. Richard's Jews would aim and fire.

There was nothing much to see, not at first. Their voices rose and fell in a droning chant. Then slowly, seeming like a trick of the eyes until there could be no mistaking it, a mist of light rose up from the paving of the gate. It limned the pillars and poured over the arch, infusing them with a ghostly shimmer. The gate itself was dark, a black maw.

The chant quickened. The light grew brighter. Shapes grew visible through the gate: walls, roofs, a glimmer of golden dome.

The Dome of the Rock. They were looking on Jerusalem.

Richard braced for the moment when he could order the army to march. He saw how the image in the gate wavered, blurring as if a shadow had slid across it. The mages' chant lost its rhythm. One or two swayed, and one crumpled to the ground.

The rest stood fast. This was a battle, and they were the vanguard of his army.

The shadow pulsed within the gate. The chant rose suddenly, fierce as a war cry. The shadow writhed, coiling like a snake. It struck; the mages lashed it with their voices. Richard felt the struggle in his own body.

For a long while it poised, with neither side the stronger. Then all at once the shadow collapsed upon itself.

Now. Richard did not need Judah's signal to know that he had to move fast. He had an army to get through this gate before the enemy came back with reinforcements. He raised his arm and slashed it down.

Templars led the van as usual. They shied a little at the gate, but their horses walked calmly through. It looked as if they simply and truly rode through a gate; the eye did not record that in so doing, they traversed the length of Outremer.

His usual place was in the center. For this he took the rear, with the Hospitallers and a few stragglers from the baggage train.

Henry was standing with al-Afdal, watching them go. Richard had said his farewells before the gate was raised, but he turned back toward them. He had nothing to say that had not been said.

The sultan bowed in the eastern fashion. Henry saluted him. Richard could only think to say, "Stay alive, will you?"

"We'll do our best," said Henry. "Win the war for us, uncle."

"I'll be damned and in hell if I lose it," Richard said.

That struck him to sudden laughter—he did not know why; hysteria, maybe. He wheeled his golden charger about and aimed him toward the gate.

CHAPTER THIRTY-SIX

There was no one home.

Teleri could tell from the street that the house was empty. It was shuttered and its gate was barred. Even the servants were gone.

It did not matter just then. She knew where there was a gap in the garden wall, which she had made sure was never found or repaired. She was much larger now than she had been when it was her regular mode of escape, but she squeezed and scraped through.

The garden was deserted. The kitchen was shut down, but she found cheese and salt fish in the storeroom. She hated salt fish. She devoured it as if it had been the loveliest banquet in the world, because it was honest mortal food and not the magic-tainted dainties that she had eaten for too long.

Her room was as she had left it, and they had left her bed alone. She buried herself in blankets and cushions, set wards as she had learned to do when she was small, and let the world slip away.

Mustafa could not rest in Judah's house. It was too crowded, with so many guests, and now Sioned and Ahmad taking a room there rather than open up their own house. He found Giuliano willing to retreat as evening drew on, to go looking for a place that was both quiet and well guarded.

The cook did not at all mind filling a basket with food enough for a small army. Laden with this and with Giuliano trailing behind, Mustafa made his way to a certain refuge.

The gate yielded to the key that Sioned had given him. The house was shuttered and silent. And yet—

He never entered any walls without deep and inbred wariness. Here, he was glad of it. It was nothing so distinct as a scent, and the floors were not yet so dusty that they held a track. Nonetheless he knew there was someone in the house.

He motioned Giuliano to stay behind him, guarding his back. Giuliano did not argue. They moved softly through the house, keeping to shadows, listening before each turn and door.

There was someone in Teleri's room, drawn into a tight knot on the bed, breathing in gasps as if caught in a nightmare. Mustafa left Giuliano at the door and crossed the room on silent feet.

He stopped where he could see the invader clearly. He would know those tumbled blue-black curls anywhere, and that oval face with its fine-drawn mouth and determined chin.

He did not give way to joy. Not yet. There was magic on her, and some of it was as black as the Old Man's heart. Cords of it wrapped about her, not quite binding her, but certainly binding her dreams.

"Giuliano," he said so softly the air barely moved. "Do you remember the way back to Master Judah's house?"

Giuliano nodded.

"Go there. Fetch the sultan and his lady. Bring them as quickly and quietly as you can."

"Shall I ward you?" Giuliano asked, no louder than Mustafa.

Mustafa shook his head. "I'll be safe. Go. Quickly."

He had spoken bravely, but when Giuliano was gone, he felt very much alone. He found a shadow to hide himself in, and watched over Teleri. Her dream went on for a while, but she never woke. In time she went quiet. She was free of whatever had tormented her, he hoped. Then, Allah willing, help would come and she would be well.

Help was a very long time in coming. Night fell as Mustafa waited. He dozed, but stayed on watch. He knew under his skin when her sleep changed.

He had time to think before she was fully awake. He could hide in the shadows, or he could sit where she could see him, quiet, hands away from weapons, offering a familiar face for her to welcome or kill, as it pleased her.

In the event, she did neither. She was awake for some time before she opened her eyes. He felt her awareness on him. He could not tell what she was thinking or feeling—that much was hidden. He chose to stay quiet until she was ready to speak.

Her eyes opened, resting on his face. She did not believe what she saw, he thought. She reckoned him another dream, rather more pleasant than the last.

"I'm real," he said.

She frowned. "Mustafa. You look different. You look . . ."

"Tired?"

"You're shining," she said. "In the dark. When my eyes are shut, I can see you."

He did not know what to say to that.

She sat up. The darkness was trying to bind her more tightly: undulating like the arms of a sea creature, grasping and slipping free, then grasping again.

Mustafa drew a knife from his boot. It was one he used seldom: it was small and very narrow, more a fang than a blade, and the steel was edged with silver. There were words of warding incised on the blade, and the hilt was the face of a jinni, an extravagance of horns and fangs and glaring eyes. He had seen the magic in it when he first found it in the bazaar in Acre.

He sprang suddenly and slashed. Teleri cried out—not loudly, but enough to bring down the fire from her mother, who stood in the door. Mustafa dropped and rolled. The bolt singed his sleeve, but did not blast him to ashes.

Teleri cried out again. "Don't! Mother, *don't*! He was helping me."

Sioned was shaking. Her face was flat white; her eyes were too terrible to meet. The lord Saphadin came round from behind her. He ignored Mustafa, strode to the bed and gathered his daughter in his arms.

She clung to him as if she would never let go. Very carefully Mustafa rose to his feet. Sioned had forgotten him. Her eyes and mind were fixed on her husband and her daughter.

Teleri lifted her head from her father's shoulder. "Mother," she said.

Walls cracked; strong defenses tumbled down. Tears ran down Sioned's face. But she still did not move from the door.

Ahmad let his daughter go. She ran to Sioned and clasped her tight. "Mother," she said. "Mother, I'm sorry."

"You have plenty to be sorry for," Sioned said. Her arms went around Teleri's body; she lowered her face into the tangled curls. "It doesn't matter. You came back. You're safe. I was so afraid . . ."

"So was I," Teleri said. She tilted her head back. She had grown: she was not so much smaller than Sioned. "Mother, he's hunting for you. He wants you dead and worse."

"I'm sure he does," Sioned said. She smoothed Teleri's hair and ran her hands along her daughter's shoulders and down her arms. There was love in it, but more than that: there was magic. The remnants of the bindings that Mustafa had cut shriveled and fell away.

Teleri breathed deep and stood a little straighter. Sioned kissed her forehead. "Can you forgive me?"

"For what?"

"For everything."

"I never hated you," Teleri said, "or blamed you. You know the Old Man—Owein—"

"I know," Sioned said very calmly. "He wants to destroy me from the heart outward. I won't let him do that. You're safe now. He'll never touch you again."

"I made a mistake," Teleri said. "I thought I could do a working and not pay the price for it. I didn't know he was going to come and take us. Benjamin—it wasn't his fault."

"We know that, too," said her father. "Benjamin is safe. He came to Damascus; he's with his father and Moishe and Aaron, and the king."

"And my cousins?"

"And your cousins, and especially the sultan."

"Good," she said. "I'm glad they'll fight together, even if it's hard."

"It's easy enough against this enemy," Ahmad said.

"He is a terrible thing," she said. "He's so strong and so absolutely evil. He loves nothing. He hates everything. He hates us worst of all. Because of us, he was taken from the light. Not that he ever wanted light, but life—he wants that more than anything in the world. He'll do anything to get it."

"You are safe," her father said firmly. "No dark thing will touch you again. I promise you."

Teleri said nothing, but Mustafa saw how her eyes lowered. She did not believe him. Nor for that matter did Mustafa. The darkness was groping after her already, distilling out of shadows. It wanted her; it would not stop until it had her.

He would do what he could to stop it. He moved, meaning to slip into shadow again and wait for them all to leave, but Sioned's eye was too quick. "Mustafa! Where are you going?"

He stopped with an inward sigh. "Nowhere, lady," he said.

"I want you to stay here," she said. "Stand guard."

"What, after you thought I was trying to kill her?"

"I wasn't thinking," Sioned said. "Now I am. She needs you."

"She does," he agreed.

"So stay."

"I had intended to," he said.

"I'm afraid," Teleri said.

Her father had had to go—there were things he had to see to, for defending the city. Her mother had left some time after him, for the same reason. They had both hated to do it, but Teleri herself told them to go. She understood how badly they were needed in this war.

Giuliano had stayed, curled up in a corner, seeming sound asleep. But his magic was awake, doubling Mustafa's guard.

Teleri had slept for a while, but Mustafa knew when she woke, just as she knew that he was watching her. "I'm scared," she said to him.

He sat at the foot of her bed, tucking up his feet. She

looked at him with shadowed eyes. "He didn't really let me go. The magic carried me away, but he has his hooks in me. He's here, whispering. He still wants me. He means to get me. And now I'm in Jerusalem, where he wants most to be."

"We'll do what we can."

"Yes, but will it be enough?"

"It will have to be."

"I'm glad you're here," she said.

"Do you know," said Mustafa, "so am I."

She smiled. She was quiet for a while, half-dreaming maybe. Then she said, "I like your friend."

"Do you? I'm glad."

"It's good to have a friend," she said, "especially one with that much magic."

"The magic isn't why I like him," said Mustafa.

"Oh, I know," she said. "He's the other half of you."

She always had been clear-sighted. He smiled and nodded.

There was another silence. Again, she was the one to break it. "You should sleep tonight. There's not going to be much sleep for anyone after this."

He raised a brow. "Foresight?"

"I just know."

"Then I'll sleep," he said.

CHAPTER THIRTY-SEVEN

When the gate opened between Damascus and Jerusalem, the mages in Jerusalem felt it in their bones.

Sioned was already on the walls, standing above David's Gate. She had had a more restful night than she expected, but a call like a trumpet had brought her out in the last of the darkness.

The dawn was just bright enough that she could see the road winding away through the barren hills. If her brother had truly been coming from Damascus, he would have come by way of Saint Stephen's Gate—but his mages had wrought otherwise. The hospice there and the Pool of the Hospital raised too many obstacles to the pursuit of a battle. The way was clearer here, the road wider, and the field more inviting.

Richard's army rode out of air. She heard the commotion below: voices shouting, arms clashing. The lepers and beggars who scraped what living they could in the heaps of rubble and scattered stone along the wall toward the lepers' hospital were fleeing into such hiding as they could find. David's Gate was opening, rumbling under her feet. She wanted to shout at the garrison, to bid them wait, but it was too late for that.

A handful of Judah's kinsmen had come up along the walls, ready with wards and protections. They could see what she saw. The hills were overlaid with a darkness that had little to do with the remnants of night. The earth was shuddering in its sleep.

The army came on at the fastest pace the footsoldiers could manage. Mounted knights rode up and down the column. Turcopoles in their light eastern armor on their light eastern horses spread as wide as the land allowed, bows strung and arrows nocked.

There were no mages in the van or the center. All their protections were mortal: bow and sword and spear. Sioned cursed Richard under her breath.

The earth heaved. Men boiled up out of it, swarming like ants.

Richard's army barely slowed its advance. Trumpets rang; drums beat a swift rhythm. The knights of the Temple drew together into the terrible wall of the Frankish charge.

There were frighteningly few of them. Far too many who should have been mounted were marching on foot. Twice, three times the number should have massed to the charge. The enemy's diversion had succeeded too well already, if it had cost so many of the destriers.

There were enough to break the line of the enemy, which was still somewhat in disarray. The mounted archers and the infantry behind them widened the wedge that the knights had cloven.

Still the army streamed out of air. They must be close to

the rear now. The press of the enemy grew ever greater. The advance had begun to falter.

Sioned glanced at the mage who happened to be nearest. It was one of the young cousins from England. He never had reconciled himself to alliance with Gentiles, but his magic was strong and he had a quick eye. He nodded.

Sioned reached into the power of Jerusalem. She had done that often before—to make, to heal, to advance her studies. But not since she came back. Not since the Ark had returned to the city's heart. And not since she had had the power to reach through the Seal.

The power rose so swift, so strong, that her body nearly went up like a torch.

She cast it as far and as hard as she could. A bolt of white fire leaped from her uplifted hand. A moment later, lightning fell again; then again, as mage after mage clove a path for the army.

It was a kind of madness. She was an instrument, a vessel for the power.

She caught herself with an effort that made her gasp. The Ark was wielding them all—aiding them, defending the city, yet they had little part in it.

This was dangerous. The Seal pressed on her, willing her to give herself to it again, to blast the enemy. She flung up every wall and shield that was in her.

The army had reached the gate. The rearguard fought off waves of assault much weakened by the mages' defense but still relentless. Sioned saw Richard on his gleaming stallion, in the thick of it as always.

She went down off the wall. She was not running away; she had no need for that guilt. She had a purpose, and it was pressing.

*   *   *

Well before the armies appeared out of air, all of the mages in Jerusalem who had not gone to stand vigil at David's Gate had followed Ahmad through the hidden door near the Wailing Wall, and made their way to the chamber in which the Ark was waiting.

When Sioned came into the hall, the Ark was still veiled. The mages stood together in front of it, apparently oblivious to it. There were more than she had reckoned: a good score of them.

They were arguing—Daniel against another of the cousins from York. Daniel expected the Ark to remain where it was, since it had chosen to be there. Gideon wanted to lift it up out of the earth.

"If we take it out of this room," Daniel said, "the Templars will know, and we'll have a new squabble on our hands. We can't afford that."

"We can't afford to lose even a fraction of its power," Gideon shot back. "If we raise it up into the Temple, under the dome, it will be stronger than ever."

"Stronger than we can ever hope to control. That's the Dome of the Rock you're speaking of. There is already so much power there that it befuddles the spirit."

"All of us together," said Gideon, "can control it—and use it. Do you want to lose this war because you wouldn't take one last and necessary risk?"

"It is not necessary," Daniel said. "It's foolhardy in the extreme. We cannot—"

Ahmad raised his voice above the babble of contention. His patience showed no sign of strain, but Sioned could see the glitter in his eyes. "Sirs," he said. Then, slightly louder: "Sirs! If you please. Time is passing."

"Faster than you know," said Sioned.

Some of them started like deer. Ahmad had been aware of

her, as had Daniel, but most of the rest had been intent on the quarrel.

"The siege has begun," she said. "By now the king is in the city. If we don't raise this power soon, while the enemy is still settling himself, we may not raise it at all."

"Then we need to take it to the Dome," Gideon said, "and we need to do it now."

"The Ark stays here." That was the second shock: a new voice altogether, sharp with command.

Teleri had not come in by the passage, or by any door that Sioned knew of. She was simply there, on the other side of the Ark, with Mustafa and Giuliano behind her.

"This is where it needs to be until it goes out to battle," she said. "If you try to move it, it will object."

"Teleri," Sioned began. "You shouldn't be—"

"Mother," said Teleri, as apologetic as she could be when she was glaring at the knot of squabbling mages. "It called me. I had to come. It needs to be woken up now. It doesn't care who does it or how many they are, but if they don't stop fighting, it's going to blast them.

"And that's another thing," she said. "You're not remembering your scripture. The Ark in the open air, with the sun on it, is a weapon so powerful it kills its own priests. You don't want it to see the sun—or the light of day—until you're ready to unleash it against the enemy."

"It's not *my* scripture," Sioned started to say, but Teleri was not speaking to her, not any longer.

"It stays here," Daniel said. He leveled a glare at Gideon. "Will you consent to that?"

Gideon glared back, but he said, "Do I have a choice?"

"No," said Teleri.

Giuliano moved from behind her. Yesterday he had borrowed clothes from Judah's sons, but today he was in armor again, blue and silver. He had struck Sioned as being very young, still in greater part a boy, with a boy's enthusiasms and callow charm. In armor, before the Ark, he was both knight and mage, bred and trained for this charge.

He bowed before the shrouded shape, hands together as if in prayer. It was a Great Ward, a spell of guard and of restraint. Such a working should have needed a circle of mages, but it was bred in his bones.

"Cover your eyes," he said.

Sioned for one was not going to argue with that cool, dispassionate voice. She drew her veil over her face. Mustafa had raised the round horseman's shield that had been slung behind him. Teleri had a disk of dark crystal that Sioned recognized: it came from Ahmad's magical storeroom. As to how and when the little witch had discovered the key to that . . .

Sioned would settle it later. Giuliano set hand to the shroud of silk. His eyes were not covered. He drew away the silk.

Sioned turned away quickly. She was almost not quick enough. The blaze of light came near to blinding her, even in the heavy veil.

"Now," said Giuliano, "it's safe."

She turned back, blinking. There was still light, but no brighter than a bright morning in the desert. The Ark stood unveiled.

It was as the old priests had described it: a chest of acacia wood, sheathed inside and out with gold, suspended by rings from gold-sheathed poles. Its lid was pure gold surmounted with cherubim, their wings upraised, their faces lowered as if in adoration.

Light glowed between those wings, a pulsing shimmer. Most of the mages had flung themselves flat. Some were praying, chanting in Hebrew.

Ahmad had sunk to one knee. His face was rapt. Maybe he heard the voice of his God, as the Israelites had been said to do. Sioned heard nothing but a ceaseless hum of magic.

There was a rhythm to it, a complex music. It made her think of the rhythms of magic, how a mage's power could express itself in a pattern of harmonies or discords. This was a great choir of voices. Every mage who had ever touched this thing, every force of magic that had ever used or been used by it, had left some of that magic in it.

It was seductive and very, very dangerous. But for the protections on it, it would have blasted them all.

Giuliano's presence was a stroke of pure good fortune—enough that Sioned could believe some god or power had chosen him. He knew the ways and the wards, and he was bred to withstand the full force of its strength. Without him they would have been in far worse straits.

Even with him, they were nearly overmatched. The Ark was straining to overcome the wards, to sink roots in the earth and send branches up to heaven. It would rule them if it could, if they had not been warded against it—as, even shrouded, it had captured the minds and power of the mages at the gate, and wielded them against the enemy without.

"Hold fast," Giuliano said softly. His voice echoed in Sioned's skull. The Ark's song was making her dizzy. "It's not time yet. When it is, we'll let go. But not yet."

"I have to go," Sioned said, too low for anyone else to hear.

She caught Ahmad's eye. It was glazed as hers must be, but he nodded, with a glance toward Teleri.

There was no shifting her. She was as much a part of this working as Giuliano. It rent Sioned's heart to see her, but it swelled her with pride, too. She was a mage among mages, as strong as any Sioned had seen.

She was safe from the dark one here, whatever the Ark might do to her. Its protections would protect her.

With that thought, her mother could muster the will to leave her. Sioned steeled herself to pass through the shields about the chamber, and to face a city that had awakened to discover it was at war.

CHAPTER THIRTY-EIGHT

The whole of Jerusalem was under siege—on every side, at every gate. The enemy were innumerable, swarming over the hills, pitching camp out of bow-shot and bringing up siege-engines that must have been made of air and ill will, for no one had seen them bring in those rams and ballistas and trebuchets.

The bombardment began near sunset. Most of it was stones and bits of rubble. Some, in a too-familiar cruelty, was less damaging but more difficult to bear: the heads of men killed in the march to the city.

Darkness only made it worse. Then the sorceries began: dark things battering against the city's magical defenses. There would be no getting out and no getting in, not with the enemy besetting them in every manner possible.

Richard had seen his army settled and fed in camps or barracks through the city: some in the Tower of David, a good number in the court of the Temple, and a scattering in the guardrooms of the gates. Those few who were left took sanctuary in pilgrims' hostels. He disposed them as much as he could by companies, so that when he called the muster, they would be ready to fight wherever he sent them.

He came late to the Tower of David and ate a hasty dinner in the midst of a war council. All of his commanders were there, with the lords and captains of the city, the Patriarch and the captain of his guard, and anyone else who might be of use. The Sultan of Egypt came in even later than Richard, and his wife later still.

The newcomers ate as Richard did: barely noticing what was set in front of them, but gaining strength from it.

"We can try to get word out to the castles," Richard said. "The enemy came here by sorcery—that means he didn't touch anything between here and Damascus. The beacons will still be intact. If my barons can get another army together, they can strike the enemy from behind."

"That supposes the enemy has directed all his strength at us," said Ahmad.

"You don't think he has? How many men are out there? Twenty thousand? Thirty? More? Where did he get them? Maybe he's stripped half the emirs of Persia and Syria of their armies—or maybe he's called them up out of hell. There's got to be an end to them. Even his power can't be infinite."

"I saw banners from Aleppo and Baghdad," Ahmad said, "from Persia and the cities of Rûm. He's cast his net wide. I doubt we've seen all of the fish he drew in."

"Still," said Richard, "if he's besieging Krak as well as Jerusalem, and harrying the army that's on its way to lift the siege, he'll not be troubling my castles overmuch. They'll be able to get an army through."

"Maybe," said Ahmad.

"Sire," said the commander of the city guard, "we can

withstand two years' siege—your foresight saw to that. That's enough time to bring a Crusade, if need be. The west will help us if it knows we're beset."

Sioned had her doubts of that. There was no Richard in the west now to raise the armies and put heart in them. Philip of France, that bloated old spider, had gone Crusading once and left in a state of pure pique, most of it directed at Richard. The Emperor of the Romans as he called himself, whose actual domain was a patchwork of German baronies, was no friend to Richard, either. As for England, with Eleanor gone, John would take the throne unless Richard returned in all haste. He was highly unlikely to come to his brother's aid. Spain, Sicily, the Italies—all in fragments, all preoccupied with their own troubles. The Pope himself would hardly wish to whip them into action, not after the audience he had had with Eleanor and her allies.

Richard was alone here, as far as the west went. Damascus was already giving him all the aid it could spare. Egypt would come if Ahmad called it. If there was time. If the message itself did not arrive too late. The rest of the east, and Byzantium with it, would be delighted to see the last of the infamous *Malik Ric.*

Richard knew all that—none better. It was his hatred of magic: he would not admit that if he was going to defeat this enemy, he would have to do it with other means than mortal steel. Steel would help—would at least put on a show of bravery—but magic would decide the war, one way or another.

Judah spoke Sioned's thoughts much more tactfully than she would have been able to. "My lord, it's well to take thought for all the possibilities of war. Here more than with any enemy you may have fought, the commander is the war. If he can be disposed of, his armies will sink back into the earth. They're nothing without his will to rule them. Once that is gone, so will they be."

"You mean they're not real?" Richard demanded.

"They're real enough," said Judah, "but their will is subject to his. Remove him and they become men again—confused, stumbling, with no memory of how they came here. There will be no army left."

"I hope I can believe you," said Richard. "God knows, the sooner he's back in the hell he came from, the happier the world will be."

"We'll set ourselves to do that," Judah said. He rose. "By your leave?"

"Go," Richard said.

Sioned followed Judah out of the hall. Ahmad stayed behind. There were still matters for him to consider; he had all the resources of Egypt to offer to his ally, if he chose—if there was time.

Judah did not glance at Sioned, but he slowed his stride slightly so that she could draw level with him. "You feel it," he said.

She nodded.

"We have to do it tonight," he said. "The enemy will block us if we wait longer. I don't think he knows for certain what we have yet—but he won't stop until he does."

"If I were an undead sorcerer," said Sioned, "I would have a traitor inside the enemy's camp."

"You think he has someone here?"

"When he was alive, if you were his enemy, you couldn't trust your own mother."

"Or daughter?"

Sioned's lips tightened. "Or son. We know what he's done to our children. They're under guard. No; there's someone else. I can feel him here, and I shouldn't, not with as many protections as we've laid on this place."

"We need you for the working," he said. "Maybe one of the boys—"

"We can't spare anyone tonight," she said. "It will have to wait."

He liked that as little as she did, but there was no choice. With the fall of night, the enemy's power grew stronger. They had to finish what they had begun in bringing the Ark back to Jerusalem.

The Ark was even stronger when Sioned came back to it than it had been when she left. She could feel the Seal about her neck, pulling her toward it.

The circle of mages had given up their squabbling and agreed to a truce. Teleri was sitting with apparent placidity, feet tucked up, hands on thighs, looking as if she had gone to sleep. Benjamin sat beside her.

Judah had not expected that: his breath hissed through his teeth. But he said nothing. He knew as Sioned did that their children were not theirs to command. The Old Man had left his mark on them. Their only hope of safety was here, in this thing that could as easily destroy as heal them.

The working was ready. It waited only for Judah, firstborn of the descendants of David and Solomon, and for the Seal, which was the key. Judah took his place in the circle. Sioned paused.

The Seal was pressing hard, gnawing at her will. She slapped it aside as if it had been an importunate dog, in a sudden burst of cleansing temper. She had had enough of waiting and suffering and allowing herself to be acted on. The Seal was made to bind the powers of the elements to its bearer's will. The Ark was made of earth and fire. For all its power, the Seal could bind it—if its bearer had sufficient courage, and great need.

Need she certainly had. She did not know if she had courage, but she was angry—that this war was necessary; that her child and Judah's child had been taken away and had come back marred, perhaps beyond healing. She wielded that anger. She focused it in the Seal and turned it on the Ark.

That great blazing thing gave way. She would not say it submitted, but it consented to obey her will. She raised its power over the city, and laid the traps that would spring when the enemy attacked.

One by one she laid them. If she faltered, the mages were ready, poised to act in her place. She could feel Judah's like a strong hand clasping hers. He had always been her friend, her teacher, her refuge when the world was too much with her. He was the rock of the Temple, and his kinsmen were the pillars that lifted it up to heaven.

Pillars indeed were lifting. The power was taking shape in walls of light. She looked up to a golden vault, and about her to a chamber transformed.

Most of her awareness was caught up in the working. A minute fraction observed that if indeed the First Temple had risen again on its ancient foundations, the Templum Domini and the Dome of the Rock must be gone—and two great faiths would be driven to blood-red madness by the loss of their shrines.

No; the Dome still stood, a jewel encased in gold. But the Temple had risen inside it and in its court, a structure of light and shadow, magic and living spirit. From it rose a new dome, a dome of light, englobing the city and defending it against the hail of sorceries that, even as it rose, began to fall.

CHAPTER THIRTY-NINE

Once the shields were raised and the Temple of light established, Giuliano and Mustafa could leave their charges to the sons of Levi and withdraw to rest and eat. Rebecca fed them in her kitchen, since they would not let her go to the trouble of setting a table for them. She would have offered them beds, too, but Sioned's house was far less crowded and much more quiet.

Mustafa would not ask for anything. They should both sleep while they could—any soldier knew the wisdom of that.

"Are you angry with me?" Giuliano asked.

They had walked from Judah's house in silence, which Mustafa had thought reasonable enough: they were both exhausted and had a great deal to ponder. Within the gate of Sioned's house, in the light of the lamp that was kept burning now that the master and mistress were home, Giuliano barred Mustafa's way. "Well? Have I done something to offend you?"

Mustafa stared blankly at him. "You? Offend me? I tempted you away from your family, turned you traitor, destroyed your life. You should be plotting to kill me."

"You did nothing without my full consent. I chose this. And so did the thing I was born to guard. It wanted me; it needed me. In the end it had very little to do with you."

Mustafa looked down abashed. Nonetheless he said, "You should hate me."

"Probably," Giuliano said. "I suppose it's my misfortune that I can't. I look around me and I know I chose rightly. I look at you and know . . . I can't hate you."

"You may die here. We've trapped ourselves. If our plan fails, we're rats in a cage. The enemy will destroy us at his leisure."

"Ah, but we will have lived. And I'll have seen Jerusalem."

Mustafa shook his head. "I think I've forgotten what it was to be young."

"I'll help you remember," said Giuliano.

That too was youth: to know nothing of weariness or the body's frailty. "Be gentle to this old man," Mustafa said, only half laughing.

Giuliano grinned. Completely without warning, he swung Mustafa up and over his shoulder and carried him off for unspeakable debaucheries.

Mustafa could have killed him: a blade in the back, his throat slit as he dropped Mustafa onto the bed in one of the guest-chambers. Mustafa had that power—and the choice to let it go. He let the tension pour out of him. This was healing, if he would accept it.

"You are a man of infinite talents," he said to Giuliano.

Infinite endurance, too, it would seem. Mustafa was not so old after all: he found his youth anew in those strong arms. It was better than sleep, and even better than magic.

*   *   *

Berengaria had come back to Jerusalem a night and a day before Richard returned to the city, slipping into her old place as easily as if she had never been gone. The thing that she had made in her image was still moving mutely about its daily round. As far as she could see, no one had noticed that the queen was a shape of earth and sorcery; that she never spoke, that the rhythms of her days never varied.

When Berengaria spoke the word to dissolve the spell, the image crumbled into dust. All that was left of it was a dark and lumpen thing like a spent coal, lying lonely on the floor.

She stooped and took it in her hand. It was heavier than it looked, and cold.

She realized with a shudder that it was the distillation of her heart. Her hand drew back to cast it away, but her magic warned her against such folly. With shaking hands she wrapped it in a bit of silk and slipped it into her bag of magics. It weighed heavy there, dragging her down.

So too did her position, the round of days that the image had pursued with blank persistence. There was a war outside these walls, but within them was nothing. A convent, with its endless prayers and daily offices, its work of the hands as well as the spirit, was less bleakly monotonous than this.

She could have left. For a few hours, the way was open. But when the great roaring fire of power came into the city, she was still there. She recognized Sioned within the power, like a single skein of thread woven into a king's mantle. Where Sioned was, was her husband, and others—powers greater and lesser, mortal and not, and one more dark than light, but of light there was enough. That one broke in the weaving, snapped asunder and flared into ash.

The Queen of the English was dead. Berengaria did not know what she felt when she realized that. Exultation—

maybe. Grief? Possibly. One could grieve for what one hated, because it was no longer there to hate.

If Eleanor was gone, then there was no Queen of the English now; only Berengaria. She pondered that as she pondered so much else, even as she began to understand what had come to Jerusalem.

They had found the Ark of the Jews. Did the dark one know? Had he suspected?

He was not going to learn it from Berengaria. Once it was in the city, the walls were up, the wards impenetrable. He was on the other side of them, and she was not minded to look for a gate. If he wanted one, he could open it himself.

Berengaria's journey had ruined her for confinement. She had learned that she could come and go, and no one would notice. That was a dangerous lesson, if she was to be a prisoner.

She had never prowled the city before, never gone anywhere without a large and cumbersome escort. She had seen David's Tower, the Holy Sepulcher, and the Dome of the Rock in its vast and heat-shimmering court. The rest of the city was lost in the curtains of a litter.

The day after she returned to Jerusalem, she went out in her worn and dusty traveling clothes. She was indistinguishable from a hundred like her, faceless and forgettable women dressed in black: servants of noble houses, wives of tradesmen, pilgrims wandering in a blissful haze from shrine to shrine.

As the day waned, almost she did not go back to her prison. It was not fear that brought her back, nor any sense of loyalty to either Richard or the Old Man. She went because she had business left to do. When that was finished, God knew where she would go, for certainly she did not.

*   *   *

Berengaria was on the wall when Richard came back to Jerusalem. She had heard the servants talking, ordering one another to prepare for the king's arrival. It was all very hasty and somewhat frantic.

She had no plan as she stood waiting, having marked the mages in their places. She was very well shielded, but they were sending off sparks. Either they were careless or they were not afraid of consequences. She was tempted to dispose of one of them as a warning, but they did not need to know yet that not all the people of the city were obedient sheep.

Even she was taken aback by the size of the army that rose out of the earth to besiege the city. Her supposed ally had not warned her to expect this horde.

He was feeding on their will and spirits and filling them with his own will and desire. She could feel him out beyond them, and almost see him: a vast shape spreading black wings across the hills.

When the power in the city's heart rose up, she was nearly caught in it. It seized the city's mages and wielded them like weapons. She was buffeted as if by a whirlwind.

Somehow, in the midst of it, she could both see and think. To fight their battle, the mages had withdrawn the city's wards from the walls. They were open, exposed—and the enemy knew. The sacrifice of bodies was nothing to him— their blood and souls were his sustenance.

He shot a dart of power across that swarming field. Berengaria saw it, knew where it aimed, and could not move.

It pierced her breast with burning cold. The dark one's consciousness was in it, a part of his essence, a fragment of himself. He coiled like a worm in her soft and beating heart.

There was nothing she could do, not for all her rage and revulsion. He had hunted her, trapped her, and made the kill. He was in her now, and therefore in the city. All the walls and guards, shields and wards and great workings of magic, could not keep him out.

She had wits enough to keep a part of herself away from him, to bury it deep and conceal it with trivialities. If he went looking, he would find a long reflection on the quality of Chin as opposed to Byzantine silk.

His will brought her down off the wall and sent her back through the city. She did not fight it. He wanted her to spy, to search out the defenses, to work her way in a slow spiral toward the Ark in its house of stone. Her feet were aching as badly as her head, long before she came to the Dome of the Rock. The Ark was below it—as she might have expected. The Dome stood on the foundation of the Jews' Temple. If the Jews' great magical weapon had come home, where else would it come but here?

The thing inside her did not make her go down to it, not yet. It let her go so suddenly that she fell against a wall. It was a long while before she could steady her knees enough to stand, and longer still before she could walk.

The streets that she had passed so easily while the dark thing ruled her seemed impossible now. They were full of people, most of them calm, but a few giving way to panic as the battle raged and the king fought his way into the city. She was jostled and carried along, no longer even knowing which direction she went in, or where she wanted to go.

She never knew the name of the man who found her clinging to a column on the street of the goldsmiths. He was kind; if she had had tears, she would have wept. He set her on her way toward David's Tower, even walked with her until he was sure that she could look after herself. He asked and expected nothing for it. "In Christ's name," he said as he left her, bowing and smiling.

That smile lingered with her as she sought the only home

she had in this city. It pierced her with pain even greater than the dart of sorcery that had made her the Old Man's slave. Of all times and places to meet a simple kindness from someone who not only saw her but was visibly glad to help her, this was the most unbearable. When it was too late—when she was lost.

Maybe she was not. It was a feeble thought, with little conviction, but it stiffened her spine enough to carry her onward. Richard had said often enough where she could hear: "No battle is ever lost until one side has surrendered and the other has accepted the surrender—and even then, the victor would do well to watch his back."

She had no love whatever for her so little devoted husband, but one thing she could grant him. He knew how to fight a war. She had suffered an ambush and a defeat—but she was not completely lost. Not quite yet.

CHAPTER FORTY

"We have to take the fight to him."

Sioned's throat was sore with arguing. She loved Judah and his kin as if they had been of her own blood. She respected them; she was in awe of their circle of mages. And yet they were the most contentious creatures that she ever had the misfortune to meet. They could do nothing, not one thing, without a lengthy and thoroughly documented disputation.

She had tried to play the game as they played it. But it went on and on endlessly while Richard's army played out its siege. The enemy's men were battering the walls and trying to burrow under them. The enemy himself waited, wrapped in shadows, for gods knew what. Maybe for Jerusalem's mages to fall apart in a storm of bickering.

In desperation she did a thing that she would have to pay for later: she silenced them all with a Word of power. They glared at her, but they could not speak.

"Now," she said in the blessed and dearly bought silence. "Listen to me. We have a weapon here. It's raised wards of surpassing strength, and that's a wonder and a marvel. But its real, its strongest use is as a sword rather than a shield. It's meant for attack, not defense.

"And," she said, "we must consider this enemy. Every day that we wait, he grows stronger. Every man who dies on that field, on either side, is feeding him. He can't lose this war—not unless we can win it without bloodshed; and he's made sure we can't do that. We're trapped. He only needs to wear us down, then when we're so weak we can't defend ourselves, he'll take us all."

They were still glaring, but one or two—Judah among them—were starting to think. She said again what she had been saying for hours: "We have to take the fight to him."

The flash of Judah's eyes told her—rightly or wrongly—that he was ready to ask a reasonable question. She released him from the binding.

He coughed, choking on enforced silence. His voice when it came was a rusty croak. "How do you propose to do that?"

"I've been thinking," she said, "of simple solutions. The Ark was carried into battle, your scriptures say. It was unassailable, and it always brought victory."

"You want us to bring it out of the Temple." Judah was not arguing, he was thinking aloud. "Even if the Ark would agree to be moved—and I concede, for a battle it well might—that could leave it open to the enemy."

"It could," she said, "but consider the circumstances. We'll bring it out under the sky to a creature of the dark, in sunlight, which transforms the Ark from a shield into the sword of your God."

"And if the sun neither frightens nor destroys him, he

takes the sword and raises it against us, and we're all destroyed. We're not that desperate yet," said Judah.

"Do you want to wait until we are? Then he'll be so strong none of us can stand against him. At least if we move now, before his siege has had a chance to weaken us and while he's still as weak as he's going to be, we have a chance of winning. The longer we wait, the smaller that chance will be."

"That's a gamble," Judah said.

"Isn't everything to do with war? Sometimes it is wise to wait. I don't think this is one of the times. Either we strike fast and hard, or we lose the opportunity to strike at all."

Not only Judah had at last begun to understand what they had to do. They did not all like it, but they had to concede that it had a long and sacred precedent. This was the use to which their ancestors had put it. Surely if their God had laid it in their hands after twice a thousand years, he meant them to use it as he had intended.

"Richard will be delighted," Judah observed rather dourly. "A battle—with blasts of fire, but plenty of work for sword and lance."

Richard was delighted. He would have marched out then and there, if it had not been nearly sundown. For this they needed the sun.

It was a long night. The city was protected, but wards and guards could not close men's ears. It was deathly still until nearly midnight, then began such a clamor as must fill the pits of hell: shrieking, howling, the clashing of metal on metal, and the booming of drums so deep they reverberated in the earth.

"You'd think they were trying to bring down the walls," Richard said. He had not gone to bed yet, and was therefore spared the anguish of waking from a sound sleep to pandemonium.

"Maybe they are," said Mustafa.

Sioned had sent him to the king, to tell Richard of her plan and to enlist him in the mortal part of it. Even at this late hour, Richard's guards had let him in. They never refused entry to the king's dog.

It was their first meeting alone since Mustafa went to Rome. That was only days ago, and yet everything had changed. Mustafa still loved this man, would love him until he died. But now there was another.

He had not brought Giuliano with him. He had told himself that the boy needed to sleep, and he was deep in it when Mustafa left him. On his way to the Tower of David Mustafa had acknowledged the truth: that he was not ready for them to meet. That would happen, there was no escaping it. But not tonight.

Richard knew nothing of this. He was as glad as ever to see Mustafa, and as willing to let him simply be there, even without the message that he brought.

The tumult began not long after Mustafa had told the king all that Sioned had in mind. It drowned out what Richard had been going to say, and distracted them rather too well. "Sound can be power," Mustafa said in such a lull as there was. "It can break stone and shatter crystal. They must think they can break our shields with it."

"Can they?"

Mustafa shrugged, one-sided. "I suppose they can. But as horrendous as this is, it's not a fraction of what they would need."

"So," said Richard, "mostly it's to keep us awake."

"I think so, my lord."

Richard sighed. "Now that I understand. It's an old trick. I've used it myself. It works: no matter how well the victims may have prepared for any and all surprises, they can't shut this out. It's with them no matter what they do."

"They'll stop at dawn," Mustafa said.

"And we'll be ready to kill them by then, just for a moment's peace." Richard bared his teeth. "There's the flaw in that plan, you know. It may not exhaust your enemy—it may incite him to fight harder than ever."

"Maybe mages could do something about it."

"Not tonight," said Richard. "Let him think he's wearing us down—and let him think our magical allies have all they can do to keep their shields and weapons under control. The enemy's contempt is a soldier's friend. The more he underestimates us, the better chance we have of striking where it hurts."

Mustafa bowed to his superior generalship, as the uproar rose to drown whatever else Richard might have said. Even through walls of stone a dozen feet thick, it was deafening. Away from walls, it would split the skull.

Richard would have offered him a bed in David's Tower, which was warded well enough at least that the clamor was sunk to a dull roar, but he had one waiting in the city. He was more than glad to come to it. Not only was Giuliano in it, but the house, like the Tower, was warded. One could stuff one's bedclothes into one's ears and find some semblance of rest.

Benjamin had not said a word to Teleri since his father brought him back from Damascus. He pretended that he was terribly busy being a mage like the rest, but she knew he was avoiding her. She could even understand it, after a fashion, but it hurt. It hurt a great deal.

The night before they were all going to take the fight to the enemy, she went to find Benjamin. It was easier to escape than it would have been on any other night. Mustafa was gone, taking the message to the king. Her mother and father were resting, which mostly meant that they were doing things she was not supposed to be aware of. Giuliano was sound asleep.

She had a pair of jinn watching over her, young cousins of the prince who loved her mother. They were strong in magic, which was why they were guarding her, but they were also a mere few eons old, and they could be reasoned with. They saw no harm in helping her to find Benjamin. They were with her, after all, and they would protect her against anything that attacked her.

Benjamin was in his father's house. He was supposed to be sleeping with some of his brothers, but he had escaped as she had and was sitting on the roof. To such eyes as the two of them had, the protections on the city were visible overhead, a faint pale sheen like a film of cloud, not quite obscuring the stars.

He was not surprised to see her. He was not glad, either. He refused to look at her.

"You had better tell me," she said. "What did I do? Was it something I said?"

His shoulders set stubbornly. Whatever it was, he was as angry as she had ever seen him.

She pulled him around and made him face her. He kept his eyes on his fists, which were clenched in his lap. "*Tell* me," she said.

"He's in the city," Benjamin said, so low she had to strain to hear. "It doesn't matter how many defenses they put up. He's already here."

Teleri's stomach clenched. "How do you know? Who told you?"

"I can feel it." His eyes flashed up. "It's you. You did it. He got to you. You gave in."

"I did not."

"You did! He's here. I *know* he's here."

Teleri shook him so hard his teeth rattled. "I didn't do it! Can't you look and see? He was tempting me and tormenting me, but once the walls went up, he stopped. He hasn't come back. If he is here somewhere, he's not in me."

Benjamin peered at her. She let him look as deep as he wanted, which was not particularly deep—he was shy, and for some ridiculous reason he had remembered that she was a girl. That made him all hot and flustered and even more annoyed than ever, but he was decent enough to say, "It's not you. So who is it?"

"I don't know. Can you tell where it is?"

He glared. "Obviously not, if you're standing right here and I thought it was you."

"You know what that means."

Maybe he did. Maybe he did not. He was not about to say so, either way.

"We've got to find him before the Ark goes out tomorrow," she said. "As long as it's in the city, it must be keeping him from doing too much. Once it's gone outside, he can do whatever he wants."

"Maybe not," said Benjamin. "They're going to keep the walls up even after the Ark comes out. They think they can do it by binding the spell into the Temple's foundations. Aaron's going to try toward morning. Then Father and Uncle Daniel will lead the Ark to the gate."

"Aaron can do it," Teleri said. "But even so, if he's here, you can lay wagers he'll do something while everyone is busy fighting."

"Well then," said Benjamin, "there's something for you to do. You can find out where he is. When everybody comes back, if they come back, they can get rid of him. If they don't come back, he'll rule us all anyway, and it won't matter."

"We need to find him now," Teleri insisted.

"We can't," said Benjamin. "We don't know where he is, we don't have time, and if you do find him, what happens if he really does go into you? At least if you do it while everybody is fighting, he'll be distracted and you can stay safer."

He was maddening, but he was right. Tonight was not the night to be hunting shadows. She was weakened already, and the dark would come into her all too easily. Like the Ark, she needed the sun.

She was not about to let him know he had won his point. She said instead, "You don't really hate me, do you?"

"What makes you think that? I'm afraid for you. I don't want him to eat you from the inside out the way he eats his followers."

"He's not going to do that," she said with as much conviction as she could muster. "I won't let him, and neither will you—and if he gets past us, he has our whole families to face. My mother won't let him touch me ever again."

Benjamin was in awe of Teleri's mother. That stopped his nonsense, though it did not trick a smile out of him. None of them would smile again, not really, until the dark thing was finally and truly dead.

CHAPTER FORTY-ONE

At sunrise the Ark was ready. Judah and Daniel had chosen the four strongest of the young mages to carry it: Joshua and Gideon from England, Moishe and his cousin Baruch from Jerusalem. If they had had time they would have put on the ancient vestments of priests in the Temple. But there was no time to fashion any such thing. They had to settle for well-forged mail and bright steel helmets, and surcoats that Rebecca and her daughters had labored over all night long. They were white, embroidered in blue and gold and purple and scarlet with the names of the twelve tribes of Israel.

They covered the Ark in its silken shroud. At a glance from Judah, the bearers took up the poles and shouldered them. They grunted as they lifted it. It was not large, but the tablets of the Law inside it and the sheathing of gold within and without made it imposingly heavy.

They came up out of the Temple by the hidden way they had all been using since the Ark returned to Jerusalem. A hundred of Richard's best men were waiting outside the door. Giuliano was with them, and Mustafa. Giuliano had chosen not to go down to the Ark while its priests attended it. He had tact, and a degree of wisdom.

And yet, thought Mustafa, he was at least as vital in this venture as any of the sons of Levi. His power equaled or surpassed theirs. He knew the Ark directly as none of them did.

He was very quiet as the shrouded thing came out into the light. Mustafa stayed close, with care not to intrude, but keeping close watch. This could not be easy for him at all. Mustafa did not expect him to break or to betray them, but he might need strength when his own began to falter.

Richard's guardsmen fell into formation around the Ark. They began to march down the Street of the Temple.

People were out. News traveled fast. They did not gather in crowds: quite the opposite. They had cleared the way, and stood on either side of it, silent, watching. No one cheered or shouted. They could not have seen the bearers in the midst of the shieldwall, and the Ark in any case was covered, and yet they knew. One by one and then in a long slow wave, they went down to their knees. Pilgrims, townsfolk, tradesmen and artisans, priests and monks and lesser servants of God, all bowed at the Ark's passing.

It was eerie, that silent procession. There was power in it—subtle, barely perceptible, but impossible to mistake. Not only the earth and stones of Jerusalem partook of the Ark's magic. Its people were part of it, as they had been since the first days of the city.

Richard's army was drawn up in and about the Tower of David. It too made way for the Ark, all but the vanguard—suitably enough, knights of the Temple. Whatever they thought of these new allies, they would fight for Jerusalem.

Richard would ride in the van, with Ahmad at his back. So

would Sioned have done, but they would not hear of it. She would take station above the gate and fight as she could from there. Mustafa had no doubt that she would fight as fierce a battle as any of the knights.

As they had all expected, the enemy's ungodly clamor had stopped not long before sunrise. The rams and the catapults had not yet begun the day's bombardment. The enemy rested for a little while. It might be too much to hope that this sally would be a surprise, but the sentries on the walls, mages as well as keen-eyed watchers, saw no sign of alarm. No one was preparing a counterattack.

The sun was rising higher. Even shrouded, the Ark had begun to draw its power.

The gates began to open. In the vanguard, the destriers snorted and pawed, impatient for the battle they knew was coming. The great iron-shod hooves rang on the paving, echoing under the arch.

The moment the gate was fully open, the charge burst out of it, thundering down the road and spreading onto the field. The enemy had been marching and riding toward the siege-engines. The Templars ran over them, trampling them. Infantry ran behind, aiming for the engines, with bars and poles and great hammers to batter them to pieces.

Under cover of the melee, the Ark advanced within its shieldwall. Battle was raging all around it. Richard's army formed a second wall, a line of defense many ranks deep.

They could not advance above walking pace. The bearers were sweating, but their breathing was steady. The Ark seemed to be growing lighter. Mustafa's nostrils twitched. A scent was coming off it, like heated metal. It had begun to hum on a deep sweet note.

They were aiming for a hill some distance from the gate, which overlooked the place where the dark one was laired.

Mustafa began to think they would not get so far. The hordes of the enemy were recovering too quickly from the shock of the charge, and were converging on them, seeing how they were protected in the heart of the army.

Richard had seen this even before Mustafa had: he was pressing the charge again, driving a deep wedge through the massed ranks. At the same time, although the sky was clear overhead, bolts of lightning began to fall upon the enemy. Sioned on the wall was fighting her own battle.

One bolt struck so close that Mustafa's skin prickled. The stink of scorched meat and hair made him gag. A company of Seljuk Turks lay in charred ruin, just before they would have fallen on the shieldwall.

There were still furlongs to go before they reached the hill. The dark one must be aware of them—nothing with magic could fail to know what was coming.

He had not, so far, taken the bait. He was letting his army batter at the defenses until they were gone. Then he would pluck the Ark like a rose from among the thorns.

They had to tempt him beyond even his great capacity for resistance. Mustafa met Giuliano's glance. He could see the same thought in those eyes, the same impulse, which Giuliano could set in words: "Take off the shroud."

The bearers checked their stride. The priests glanced at him. None of them, even Judah, moved to do his bidding. He was a mage and an ally, their faces said, and they owed him a great debt, but he was not their commander.

He was not about to wait for them, or to argue, either. He swept his hand in a swift gesture. The shroud leaped toward him as if it had been waiting for exactly that.

Almost too late, Mustafa shielded his eyes. The Ark loosed a sound like an exultant shout. Light erupted from it, a storm of brilliance.

Slowly Mustafa lowered his hand. He had not gone blind. He was not even terribly dazzled. Nor was any other man who fought on this side of the war. Richard's men had been spared. The enemy's men screamed in agony. Those closest had been blasted to ash. Those farther away were seared, their eyes melted from the sockets.

The enemy took the bait. He reared up above the hill, a wave of darkness, spreading great wings across the field. His presence was living terror. Where his shadow lay, all light died. Men withered where they stood, and fell mewling to the blasted earth.

Judah spoke quietly, as calm as if he had been in his hospital, standing over a man who might be dying, but who might be saved. "Stand fast. Wait."

The darkness roared upon them. Men scattered, crying in fear. Even the light of the Ark was quenched.

But the priests and the guards stood their ground. So did Richard and the knights of the Temple—some with difficulty for their horses were half mad, but they held on. They drew back, making themselves a wall, a half-circle of armed and utterly mortal defense against immortal power.

"Hold," said Judah, soft and steady.

The storm was all about them, a whirlwind of darkness and cold, emptiness and black despair. It rocked Mustafa on his feet, lashing him with dust and the acrid stink of ash.

Judah began to chant, still softly, but the resonance of his voice trembled beneath Mustafa's feet: "*Sh'ma Yisroel, Adonai elohenu, Adonai echod* . . . Hear, O Israel, the Lord our God, the Lord is One. . . ."

It was the simplest and one of the oldest prayers of all, and the greatest magic that his people knew. Even here, even under the darkness, it woke the light. It called to the sun and the powers of heaven, spirits of the aether, forces of the elements, summoning them to the battle.

Between the wings of cherubim atop the Ark, a cloud of light began to form. All the hairs on Mustafa's body stood on end. The Power that was coming was greater than any he had ever known—greater than mortal mind could encompass. All that contained it was the will of a handful of mages, two pairs of golden wings, and a box of acacia wood sheathed in gold.

Their enemy was terrible, but what they had raised might be more terrible still. Raw power of the Infinite, utterly divorced from mortal substance. Whatever qualities of mercy or compassion that the Prophet had attributed to it, here it had none. It was too old, too remote, too perfectly alien.

Other voices joined Judah in the chanting of the *Sh'ma Yisroel*. Some wavered; one broke, and one of the mages crumpled to the ground. No one moved to help him. From where Mustafa stood, just within the shieldwall, it was obvious that he was dead.

Giuliano had not joined in the working. Somewhere he had lost his helmet. His head was tilted back, his eyes on the shadow that stooped above them. It was reaching slowly, with utmost care, downward to the Ark and the half-wrought spell. As potent as was the thing the mages called upon, it was neither fully summoned nor fully reconciled to the summoning. If the spell was broken or interrupted, all that power would turn against those who invoked it.

Mustafa wished to his God that Sioned had been there and not in solitary exile atop David's Gate. Fools that these men were, to keep the strongest of them apart, because she was a woman.

He laid his hand on Giuliano's shoulder. Giuliano neither started nor shook him off. The power that had surged between them before was there still, waiting to be called upon.

Giuliano nodded, half-smiling, as if Mustafa had answered a question that he had happened to ask.

Sioned was there, inside him. Mustafa would not say that she was smug, but she had a certain air of satisfaction about her. None of the mages who had relegated her to the woman's place could wax contentious with a man in armor who happened, most conveniently, to be a mage of an order that frequently and easily blurred will into will and self into self. This was one of Giuliano's many gifts, and most useful now.

Mustafa's hand slid down his arm to clasp his wrist. It was half a caress. He was keenly aware of it, even as he looked up into horror.

The dark one had opened a gate—the gate of all gates: the gate of hell. His laughter was all around them. Such a lovely trap, so beautifully baited, with such sweet morsels of mages, and in the heart of it, the best lure of all. He fed on its power, that was sweeter than wine, more precious than blood.

They had given him exactly what he wanted. When he had swallowed the Ark with all its priests and mages, he would be more powerful than a god—powerful enough to challenge Iblis himself.

"Or so you fancy." That was Sioned's voice, as brisk as ever, clear and sharp and undismayed as she looked into the abyss. The wind was plucking at them, striving to tug them free of earth and whirl them into the darkness.

She was completely unafraid. "Sinan ibn Salman," she said, making no effort to raise her voice above the shrieking of the wind, "who was called Sheikh al-Jabal, the Old Man of the Mountain: can you not remember that you are dead?"

The darkness roared, half in mirth, half in rage, and swatted her as if she had been a fly.

Like a fly, she eluded him with maddening ease. She was not here in the flesh, nor could he touch her body—it was protected by the wards of Jerusalem. Only her spirit was here, riding lightly in Giuliano's consciousness. Other spirits made themselves known, circling about her like sparks from a fire: the jinn, all who were not protecting Jerusalem, swirling and dancing and mocking the dark.

Did the wind waver the merest fraction? Sioned grinned in the teeth of it and said, "No matter how much power you seize, no matter how many souls you swallow, no matter how much blood you drink, you will never be alive again. Never while you cling to this unlife. Only if you let go your self can you live once more in flesh."

"Lies," wailed the wind. "All lies."

It smote the mages with renewed force. Not all of them withstood it. Even the bearers of the Ark swayed on their feet, and Baruch dropped to one knee. The wind battered him, flailing him with dust and sharp-edged stones. He could not protect himself, not with the Ark weighing him down. Blood streamed down his face. His eyes had swelled shut.

"You can swallow the world," Sioned said, "drink every drop of blood in it and consume every life, and still hell will be within you. You can never be free of it."

The wind went mad. Baruch fell, and this time he did not get up. The Ark rocked and tilted dangerously.

Just before it fell, Judah set his shoulder to the pole, straddling his kinsman's body. The cloud of light above the Ark glowed visibly brighter.

The darkness gaped to swallow them all. Mustafa looked into the pit and knew with despair so perfect it was almost hope, that there was nothing he could do. Magic was useless. They had gambled their lives and souls, and lost. Sioned's defiance had amused the darkness for a few moments, but now its patience was exhausted.

It shot down a claw of endless night and clasped the Ark, ripping it from the hands of its bearers.

"Now," said Sioned perfectly calmly.

Giuliano spoke two words. They were in Latin, which Mustafa had not expected. And yet they were perfect, flawless, bound into the fabric of the world.

"Fiat lux," he said: "Let there be light."

And there was light.

It seared the very depths of hell, and silenced the chorus of the damned. It shut and sealed the gate and swept the darkness from the sky. It pierced the dark one to his center.

He burned like a twist of straw: smoldering, then bursting into flame. There was no sound, no scream. The silence was more terrible than any howl of agony.

As suddenly as it had erupted, the flame collapsed upon itself. Not even a fleck of ash remained.

CHAPTER FORTY-TWO

The sun shone in a cloudless sky. On the field, the remnants of the horde wandered aimlessly, lost and empty of memory. Richard's captains called their companies together; his army formed anew, to surround and capture their erstwhile enemies. Richard led them all, riding like a man possessed, or one freed from long imprisonment.

They all gave the Ark a wide berth. The priests recovered themselves, such of them as could. Baruch and Gideon were dead.

Judah and Daniel, with the bearers who survived, covered the Ark once more. The men of the guard made biers of cloaks and spearhafts, to carry the dead and wounded back to the city. Judah was already tending the latter, his priesthood laid aside in favor of his other and older calling.

Mustafa could find a horse and ride with Richard, or he could stay with the Ark as Giuliano obviously intended to do. It was an exquisite dilemma. The war was over—they had won it. But as with all wars, there was a great deal of after-math to contend with.

Giuliano settled it for him by catching the rein of a loose horse and tossing it into Mustafa's hand. His smile was almost as good as a kiss. "Tonight," he said: both command and promise.

Mustafa sprang into the saddle without touching the stir-rup. The horse was much to his taste: desert-bred from the look and feel of her, still fresh and eager although she had seen hard fighting. There was blood on the saddle and spat-tered on her sides; she looked as if she had waded through a pool of it.

None of it, thank Allah, was hers. He thrust feet into stir-rups and turned her toward the king. She leaped gladly into a gallop, hurdling the bodies of the slain, veering lightly round the dazed and the wounded.

Richard greeted him with a glance in which gladness and relief were mingled. He settled into his old place, a few paces behind, watching the king's back as he made order of chaos on the battlefield.

Now that the glory was past and the real work had begun, Sioned was allowed on the field in body as well as in spirit. The surgeons' tent had been pitched near the shrouded shape of the Ark. She had a place in it, which she was glad to fill.

She felt strange: light, giddy with freedom—from fear, from the worst pain of grief. The Old Man was gone. He would not, gods willing, rise again.

He had left a terrible wrack and ruin behind. Some of his former slaves had seen where they were and remembered, if not how they had come there, then that they were of Islam and this was holy war. They had mustered in hastily ordered companies, hoping to die for their God and so win Paradise.

The Templars and the Hospitallers, with a fair few of the knights of Outremer, were more than glad to grant them their desire.

It was the same promise the Old Man had made, but he had given them nothingness; he had drunk their blood and swallowed their souls. At least if they died under Frankish swords, their souls would come intact into the garden of Allah.

She stitched wounds and salved burns and set bones. She was not at all aware of the passage of time, until she looked up from tending a deep sword-cut to find her husband watching her. He was smiling faintly, a little wryly, as if he had been waiting a long while for her to notice him.

She bound off the bandage and assured the wounded man that he would live, if he kept the wound clean and did not let it fester. Then she could straighten, working the knots out of her back and neck, and say to Ahmad, "Are you as hungry as I am?"

"Possibly," he said. "I'm sure they've kept dinner for us at home."

"I won't survive that long." She swept her glance over the tent, which had gone from daylight to darkness without her noticing. The lamps were lit, and through the open flap she saw the flicker of a campfire.

No new wounded had come in. Everyone had been tended and either let go or given a bed. She could leave for a while at least, and find something somewhere to take the edge off her hunger.

"As to that," said Ahmad, "come with me."

He held out his hand. She took it. It was not dignified for people of their age and rank to walk hand in hand like children, but she did not care. Tonight, nothing mattered but that this brief but terrible war was over.

Cooks had come out of the city and set up a tent not far from the gate, and proceeded to feed the army. These were not the usual rations: the bread was fresh, the meat well spiced and seasoned before it was roasted, and there were pastries and sweets such as soldiers for the most part could only dream of. It was a feast, varied enough for a king, and there was dancing and singing and all manner of revelry. Later there would be a proper celebration of the victory, after all the flotsam of battle was cleared away. But tonight outside the walls of Jerusalem, the people's joy was immediate and their gladness heartfelt.

Sioned might have lingered after the edge was off her hunger, but she had a daughter at home, and she was suddenly desperate to assure herself that Teleri was safe. Ahmad had had the same thought. Hand in hand again, they entered the city between a company of crossbowmen from Genoa and a flock of pilgrims who had gone to gawk at the battlefield.

Teleri was asleep in her bed, attended by her guard of jinn. Sioned wanted to gather her up and hug the breath out of her, but that would be cruel. She had been distraught all day, the guards said. Rebecca had had to come and dose her, to make her stop insisting that she should be outside, in the battle, with the Ark and the dark thing.

She was quiet now, slightly flushed but not feverish. Her dreams when Sioned touched the surface of them were placid enough; no nightmares. Sioned laid a wishing on her, to drive away the darkness.

It hurt that that was the best she could do, but it was better than nothing. She lingered as long as she could, but unless she was going to sleep in this room, she had to tear herself away.

"Be at rest, lady," said the more outspoken of the jinn. "She will be safe. We will watch, and call you if she wakes."

Sioned sighed and let herself be persuaded. She was beyond exhaustion. If she did not rest soon, her body would settle it for her.

She let Ahmad lead her to her own bed, which she had seen too little of for too long. When this was truly over, she thought blurrily, she was going to sleep for a week—and woe betide the fool who tried to keep her from it.

Teleri pretended to sleep for some time after her mother and father left. She would have given much to be able to tell them not to worry, but that would have to wait until later.

She glared at the jinni who talked too much. "What did you tell them I was upset for?" she demanded.

"Because you were," he said. "You were screaming. The servants were horrified."

"The servants are silly nits." She was in a fair temper, and she did not care. "I wanted to be out there. I *needed* to be out there. Why did you stop me?"

"You would have died," the jinni said, "or worse. The dark thing would have eaten you. He wanted you, to feed on your power, to destroy the one who was destroying him."

"I would have fought," she said. She flung back the coverlets and got up. She was dressed; it was well her mother had not looked too close, or she would have seen that Teleri was up to something.

"Where are you going?" the jinni asked her. "He's gone now. There's no need to—"

"There's still something wrong in the city," Teleri said. "I have to find it. He left something behind—a seed, a canker. I have to root it out or it will grow."

"No," said the jinni.

She stared at him in absolute shock. "What do you mean, 'No'? I *am* going."

"You are not."

"You can't stop me."

That was not true, and they both knew it. She was all muddled and weak. He was a spirit of fire, even if he happened to be looking, just then, a great deal like Mustafa's beautiful young Roman.

Mustafa's Roman did not have finger-long fangs and a serpent's tongue. The jinni bared his fangs at her and dared her to try something.

She almost did. But her head was aching again, and there were voices trying to get in. If she started screaming, her mother would come, and then she would never get away at all.

She had to give in—for the moment. She let herself be put back to bed, though if she did not choose to sleep, there was nothing any son of the jinn could do about it.

Chapter Forty-three

It took Richard a week to clear the field in front of David's Tower. He saw the enemy's dead buried or burned, and the living at last either sent home or taken captive and held for ransom. Those who went home had offered no resistance; they had been baffled and helpless. Those whom he put in chains had fought, sometimes fiercely, in the name of holy war. They were not very many. Most of their fellows had flung themselves on Frankish swords or spears, or fought so hard that Richard's raiding parties had to kill them or be killed.

Now at last it was over, and he could come home for more than an hour or two. His cooks had been waiting in growing impatience; once they were assured that this time he meant to stay, they flung themselves into preparations for the feast of victory.

The city had been celebrating for the whole of that week. Richard's stewards had some little trouble to find an adequate supply of wine, oil, or sugar; they had had to send to Acre and Jaffa, and tax a demesne or two for its sugar and oil.

It was not, in the end, too shabby a feast. The Sultan of Damascus had come: the siege of Krak had broken when the Old Man fell, and al-Afdal had come with Henry to see the end of the war in Jerusalem. The Sultan of Egypt was there, of course, laying somewhat reluctant claim to his proper rank and station. It trammeled him after his too-brief respite, but it was a captivity he had chosen. He was gracious in it, taking it on like a mantle he had laid briefly aside.

The two sultans shared the feast with the lords and commanders of the Franks, and their priests, and a company of noble pilgrims who had come from the west just too late to see the strange battle before David's Gate. There was also, for the first time perhaps in a thousand years, a small but proud delegation of Jews, there not by the king's sufferance but as his guests and valued allies.

That was an uncomfortable prospect for certain of Richard's court and following. The Pope of Rome was far from alone in his hatred of their kind. It went beyond reason—

"Beyond sense, too," Richard had snarled to Sioned when the first rumblings of discontent reached him, not more than a day after the battle. "But for these hated Jews, I wouldn't have a kingdom, and we might all be in danger of losing our souls."

Richard, as those who knew him knew too well, did not take kindly to the less subtle modes of persuasion. When a delegation of priests and nobles approached him to demand that he repudiate his allies and take their Ark by force, he had laid about him with the flat of his sword. They had meant to argue that he was ill-advised to continue in this alliance. They had succeeded only in convincing him of the opposite.

Therefore, tonight, he had invited Judah and Daniel and

the rest to share the victory with him. They were seated at his right hand with the sultans and the noble infidels. That whole table was served by its own kitchen and its own cooks, who had prepared a banquet according to the laws of both Moses and Muhammad. It was a mark of rare and striking grace, and Sioned hoped they were all aware of it.

There was going to be a price to pay for that. She hoped it would not be impossibly high.

Richard seemed to be thinking of no such thing—at least not tonight. He was in great good humor. He had had himself a war, if not exactly to his taste; and he had won it, as he always did. Later he would let himself be persuaded to sing— and that would be worth hearing: Richard was a fine poet and a sweet singer, in among his battles on the field and in the council chamber.

She was sitting between Judah and Ahmad. Teleri and Benjamin were farther down the table with the rest of Judah's offspring. In the way of children, they seemed to have forgotten their ordeal in the Old Man's garden, although Sioned was watching her daughter closely. She did not altogether trust Teleri's semblance of normality.

Mustafa, at terrible cost to his self-effacing nature, sat at Ahmad's right hand, with Giuliano beside him. Giuliano was nominally a Christian, but no one would have expected him to be anywhere else. He had come with the Ark, and in everyone's mind, he belonged with its priests.

He did not seem to mind. These were his friends, far more than the Frankish knights who eyed him askance and muttered among themselves when he passed. To them he was an unfathomable thing, a knight and a nobleman beyond doubt, but friend and more to infidels and Jews. Even in this country, where minds were unusually supple, he was out of their reckoning.

But then so was she, and she had done well enough, all things considered. She should follow Teleri's lead: forget her troubles and everyone else's as well, and set herself to take pleasure in the banquet and the company.

Berengaria watched the revels from the latticed window of her solar. Just so were lepers set apart in churches, forced to look down on the rites from hidden rooms high up near the roof.

If she had been a leper, she would hardly have been less regarded than she was now. No one had come to bring her word of either the war or the victory. She had not been invited to the banquet, of course; Richard had not troubled himself any more now than he ever had, to remember that she existed.

She had considered making an appearance as she had before he led his army toward Krak, to remind them all that England and Jerusalem still had a queen, but that might betray her hand too soon. They thought it was over; they preened and boasted, and told one another that the Old Man was destroyed.

She knew that he was not. She had felt the terrible power that rose up and blasted him, just as she had felt the powers he had raised. In the moment of his dissolution, she had been pierced with dazzling pain, worse by far than when he had set his worm in her heart.

This worm had driven itself into her belly, in the life that grew there, and woven itself through it. Rage, curse, grieve though she might, she could not get rid of it—not without destroying the child.

She was past prayer and almost past sorcery. But she still had a few wits left. She waited and watched and cast a working here and there, a small spell to feed Richard's weariness and cause him to grow bored with the banquet.

That was not a difficult spell. Richard had labored hard and long, and he was not as young as he had been. He was glad enough to contemplate rest and quiet.

He still took a tediously long time to make his excuses and withdraw. It seemed half the court tried to follow him, and he laughed and pretended to indulge them. But by the time he had closed the door of his bedchamber, they were all gone, even the squires and the servants. He was alone in rare solitude.

He never knew who watched him from the hidden passage that must have served some long-ago king or sultan to bring in his wives or his spies. He stretched luxuriously and yawned. He began to undress himself, a skill not every king was willing to acknowledge, but she had never known him to care what anyone else did or thought.

He was not as good to look at naked as his nephew Henry. Part of that was his age; he was a dozen years the elder. Part was a simple matter of taste. She liked a lighter, less muscle-bound figure, with smoother skin.

Even so, he was attractive enough. The years had not thickened him overmuch. He had a fighting man's honed strength, and he was still surprisingly light on his feet.

He lay on his bed but did not at once draw the draperies of sheer muslin. He sighed deeply and stretched, and groaned at some small but pressing pain. Almost miraculously, he had taken no worse than bruises in the battle—and that in spite of being in the thick of it as always.

She waited until he was lying loose, arm over his eyes, breathing steadily but not with the rhythm of sleep. Then she slipped through the hidden door.

She considered the working that had served her with Henry. Maybe it would serve her here. But she could not bring herself to perform the spell. She sat in the chair beside the bed and watched him become aware of her.

He lowered his arm, blinking, then scowling as he made out her face. "You. How did you get in here?"

Not even a word of greeting, let alone a scrap of courtesy. If her resolve could have wavered, that put an end to it. "I come to offer you a bargain," she said.

"No," he said.

She ignored him. "I know that you are not capable of making a child with any woman. That was evident long ago. It could be done, one supposes, with magic and deceit, but what use? Here is the bargain I offer you. Let me provide you with an heir—never ask how or whom—and I will swear on holy relics that the child is yours."

His mouth had fallen open. She could read his estimation of her in his face: mealymouthed little half-nun, untouched and unwanted by any man. That she should speak so bluntly left him speechless.

She was beyond mercy. "Think for once, King of the English. Your mother is dead. Your brother will break free of his prison soon if he hasn't already. He'll be your heir whether or not he seizes your throne—there's no one else. Unless you let me take care of it."

Richard had not heard a word of it, except one. "Dead? My mother is dead?"

She arched a brow. "What, your sister didn't tell you? She died getting the Ark out of Rome. I suppose there's a fetch lying in state in some abbey in England, so that people will have something to bury."

"She died? My mother is dead?"

A great rage was rising in her, surging up out of the thing in her womb. She was sitting in front of him, demanding that he take notice of her, and he had seen and heard nothing but the few words she had spoken of his mother. She was less than a shadow to him, less than nothing. She could not even threaten him; he did not notice.

"Your mother is dead," she said, driving the words hard. "Do you know what that makes me? I'm the queen—the only queen. Hate me, ignore me, despise me though you will, I wear that crown on my head. And I am done with suffering your neglect."

"I knew it," he said to himself. He had not heard her at all. "I felt it. I didn't know—I let it go. I didn't—"

She struck him. It was no light blow, no weak woman's slap. His head rocked on his neck. The skin had split over his cheekbone.

At last she had his attention. His eyes were on her. His expression was blank.

It was all too clear what she had to do. If he would not accept the bargain, then she would have to settle matters in another way. Her child must live to be born, and must grow up to rule. If that required that Richard be got out of the way, then so be it.

"Forget your mother," she said, deliberately cruel. "Your mother is gone. I am not. I will give you an heir. You will swear that it is yours. A certain decoction of herbs, a charm and a small working, a few eastern wiles—the world will believe, because it wants to believe. There will be a child, and he will rule after you. John may gnaw his liver. He will never have what is yours."

Almost—almost—that caught him. But he despised her too completely. "You're mad," he said.

"Probably," she said. "I am also queen, and you are a king who cannot or will not do your dynastic duty. Either I will see that it is done, or . . ."

"Or what? You'll shut yourself in a convent?"

"No," she said.

It was there in her hand. The thing inside her had shaped it and nurtured it and made it ready. He was altogether unwary, naked and defenseless; she had only to let it go, and it would be done.

She gathered it together, every scrap of killing power, and aimed it at his heart.

CHAPTER FORTY-FOUR

Long before the king's banquet was over, Teleri knew for certain that the dark thing was still in some fashion alive, and that he was in the king's palace. He was very close—she could feel him like a crawling in her skin. He was watching them, laughing inside as they celebrated his destruction.

She was going to tell Benjamin, but he and his brothers were up to something with some of the young men from Damascus, with a great deal of hilarity. She had not seen him laugh since before the Old Man took them.

Let him be happy. She could do this alone. Then if she succeeded, everything would be well; and if she failed, Benjamin would not be sucked into it.

For once since she had come back, her mother and father were not watching every move she made. The jinn were not guarding her. Even Mustafa had other preoccupations. He was so obviously torn between watching the king and yearning to be with Giuliano that she wanted to pat him like a nervous horse and tell him to steady on. Richard would stay Richard, and Giuliano was not going anywhere. Mustafa could have them both.

Later she would do that. She slipped away now, while all her guardian hounds were occupied elsewhere.

There were so many people here, between the guests and the servants and the entertainment, that she lost herself easily among them. Soon enough she was away from the hall and the crowds, following the darkness in her heart.

She had been afraid before, very much. The voices that whispered and whispered were wearing her to a shadow. But now she was on the hunt and the prey was close, her fear had gone away. Whatever she did, whatever happened to her, after tonight it would be over—truly, and not only because everyone wanted it to be.

She followed the trail up away from the hall, past the solar and toward the king's apartments. The flutter in her belly was coming back, but not for herself. The king had left the hall— she had felt him go. He was up here, and so was the dark thing.

If she were a spirit of darkness, and she wanted to destroy a king and his family and his whole kingdom, she knew what she would do. She would kill the king. Then she would kill the rest. Then she would lair inside someone who could not fight her off, some servant maybe, someone that no one ever thought of, and make that person hers, and everything would belong to her.

It scared her to see how clear that vision was, and how simple and obvious it seemed. She began to run.

The king was lying in his bed. The dark thing stooped over him. It was all black, with black wings, but its hand was small and thin and yellow-white. There was something in that hand, something that twisted and coiled, a little like smoke and a little like poison. It strained toward his heart.

Teleri struck it away with power she had not even known she had. The black shape squawked and spun about.

It was a woman. After a shocked instant she recognized the face. "Your majesty!"

Berengaria's eyes were full of darkness. They laughed to see her. So much the better—first Richard, then Teleri, then her mother whom the dark thing hated most of all. What delight; what black joy.

"No," she said. It was an empty sound. The darkness was sucking her in. It already had Richard, even if the poison had never touched him: he was motionless, enspelled.

With a kind of despair, she heard the running footsteps and felt her mother behind her, and her father, and more in back of them. This was just what the dark thing wanted. The more there were, the more magic they had, the more it could feed.

It had laid its traps, and because Teleri had learned absolutely nothing since the last time she tried and failed to get rid of the dark thing, they had all fallen in. Now they were all here, ripe for the taking. And there was nothing anyone could do. Not one thing.

That was the voice again, whispering and whispering.

All at once she could not stand it any more. She had a temper—her mother said she got it from her grandfather, from the old devil's line of Anjou. It was black and it was wild, but next to the dark thing it was as clean as a storm of fire. She let it rage through her. It burned away all the darkness; the roar and hiss of it silenced the voices.

The dark thing leaped past her at her mother, snatching with Berengaria's hands, clawing for something that she wore under her gown.

The Seal. It was trying to get the Seal.

If it had that, nothing else would matter. It would crush them all and seize the Ark and hold Jerusalem.

Sioned was taken by surprise. She reeled back into Ahmad's arms.

Teleri flung herself at Berengaria. She had no weapon but her anger. It made her strong, stronger than a thin and tormented woman who had spent years sitting in closed rooms, growing weak and soft.

She wrenched the queen away from Sioned and swung her about. Someone else was moving, quick as a cat—Mustafa. He was much stronger than Teleri, and faster. The darkness could not find purchase on him. It struck like a snake, over and over, but it was as if he were cased in armor. None of it touched him. Those were Giuliano's wards, shaped to defend the Ark. The dark one in this weakened state was no match for them.

While Mustafa held the darkness, Ahmad raised a swift working to trap and bind it. Sioned sealed it with the Seal.

Suddenly it was very quiet. Teleri was shaking. The rage had gone away, leaving her cold and empty but somehow clean. The darkness was gone from inside her this time— really gone. The voices were silent. She was free.

Berengaria lay on the floor. Her face was empty, her eyes blank. She was a shell, and the dark thing was still in her. The binding and the working had driven it deep. Teleri could see where it was and what it was. It was horrible—and sad.

Sioned stood over her. "Berengaria," she said. "We should have known. We should have noticed. None of us— not one of us—ever so much as looked at her. Not I. Not you. And certainly not my brother, in whose charge she was, and who never gave her so much as a moment's thought." She looked ready to spit, though precisely at whom, Teleri could not tell. "Damn him. Damn us all. We were fools and worse than fools."

"We are all at fault," Ahmad said. "It's only Allah's good fortune that we caught her at the end."

"Teleri caught her," said Sioned. "The rest of us would never have known. And my brother would be dead."

Her father's arms about her were no warmer than Teleri's heart at her mother's brisk and unassuming praise. She wished she could bask in it, but she had to say, "The dark thing is still alive. Nothing we've done has killed it. It's in her baby, can you see?"

"I . . . see," said Sioned, not willingly.

"So kill her," Richard said. Some of them started. They must have thought he was unconscious. Teleri had known he was not. Once Berengaria was bound, he had started to come to himself. He knew how to do that quickly—any soldier did if he wanted to survive in battle.

He sat up, and she could see that he had taken stock of everything and everyone, and decided a number of things.

"We can't kill her," Sioned said, "much as some of us would like to. That will free the Old Man again."

"Are you telling me he can't be killed at all?" Richard demanded.

"There are ways to send him back to the pits of hell and bind him there for eternity," she said, "and believe me, brother, I am tempted to use them. But there is another way."

Richard did not look as if he wanted to hear it, but he knew Sioned too well to say so. He wanted the simple solution. He had never loved or liked his wife, but what she had done tonight had shifted him over from indifference to hate. He wanted her dead, the sooner the better.

"Listen to me," said Sioned, "and think. Your wife is

pregnant—and very recently, at that. It seems she finally decided to take matters into her own hands. I would wager that
the Old Man had somewhat to do with it, though he
wouldn't have had to do much: she's wanted this since your
mother made you marry her. I doubt very much that she had
any intention of creating a body for our old enemy, but in the
end, she did exactly that.

"Now consider. If we kill her, the Old Man goes free. We
can bind him with a great working through the Seal and the
Ark, and pray he never finds a way to escape. But what if we
bind him in another way? His soul has passed as it should in
the natural order of things, out of death or undeath and into
new life. He thinks to keep his consciousness intact in the infant body, and be born and grow in the full awareness of his
former self."

"Ah!" said Giuliano in sudden understanding. "The Spells
of Lethe. But we would need water of that river, and one of
us would have to journey to Tartarus for it."

"Not while we have the Seal and the Ark," she said. "We
can bring it to us, and work both the spell and the binding
through their power."

They went on, but Teleri stopped listening. The dark
thing was bound, but it was not either deaf or unconscious.
It heard what they were saying and what they intended, and
it did not want to be scoured of its memories or cleansed of
its darkness—not at all. It woke Berengaria, who was a great
deal more of a sorceress than anyone might have believed, and
made her rouse her power.

Teleri could not tell if she meant to blast them all or escape through a gap in the world's fabric or both. Probably
both.

Teleri's father was still holding her as if he would never let
her go. She touched him with a brush of magic. He was

quick: he joined with her, looked through her eyes, and saw what the enemy was doing with Berengaria.

He laid his power in her hand, as gently, as graciously as if it had been a gift of great price. And it was. It was beyond price. It was hers to use as she judged best.

Time slowed and stretched. Her mother was still talking. Richard wanted to argue. Giuliano wanted to talk about the spells, how best to work them. Judah was getting into it, and Aaron—when had they come in?

It was all very crowded and slow. Teleri reached past them toward Berengaria. She was starting to get up, calling in her strength as well as the Old Man's.

Teleri did not know the spells that Giuliano knew, but she had her father and she had herself, and she knew what she had to do. She had to take away the darkness and only leave the light. She had to empty the soul of memory, make it all clean, so that it could live inside its clean new body.

It was hard. Without her father she could not have done it. The darkness was set deep, and the light was very, very far down inside it. She almost did not think there was any, but somehow, through all that he had done and been, Sinan ibn Salman had managed to keep the core of himself intact. It was very tiny and very remote, but it was there.

She made herself into a bath of fire. Her father showed her how. It was an old Persian spell—and that fit, because Sinan had come from Persia. It sent the soul through the River of Ordeal and cleansed it in sacred flame. She became the River and the flame.

The darkness fought hard. Just when she knew she could not do it, a new and different fire came to strengthen her.

Her mother had seen what she was doing, and bound the Seal with the Ark and given her what she needed. They burned that soul clean, and the body it lived in.

That body's mother was not so simple. Maybe it would have been kinder to empty Berengaria of memory and let her start new, but Sioned did not want to, and neither did Teleri. Some penalties had to be paid. Berengaria had committed terrible treason. She should know and remember, and atone for it.

CHAPTER FORTY-FIVE

Teleri came out from inside her magic. Hardly any time had passed, though it had felt as if she spent eons working the spell. She slipped out of her father's grasp and went to kneel beside Berengaria.

The queen was sitting up. Teleri saw where her eye was looking. The nearest dagger was in Mustafa's belt, and he was busy watching Giuliano.

Teleri caught her before she could leap. She fought like a mad thing, but she had little strength left. Then Mustafa was there, keeping his weapons out of her reach, and holding her until she stopped struggling and trying to scratch and claw.

Tears were running down her face. "Why don't you let me die?" she railed at him. "Why do you make me live?"

"Because you deserve to live," Teleri said before anyone else could speak, "and not only because you have a great deal to make up for. You were wronged, which is something my uncle is going to have to face, and you did wrong because of it, but now you can make it right. You'll stay alive, you'll have your baby, and you'll raise him to be as good a man as he can be."

Berengaria's eyes narrowed. Even in her grief, she could be crafty. "As the king's heir?"

"No," said Richard. His voice was flat. "I don't care who his father is, and I never want to know. My heir in Jerusalem is Henry."

"And your heir in England?" asked Berengaria.

"If it has to be John," Richard said, "at least he's of my blood—and he didn't come to this life as the Devil's rival."

Her lips were tight, but she was keeping a tighter rein on her temper than Richard was. Teleri almost admired her. "What if this child is your kin?"

"I do not want to hear it," Richard said, so calm and yet so firm that her teeth clicked together and her face went pale. "I will not undo our marriage and I will certainly not execute you as I'm entitled to do, but you will be removed from Jerusalem. There must be somewhere that I can put you, where you'll be safe and guarded, and your offspring will be raised properly."

"There is," said Sioned. "Brother, give her Montjoyeuse. Let me choose her guards and her child's tutors, but let her be lady of the domain."

Richard stared at her. "You mean *give* her your demesne? Let her rule it? Has she corrupted your wits?"

"No," said Sioned. "I don't want it; there's too much grief in it, and too much memory. It's a good place even so; its soul is clean. Don't you think it would be eminently right and fair that she should be entrusted with the care of it, and her son should become lord of it and be responsible for it— after what he did to my son? Let them be bound to it as old kings were bound to the land, so that its prosperity is theirs, and if it fails, or they fail it, they suffer with it."

Subtle solutions were not Richard's usual way, but that did not mean he was incapable of appreciating them. A slow grin spread across his face, replacing the scowl. "Oh, indeed," he said. "He wanted life; he gets life, but without any of his old one to taint him. She gets freedom and responsibility and honest standing in the world, but she can't give them up once she has them. That's fair, and just. It's even merciful."

"There is one thing," Sioned said, "that you must do. Because a good part of the fault in this is yours, and you owe her a debt for your years of neglect. You must look her in the face and forgive her for what she did."

Richard had gone crimson. Teleri braced for a bellow of rage.

But Sioned stopped it before it could begin. She never had been afraid of her brother, no matter how violent he might threaten to be. "Be honest, Richard. Admit that I'm telling the truth. You never loved her, but the least you could have done was remember that she existed."

Richard snarled, but the edge was off his temper. With his sister's hard eye on him, he turned to Berengaria. She was standing with her chin up, obviously trying not to shake. She looked more like a queen then than she ever had.

Maybe he could see that. Maybe he could not. When he spoke, he was polite enough, though there was no warmth in him. "I forgive you, lady. If I've wronged you, I'm sorry for it. I wish you well, and I hope for your sake that you prosper."

Berengaria inclined her head. She did not speak to him.

That was fair, Teleri thought, though Richard looked as if he was waiting for her to apologize to him. Maybe someday she would, but just now, the wounds were still too raw. She was doing well to accept what she was given, and not to cast it in his face.

When she did speak, it was to Sioned. "You are merciful," she said, "and maybe a little cruel. I would rather you had put me to death—and with me the monster that grows inside me."

"It's not a monster now," said Teleri. "It's a baby. He won't be a bad man, particularly; that's all gone. He'll be mortal, and he'll make mistakes and do foolish things as men do. But the great evil has gone back to the hell he got it from. He'll be warded against it. It won't possess him ever again."

Berengaria turned to stare at her. "How do you know that?" she demanded.

"I know," Teleri said. She paused. "There's another thing. We'll have to take your magic away from you both. It's not that we want to hurt you, but it's too tempting. You'll leave here mortal, and so will he. If you try to get it back again, we'll know, and we'll stop you. I'm sure you understand."

"I understand," Berengaria said with surprising lack of sullenness. Maybe she was relieved. Magic could be a heavy burden, and hers had been worse than most. "And yet, I must ask. Whose name will this child have?"

"His own," Sioned said. "He'll be a bastard without a father—and that's not easy to bear, but others have done it and done well. See that you raise him to be strong, and teach him to know what's right. Never let him be ashamed to be what he is. The rest should take care of itself."

Berengaria was silent for a long moment. Maybe she was thinking of the fact that Sioned had not been born legitimate, either, although she had certainly known who her father was.

Whatever Berengaria thought, eventually she said, "This is far more than I'm entitled to expect. I'm not going to thank you—I'm not ready for that. But I will promise to do my best. You won't have cause to punish me again."

"I'm sure I won't," Sioned said.

*   *   *

Berengaria left for Montjoyeuse in the morning. Richard sent two of his steadiest knights with her, and a clerk who was young but skilled, and who had a gift for keeping people from each other's throats. He was also a mage, although Berengaria had not been informed of that. Sioned had taught him in Judah's hospital, and he was as solid a creature as she knew. They could trust him to do his duties well, and to see that Berengaria raised her son as he should be raised.

Berengaria seemed almost happy as she rode out. For the first time she had a life of her own. Sioned hoped that she would blossom in it, and in time learn to forget her descent into the darkness. Any human creature deserved that, and Berengaria had had a worse time of it than some, with neglect and disregard and unearned contempt.

Sioned surprised herself with a pang at the thought of another lady in the castle that she had loved so much. But she had spoken the truth. She did not want to go back—not now, maybe not ever. She had moved beyond the darkest grief for Owein, but some things would not go away.

She was going to Egypt. She had never been—surprising, a little, but she had been so busy here with her demesne, her family, her work. And, to be honest, she had been avoiding the rest of her husband's life. His sons she knew, and some she loved; they were fine young men. But their mothers, Ahmad's elder wives and concubines, she had never met. Of them all, she had only known the first and eldest, the great mage and teacher Safiyah, who had died fighting the Old Man while he was alive.

It was time Sioned saw the country in which the art of magic had been born, and came to know the family into which she had married. Ahmad had never forced her, never said a word in fact, but she could tell that he was glad—deeply so, all the way down to the heart. She had held back a part of herself in evading this part of him. It was a new rite of marriage, a new binding, this time to all of him and not only to the man he was when he was in Jerusalem.

The night before they were to leave happened to be the Jews' Sabbath. Rebecca had asked them to share the rite with her family. It was a great honor, and one Sioned had no inclination to refuse.

They were all there: all the sons of Levi who had come to serve the Ark. More were coming now that the ban had been lifted on Jews dwelling in the holy city. The Temple of light had drawn in upon itself once the great working of the battle was done; the knights' Temple and the Dome of the Rock stood where the ancient walls had been, and those would not change. If a new Temple of the Jews' God was built, it would not be in this age of the world.

But beneath the paving of the Christian and Muslim shrines, the Ark rested in its chosen place, guarded by its chosen priests. Nothing now would shift it, though the Tiresi might try—as might the Pope and the caliph and any other power that craved greater power.

Those were worries for another day. Tonight they celebrated the Lord's day, the day of rest. Sioned had not grown up with the rite and she did not believe in its doctrine, but she took comfort in the cadences of the words, in the light of candles on familiar faces, in the knowledge that here she had family, although there was no bond of blood between them.

But who knew? Someday there might be. Teleri and Benjamin were children now, given to squabbling and not at all inclined to sigh over one another's beauties, but Sioned could see how they were together. They would be friends at least for their lives long, and it was rather likely that in time they would be more. There was something about them that reminded her of how she was with Ahmad.

That would come when it came. She ate and drank with honest enjoyment, and listened to the flow of conversation up and down the long room. She had not said much; there was nothing to say that could not be said with a smile.

After the first passing of the wine, one of the servants announced new and belated guests. It was Richard, with Henry for escort, but otherwise alone. Judah rose to welcome them, and Rebecca had left room at the table for them.

Richard was unusually apologetic. "I am sorry," he said. "There was a crisis just as I was getting ready to go, and we had to settle it then or not at all."

"We understand," Judah said—as indeed he of all people would. "It's enough that you're here; we're very glad that you could come."

"I wouldn't have missed it," said Richard. He looked about him, bright-eyed with curiosity. "You'll have to tell me what to do. I've never celebrated a Sabbath before."

Rebecca smiled as she poured wine for him. "Why, it's very simple. You eat and drink. You thank the Lord for the privilege of both. And you enjoy the company."

"That's almost too easy," Richard said.

She laughed. "Isn't it? But some things are easy, and that makes them beautiful."

As the evening began to grow late, Sioned slipped away from the crowd and went up to the roof. It was not any desire to escape that moved her, but she felt a need to stretch her legs and an inclination to see the stars.

When she had been there for a while, someone else came to stand beside her, leaning on the wall that rimmed the roof. She glanced at her brother, but did not speak.

"So you really are going to Egypt," he said.

She nodded. There was enough starlight to see by, and the

moon was waxing. Even without magic, he could see her clearly enough. "I suppose you'll be off to England now," she said.

He sighed deeply. "That was the crisis that made us late," he said. "The letter came—the one about Mother." He said it steadily; he had had time to grow accustomed to the fact of her death, although he would never stop grieving for her. "As far as the world knows, she died in her sleep in the castle at Windsor. John's broken out of Rouen. The message from my justiciar was to the point: 'The Devil is loose. Look to your crown.' "

"So you'll go."

"It's odd," he said. "Just before I was crowned, I suffered a plague of soothsayers. Everywhere I went, there was some weird sister or peculiar gentleman offering words of doom. Every one of them said the same thing. My coronation was a day of ill omen, I'd never see Jerusalem, I'd bankrupt England with my follies, and I'd die a fool's death. So far none of it has managed to come true."

"Your fortunes have been better than your stars," she said. "Maybe that's magic's fault. There's been a great deal of it about you since you came over the sea."

Richard grunted. "Too bloody much. I hope I never fight a war again like the one we just fought."

"You probably won't. John has no magic to speak of."

"You think I'll fight my brother?"

"You think he won't fight you?"

"Now here's a conundrum," Richard said. "One thing that a soothsayer did say has been more true than not. That one said I'd be no kind of king to England. I'd take the crown and run. My first love, he said, was Jerusalem, and England was nothing more to me than a treasury to rob for my Crusade. I know I've never missed it when I'm away from it. It's part of my domains and I try to see that it's ruled well, but it's the last and least of them when I order them in my mind.

And that's not logical—because without England I'd be a count or a duke, but I'd never be a king."

"You'd be king of Jerusalem."

"Would I? Would I be able to claim as much as I have without a crown already to my name?"

"You wouldn't be the first," she said. "Godfrey wasn't a king. Nor was Fulk—nor Guy who lost it all to Saladin."

"The trouble with England," said Richard, "is that I don't want to go back. Mother's gone. There's nothing else there but rain and mud and obstreperous barons. While I was reading the letter and thinking about what it meant, I was also thinking about the war we just fought. It's over—thank God. But it's bought more trouble than it's settled. With the Ark, the Jews, the agreement I had to make with al-Afdal and your husband to win and keep their alliance, that Muslims would continue to be admitted as pilgrims and allowed to worship at the shrines—I've ruffled an excessive number of Christian feathers. The Pope is not a happy man when he looks eastward, and he'll be even less happy when he hears what we've been doing here.

"It's not just that I want to stay," he said. "It's that if I leave, everything I built will start to crumble. Henry's good, he's a strong ruler, the people love him, but if we change kings now, we'll rock the foundations when the earth underneath them is none too stable itself."

"So stay," she said.

He scowled at her. "You're supposed to tell me England needs me."

"It doesn't," she said. "It's done perfectly well without you for over a dozen years. John has little charm and less humor, but he has a gift for order. If you name him your heir and regent and give him a free hand, he'll rule well enough—and he'll be there to do it."

"Which is more than anyone's ever said of me." Richard ran his hands along the stone of the parapet. His eyes were on the Dome of the Rock, which floated above the roofs of the city, frosted with moonlight. "God, I love this place. Heat, dust, flies, blasted fevers, hordes of infidels, damned bloody magic—I love every bit of it, even the parts I hate."

She laughed a little painfully. "I do know what you mean. I think of Gwynedd, and all I can remember is chilblains. My blood has gone as thin as a Saracen's."

"That's well for you—you'll need it. Egypt is even worse than here."

"Egypt is Egypt."

"And Jerusalem is Jerusalem." He yawned, groaned, stretched. "Henry says he doesn't mind. I suppose he'll forgive me eventually, though his wife may not. She's been waiting much too long to be queen."

"She can wait a while longer," Sioned said. "You are right, you know. This is where you belong."

"Are you speaking as a soothsayer?"

"You know I don't have that gift," she said.

"Sometimes I wonder," he said. He spread his arms wide and threw his head back, embracing the city and the sky.

That was how she would remember him from the white walls of Cairo: standing under the stars and waxing moon, with the golden dome rising behind him, and all his heart and soul given to this blessed, blood-stained city. There had never been a woman, or man either, who could rival it—not even his mother.

He lowered his arms. His eyes were glinting, but his face was quiet. He bowed and offered his hand.

She took it with as much grace as she could muster. Regally then, but with a flicker of laughter, they went back to light and mirth and the warmth of friendship.